Kim Kelly lives in the upper Blue Mountains of New South Wales. *Black Diamonds* is her first novel.

BLACK DIAMONDS

BLACK DIAMONDS

Kim Kelly

HarperCollins*Publishers*

HarperCollins*Publishers*

First published in Australia in 2007
by HarperCollins*Publishers* Pty Limited
ABN 36 009 913 517
www.harpercollins.com.au

HarperCollins*Publishers*
25 Ryde Road, Pymble, Sydney, NSW 2073, Australia
31 View Road, Glenfield, Auckland 10, New Zealand
77–85 Fulham Palace Road, London, W6 8JB, United Kingdom
2 Bloor Street East, 20th floor, Toronto, Ontario M4W 1A8, Canada
10 East 53rd Street, New York NY 10022, USA

National Library of Australia Cataloguing-in-Publication data:

Kelly, Kim.
  Black diamonds.
  ISBN 13: 978 0 7322 8413 8 (pbk).
  ISBN 10: 0 7322 8413 9 (pbk).
  1. World War, 1914–1918 – Fiction. I. Title.
A823.4

Cover concept by Darian Causby, Highway 51 Design Works
Cover design by Darren Holt, HarperCollins Design Studio
Cover image of woman by Corbis; apples by Shutterstock; lace by Shutterstock;
background texture courtesy of Darian Causby, Highway 51 Design Works
Typeset in 12 on 17pt Bembo by Kirby Jones
Printed and bound in Australia by Griffin Press on 70gsm Bulky Ivory

7 6 5 4 3 2 1   07 08 09 10

For my darlingest

[Australian history] does not read like history, but like the most beautiful lies … but they are all true, they all happened.
Mark Twain, *Following the Equator*, 1897

Laugh, Kookaburra, laugh, Kookaburra
Gay your life must be.
Marion Sinclair, 1934

Australian sons let us rejoice
For we are young and free.
'Advance Australia Fair', 1879

Don't go to Hell in order to give piratical,
plutocratic parasites a bigger slice of Heaven.
Direct Action, Sydney, 1915

ONE

MAY – JULY 1914

FRANCINE

The first part of him I see is his hobnail boots, soot-black and massive, a few feet from my nose. I'm crouching, about to pick up the apples that have fallen through the bottom of the string bag, and there they are among the rolling red bobbles, and then his hands reach down, and then there's his face, black as his boots, black crescents on his fingers. I look away quickly, over my shoulder; not sure if I'm embarrassed about the apples, the man, the grime, or myself for being here in this place.

There are others, grey streaks of charcoal heading home from the mines after the shift, I presume. I don't know any of them, and have no reason to. They are just parts of the machine that digs the coal from the earth and keeps us in apples — and the rest. One of them glances at me, a flash of blue-white question, but keeps going, talking to the one he's walking with.

I can't ignore the one in front of me any longer. He's holding out the apples he's gathered for me, three in each huge hand. I don't know where he's going to put them; the bag is no good. So I look at him, finally. My cheeks are scalding already and then he smiles, teeth startling out of the black, and his eyes are green, glinting amber. Oh dear.

There's nothing else for it: I grab up the rest of the apples from the ground, four of them, and put them in my lap, scrunch two handfuls of skirt to hold them there. He's on his haunches, staring at me. Then he lets the apples fall, slowly, not touching my skirt;

3

they roll in and bump against the others, and for the smallest of moments I watch them. And he's still looking at me.

He's going to ask me if I'm all right, I can feel it coming, but I don't give him the chance. I stand up and fairly fly away across the street to the trap, skirt still hitched up over my dun-dusty black-stockinged knees as I drive off and I don't care. I didn't even thank him. There's no real reason why I should have acknowledged him at all, but by the time I reach the house, I feel more scalded than ever.

'You took your time,' Polly says from the kitchen when I get in. She's the housekeeper, and always rude. That's the way things are here. She's unaware that she's a servant, it seems; unlike our old housie, Hanna — for Mrs Hanrahan — whom I'd always thought to be about as animate as congealing porridge, but now, belatedly, appreciate for that very virtue. In any case, I suppose I have taken my time. Polly wanted the apples two hours ago, for a pie, and I said I'd go, just for something to do, but I went to the post office first — I'm waiting for a copy of *Native Flora and Fauna of New South Wales* I've ordered from Sydney; still not in — and then I took the trap a little way out of town to watch the sunset. At least, not the sun setting, but the way it hits the mountain foothills as it begins to sink: the rocks sticking out of the scrub look like fire trapped in glass, and the scrappy gums almost look graceful, the white patches on their peeling trunks like streams of pearl shell. There's so little else of colour here, except the sky that screams so blue into the valley it hurts sometimes; it's autumn now, but what'll it be like when summer comes? Anyway, I got my tiny glimpse of beauty before I had to turn around and face the town again, with its belching smokestacks like fat cigars, and its hills bald around the edges from all the poison; I only just made it back to the grocers before they closed.

No point in telling any of that to Polly as I tip the apples from my skirt onto her kitchen bench.

'No time to make a pie now,' she says. 'I'll poach them with brandy instead. It'll have to do. My pastry's gone to waste, mind.'

Tisk, tisk, tisk. Wouldn't matter what I said, she'd heave her great bosom in weary contempt. She came with the house; we're just pesky interlopers to her, my father and I. No doubt she thinks me a brazen little thing, too, wandering about on my own. I have no interest in her opinion; if she thinks I think I'm too good for this place, if she thinks I don't belong here, then she'd be right.

Polly sighs as she inspects the fruit: 'These are bruised.' But I barely hear her. I'm still thinking about that incident with the miner. Or not thinking of him exactly, but me, and why my face is still burning. It's not like me, not like me at all, to blush and flutter like this. I tell Polly I'm not feeling well and I can sense her eyes rolling as she washes the apples, and I'm glad she never seems to look at me. She says, 'There's dust on them too,' with disgust, but I've already left her. I see a faint black smudge on my skirt as I climb the stairs to my room; something else for her to be disgusted with.

Upstairs is some kind of refuge, but there's nothing *mine* about this room. It's just a place where my things are now, since we lost the house in Sydney, almost a month ago, though I'm sure few here in Lithgow know that, apart from my father's partner in the mine, Mr Drummond, who organised this new *place* for us. I don't pretend to know how the world of business works, but if you read the newspapers it appears that Sydney is one big betting ring of booms and busts; everyone's a gambler and a skiter for it. My father especially. He even tried to convince *me* that we were moving over the mountains because the mine needed his full attention for a time. Why, then, were we taking every stick of our furniture with us? I didn't bother asking. I might be somewhat ignorant, but I'm not stupid; and I don't need to rub it in for him. He's busted. Why else would he have sold our home, my beautiful rambling sandstone home, the only home I've ever known, on the water at Rose Bay?

He'd say I shouldn't crinkle my lovely brow with any such thoughts, but there's not much frowning involved in putting two and two together: he's hung on against some kind of ruin only because of this mine, which is doing very well, he's boasted. But I have to presume he's had to sell off just about everything else to square up his debts, and now here we are, with all our eggs in a coal basket, or whatever you call those little rail trucks that carry the stuff all about. I don't think Father knows anything much of mines or making anything apart from money — he's an investor, someone who puts up the finance for ventures, then takes his portion of the profits. Mr Drummond is the one who actually runs the mine and has for as long as I can remember, so there's no reason for Father to have come here, except that property is cheaper by far, and since the town is growing such apace there's no real shame in being here. Father still gets to strut and tootle around in his motor car and proclaim that Lithgow is the next best thing. *The Birmingham of Australia!* And it is, I suppose, judging from its growling pits and furnaces, factories and mills, turning out everything from iron and copper to chimney pots and tweed, rifles and bricks. And mountains of coal, of course. The whole town is black with it — truly. A grey film lies on every surface.

As much as I loathe this town, at least we're here together, Father and I. He's always good company, when he's about; he's quick to cheer me, mimics Polly's heaving and sighing to perfection, and pours forth his rich raw baritone against clumpy piano when he's had too much drink after dinner, which is most evenings now: 'There once was a boy from Dublin who …' he begins and makes up a different song every time, sometimes fabulously vulgar, depending on consumption. He's a marvellous disgrace, and bleary or not his eyes sparkle when he looks at me. He is an Irishman, a drunk and a devoted punter, the full cliché, who came here, he tells me often enough, as a boy on a freighter from Dublin, and skipped off in Sydney*town* to make his fortune. What he never talks about is how he made that fortune; I suspect that's probably too vulgar for my ears. And it doesn't really matter in this country where wealth in itself buys respectability; if gossip is to be believed, then there are plenty here who are coarser than my father, and they are not all Irishmen — or the progeny of felons, as the English like to call us all.

There's another thing we never talk about and that's the future. There's been no mention of beaus or belles or, God forbid, marriage — for him or me. I turned eighteen on Sunday, and Father said to me after dinner, as he does: 'Lord, no, you can't be more than twelve, my girl,' slid his present of a silver filigreed pen across the table and then changed the subject. I do, however, fancy I understand the reason for this. My mother died suddenly in 1901, of influenza, when I was nearly five; three days after Queen Victoria, and I remember thinking all the black armbands were for us. Father still gets tears in his eyes when he speaks of her, his Josie, or when he sings 'My Little Blue-Eyed Nell', and sometimes I know when he is thinking of her; he has a look that pulls at my heart. But my mother is little more to me than a photograph of a pretty woman, the smell of hyacinths and the memory of a soft hand on my plump little cheek; before a lady called Miss Una came to take me up the hill to school, before the tram came and I learned to take myself. I know that's somehow much more a part of why I feel so strange this evening; how could I ever leave Father? But it's ridiculous to imagine I would stay with him forever in this hole in the ground just because I can't bear that heartbroken look of his. It's even more ridiculous to imagine that my present confusion has in any way been provoked by the filthy, nameless miner I stumbled upon in the middle of the road. The problem is, I can't imagine … anything.

My days were clear in Sydney, calm and contained as the harbour I looked out across every day. I had my garden that tumbled down to the sea, and my painting — watercolours, of animals mostly — to keep me busy. While Father was out, I'd ramble about, catch the tram into town to lose some hours at the David Jones emporium, or go riding out to South Head, or walk the foreshore near home, most often alone, sometimes accosted for a chat about nothing by Sister Terrence from the convent taking her constitutional. I've never really had any friends to speak of; never made a connection with any of the girls at Our Lady, not a lasting one anyway. I'd sometimes go on picnics and attend parties with the local crowd, naturally, but really I've always preferred my own company, and Father's, or that of a decent, fat novel. Or the water, swimming alone at sunset at the edge of my garden in my little sea pool … But now I don't even have a garden, just gums towering over a yard of spindly grass in the back and a small spread of mangy flowerbeds and moth-eaten hedge in the front of the most hideous dark-brick monstrosity that was ever built: it looks like a two-storey temperance hall whose grounds have been attended by a wayward member. And as for painting, I've had to resort to ordering *Native Flora and Fauna of New South Wales* for the colour plates as inspiration, since there's little else but ugliness outside my windows here. For the first time ever I am, I think, lonely. That's what's wrong with me, of course; I'm simply burning with resentment and have no one to tell it to.

I'll talk to Father again tonight about the yard; there must be someone in this town who can help me make a garden. Then, in the morning, I'll go to that early Wednesday Mass and talk to Father Hurley about seeing if there's some way I can make myself busy. He seems a pleasant, approachable sort of a man. Perhaps I can teach at the school. Is there even a school? There must be. Regardless, I need to spend less time in contemplation of things I can't change … and adapt. I've never done a day's work in my life, but perhaps a job is the thing — everyone else here seems to have one. It's a *workers'* town.

The sun has well and truly vanished now, and from the window I can only just make out the lines of cottages dog-tailing beyond Main Street, away from the town, or peppering up the hill towards this house, fuzzy splotches of light here and there. And then my stomach lurches: that miner's eyes loom out at me from the darkness. He lives out there somewhere; what does he see now? His town. Perhaps he is remembering a strange, rude girl. Why I should care I have no idea, but somehow I do.

I hear the engine of the Austin putter up the drive, the creak and bang of the front door; Father is home. Thank God.

DANIEL

I've hardly slept. Keep waking up, then waiting for the wake-up whistle, then dozing again. I can hear Mum by the stove, checking our clothes, turning them over. She's washed them all, even though it's only Tuesday, or maybe Wednesday by now. She has to go to Bathurst in the morning and she's not sure when she'll be back; Miriam's expecting another baby and Mum's going to help with the others. Mim's got six already, and getting dippier with each one, is my sister, averaging a kid a year … fascinating. She's so quiet, Mum, I can barely hear her. She's quiet anyway, in everything she does. Wish my own quietness would shut up.

Stop telling me I don't want to go to work tomorrow, today, again. I keep seeing pit top in my mind, and I just don't want to go in. Everyone flows round me and down, and no one says a thing, not even the ponies. I've not choked, and I'm not worried; I'm just invisible. And I walk away, float away, back into the light.

Anyone'd think I've got a mental problem if they could hear what my mind's like when I'm like this. Yes, I'm so bloody different, aren't I. Remind myself now that I do actually have to go to work tomorrow. And go to bloody sleep.

Can't.

Any more than I can help being … a bit separate. Why? I don't know: it's obvious one second and nothing the next. It'd be easy to say it's because I'm German, except I'm not. Just Australian, but not quite. Can you know that sort of thing? I know Dad would disown me if ever I was caught singing God Save The King, but he is German, except he's not. And he'd laugh himself stupid if ever he caught me with a Bible. No fear there. Though having an Almighty to jabber to in the middle of the night might've been handy at the minute. Can't just make one up for yourself, can you. Not when you're a red flagger from nowhere with no idea. No one'd ever rag us for a lack of religion, though, or lack of loyalty … no one'd ever rag Dad, for anything. Except me, within reason.

He's a legend is Dad: isn't everyone? More than obvious with him, though, I suppose. According to legend, he came off the boat in 1882, said he wanted the gold mines, but with his bad English and heavy accent and bad timing they told him to go off to Kembla — lots of coal there. He turned up, got a job first day spragging and shovelling shit, and worked out pretty fast that all the gold was black at Kembla. He went to the face quickly and he was champion, one time taking three ton a day for seventeen days straight on his own, including Sundays, unbeatable effort, and not just because you'd get arrested for working Sundays now. He took my eldest brother in with him when he turned thirteen, and in his first week there my brother, he was Daniel too, got his face blown off from left shot and he died where he fell. No one said a word either way, but the firer moved on quietly. Wasn't his fault, apparently; he was working like he had a bee up his arse to keep everyone going. I know there's more to it than that, of course, and half of it is no doubt bullshit, but Dad's not likely to fill me in: he doesn't talk about the past beyond 1894. Ever. And I wouldn't dare ask Mum about it. Jesus.

Can't fail to know that that was the year I was born, a few weeks after the first Daniel copped it, and that eight years later, after Kembla blew out, killing nearly a hundred, my father moved us on too. Here, to Lithgow, since there was an amalgamation of the mines and a stronger labour movement to match it. Joke. A union of capitalists talks louder than a miners' federation, does it? Pull the other one. The other mines here are mostly all tied up together with local iron, steel and copper, or swapping grades with Sydney and Newcastle, and the owners are all mates, with government mates, setting prices and gipping the workers; but pretty much all we do is feed the railways with clean black bituminous coal and aren't amalgamated or associated with anything much other than steady government contracts, and we get gipped just the same.

Things are just as good or bad, wherever you are, but in all this time no one's been blown up here, not at Wattle Dell at least. Dad doesn't say anything about it, but he's more responsible than anyone else for how few serious accidents we've had. He's been there since just after it opened, and he's been doing the bastard fixing ever since: blowing and stabilising the worst spots, as necessary, or as others won't touch them; and it's him others go to on questions of stability, more than manager or deputy. We've also got compulsory safety lamps because of Dad; another chapter in the legend: four years ago he raised half the money passing round the hat and then went and had a quiet word with the boss, Drummond; no one seems to know what was said, but it was obviously very effective. I asked him about it once and he only said: 'Some things are no one else's business.' End of story. Typical. But if Dad catches you with your lamp open in-pit, he'll give you a mouthful.

And I should remember to be grateful. I am too. By comparison, we're well off because of Dad: he gets paid a quarterly extra for the time out with the fixing, and so do I, since that's what I do now too, when we're not just hewing, and even when we are just hewing, as we are at the moment, we earn above maximum. Always together, and always on day shift, special privilege of always reliable father and son, there's no competition for our hauls at the Wattle and no financial concern in our house. Unlike others who only make enough to live on, and even then miners are better paid than most other workers, before expenses and contributions and lay-offs anyway. It's enough to turn you red, what others have to put up with.

But Dad's not a fist thumper and neither am I. We keep well out of trouble. He keeps the records for our meetings, keeps a note of everything, he's that meticulous about it, about everything he does, and staunch for the union, obviously, everyone of all persuasions is, but I think he takes most of his fight to the coal; lays in like he'd rather kill it than hew it. He says to me, 'Where would I be if I lost my temper one day? In prison, that's where.' They say you've got to watch the quiet ones.

Like me, driving myself round the bend turning all this over now. Looking for sense where there is none.

Avoiding thinking about what's really cut me. Dad's dusted. He's started coughing it up, a lot now; had the wheeze for I don't know how long; still ignoring it. And he'll push on, as he'll expect me to, even when he can't ignore it any more. I'd like to think this is stupid, to tell him to stop, but you don't tell my father anything, and if he's going to die, then he'll want to be earning up till the day he does. He's never seen a doctor in his life, and he's not about to start; unlike me: I average a trip to the hospital once a year for some little thing or other. When I burned myself again last year, Dad said to me: 'If that quack could fix your clumsy head, he'd go broke.' Nothing the doctor could do for Dad, though, even if he got seen to. Of course I'll keep on, look after Mum. Worry about financial concerns when I'm looking at them.

And I'm the only one who will be looking at them, since my other brother, Pete, took off four years ago, to Newcastle. Twenty-five and he'd had enough; talked his way into a job on the docks doing bugger all, directing traffic; he writes to Mum now and again, says he doesn't miss Lithgow winters. Dad doesn't say anything, never mentions him, and wouldn't go up to Newcastle even when Pete got married last year. I can understand, sort of. As much as I've been thinking I'd rather never go in again, I could never walk away like that. There's too much of me here. Don't have to think too hard about it: I can still see Jimmy Skelton too clearly, same age as me, on our first year in, caught by a runaway skip and cut almost in half. I had to run on to his family, because I knew his mum well, to tell her before they brought his body home; his father was a wreck; died the year after from the shock of it, they reckon. That's a lot to walk away from, just there. Not to mention letting Dad down; I'd never do that.

But I also don't have to think too hard to remember that Mum didn't want me to go in in the first place. She argued with Dad, the only time I can remember them arguing, the day I came home from school and said I'd go in with Dad, as the other boys from school were going in with theirs. He came back at her in German, which he never speaks unless he's really shitted-off, and he'd have been thinking I wasn't following the conversation through the bedroom wall. But I was. Thanks to Mum who, up until that day, had taken a particular interest in my education. Always making me read, despite the fact that I've always hated it; asking me about school all the time, which I hated even more, because I've never been the best at sitting still doing bugger all; and teaching me German, talking to me in German every day after school, on the sly from Dad. I don't know, I'm the youngest by a long way, and I suppose Mum had time to put the effort in. She speaks French as well, and reads like it's going out of fashion, and when I was younger I was impressed by it, but by the time I'd made the decision to go with Dad, I'd dropped the Deutsch.

It seemed disrespectful to keep going with something he disapproved of — 'This is Australia — speak English, not that ugly rubbish,' he'd say whenever she'd let it slip in front of him — so I stopped listening, and Mum stopped bothering. Still, I have to call Dad *Vati* on occasion, because, well, he does love his cabbage. Anyway, what else would I have done with myself? Miners can earn more than government schoolteachers and there wasn't much alternative. Getting fried alive at the furnaces? Good money, and it'd want to be; same difference as mining. Be a plumber and deal in shit all day? Or some other idiot trade job trying forever to edge into the middle class? Like my brother-in-law. No thanks. So I went in. I read *Australian Worker* and *Radical* and that new dippy one, *Direct Action,* while we're all waiting for the socialist revolution; that'll do. How's that for a desperate shot at justification?

Don't think Mum would buy it. She never makes a disappointment known; not to me anyway. But somehow I can hear it now, in the way she's turning our clothes again. There are secrets in her that are not legends and maybe I want to live long enough to catch wind of them.

Maybe I should hit myself over the head with something to shut off this rubbish.

My head is like stew. And now here comes Francine Connolly, making her hundredth appearance, scrabbling for her apples in the street, not looking at me while I help her pick them up.

I've seen her once before in town, and Evan Lewis, who's Dad's best mate and our representative to the union, and whose socialism is matched only by his Methodism, saw me looking and said she was one of the owners' daughters. I put her out of my head then. It's not that hard to be a stand-out in this town full of so many men, and married women, but even with her red hair falling out of the coil under her hat as she walked up Main Street, her pretty body hugged by that slim grey skirt, I looked away again. She's an owner's daughter. And probably only here for a spell, and certainly out of bounds. But when I saw her again today, yesterday, when I picked up the apples, she made me feel a bit worse than invisible. Sure, I did just want to get a closer look, but I thought I was being polite about it. For me; I'm not usually known for my politeness. She looked at me like I was some kind of an animal, and ran away from me. I don't know why I did it. Maybe just for lack of stand-outs. I hardly ever go into town looking like that; I only wanted to ride in quickly to pick up some linseed oil before the co-op closed. But what difference should it make? I'm a fucking miner. That's what I look like after work, and I'm not on my own there: there's a couple of thousand of us round about the place.

Forget it, for the hundredth time. She's bourgeois rubbish. What else did I expect?

The whistle sails across the valley, and I get out of bed like my legs know what they are doing before I think it. I look out the window into the blackness and the tree next to the house lights up in a cloud break. It's an apple tree, standing there like a ghost looking at me. No fruit on it.

I hear the pan hit the stove as Mum starts breakfast. I hear Dad yawn, cough and scratch his head in the next room. I open the window and piss on the tree and already it's just another day.

FRANCINE

For the third morning in a row I've been woken by the kookaburras. It's hard to believe they don't do that deliberately. At Rose Bay they were so bold that they'd sit on the balcony rail and look at me; they'd say, *It wasn't me laughing*, unconvincingly. Then, just to rub it in, one of them would dive headlong into the garden below, as if in fright, only to reappear with a lizard in its beak. I look into the tired old gums of now, drearier for the hazy dawn. I haven't seen a single one of those puffy-chested, cheeky birds here, though I can hear them loud and clear; perhaps Lithgow kookaburras mock by stealth. Oh, stop it, Francy. I break my resolutions against negativity so easily.

I should be pleased. Father said last night that he'd already approached someone to help me with the garden design and choosing the plants. Some friend of Mr Drummond's knows some fellow in Bathurst, and he'll be coming on Friday on his way through to Sydney to have a look at the yard. Father seemed very chipper himself, too, said that the mine would turn a healthy profit this quarter and there was more to come; whatever that means. Always good news he gives me. Still, when I went down to meet him in the parlour last night I could smell the sharp whisky sourness on his breath already. Not like him to drink spirits before the sun goes down; he's always been strict about that, if nothing else. Perhaps he'd been celebrating impending healthy profit with Mr Drummond.

I wash and dress, shifting flowerbeds and feature trees around in my head and, downstairs, gulp a glass of water in the empty kitchen. I'm sure it tastes of coaldust, but I tell myself instead how pleasant the kitchen is at this hour of the morning — with no Polly in it. She's still asleep, not to be woken before seven o'clock, *thank you*, and she'll have done breakfast by the time I get back from Mass, so I can fix myself something to eat then, when she'll be out the back doing the washing.

Hayseed, my new little chestnut pony, greets me with a snort and a nod outside his stall in the rear of the yard, and the ancient McNally, who looks after him and other odds and sods — and also seems to have come with the house — has already got him ready with the trap, as I told him to yesterday. No sign of Cranky McNally, though; lucky day!

He's a dear pony, Hayseed, most delightful being I've met so far. He snorts again as I climb up, and we set off down the hill towards the town.

Already the place is alive with bustle and the sun is barely risen; I can feel it seething as we come closer, carts and traps and bicycles and working men, feel it all press in upon me along Main Street, and I rush too, turning off and up again to the church, as if I don't have all the time in the world to get there.

Inside, it is still, and the cool old bricks smell fresh, like river pebbles steaming rain. Cross myself, genuflect, I can hear myself breathe. There's hardly anyone here. Just a few old women and some working types scattered amid the pews. Father Hurley has put on this extra midweek Mass for Lent, so says his yellowing notice pinned on a little board inside the door; clearly the enthusiastic response has caused him to extend it well beyond the season of sacrifice. Not many have chosen to extend themselves this morning.

I go through the motions, let the Latin wash over me. *In*

18

nomine Patris, et Filii, et Spiritus Sancti, burble, burble, burble …
I've never listened at Mass, but I am bound to the ritual of it. It's
dreamlike, removed, and induces me to meditate upon higher
thoughts; I always feel cleansed afterwards, and always feel
compelled to return, as if prayers are more significant here. Father
Hurley's voice is wondrously dull and does the job. He looks like
a dirt farmer from one of those *Bulletin* sketches with his thin,
lined face and pale eyes tired from squinting eternally in a
paddock in the middle of nowhere, mourning for his drought-
stricken flock. I'm thinking about my attitude, which is my
higher thought for the day, and how I shall improve it and
impress upon Father Hurley that I am indeed keen to find a
purpose here, so he will provide an interesting suggestion for me.

Father Hurley wearies himself and it's all over remarkably
quickly. I've barely crossed myself before I'm down the aisle to
accost him before he leaves for the vestry. 'Ahem.'

He turns around, peering through the motes.

'I was wondering, Father, if I might have a quick word with
you, if you've a moment?'

His squint opens a little with a slim but kindly smile. 'Ah, Miss
Francine Connolly,' he says, emphasising the *Francine*, I imagine,
to remind me of my saint, my best intentions, and the fact that I
haven't been to confession since I arrived in this town and am
therefore not entitled to sacraments of any sort. 'Yes, of course.
Tell me, how is your father? We didn't see him on Sunday.'

'No, that's right. He was unwell,' I say, with one part gravity to
six parts mortally coy. My father's attendance at Mass is ever
sporadic to say the least; he only went the week we first arrived
because I badgered him. 'How odd will it look, me turning up
alone and introducing myself?' I'd snipped at him and he'd
indulged me.

A look of concern from the priest: 'Is he recovered?'

'Oh, yes. He's very well now, thank you. In fact, he's sent me here to ask you if you might suggest some sort of work for me, to keep me from idleness,' I fib, having decided during my meditation to give my enquiry more weight this way. Father's not the slightest bit interested in what I do all day when he's out.

Father Hurley's pale slots brighten; he thinks for a moment and then says: 'What sort of work do you think might suit you, lass?'

'I thought perhaps teaching? Is there a school where I might be useful? I especially love the little ones.' That's true enough: very little ones are the only little ones I might abide; most children are ratty or dimmed above the age of five, I suppose because that age is the threshold for strapping and rote. Oh, but little ones smell of all sorts of foul and mysterious things, don't they. At this point I have to admit to myself that this is a lost cause; despite my prayers, I don't really want to do this sort of work at all, noxious odours, preparing youngsters to have their spirits broken. Much as I owe the convent sisters for my education, they beat something out of me, or into me. I'm not sure which.

'There are a few schools here,' he says, looking at me thoughtfully again. 'But none that I know of that require a new teacher. I shall enquire for you, if you like.'

I'm about to say, *Don't go to any particular trouble on my behalf,* when he adds: 'They do need a nurse at the hospital, though, quite urgently, I hear. Mrs Moran, the matron there, is stretched to her limit. Do you have any experience at that?'

I am horrified, couldn't think of anything more hideous than tending the sick. I say, ruefully: 'No, none at all. I think I'd be all fumbles with that.'

He smiles his kindly smile again, knowing, I'm sure. What a silly, spoiled girl I am. I thank him after he says he'll have a further think on it, and I leave for the post office, perhaps my book will be in this morning. I shall go back to pretending that I can be an artist instead, fill my days communing with the sublime in order to create … what a load of old rot.

'No, it's not in,' Mr Symes, the postmaster, grunts without looking for my package from Angus & Robertson; I am becoming a pest. But he adds, for my crestfallen face: 'Why don't you call in at the bookshop, they might have something for you instead, while you're waiting? Or the library?'

They have a bookshop here? And a library? Well, that's something. But I'm too glum to ask him where they are, and embarrassed, yet again. I nod a thanks and slink away back to Hayseed tethered to the verandah pole outside. As I climb into the trap my eyes wander along the railway tracks to the buildings backing off Main Street — and fall directly on the bookshop just down from the bakers. I must have passed the front of it at least half-a-dozen times. Why didn't I see it? Then, within a blink, I see a flicker of red apples rolling through tawny-grey dust. My cheeks are burning again and my heart is hammering all of a sudden. I grab at the reins and thwack them, swimmy-headed and the blue light blinding me as we move out from the shade. What on earth is wrong with me?

DANIEL

Dad's always that careful, I can't help ragging him for it, but I don't this morning. Too busy yawning. I watch the way he smells the air as we come back round after firing, then he listens as he's tapping everywhere above the fall with his pick, like he's talking to God, as if, before laying in. There is a point to it here, though, round this blind pinch in section three; we've cavilled that for this quarter and the place is full of bumps and low-roofed with cranky shit shale — I've got a ridge of scrapes down my back to prove it. I'm way too big for this sort of thing, they should make it Taff-only work; I didn't mean that. The rock above us groans softly, and we wait a little longer: tap, tap, tap. It settles and Dad says: 'Yep.'

I'm fighting my pick before I lift it, and already thinking about crib break, already blinking. Next time I have trouble sleeping I will hit myself over the head. The light's streaking in my eyes like there's water running down the face, and I'm boiling after five minutes. It's always hot of course, but it's too hot too quickly. It feels like there's a fire above us, gusting down. I take off my shirt, but it doesn't make any difference.

I'm turning around to look at the brattice cloth, back towards the fan shaft, to see if the ventilation's right or if we are on fire, when it bumps again, very loud this time, with an unscheduled spill of rock somewhere, and we stop. Even the rats stop. There's dead silence; we've all heard it. And we all wait.

I hear Robby Cullen say, 'Jesus Christ' and hoick from the next stall up. This section is so slow in parts he hasn't met his present darg of two ton a day for a few weeks, and it doesn't help that it takes the ponies ten years to get down here to collect. His wife is having her second one already and he's feeling the pressure. Stupid bugger, shouldn't have got married so young. He's only a year older than me.

Then it comes again, and somehow I know this time it's going to come down in a big way. I see myself at pit top, going in. And everything speeds up, I'm flying down the drift to the face. Here I am. And now I'm not. I've dropped the pick and I'm running back. Not panicking. Just running, as if I can outrun whatever the roof has in mind.

'Move!' That's Dad, behind me, with a shove: '*Achtung!*' Don't worry, I'm fucking moving.

It keeps coming and the sound is everywhere. I look over my shoulder and it's just black, and dust flying towards me like a fist. I keep running, and even as I'm running I'm thinking this is no good, I can hardly see a thing, but I keep going. Then something catches me on the back of my leg and I'm flat out, winded, and I definitely can't see a thing. And I reckon it's all over. I'm waiting for the rest to hit me.

I lie with my face on the floor and I think I can't breathe for a second but I am breathing and I must have moved because I feel the roughness against the side of my face. And it's warm. Just warm. I hear the trapper above, it's Billy, with his high voice, calling down something, and then it's all quiet again.

I wait.

A light swings through the dust way ahead with footsteps. 'Jesus fucking Christ!' That's Robby, loud and to my right; I can hear him frigging around for his lamp, and I try to get up now, but I can't. When I try to push up against the floor, pain rips through me like you wouldn't believe. I must have made that plain because Robby says: 'Hang on, mate.' I can't see him but he's right near me now. I'm staring up at the light ahead and the footsteps coming closer and I'm wanting it to be Dad but I know it's not. He's behind me, where's it's come down. I close my eyes, I can hear the others now, I don't want to know.

There's a hand on my shoulder and it's Evan, Evan Lewis saying, quiet and steady: 'Who's here, then?' And Robby says: 'Just us so far, this way.'

I can't say anything. The weight is lifted off the back of my leg and it wasn't much after all, only a prop; probably one I laid up: I hear it thud next to me. The four whistles blow for evacuation; says it all.

Hands slide under me, one two three, and I bite down against it this time as they lift me onto the stretcher that stinks of iodine; it's so old it's a wonder it holds the weight of me. I keep my eyes closed, I don't want to know. I wonder if Mim's had the baby yet. I panic for a minute thinking Mum's not at home, and then I'm thankful she's not. Evan says, 'Easy!' and I'm out to it then. Won't be riding my bike home today.

I'm in and out, not thinking, but every step they take up that drift is branded into me. It takes ages and it doesn't take long enough and on reflex I open my eyes when we come out and they put me on the ground, but I can't see anything through the brightness anyway.

Evan's saying something next to me, but I don't catch it; everyone's out and milling around, wondering what's going on, wondering in the back of their minds whether they'll get back in today, though no one would ever say that. When I focus there's a man looking at me I think I've seen once or twice before, and he pats me on the chest. Who the fuck is he?

Evan says across me: 'Well, that's very good of you. All right, then.' And then he says to me: 'Well, up with you then, boyo.' I'd rather stay here, thank you.

My head's spinning right off as they get me up and onto the back seat of this new beaut motor car. Light blue panels, black leather: very flash; in any other circumstances I might be impressed by the service. I know every pothole in the road up to the hospital too by the time we get there.

Must have known I was coming because there's Mrs Moran shoving a brandy at me. I push it away — can't stand the taste let alone the smell of grog — and she says to me: 'Drink it, Danny. Be a good lad, and I'll knock you out in a minute. The brandy won't kill you but what's coming might.' I drink it, and she strips me and washes me down. It hurts to buggery but somewhere I'm grateful to feel in my skin again. Till Nichols, the doctor, gets started prodding; he says it's not too bad by the looks of it, though, not too much bleeding inside. 'X-ray will confirm it.' X-ray does, apparently, and in any other circumstances I might be impressed by that machine too.

'Hold on, Danny,' Nichols says as he goes round to my feet. I look down at my left leg, doesn't look like there's anything wrong with it to me, but I start feeling it worse before he has a proper go at it, and I can say that the brandy does not help.

Now Mrs Moran knocks me out. Thank Christ. When I come back round and it's all over I don't argue about more brandy. A lot more. There are tears in my eyes now, and they are not all for me. There's someone yelling over the other side of the room; I can't see him and hope it might be Dad. Know it's not. Dad wouldn't carry on like that.

FRANCINE

So, I've tried to sketch a kookaburra from memory today — it looks like a duck — and I've paced around the garden imagining it till it bored me witless. At least I've calmed down now. Halfway home this morning, my heart still battering like a bird hitting a window, one of those work whistles started blowing shrill above the incessant crunch-crash din of the place and I just about jumped out of my skin. As if it were demanding, *What* are *you doing, Miss Connolly!* before setting off a chorus of every like whistle across the entire valley. This place is conspiring against me.

Good God, I even contemplated looking for my old needlework, which I haven't touched for at least a year — a twee thing of violets and lobelia I had planned to place under glass on my dressing table before the tedium set in: didn't get halfway round the border. It's here somewhere, in one of the packing cases in the spare room. Leave it there. I had a long, hot, drowsy bath instead. I suppose I could have done a little more unpacking to wile away some time, but I can't face it. Really. I'm turning into one of those girls I've always despised; next I'll be peering into the mirror worrying about the fashion of my hairstyle and reading cheap romances to assuage the meaninglessness of my existence.

That's it, I'm going out. I'm not the best at landscapes, but I'll go and have a shot at the hillsides out of town, wait for the sun to come around. I gather up my sketchbook and pencil box and

I'm heading for the stairs when I hear the Austin pull up. Father's home, from whatever he's fortunate enough to have been doing out there all day.

'Francy!' he's calling as his head appears around the front door, waving at me to come down, before disappearing outside again. He's in a terrible excitement.

'What's happened?' I say, following him out, and I can smell the whisky lingering around the doorway. Oh dear.

Oh dear indeed. There's an unconscious man in the back of the vehicle, he's covered in a blanket and there's a graze on his cheek, and I think the worst. Father's run someone down. Well.

'I'll explain in a minute. Stay here while I get McNally to help me,' he says, already striding down the side of the house. Help you do what?

I step closer to the Austin and look at the fellow. His head is lying back on the folded canopy and he's frowning; he winces, then sighs. He's wearing pyjamas and there's a cast on one of his legs sticking out from under the blanket and shoved up diagonally against the front seat. He looks extremely uncomfortable, and quite young too. This is not quite real. I'm still holding my book and pencil box and have a strange compulsion to sketch him.

'Go up and turn down the bed in the spare room, will you, Francy?' Father says behind me, McNally lumping crankily along with him.

'Shouldn't he be in a hospital?' I say; he surely shouldn't be here, should he?

'No,' says Father, quite sharply, and that jolts.

So I go back inside the house and Polly meets me in the hall saying: 'What's all this fuss?'

I shrug, casually, and say as I walk past her: 'We have a visitor, apparently.' My grasping for a small moment of condescension overriding my sense: I should have told her to go upstairs and turn down the bed. No, I should have asked her to help me. I am a first-class fool: there is no bed to turn down. Well, the bed is there but it's not made up. I have never moved so fast in my life. It's a sloppy job, in accordance with my inexperience and haste, but I don't imagine our guest will care. I can hear them awkward and heaving on the stairs. I push the higgledy-piggledy cases into some order against the wall and feel like saluting. Five minutes ago I was wondering what to do. Asketh and the Lord shall provide.

Father looks as if his face is about to explode as he and McNally come in. Our visitor dwarfs his bearers ridiculously; I can't believe they made it up the stairs. Father looks at me urgently and I take the poor man's feet, trying to be gentle against the weight, and help heft him onto the bed. The man lets out a pitiful groan but he doesn't rouse. I look at my father, my eyebrows fairly off my face. He cocks his head; he'll speak to me outside. I look back at the man as I turn to leave and realise we've just left him sprawled there, with his feet off the end of the bed. Nothing I can do about the length of the bed, but I pull the covers up over him, and follow Father out of the room.

What? my eyes are saying to him; he's still catching his breath.

Then he runs a hand through what's left of his hair and he says: 'Oh, Francy.'

My eyes are still asking but I'm waiting for him to tell me that he ran the man over.

Instead he says: 'There was a terrible accident at the Wattle today, a cave-in. Three men killed. One of them this lad's father.'

That is unspeakably awful, but I still don't understand what he's doing here in our house. He's a *miner*.

'And his mother's out of town,' Father adds, shaking his head, but that's not an answer.

28

'Shouldn't he be in hospital?' I repeat, with some proper compassion this time.

'No. There's a man they've got in there with gallstones, moaning to wake the devil. And that Doctor Nichols said the lad'll be all right; just groggy from too much brandy — he passed out on the way here. Needs a comfortable bed, that's all. When I realised he had no one at home, I said we'd take him, till his mother comes — just overnight possibly. It seemed the very least ...' He grabs at the top of the balustrade as if off balance.

'Are *you* all right?' I ask. He looks ill himself, face pale now, and tired.

'Yes,' he bellows, summoning a grin at my concern and heading down the stairs with the spring back in his step. 'Nothing a malt won't fix.'

I follow him down, wondering why it is he feels so personally responsible. I'm sure Father doesn't know a jot about this mine of his, and a sense of responsibility is not generally known to be a high point in his repertoire.

But I don't get a chance to ask any more questions before Mr Drummond clumps through the open front door.

'Francine,' he says, taking off his hat as he sees me at the bottom of the stairs.

'I'm so sorry to hear about the accident,' I say to him above my own confusion.

He nods very gravely in my direction but he's looking at Father. 'I need to have a word, Frank,' he says and, although Mr Drummond has never displayed too much good humour at the best of times, he appears positively grim now.

Father nods in return and they head without further word for the parlour. The door closes with a soft click behind them. I have never eavesdropped in my life — I'm confident that the majority of closed-door conversations between Father and his associates would not be worth the bother — but, naturally, I can't help myself now. I slip over to the parlour door and press my ear to the wood.

I don't hear anything at first since Polly heaves down the hall behind me and shuts the front door with a forcible sigh. She stops as she turns back, and stares at me, but I have no shame; I wave her away with a scowl.

The first thing I do hear is Mr Drummond saying: 'You've no business taking this sort of thing into your own hands. You're a bloody liability!' I couldn't fail to hear it, since he's not making much effort to keep his voice down or hold off the expletives.

I can't make out what Father says in reply but there's a dismissive quality to it, followed by the stopper plipping out of the decanter, then Mr Drummond says: 'What message does that send the men, you strolling in here and promising Lewis such terms? Every bloody industrialist in this country would think you a fool — a dangerous one. You've got no bloody idea!'

'What difference will it make to the company ledger?' Father says and I can hear a scoff in his tone. 'They are my profits too — I can do what I like with my bit.'

'The difference is that it won't stop at compensation, Frank. Give them an inch on this issue and we'll never hear the end of it. The union could well use this as a precedent and run with it.'

'And they'll hit a brick wall, won't they, in you and every bloody industrialist in the country. But three men died today, in *our* mine, that's all that concerns me. And their three widows. The piddling payout from their own fund won't amount to enough for those families to live on beyond a few months. The lad upstairs will be off for weeks — is it his fault he won't be able to work?'

'It's not ours either. This was an accident, pure and simple — as the enquiry will show. We're not culpable for something so completely unpreventable. As *that lad's* father would have known: he was one of our most valuable workers; where's our compensation for losing him? This is not a charity. You can't act on your emotions here.'

'I've never acted any other way, John,' Father laughs, then cuts it off. 'I'm going to make them a reasonable offer and be done with it.'

'Why?' There's genuine bewilderment from Mr Drummond now. 'This is madness. You've never shown the slightest interest in ten years and now …?'

'And now I am. Look, John …' and it goes to mumbles now. Mr Drummond says, 'Oh,' a soft blow. Father laughs again, more mumbles. Mr Drummond says: 'All right, but make certain it's unofficial — just between you and them, and don't involve Lewis. Keep the union out of it. I still think you're mad, though.' He no longer sounds angry, just resigned.

'Done,' Father says cheerfully. 'And I'm going to build a lavatory as well, if it's the last thing I do!'

'They won't thank you for it,' Mr Drummond adds, 'if that's why you're doing it. Believe me.'

'Oh no, it's far more indulgent than that.' Father's moving towards the door. 'Stay for dinner?'

I scurry to the stairs and bound nearly to the top before they come out.

'I think I've had enough excitement for today,' Mr Drummond says; he's so terribly dour; Catholic like us, but from Yorkshire. He adds: 'And so have you. I'll see you tomorrow.' And he's gone.

Well. That all says a lot and a little. Father's had some kind of epiphany by the sounds of it and appointed himself philanthropist, which is at once as baffling as it seems fabulously noble, but that soft 'Oh' echoes. I shall make a big deal of his kindness at dinner tonight, since it is evidently so important to him, whatever the reason. I frown; can't put two and two together with this lot.

I look across the landing into the open doorway of the spare room and another whisper slips through me. I can see through to the window, and see myself sitting on a rock futilely trying to capture the sun on the hills with a piece of charcoal. That's where I'd be right now. While this man in the bed … I can't begin to think. I don't even know his name.

DANIEL

I've gone in again, and I can see the face ahead of me, black and shiny, even though it's a fair few yards away yet. I'm telling Dad it was lucky the prop didn't break my neck yesterday and he laughs; he says: 'Pity it didn't hit you on the head.' Then my lamp goes out but I'm not bothered because I can still see his. But then Dad's goes out too. I'm still not worried, though, because I can feel his shoulder rubbing against mine and we just keep walking. Then I feel the roof scrape the top of my head and I think I know where I am. I sing out to Dad but he doesn't answer; I grope around for a bit but I can't find him. Then the roof starts pressing down on my head. But I've stopped walking now, so how can that be? It keeps coming down, slowly, and I try to crouch but I can't bend my knee. It's grinding against my skull now. Coal fills my mouth. And I am thirsty like you wouldn't believe.

Then I realise I'm dreaming and pull myself out of it. But the roof is still laying into the back of my head. I know I'm going to chuck. I can taste the stale grog in the back of my throat and it doesn't want to be there any more. I sit straight up and the rest of me doesn't like that at all. I feel for the edge of the bed in the dark, lean over the side and let it go.

That's better, except for everything else. I lie back again. I don't care. I don't want to know.

FRANCINE

What on earth? I'm halfway into my nightdress when I hear it. Oh no. I step out onto the landing, dreading what I know I'm going to find. I've heard Father retch into the night pot often enough, but that was not Father. He does not tend to yell obscenities before he vomits, and he's also just appeared from his own room. We glance at each other with feeble resolution before I open the spare room door.

I feel for the light cord and pull but the stupid thing doesn't go on — of course. Electricity's more trouble than it's worth here too. Urgh, I might not be able to see what's happened, but I can smell it clear enough. I grope about for the little oil lamp on top of the chest of drawers. And knock down my pencil box, which I'd left there earlier. 'Are you all right?' I croak into nowhere and there's an affirmative grunt in reply. I've got the lamp glowing now and peer through the gloom at him. He doesn't look too well to me; he is a study of grey. I turn back to Father, who's swaying slightly in the doorway, full as a boot after those *fixing* malts; despite the intent look on his face, he'll be no use. 'Go to bed, Father, I'll deal with it,' I say, sounding very grown up, feeling hopelessly daunted.

'You're a good girl, Francy,' he says, lilting thickly. If I weren't such a good girl I'd curse him for this. So much for philanthropy. What was he thinking? He shuffles back to his room, hand raised in benediction.

34

What to do? I don't want to, but I'll have to call Polly up. I have no idea where to begin. 'Polly!' I call down the stairs, and somehow that shakes my brain into action: I go back to my room for my basin and the cloth I was just about to wash my face with. It occurs to me that our guest might appreciate it more, sans rosewater.

When I return across the landing Polly's already hauling herself and a mop and bucket up the stairs; evidently she heard it too. As I now realise she would have, her room being directly below at the back of the house. 'Poor lad,' she says as she reaches the top, and even manages to make that sound like it's my fault.

I ignore her; she can deal with the vomit on the floor. I put the basin and cloth on the bedside table and take the lamp from the drawers and put it there too so I can see him better. I soak the cloth and wring it, then hover over him, hesitating. I've never washed someone's face before.

Polly slaps the mop onto the floorboards over the other side of the bed and he opens his eyes and blinks straight into mine. Green glinting amber. It's only then that I recognise him. The miner from the street. It shocks me more than anything else that's happened on this very strange day. His face is fierce, not smiling now, not smudged with coal; his eyes impale me as he takes the cloth that's dangling in my hand. He wipes his mouth and gives it back to me, then lies back again, turning away from the light. The embarrassment I felt before is nothing compared to this moment. I am suspended in it.

Polly gathers up the bucket and mop and says: 'I'll get a cloth to finish off.'

'No. I'll wipe it,' I say. 'You can go. Thank you.'

I sound mean, with the meanness of incompetence, and it sticks in my throat.

'Suit yourself,' she says and I don't hear her leave.

I sit down on the packing cases. I won't get a cloth right away.
I am having a higher thought: shame.

And I remember his name now, Father told me during dinner.
Daniel Ackerman. And that only makes it worse.

DANIEL

There's a light rain spitting on the window, mist circling through the gums outside. If I was dry before, then I'm screaming for a drink now. Francine Connolly is sitting near the window, on a box, her head against a chest of drawers. She's asleep, like a doll in a shop. There's a small wooden container at her feet that's flipped open, showing the pencils inside. When I saw her in the night I thought I was dreaming again, but I've worked it out now. Though why I'm here is a mystery I couldn't be arsed thinking about. Her stomach grumbles, she makes a small mewling sound and she's coming to. Thirsty as I am, I don't want her to wake up yet. Lying here looking at her and the rain is keeping me blank. If I look at her I can't see Mum's face. I remember Evan telling me somewhere yesterday that he'd sent off word to her. He didn't mention anything about Dad. Didn't have to.

If I look at Francine Connolly I can feel the anger settle hard in me.

She opens her eyes and sits up with a start. She's wondering where she is, sitting on a box in her nightdress.

'Hm. Hm. Hello,' she says, brushing her hair off her face, like she sleeps there every night.

'I need to piss,' I say.

She blushes all over her cheeks, hands me the pot and leaves. She can fuck off now. I should have asked for a drink first, though. As for the other, it's not an easy job and I end up pissing half on the floor. What an animal I am. I'll be able to watch her clean it up.

Hello. She's back, all tucked into her slim skirt, with breakfast. I throw down the water, but I can't eat. As she leaves again I want to tug the back of her hair and ask her why. Another, older woman comes in, I've seen her in town once or twice but I don't know her. She smiles plainly at me and cleans up my mess and I feel like a pig.

A little while later Frank Connolly comes in. Unbelievable as it is, that's who he is. Overfed and puffed out for it. Asking me how I am, telling me he'll make sure my mother and I are looked after. I can still see him patting me on the chest yesterday, wanting to shove him off. I can see him driving his flash motor car. I'll take whatever money there is, but I don't want his sympathy. He, and everyone like him, is the reason for this. Why my father is dead. Why one brother is dead and the other one taken off. Why my mother is quiet. Why I've been cut or bruised or burned in some way just about every day for the last five years. Maybe from a different view I might think he was a good bloke, but his generosity squashes me like an ant here. I get lost in the tiny red lines that snake out across his nose, and say nothing.

Then they all leave me alone. I push myself up against the back of the bed so at least I'm not lying down any more. That's all I can do at the moment and I just sit here like my arse is drilled to the mattress. It stops raining, but the mist thickens and fills the window. I get lost there too. I'm thinking about that day I ran ahead to warn Mrs Skelton about Jimmy. I was fifteen and skinny and I flew and I didn't really know what I was doing. I knew what to do, and why I was running, and what to say, but I didn't know what it meant. That's how they want you to be: to do as you're told and not think about it too much. Everyone. Them and us. But that look on Mrs Skelton's face … I want to see her now and tell her properly, but she moved away; don't know where she is. It's not even anger in me now, it's just white, hot, and I've got to get out of here, and forgetting I can't, I go to get up. And I'm biting down against it when Evan walks in.

He tells me, finally, what I already know about Dad, and the others, Fred McNally and Matt Jones who were in the stall after ours, and that Mum'll be here in the afternoon sometime, and that I'm not to worry because Connolly's paid the doctor's bill and sounds good for some figure of compensation regardless of the enquiry, which Evan'll keep me well out of, and his low smooth voice fills me so that I'm not hearing the words so much as the sounds of him talking to me, until he says, 'How's the leg, then, boyo,' and I lose it like a girl. He sits down with an arm around my back as I do, for everything, and for knowing that this is the last time a man will touch me like this. My father is gone. He's gone. And I'm still here, but I've gone somewhere too.

FRANCINE

Not only am I shame-filled in a dozen different ways, I am altogether irrelevant to this day, this drama, this other person's being. How mortifying, falling asleep in the room like that; flushing, mute, idiotic. And the way he glared when I brought the tray in: he despises me. That rankles — how dare he! But then I think of the state he's in and how he quite possibly recognised me, too, as that strange, rude girl in the street, and I can't blame him. And I flush and flush in waves of indignant humiliation and something else I cannot name, more a feeling in the very centre of me that's soft and waiting to be stabbed. I also have a sharp, irritating strain in my neck.

I spend the rest of the morning hiding in the empty parlour pretending to read *My Brilliant Career,* can't get past: *My Dear Fellow Australians, just a few lines to tell you that this story is all about myself* … Father's out and Polly's gone to the shops for something or other. She'll be back to fix lunch, and praise be, because there is no way I am going back into the spare room. I can't face him. Father will take him to his own house this afternoon around three, and three can't come around soon enough.

There's a knock at the front door and my heart just about leaps through my ribs. My face must be fairly incandescent as I open the door. I cannot make my mouth function.

'Francine, isn't it?' There's a woman there, tall and broad and already impatient with the cretin she's speaking to.

40

'Yes,' I manage.

'Ada Moran,' she says, and I'm not sure at first if it's an introduction or an instruction. She's holding out a bundle of neatly folded clothes that she's retrieved from a basket at her feet. 'For Daniel. Daniel Ackerman,' she explains, because I clearly need telling.

'Oh. Thank you. That's very kind of you,' I splutter. 'I shall see that he gets them. Very good to meet you, Mrs Moran.' Mrs Moran, who I now remember is the *stretched to the limit* matron at the hospital. There's a wrench of gallstones in my belly.

'Must rush,' she says after one last mystified glance and she's already off and away to the trap waiting for her in the drive.

I look at the bundle in my arms and do as the circumstances dictate: I write Polly a note and leave it for her with the clothes on the kitchen table. *Gone out, not sure when I'll be back. Please see that Mr Ackerman gets lunch & clothes.*

I can now add abject cowardice to my growing list of shortcomings.

Hayseed makes no comment as we ride up into the hills, but I'm sure he looks askance at me a few times. The air is wonderful, though, once we're out of town. Damp from the rain and the mist that's now been burned away by the sun, which is warm on my skin one moment and cooled by the breeze the next. A perfect May day. Even the scrub looks more appealing, brighter, greener, and at last I can feel myself settling to the rhythm of Hayseed's gait.

From up here I can look down on it all, the smudges of smoke and the scars on the land. I try to imagine how it might look if there were no people here; how it would have been to the native Aborigines and the first explorers, long since passed through, inexorable Progress on their tail. The shape of the valley itself is

41

really quite beautiful: it looks like two ancient women lying down around a campfire. Their rounded breasts and thighs encircle devastation as if caressing it; they are melancholy and serene at once. More melancholy today, I think. There is still a tightness in my chest but I'm made tranquil looking at them. Beyond are hills and more hills, their steep crags and boulders plain brown now in the high sun. Beyond them are the mountains, which are indeed very Blue, dark and hazy shapes that from this vantage seem to encircle too, folding and rolling away forever. Like the sea. And I am homesick again for the home I no longer have.

I'm also not wearing a hat and I can feel the sun searing the skin off my nose. What else can I manage to make a debacle of today?

We ride slowly, very slowly, back, and I try to shade my face with my hand as we go. Hopeless. Still, I take the long way round the edge of town before turning up again to our eyrie by the slagheap. My dull but insistent hysteria returns as we near the house. But it's all right. I'm only halfway up the road when I see the Austin pull out of the drive and putter down the other side of the hill. He's gone, then.

When I go inside I tell Polly I'm not feeling well and there's no fib in it this time. I flop down on my bed and fall straight to sleep.

Father wakes me, gently rubbing my shoulder, asking me if I want dinner. He thinks I'm exhausted from tending the sick last night. And the rest, I think blearily as he's smiling at me. I tell him that I'm famished and he says, 'Good girl.' He winces as he stands; he's done his back in, poor thing, and I'm not surprised. I stretch and stare into the dusky gloom as he leaves and I tell him I'll be down in a minute.

I am famished too; I realise I haven't eaten all day, and I'm at the table in a blink, devouring plates and bowls without drawing breath. When Polly has deigned to clear the carnage, Father pours himself a port and leans back in his chair, regarding me thoughtfully. He's been unusually quiet and conservative tonight; I imagine he's exhausted by his benevolence. Then as he lights his pipe he says to me: 'There's something I want you to do tomorrow, Francy.'

Joy brims: something to do! What?

'It's time, I think, you took more of a part in things …'

Yes?

'You've not been out in the world much and …'

He's sending me abroad?

'God knows the world is a tangle of a place. You must know something of its realities, Francy, and it's my fault that I've let you run a bit wild, follow your own mind, without better guidance …'

Where is this going? He doesn't seem soused, either. His eyes are bright and serious as he puffs on the pipe.

'I suppose I thought as long as you were safe and happy then there was no need. But there is a need. I can't have you stay my little girl forever. One day you'll marry …'

What? Oh … he's got someone in mind? He sees the confusion on my face and puts up a gentling hand.

'But more important, one day you'll inherit whatever I have at the end, and that may be considerable. May not be!' He laughs, then resumes the sombre tone: 'I want you to be wise enough to know what to do with it, whether you marry or not.'

'That's very modern of you, Father,' I interrupt, intrigue turning to caution. 'But what is it exactly you want me to do tomorrow?'

'Oh yes,' he says, smiling, as if come back into himself, and I must say that although Father is peculiar, this solemnity is more peculiar than anything. And then: 'I want you to go to the Ackermans' tomorrow and give them the compensation payment I've drawn for them.'

I feel in turn the muscles of my face range through naked surprise, perplexity and suspicion. Father really has gone mad. Where is Mr Drummond to back me up?

'There's reason here,' he holds up his hand again. 'You've met the lad, and he's not in a good way, in his spirits. I don't think he'd appreciate me turning up, one of the bosses, you know … no, you don't know, and that's the point … But you, in your blessed innocence, won't offend him or his mother as I might; you might soften the exchange, and at the same time see what it means.'

'What what means?' I ask, beside myself. I cannot imagine The Lad is very likely to think me a softening agent, but I can't gather my thoughts swiftly enough to express that right now.

'I know what it means to be poor, Francy, very, *very* poor; you don't. I've spent the last twenty years denying it. I have been blessed, in so many ways, with you, your mother … and most times more money than I needed. I wouldn't take a minute of any of my good fortune back — nor any of my indulgences, wise and unwise. But I've climbed over the backs of others to have the means for it all, pretending all the while that I'm only playing with the pennies and the rest has little to do with me, and you can't remove yourself from that kind of hypocrisy indefinitely. It comes back to bite those that leave themselves open to it, and I'd rather you never get bitten.'

I have no idea what he's talking about, and plead into his ramble: 'But what if they don't appreciate the boss's daughter either?'

'Well, that will be worth your understanding too. It'll be all right, Francy. Trust me. It might not make too much sense to you now, but it will, in time. I want the best for you, but having it, really having it, requires knowing the score. I'll be plain: you're too naive, too sheltered, and that makes you vulnerable; it's also a waste on a girl as clever as you are. I never want you to know poverty, of course, but I want you to know what it means to work, and what it means to be good. To be decent. The things the sisters couldn't teach you, because they must be learned in themselves. I'm afraid, on balance, I've not been a good example, my darling girl.'

His eyes moisten, and he hasn't even touched the port. He has that heartbroken look that makes me spring to his defence. 'Of course you're good! Silly thing. You're overtired, that's what you are,' I say, although what I really want to ask is what this is all about. But I don't and I won't, because I know he's going to change the subject as he always does when he's said as much as he's going to say.

'You got some sun today,' He nods with the pipe, and winks. Sparkling at me.

I put my hand to my face. It's broiled. At least The Lad won't be able to tell whether or not I'm blushing when I make my preposterous errand tomorrow. This is too bizarre for contemplation. I go off to bed with Mr Drummond's *Oh* whispering to me again, and a nagging expectation of failure. Father has, as he said, let me be, and letting me follow my own mind has apparently not been for the best thus far.

DANIEL

Mim's had another girl. Isobella. She already had that name pegged. She came before Mum even got there and for a second I want to ask Mum what time she came, to know if it was before or after. Like me and the other Daniel. But I don't believe in all that rubbish anyway and doubt that Dad would agree to come back as a girl. Mum tells me about Isobella down to the way her hair sticks up on her head and I know what she means. We've all got that hair, like Mum's — dark and straight as paint bristles; you don't want to cut it too short. There are tears coming from the corners of her eyes as she speaks, but you wouldn't know she was crying unless you were watching them fall. I don't know why I was so angry this morning, why I didn't want to see Mum's face. She's so small sitting on the bed next to me, but bigger than everything. I touch her hand, but she only lets it stay there for a second. I know. And I don't know anything.

'It's cold tonight. You're going to need another blanket,' she says, and when she leaves to get it I am black again.

Dad was going to die from the dust anyway, eventually. He would have been grateful to go not knowing about it. Out like a light. Having a laugh at the Methodists who'll bury him at the bottom of the ridge below the paddock at the Wattle tomorrow, as he wished, knowing that he was an atheist through and through, but praying for him anyway. That's the way Mum's telling it. But I just see filthy animals sweating and grunting in the bottom of a cave. No, I'm not angry now. I'm nothing.

She will bury him tomorrow, without me there; Mrs Moran came round earlier and told me to stay in bed, which I am unlikely to do. But I don't want to go to the burial anyway, even if I could get down the ridge without being winched. Mum says she'll be all right going alone; but she won't be alone at all. It's not Dad I can't face, it's the others. Evan, Robby, everyone. The whole bloody lot of them.

FRANCINE

I have to go to the Ackermans' this morning, since the garden fellow is coming at two. Father scratches out a little map on the back of the envelope he's holding, to show me where to go. And hands it to me; this contains the cheque: branded with my ignorance before I even step outside.

Hayseed appears impartial when he sees me; but then he sighs as we set off. He's right. This won't do, there must be more of me in this, so I stop in town to buy … I don't know what's appropriate so I take nothing but the cheque. Mr Symes sees me as I pass the post office, but he needn't worry. I'm off to bother someone else today, several miles away.

I could turn around and go home, tell Father that I became impossibly lost and vaporous, claiming unspecific feminine deficiency. That won't do either. For the first time I can't come home glib. Father sent me off with a kiss on the top of my head as assurance that I will fulfil his unfathomable plans for me, while he spends the day doing the rounds of the other two widows. This is too awful.

What does he want me to do? I know what I want to do: slip the envelope under the door and run away.

The houses are dark brown brick along Dell Street, miniatures of ours. Gables and windows trimmed with plain white fretwork, whiter for the shade of the hill they sit snug beneath. There's no grey film on anything here, so far from the smokestacks. The house I'm after is at the end of the road, which breaks away from the hill and opens to a gully that funnels the sun. Here we are then.

There are two camellias either side of the small front verandah and a huge climbing rose covering the fence on the left-hand side, all well trimmed in preparation for winter, only a few blooms left on the climber which are so pale they might look white but for the gable above that shows they are pink. It's in better shape than the front of my house. On the right there is no fence; the ground tumbles away into the scrub as if this really is the end of civilisation. Well, that's about it for procrastination upon the flora, and I broach the front step.

The door knocker is cold in the palm of my hand and I bang it once, too softy, how pathetic. I bang it again, twice. How bad can this be? These are people with well-cared-for shrubbery; they won't bite me. And it seems they are not home! What luck, I think before I hear: 'Come round the back.'

It's The Lad. Said with the same sharp, tight-jawed truculence as *I need to piss*. This cannot go well. I should just leave. Take myself and my faulty, disappointing mind back to my father and demand to know what on God's earth he hopes to achieve by making such a fool of me.

But I can't. I look down at the envelope I'm holding and it appears rather more important than my own distress. I shall simply go round, deliver it, ask after his health and bid him good day. Him, who appears to exert a greater influence upon my existence than I do at present, I think as I plod along the gully side, snagging my sleeve on a gnarl-laden tree opposite one of the windows. I can see a neat vegetable plot and there's a black and white cow tethered a few yards off down the back; she looks up and moos at me as I reach the rear of the house. She's in on this too.

And there he is. Oh —

I stop dead still at the sight. He is wearing no shirt, which is shocking enough in itself, but he's so … sculpted; he looks as if he is cut from marble or cast in bronze and should be adorning a fountain rather than a lean-to verandah at the back of this little house. An image confused by his broken leg, which is propped on another chair and startling as it emerges from the cut-off trousers; and he appears to be whittling a little knife into a small block of wood. He is utterly sun-drenched and I see that his hair is not black at all, but a very dark auburn. Then he looks across at me and I'm sure I've just gasped. My face is a waratah in full fire beneath my sunburn.

He picks up his shirt and puts it on, far too slowly; says, 'The sun,' gesturing at it by way of explanation. And says nothing else. Goes back to whittling.

I drag up my voice from somewhere in the pit of me and very quickly get to the point, the quicker to get out of here. 'My father would like you and your mother to have this,' I say quite levelly, considering, moving a few steps towards him, holding out the envelope. 'Is your mother in?'

'She's burying her husband,' he says, still whittling.

'Oh.' I breathe out the sound that snuffs my self-absorption. 'I'm so sorry,' I say, and mean it to my core, for his loss and my tactless intrusion upon it at this time; Father should have checked such arrangements … I should have guessed. My eyes settle on him properly again, a little more easily now; I can see the bruise on his grazed cheek purpling and I feel compelled to touch him in some way so that he knows I mean it. But there is an ugly chasm between us.

He doesn't look up.

'If there's anything you need, anything at all, you must let my father know,' I say, and somehow I know this is precisely what I should say. I put the envelope on the chair, the corner tip tucked just under his leg. It's the only place I can put it without giving it to him or leaving it on the ground.

'Well …' I get that far and I can't say good day because my throat is completely closed over with the agony of this. It's done, then, and I'll leave now.

DANIEL

'Wait,' I say. I didn't want to make her cry. It's not her fault the rock fell down, is it. I've been enough of a pig to her already. A pig all round. I've had all morning since Mum left to wonder about that and make me want to lift my game.

She stops and looks at me, and she's close enough that I can see it's sunburn not blushing all over her face now. She's an odd one. She squeaked at seeing me half naked, and I couldn't help that; spending most days underground makes you want the light on you when it's there. But then she's here on her father's business and very direct about it too, and then she's barely holding in tears. And she's something to look at, even with the sunburn.

'Thanks,' I say, looking at the envelope. Then I look at her again. 'I would like you to do something for me, if that's all right,' I say and her eyebrows go up, blue eyes blinking. She is a doll. 'You couldn't get me a drink, could you?'

I couldn't be arsed dragging myself back inside for one — it took me long enough to get myself out here in the first place — and it'll give me an excuse to thank her again.

'Of course,' she says. Blink, blink. And I tell her where she'll find a glass inside and that the tap's just here by the back wall. She goes in and I hear her rootling around, then the crash of something heavy. And, 'Oh dear.'

'You right?' I call out to her.

'Yes,' she says as she comes out, 'I knocked the kettle off the stove.' As if she does that every day; as if that's an easy thing to do. Then she goes to the tap and fills the glass, her hair coming out of its coil again and falling down her back. I feel like the worst pig remembering I wanted to yank it. Was that only yesterday?

'Thanks,' I say, and I don't have trouble smiling at her. My face feels like it hasn't smiled in ages. Probably hasn't.

She says: 'That's a pleasure.' And stands there. I don't know what to say to her, so I just drink it.

Then she says, 'What are you making?' pointing at the carving. I pick it up and show her. She laughs: like a bell.

She's an odd one, she is.

FRANCINE

It's a tiny kookaburra … its head popping out above the wood block, rough and only just begun. He looks at me like I am a lunatic. Him and the kookaburra both. I can't explain myself to him; where would I begin? And I doubt very much that he'd be in the least interested. But relief is sweet: he does not hate me, and I have accomplished my mission.

Then he smiles at me again, that same about-to-say-something smile from the street. That does me in. It's an outrage that I should ever have not wanted to see it before; and it's an outrage that I want to see it now.

Before the thought is formed in my wayward brain, I say: 'I have to go now. But I could visit again, if you like.'

Looking at me like I am a lunatic again. Why did I say that? What an impertinence. How could I presume that he would even want me to. The Boss's Daughter no less. What must he think of such brazenness? Now I've insulted him, yet again.

'Suit yourself,' he says, but bemusement seems to creep into his frown.

I leave him then and I am a walking scandal. Not sure that's exactly what Father intended I achieve this morning.

My heart is thumping to burst and I am swimmy-headed enough to drown, and I don't care how utterly inappropriate that is. This Lithgow conspiracy is too strong and I'll just have to surrender.

DANIEL

Three hundred pounds. I didn't expect it would be that much. There goes the balance of payments on Mum's piano. Bugger that. It could buy Mum this house, if they'll sell it to her. It will cover us for months, a year, more. I don't understand this amount of money in one go, not that we don't deserve it, but … It's too much and not enough, and Dad has died for it. I don't know what to think. One and a half times more than I can earn in an ordinary year. Mum puts her face in her hands when she sees it, and that says it all. I look at the cheque again; I can't remember having ever even seen a cheque before. It's drawn on the Bank of New South Wales by Francis Patrick Connolly — there's a Mick — in favour of Mrs H Ackerman. Dad looks up out of the paper at me. H for Harry, or Heinrich as he really is, was. Mum called him that whenever she had something serious to say. He says to me now, 'What are you looking at?' the traces of his accent making flat words flatter. And I think I see him stalk across the room as I've seen him do thousands of times. Well, he's not in any heaven, that's certain. He's on the face of a cheque and on my face and in the shape of my body and in my dreams and in the dust in the mine and in this room. And in this bloody payout.

Evan, who's come home with Mum, says: 'Connolly told me he wanted to make it more, but three hundred was all he could afford each split between all of you. It's come out of his own pocket. How about that? Says this is all very "*unofficial*". Can you believe it?'

Out of his own pocket? I can't hold anything else Evan's saying for a minute. Connolly, as well as his daughter, must be dippy. But I'm not complaining on either count.

Evan's going on: 'If only there were men of his sort filling the parliament, to make it official, eh. It's only commonsense — that such payouts force better safety all round; and better safety means men stay on; men who stay on are better at what they do, and so it goes. Better for everyone.'

I hear that all right. And so it doesn't go. Dad was the best, the safest, the most reliable, and no act of parliament could stop the coal from killing him or anyone else one way or another. I've made a decision: I'm not going back in. Not ever.

'You deserve every penny of that,' Evan says to us both, and his Taffy accent rolls out the words as much as Dad's would have squashed them. 'Harry was champion, he was.'

Amen. But I'm not going back in.

FRANCINE

By the time I get home I have regained my wits, sort of. Of course I cannot have an acquaintance with a *miner*. That's plain ridiculous. What would we possibly talk about? *How black was the coal today? Oh, quite black. That's good. Anyone killed or maimed today? No, not today.* We have nothing in common. I shan't see him again, and he won't really expect me to.

The garden fellow, a Mr Saunders, arrives promptly and we roam around the backyard discussing magnolias and rhododendrons and all things frost-hardy, since the frosts are bitter and it snows once or twice in winter, sometimes heavily. He suggests massed bulbs: daffodils and irises. Ornamental maples. Dwarfed conifers. Box hedge at the verandah edge leading out to … it all floats about in my head, unframed and nonsensical, and I say: 'And an apple — over there, in the very centre.'

'An apple tree?' he asks, flummoxed by my interruption upon his vision.

'Yes.'

'Just one, on its own?'

'Yes.'

'It might appear … perhaps … a little out of place there. A little common. Ordinary.' And he doesn't care how rude and patronising that sounds.

'Well, make it two then,' I tell him.

And I know then that I am not quite recovered from my incident with The Lad. I want red bobbles to remember him always and this is not a higher thought — it is nauseatingly romantic and daft. But when this Mr Saunders from Bathurst persists with, 'It's not the most attractive tree, for a formal garden, Miss Connolly. A pair of maples, I'm sure, will be better there, as a subtle focal point. Shall we let your father have a say too?', he speaks as if to a child and that steels me.

'I want two apples trees,' I say. 'Red ones.' And that's final. 'My father would not know the difference between an apple and a maple if it hit him across the face. But by all means, ask him if you think it's for the best.'

'Very well,' he says, cowed and surprised. 'We'll include these apples, if you wish.' I do wish, and I'm delighted. But it's a hollow victory. I'm not altogether certain what an apple tree looks like. Apples, they are such a staple, but where do they grow? How do they grow? I have a vague idea of the fruit on the branches, but what does the tree itself look like? Perhaps they don't grow on trees at all but the devil pours them into the bins at the grocers when we are not looking.

The obsequious Mr Saunders slithers away with his instructions and says that he'll contact my father with a quote next week — he needs to confer with Beelzebub first. The fun's gone out of it altogether. Perhaps I won't have a garden at this house at all. I look up at the gums drooping over the stubbly brown grass and I droop too.

Father putters home, he looks tired and painfully sober, and suggests we retire to the parlour for a sprawl. He pours himself a fat finger of malt and it disappears into him before he says: 'So how did it go with the Ackermans, my girl?'

I tell him all about it, leaving out my idiotic rhapsody at the end, of course, and emphasising that The Lad appeared vastly improved in spirits, leaving out that he appeared magnificent, actually.

'Good, good,' he nods, well pleased with me. Why, I don't know; it seems such a simple exchange as I told it just now. What lessons as to the tangled world and poverty and hypocrisy was I supposed to take from it? The questions are on the tip of my tongue when he says: 'It'd be a fine idea to go back in a week or two to pay a call on Mrs Ackerman, introduce yourself and let her know she's not forgotten, hmm?'

I stare.

'The lad'll be starved for company too no doubt.'

Hmm indeed. The Lithgow conspiracy envelops me again and I am fast beginning to suspect that my father is its ringleader.

DANIEL

She's come back all right. I'm exactly where I was before, exactly a week later, except I'm fully clothed, because it's freezing, waiting to see who's coming round the back. And bloody grateful now that someone's coming because I've never been so bored in all my life. It's just me and Mum all week: I watch her cooking, sweeping, dusting, and in the garden, and milking Beatrice, and doing the washing, folding it and putting it away, then reading something or other out here in the sun, and I realise something as I watch her: she's peaceful in her quietness, and maybe she steadies herself in her routines. I'm lost without mine. And out of sorts about it. Which side of my arse needs a break now? How long will it take for that itch under the cast to shove off? If it happens beyond my knee, I can't reach it with anything. Jesus. And every time I get up and lurch around, my head spins from the rush of blood. Mum says: 'Stay put. It will heal quicker.' No it bloody won't. I'm nearly ready to beg to be let back in the Wattle. And that thought turns my head inside out, running through everything again. Shut it off. I even wonder once or twice if Dad got the better deal. I don't really, I'm just that bloody bored. Soon I won't be able to sit out here at all; winter'll be here in the next five minutes; don't want to think about what I'll be like indoors.

Mum's gone on her peaceful and steady way up to town to get flour and eggs, half her luck, and I hear that pony and trap pull up. I think I'm imagining it, I'm that badly hopeful, then I think it must be Mrs Moran, who said she'd stop by again to check my circulation. On Saturday she told me it was important I keep moving my toes, meaning that failure to do this might result in worse things. That's been another thing to think about. But when I hear the knock I know it's Francine Connolly. Still, I don't believe it. Until she comes round, trips up a bit on nothing that I can see on the ground, like she does it every day, and says: 'Hello.'

And I don't know what to say. All I can think of is that I haven't had a shave yet today, which is very unlike me; won't let that go again. After ten years I make my face smile and say hello back. I've spent that much time thinking things I should not think about her. She is that far out of bounds.

'Is your mother in?'

Obviously not. 'She's gone up the road.'

'Oh. I was hoping she would be here.'

Why? She doesn't say; she looks at Beatrice the cow, like she might want to talk to her instead. She's … something to look at all right. Like you wouldn't believe. I can't tell you what she looks like.

She looks at me again. Blink, blink. And says: 'So how are you?' Lips round and pink over the words.

You really don't want to know. I say: 'Good.' Barely.

'How's the kookaburra?' she says.

I don't know where I get the reflex from but I pick it up from the ground beside me and toss it to her. I oiled it yesterday, and it's only just dry. She's so close. She nearly drops it, but doesn't. And laughs again; it's a loud sound that you wouldn't think would come out of her. But it does.

'Where did you learn to do this?' she says through her laughing.

From Dad; a thousand Sundays of sitting out here with him cut into me. I just shrug.

'You don't say much, do you,' she says, frowning, like she expected something different.

'No,' I say. That's true, most of the time.

She lets that laugh out again, and it's hard not to join her. Don't know what she finds so amusing but it's good to hear that sound come out of me. I can't remember the last time I heard it.

The breeze catches the hair that's fallen down her back and it drifts across her face. I'm gone. I could look at her forever.

And I reckon she knows it. She lets me. After ten years she says: 'Well, I'll come back another time to call on your mother. Next Friday, about the same time?'

'Sure,' I say.

'In the meantime, is there anything that you need?'

Not that I can tell you about. But there is something, and I get my head out of her hair for long enough to say it: 'Can you tell your father that my mother wants to buy the house? The mine owns it; she wants to know if they'll sell it to her.'

'Of course,' she says. There's that little frown again.

I want to make her a cup of tea or something, to make her stay, but that's not likely. No chance I'm going to lurch around in front of her. I'm not going to ask her to make me one either; I'm useless enough as it is.

She goes to hand me back the kookaburra but I say: 'You can have it.'

Her face blooms out in red, and I've embarrassed her. She probably doesn't want it; why would she? She makes that little mewling sound like a kitten as she's looking at it. Finally she says, 'Thank you,' and her fingers curl back around it. 'I shall treasure it,' she says, suddenly smiling like we've shared a joke. Then she's off.

The breeze tears up through the gully, but I'm not feeling it. She's that far out of bounds, but a bloke can dream. Maybe I dreamed the whole thing, I'm that bloody bored.

FRANCINE

Good God, Francine Connolly, what are you like? I waited a week, and couldn't bear it any longer. Like he's thrown a rope around my waist. And I flirted with him! I have little experience of young men; well, none to be exact, since the only fellows I ever seemed to meet in Sydney were from St Joseph's, all of them so stitched up, and barely more articulate than The Lad himself. This is cruelty. Do I have a streak of wickedness in me that allows this? Likely. The way he looked at me! And I virtually encouraged him! I have no business doing any such thing. As if I'm practising wiles upon this fellow. I am a disgrace.

But every time I look at the kookaburra my self-admonition is arrested. I don't know what I imagined working men did in their spare time, but it certainly wasn't that. The Lad may be reticent but there's apparently something going on upstairs. How else could he have created this? My copy of *Native Flora and Fauna* finally arrived this afternoon, but I haven't even opened the package. My watercolours, any watercolours, are pale dribbles compared to his abilities. And it is not the fact that is it so tiny and so detailed he must have gone half blind doing it. Neither is it in the practical skill of doing it at all. It's the way the bird looks at me, on the verge of laughter. The way its claws reach around the bit of branch it sits upon as if poised to fly. The Lad is something of an artist, I'm afraid. That makes this all the more excruciating.

I even tried to hide it when I first got home. Put it in the bottom drawer of the wardrobe where I keep things I never look for. Shame bit, and I had to take it out again and put it on the dressing table, where it sits now, looking at me.

I tell myself that it is the fault of my inexperience. That I really am a child and have no idea of these things. That I'll get it over with as soon as I find something sensible to do with myself. But I know all that is rot. I know, I don't know how, but I know I am in love with him. Oh, but there must be a hundred girls dizzy in love with him. I see his sun-kissed chest, the knotted thickness of his shoulder, the fire-glimmer in his raven hair as it falls in a thick curtain across his forehead. His green eyes looking at me as if I am gaga, and wanting his opinion, wanting him to look at me.

I shall have rather a few higher thoughts to contemplate at Mass on Sunday, if I can make it past the thoughts I should not be having at all.

Father relieves me of my misery by coming home at four. But there is no relief, since I have to give him the message about the house, which requires me to mention His name.

'Good, good,' Father says, well pleased, and I can barely hear him above the rushing in my ears. 'I'll have a word with our John Drummond and get an answer shortly, shouldn't be a problem with that, money's money to him.' Then he peers at me as I perch like a statue on the edge of the sofa. 'You look a bit wan, Francy. What's the matter?'

How I want to tell him the whole terrible thing; have him make it go away with a jocular wave of his hand. But instead I force out a chuckle that I hope sounds dismissive but in fact sounds as if I am being strangled. 'Nothing!' I say. 'I just drifted off for a minute.'

'Where did you go, my girl?' he asks and he's sparkling above his pipe, damn him. I am so overstrung I suspect he knows, and is enjoying this torture along with everything else he's put me through these past weeks. This is all his fault.

Mine too, though. I was the fool who said she'd go back for more next Friday, and there's no getting out of it this time.

Oh the melodrama! But I simply can't help it. This is hideous. *Hideous*. And even my own hyperbole is making me ill.

'Actually, I am a little tired,' I tell him. 'I think I'll just have some toast and go to bed.'

He puffs on his pipe and nods. Leprechaun!

Mass does not go well, as if I thought it would. I am contemplating how tall He might be standing up when Father Hurley spies me from the pulpit with his careworn forbearance. I'm sure he knows, as does everyone else here. The place is packed full of decent working people who are married and goodly with pure and simple lives, full of faces I don't know, except Mr Drummond's tight-shut dreary-old-bachelor face, and I studiously avoid looking at him. But everyone else knows me — I am the lunatic, too-good-for-this-town hussy who teases hapless miners. An injured, helpless, bereaved miner no less. Look at her! But I say in my defence that he tempts me. That God created him so well to punish me. I see apples rolling into my skirt — his hands putting them there. I am no Eve — he gave them to me! God is conspicuously quiet on the matter, as always. I should, like Father, give this farce away. There is no God that puts some people in mines and kills them, while others gather the profits in the parlour; no God that gives a widow compensation money only to have her pay it back to the mine responsible for her husband's death, so that she might have what should be hers anyway: her home. No God that delivers me Achilles in the flesh and then says I can't look at him.

So much for Mass. Seems I'm being converted to, what's that fashionable hoity-Melbourne heathen philosophy called again?

Socialism? I have also just had a glimpse of the highest thought
I've had to date. Father is right, it is a tangle, and I should know
more of what things mean beyond myself. For the first time I see
the vast realms of my ignorance and I am not afraid. Why should
I be? They, at least, are mine.

Even still, when Friday comes around again I find myself in a
bother over what to wear. Despite the fact that I will be going
now on serious business — I will carry the Transfer of the Title
Deed with me. After calling in on Mrs Ackerman to agree on a
price, Father went to the lawyers in Sydney during the week to
arrange the papers, and he's given me instructions as to where
Mrs Ackerman will have to sign, and she will give me her bank
cheque for one hundred and eighty pounds, and it will be done.
I was surprised — what can surprise me next? — that he didn't
want to take it himself, pronounce his good news with a fanfare
in his pipe, but perhaps, as he'd said to Mr Drummond, it's not
personal thanks he's after in this. What then? My education in the
tangle? Blow'd if I know, as they say in the classics. Father is a
tangly paradox in himself. With a magic hand for all but me.
Evidently there was no *problem* with Mr Drummond, and I find
myself remembering the outraged way he talked about the
miners that night; that gives me a bit of a chill now. I do know
that business is designed to *make* money, rather than give it away,
but it also seems to me that human beings should be rather less
expendable than he was suggesting.

In any case, my thoughts are quickly swamped by
remembering my own appalling behaviour at that time. *He's a
miner? Filthy, nameless. Please see that Mr Ackerman gets lunch &
clothes*: and is forthwith removed from my conscience. It calms
me a little to self-flagellate about my craven incompetence. Keeps
me from dwelling upon the impossibility of my Great Romance.

I am, today, extremely grateful to have a significant purpose to my visit: I can't have Achilles but I can hand over his house to his mother. Well, you can't have everything, can you?

The kookaburra looks at me.

I feel my throat close over.

DANIEL

She's sitting there with Mum at the table, showing her where to sign. She's wearing a brown jacket buttoned right up her throat, the sort that makes a girl look like she actually wants to be a spinster; bloody awful, but somehow she makes even that look all right. Little splash of freckles on her nose. Not that it matters what I think. I'm over in the corner like a spare shovel. She hasn't looked at me square on since she got here; just a quick hello and into the business. So much for dreaming; she really was after Mum, and was only being polite last time.

'And that's it, Mrs Ackerman,' she says, packing her flash fountain pen away in her pencil box. She looks up at Mum again and smiles, regret in the blink. Mum smiles back and says to her: 'You and your father have made this so easy. I can't thank you enough.'

I can't believe I've been hanging on a line all week for this.

'It's the very least …' she says. She and Mum get up with a scrape of chairs on the floorboards that grates right through me.

Mum looks like she's about to say something to her, but doesn't, and there's a look between them, like they're having a chat without me. Excuse me for breathing. Francine Connolly. She steps around the end of the table, she's leaving now, and she catches the toe of her shoe on the leg. And then she looks across and sees me.

She says: 'Oh. We should … Hmmm.' She looks at Mum again. 'I … think I should like to visit you again, Mrs Ackerman, if that's all right with you.'

Mum's not expecting that but you wouldn't know it unless you were looking for it. She says: 'That would be nice.'

They go to the door talking some rubbish about the camellias out the front. Then I hear her say, 'Oh. I forgot my pencil box,' and she whips back down the hall to grab it. She whispers to me: 'Next Friday.' And she's gone.

When Mum comes back she says: 'Well, we have a house, then, *ja*.' Not yes, but *ja*. And she sits at the table staring at nothing for a second, then she whispers, '*Ungerecht*,' and puts her head in her hands: unjust. Yep. Dad was never interested in owning anything, but this house is him; now it's Mum's, without him.

Her back shakes once and that's the only clue to her crying. And I want to shake the rest of it out of her, shake out everything that she's never said.

But Mum heaves up a big sigh and shakes herself out of it. She says: 'This Francine Connolly. She's … unusual.' Raising an eyebrow.

Too right, but I say, '*Ja*,' and we crack. Mum knows, without me saying anything, everything I've seen, plus some. When Mum laughs it's like rain on the roof.

FRANCINE

It's Wednesday morning and unsurprisingly I haven't made an appearance at Mass. Instead I'm sitting on the back step looking up into the fat white clouds brushing the tops of the gums. I am unrepentant, and wallowing in my dreadful secret. I as much as hurled myself at him. After almost making it through the whole ordeal with faultless decorum, and without paying him any particular attention. What must he and his mother think of me, being so forward, inviting myself back like the lady of the manor? Now I know what I am like. Desperate. When I'm not imagining a bleak future free of him, then I'm revelling in a future comprised entirely of him, which is fairly much all the time. It's a terrific time-waster. It is torture. It is not reasonable. We've barely said two words to each other and that's no exaggeration. All I am certain of is that the rope will drag me down Dell Street come Friday, and somehow that will clarify this mess. Perhaps he will make sure they are out for the day. If that's the case, then that's my clarification; if not …?

Big stupid sigh at the trees. Mr Saunders's quote has come and gone. I was not interested in his vision of well-designed, overpriced, so-uncommon-everyone-has-one-now, possibly Satanic loveliness after all. I shall have these messy melancholy gums, and I will get myself two apple trees to place amongst them to remind me of … the lowest thoughts I've ever had.

But then, even as I'm miserable, ludicrous floods of hope sweep through me and I can see Him sitting in the trap with me as we

70

go out to find these mythic trees, and we're laughing just as we did that one perfect moment. Except he's not inarticulate now; I can't hear what he's saying but whatever it is it pleases me. Then reality merges with fantasy and I think, could we go in the trap? It might be too hard for him to climb in with his leg that way. Then fantasy swamps again and I take the Austin instead. Could I learn to drive that horrible, spluttering thing in the next two days? Can't be that hard, if Father can do it, soused too. To mock me, the vehicle itself splutters home this very moment and delivers Father.

It's only just after ten and I wonder why he's back so soon. To speak to me, apparently, and he suggests a sprawl. In the morning? And he's pouring a malt. Look out, here comes something. Oh dear. The last time he behaved like this was the day he told me we were off to Lithgow, for a wonderful spell in the country. He's busted further, I know it. My stomach turns with apprehension and I wish he'd just spit it out.

He's holding the malt, still hasn't taken a sip, when he says: 'There's no easy way to say this, so I'll get straight to the point.'

Yes please.

'Francy.' I'm sitting down and his tone says I should stay that way.

He stands before me, looks down into the tumbler, swirls the amber spirit about, and there's a sadness in the set of his shoulders that confirms he's beaten, that makes me want to jump up and say, *Oh it doesn't matter, it's only money, boom'll come round again, let's sell the furniture, it's out of date anyway. You don't have to tell me.*

But he does: 'Verdict's in.'

He looks at me again, but his eyes glitter diamond-hard, and the first thought I have is: it's the mine, isn't it. Mr Drummond was wrong and there's been a court hearing or some such thing and they've closed you down or fined you out of business because of the accident. Hardly fair, after your personal largesse.

71

No. It's not that.

He sits down next to me, tumbler clunks onto the side table, and he takes my hand.

'Francy.' Then: 'My liver is failing me. Predictable as it is incurable and reprehensible, but there it is.'

Whack, as if this liver of his sits there on the floor at my feet: 'I'll be dead within weeks — a few months at best.'

Oh. Oh. It's all I can think. Oh.

'I don't believe you,' I tell him, after I've tried to run out of the parlour and he's pulled me in again and sat me back down.

'You'll have to. That Doctor Nichols did some more tests to confirm the inevitable. Not promising at all. Thought I'd have longer, but ...'

Thought you'd have longer? 'How long have you known?'

'I suppose I've known for a long time, a year or so, but put it off. I didn't really start feeling it until we moved. Kept drinking to put it off some more,' he laughs.

It's not funny, and funnily enough I no longer seem to have a sense of humour. But two and twos are assembling fast in my brain now.

'So that's what all this has been about.' I don't need to say more: this was his epiphany. My world, no, my universe is tilting around wildly.

'Yes, but it was about time anyway, Francy. I was never going to live forever, was I? So you're going to have to know what to do with the business you're left with, decide whether to take an interest yourself.'

I do not wish to discuss this, I would like to sit here in a state of shock for eternity, but he ploughs on.

'The Wattle is doing well and set to do better. You'll have half that mine and all its assets, held on your behalf by Stanley and

Bragg in Sydney. In my will I say that you can instruct them yourself to handle all matters of the investment however you wish, so long as it remains in trust until you are twenty-one. Then you can cash in the lot and kick up your heels.' He tries for a laugh again but I stare into it. This is too much, and I am not taking it in properly; can't he see that? But he goes on: 'What if I died in my bed tonight and you didn't have a clue in the morning what you should do? I can't leave you like that. You must know.'

Another two and two: 'That's what you were doing making me deal with the Ackermans, was it? Practising for business? A safe little experience to cut my teeth on?' This easy manipulation of me is confounding, but it's so clear now.

'Yes, of course. But I meant what I said: I want you to be wealthy and I want you to know what it means: where it comes from, where it goes, who it touches and how. You have a fine mind ...'

A fine mind! I have no mind at all at present.

'... and it needs to be used for more than dabbling with paints and trotting about and whatever else it is you amuse yourself with these days. You can refuse if you like, I won't hold you to it — can't when I'm gone anyway — but I will have unfinished business that I would like you to take on yourself.'

'What?' You're going to tell me anyway.

'I have made arrangements for another trust, a compensation fund, I need you to administer it — you'll own it, separately from the mine, though it is funded directly from the profits, your profits — a small percentage each quarter. You'll have to learn how it works, who gets what and when. I'm also building some facilities at the mine itself, which you'll need to keep an eye on if they are not completed before I go. If you don't pay an interest in them nothing will happen — it's nothing to do with John

Drummond. He disapproves as it is, and will be glad to see the back of me, but I want you to be able to stand on it and not be daunted by it all. I want this, Francy — last wishes and all that.'

'But why?' Amid the fog, I really do understand why; what I am really saying is: *Why me? Why are you leaving me?*

Father says: 'I've already told you that.' His voice is softer now, the urgency diminished. 'I've been very blessed and it's time to atone. Always had an eye out for an opportunity and taken every one, from taking bets on the ponies when I first came here, to playing the stock exchange. Do you know what winning at gambling is? It's fancy thieving, all of it. And when I lost your mother I no longer played the game, it played me. I even neglected you, in wanting to indulge you with the benefits of winning, only wanting to see you smile your clever smile at me when I was high on a roll. But every punter gets well cronked sometime: we lost the house in Rose Bay to an aeronautical company I believed would go through the roof; it didn't so much crash as plummet into the centre of the earth. Francy, coal has always been my best bet, and with this ridiculous loss and then knowing that I was on the way out, I … When I saw them bring that lad out of the mine, and heard that the three others were dead, I knew it was time and I knew what I wanted to do; it's men like them I've lived off most. I don't want to save my soul, don't think that could be rescued; I just want to even the score a little.'

I want to collapse into a piteous heap, but Father will not allow it. 'I know it's all a rush, my darling girl, but that's the extent of it: no more nasty surprises.'

I stare at him, still disbelieving, and he winks. 'Not unless the Dublin constabulary catch up with me at last, but I'm sure that after thirty-five years they've given up the search.'

Well, go on, tell me about it, my eyes say to him; but he shakes his head. 'I threw a brick through the window of a grocer's shop, because the mongrel in there wouldn't give my mother any more credit, to feed us, while my father was at sea. And that's all you need to know about Dublin.'

Meaning that's all he's going tell me. But he hasn't finished handing out his last wishes. 'Again, I can't hold you to it, but I want you to stay in Lithgow, till you know what you're about. I don't want you going back to Sydney where the sharks are thickest and some smooth Johnny will have you handing over your money or your spirit as soon as you're not looking. Get yourself connected here, among decent people, like Mrs Ackerman. I was perhaps a little underhanded in the way I got you involved, yes, but not wicked on that count.' He lights his pipe and finally he is quiet. No heartbreak in his eyes; glittery sparkles all round.

'Not wicked?' I squawk through slow, burning tears. Somewhere I know that everything he has said is logical and not a little tender for the depth of his care as well as his faith in my abilities to take up his wishes, but I say, bursting: 'Was it part of your plan to make me fall … make me … make me mangle my heart on a definite lose? Because that's what you've done.'

His turn to be astonished, but then he looks utterly pleased. 'Who is it?' he asks, fairly excited.

'Who do you think? You are the controller of my universe, you should know.'

'Ah …' And then there was light; I don't know anyone else in this town, and it certainly isn't Mr Saunders. 'Why is it a lose?' he says.

That infuriates. I squirm away to the edge of the sofa.

'Isn't he keen?' he asks gently.

'How should I know?' I glare. 'We're not about to start courting, are we?'

'Why not?' he says, and I could slap him, regardless that he's ill and dying, for making me talk about it any more. Well, I won't answer; he's supposed to be remorseful and sympathetic. Naturally, he's not. 'Your mother married me when I was working at the Glebe abattoirs, and I was a shady player back then, skinning more punters on race days than carcasses.'

My universe tilts again.

'You said you didn't want me to know poverty, and now you think I should romance it?' I say; my last grasp on my former reality.

'He's not poor! Nowhere near it — his mother owns her own home, doesn't she. And you're not poor, are you. An independently wealthy lass like yourself can do as she pleases, eh? And look at Joe Cook.'

'What's the prime minister got to do with it?' For heaven's sake.

'He was a Lithgow coal worker once.'

And my father is a leprechaun, I'm sure of it now. I bawl and bawl, and he holds me there on the sofa in this house that is still strange to me. Nothing of much note has happened to me for eighteen years, and now …? Oh Father.

DANIEL

Mum's gone for more flour; we went through that lot quickly. I told her what Francine Connolly said when she came back down the hall last week and we laughed again. But that was all. Now Mum's had to go out. She knows Francine Connolly is not coming to visit her, and so do I. But I'm not laughing now. I'm sweating and it is freezing out here this morning like you wouldn't believe. The clouds banking up in the south-west look like they're carrying snow, and it's only the end of May. But I'm not going inside; I want to see her come round the back again, in the light. If she comes. If the clouds hold off so that I can see her in that light. I can hear Dad scratching his head; he wouldn't know what to make of that. We never talked like that, about women. But then I wouldn't know what he thought about these things, would I? I never bloody asked him.

Maybe she's had second thoughts. Maybe she really is dippy and I should stay well clear of her. It doesn't make sense that she should take an interest and it's not going to lead to anything, so … maybe she's just curious. About the other half. And that's all right. While she's here I can be curious about her too. And I'm in a sweat again at that thought. But my toes are about to fall off my foot; they're blue. I'm going to have to get a blanket. I reach behind me to grab the crutches — which Mrs Moran has now allowed, after I swore on the Bible not to put any weight on my leg; and I swear I haven't — and it's then I hear the trap. The crutches slip out of my hand and crash over the back step. I'm not going to lurch around now anyway, so I sit here and wait. Then pick up my carving. She's not going to catch me doing nothing either.

But there's a heavy scrape and clatter on the step out the front. What's she got with her? And quick out of the trap too. I hear the door knocker crash down: one two three. It's not her. 'Round the back,' I say.

'Hello there, layabout.' It's Evan, and he's got my gear with him. I'd just about forgotten I owned it. 'Kept forgetting to bring these round,' he says. Pick, shovel, drill. He didn't forget; he's been keeping away, giving me time. He leans them against the wall near me. He's put a new handle on the shovel.

'Thanks. What are you doing out of the hole?' I ask him.

'Bad air, we're all up,' he says. 'Have to cavil out tomorrow anyway. So how long before we see you back, eh?'

Never. I can't tell him that, so I say: 'Don't know. A month maybe.'

Then I realise he doesn't have a trap, he rides a bike if he's not walking, like me, but I know that I definitely heard one; the pony's just snorted out the front. Must be her. But Evan must have seen her. Maybe I'm imagining things again. A bloke should not spend so much time alone with too little to do.

But I ask him anyway: 'You see a trap out the front?'

'Pulled up as I turned in here. Outside next-door's, I think. You expecting someone?'

Yes. 'No. Just thought I heard someone pull up.'

'Well, you're cavilled on with me, when you come back,' he says, like he knows what my mind's like; bit too quiet. If only.

He's rigged the cavil. The boys pick our tokens from a bucket outside the manager's office. I did it too, in my last year at school, waiting to go in with Dad. Evan's slipped one of them an extra penny to swear off their pledged-to honesty to put me on with him for the quarter. You wouldn't say no to Evan Lewis, not our fearless leader who knocks his head against all the others at union get-togethers condemning tyranny and corruption.

'Where?' I say, before I've thought it.

'One.'

Easiest section; like splitting chalk. So he might have slipped more than a penny then.

He knows I don't want to talk about it, but he's got to have another go: 'You want to take over with the records, or hand them on to someone else?'

Dad's records, of our meetings, and of this and that. They're in boxes under his bed. Mum's bed. They're full of the facts of our matters, Dad would say, and nobody else but us is going to bother with them. They're full of who said and did or copped what and when ... They could have sunk into the floor for all I've been concerned about them. I don't have the bottle for this right now, so I don't say anything.

'Tell me when you're ready,' he says. When I'm approachable, he means. He's only trying to tell me, in his way, that it's all there for me, that nothing's changed, despite what has. Someone else will keep records; doesn't matter who. And he leaves it there. 'You've had enough of this then, eh?' he says, pointing at my leg.

No. Not at the moment. I couldn't be more grateful. I say: 'It's God's own torment.'

And he rolls his shoulders around the blasphemy, can't help himself. He's a devout Methodist of course. But I had to say it to get my humour back.

He says: 'No, it's only man's lot, sad truth.' And he reminds me of that shoulder of his that pops out all the time now, never been right since he was a boy, in the Rhondda, in Wales, when a skip rolled back and caught him. I've seen it pop. He's laughing about it; it's not funny. But I laugh back and I tell him all about it like it's a barrel being arse-bound watching Mum doing what she's done every day for the last thousand years. Which makes him talk about Mae, his wife, who passed away years ago, and Enid, his daughter, his only child, who's had only daughters, three of them, *sweet wonders* every one, and he proclaims the laws that protect them from working as we do because it's only the ugly that should be allowed, as if he had something to do with it.

And maybe he has, he's that large, not in height but in the power of him. He's pretty ugly too.

I've given him what he came for, almost, and I want him to leave me be.

But he's got to have one last go, doesn't he.

'We're having a game on Sunday. Someone's got to rag us. Come along if you can.' Evan's only point of difference with Methodist doctrine: compulsory once-a-fortnight rugby on Sundays for the youngsters. Rugby *union*, mind, not *league*: there is only one sport God approves of. And God is Welsh apparently.

I want to put my shoulder into someone, that's for sure, but I'm not going to watch, and not there, at the paddock. A game would fix me up right now, just having a run would, and he's a bastard for reminding me. No, he's not. But he sees and he'll 'be off then', quietly. That cuts, and I tell him maybe I'll come and he waves off down the side of the house like he knows. Like I have better things to do. And it's been three weeks since I've seen anyone; except for Robby, who popped his head in for ten seconds a few days ago on his way home — just long enough to make sure that I was still actually alive and being a bit more separate than usual.

And I'm sitting here enjoying our miraculous wealth, which Evan hasn't mentioned, like he hasn't mentioned the enquiry either, because none of that means anything. Because Evan's lost

Dad too. While I'm thinking about that I hear, 'Oh dear,' from down the other side of the house.

And there she is, Francine Connolly, holding her cheek. She says, 'I scratched myself on a thorn,' standing there as if you always squeeze between a wall and a rosebush to get to where you're going. She's got that grey skirt on, *that* skirt, which is not really grey, but sort of … don't know what colour it is … it's got another little skirt thing round the top of it, and she's wearing a shirt, white one, girl's one that sort of crosses over itself at the front. Awch.

There's nothing else to say but, 'What were you doing coming round there?' Don't know yet if I'm amazed that she came or that she's now telling me: 'I saw Mr Lewis coming and I didn't want him to see me, so I came round this side and a left cane got me. See?' She lifts her hand from her cheek for a second and there's a purple welting streak right across it.

'I should see an optician, get some spectacles,' she says. 'Can't believe I did that.'

For sure.

Except she starts to cry, pretending she's not. She's ten yards away from me and there's not much I can do.

I say: 'It's not so bad, is it?' It really is just a scratch.

And she says, 'It's a bit worse than this,' showing the welt again. 'I presume your mother is not in, but I should like a cup of tea, if that's all right with you.'

'That's all right, go inside, I'll make —'

She cuts me off: 'You can't do that. I think I could manage to make it.'

'No. I'll make it.' She's heading towards the back steps and she's not looking where she's going; she's squinting over my shoulder at the gear leaning on the wall; I slide the crutches out of the way before she gets there. If I let her make the tea, she'll break something this time.

And of course she stands there looking at me as I lurch into the room and around the stove, until I say: 'Tell me what's worse then.'

Then she stares at the table and says: 'I've formed an unfortunate attachment to you.'

Just like that. That stops me for a second, and I think what the hell: 'I might have unfortunately done the same.'

She laughs, and that's what I was after, except she's still tearing up and holding it in; she's still holding the side of her face as if that'll help.

'Come on, it's all right,' I say, and obviously it's not. 'So your father's generosity won't go that far with me?' I guess.

'Oh no, it's not that.' She shakes her head, staring into the table again. 'He's all for me ... he's ... He knows precisely how I feel and his approval is unconscionable. It's that ...'

What? I wait for ten years, trying not to think about what she's just said so that I won't miss what's coming.

'My father is very unwell ...'

Another ten years. 'That's no good.' Like an idiot.

'He won't live for much longer.' Then out in a flood: 'And I don't have any friends, not proper ones, and no relatives — I've been ripped up and transplanted here to Lithgow where I know no one except Mr Drummond and Father Hurley, and you and your mother — barely. Not counting Mr Symes at the post office, who knows me for a pest. My mother died when I was small which means I'm soon to be an orphan, and I'll own half the Wattle mine in my own right. And this, with you, well, it's not reasonable, not any of this, not anything I feel.'

She pauses, thankfully; I'm struggling to follow.

Then she starts again: 'So I thought you should know, to explain my behaviour. I don't have a habit of imposing myself on young men I don't know, men who ...'

But she runs out of steam there. Then finally looks across at me. Blink. Blink. I want to kiss her, like I've heard only about her attachment and her father's approval of it. She's a fair bit more than unusual. I've never met a girl that comes anywhere near to her, and I've met a few, pretty enough and lively enough, but no girl that makes me want to … I'm not thinking about the consequences other than the ones I'm after, which are, well, only one right now: to kiss her. I know I'm not going to but …

'That's a lot to think about, but it's not all bad, is it,' I say, not asking but telling her. I'm not going to let this go.

'No.' Bit of a smile.

'No.' Definitely; very badly hopeful.

'Then I suppose that means the exploration of this unlikely possibility is begun,' she says.

'You could say that.' Through those words that she threads all around like string, I hear that she's not going to let it go either. Somewhere I know that she's still out of bounds and I shouldn't be doing this, but: 'I'm fairly desperate to get out of here. You want to go for a drive in the trap?'

'Of course!' she says, like she's been shaken from a dream.

'You still want this tea?'

'No!' That bell that comes out of her bounces round the walls.

And I know I won't try to kiss her, because I feel like I already have.

FRANCINE

So, reality was wrong: He, This Lad, gets up into the trap without any trouble, at least not much anyway; and I have jumped across fate's railway tracks, without getting run over, yet. I can hear Father chuckling and applauding my bravado from across the other side of the town. Even as my hands are trembling, very visibly, holding the reins. Hayseed nickers into my terror and thrill, I imagine in concord, but more probably because he can feel the extra weight, rather a lot since The Lad is not small, and quite a bit taller than I had estimated; inordinately tall, in fact. Never seen a man so tall — he had to duck a little to go out his front door. But it is not this massive shift in my own reality that terrifies and thrills; it is that The Lad evidently feels something of the same thing I do. I had hoped, but didn't dare think it, not really. Yet it must be true: if hiding in the rosebush, then blathering and weeping didn't put him off, I don't know what would. But then, even as I glance at him to check I am not dreaming, it strikes me that I might have got this all wrong: what if his intentions are no good? And calm myself as quickly: I can simply run away; he's not going to chase me, is he. What I would do if he did is something I cannot consider for fear of spontaneously combusting.

'Where shall we go?' I ask him.

'Down the track into the gully. I want to show you something.'

Fear redoubles; he sees my alarm and adds: 'The view.' Laughing at me.

The way the brightness in his eyes makes them greener is positively sinful; but that's not his fault. All mine, and I have given up on God anyway, truly, for more reasons than I can count, especially the most recent injustice. But I shall not think about Father's predicament now, I shall think only of what he wants me to do for his last hurrah: be a good girl, and a happy girl, and a student of industrial philanthropy. With a beau, perhaps. Who's a decent working man. With a broken leg. Here, with me. The Lad knows I am considering him, because I am staring again, and I swear the amber flares brighter still.

Oh, stop it, Francy, and just get going before he changes his mind!

Our shoulders bump as Hayseed sets off; this is our first touch. Oh my goodness. The first of many as it turns out: it's a rather rough track that winds down and around the gully's left flank. I wonder if we should turn back: 'Are you all right? You can't be comfortable.'

'Just fine,' he says, and he doesn't seem to be pretending stoicism as he drags his eyes from the trees to me; he really does want to show me a view. 'Not exactly comfort, but … Not far anyway. Pull up at the top of the rise ahead.'

The gully closes and closes around us as we head up the rise, till the tops of the gums join and arc above us; on either side huge ferns fan out and the smell of damp earth is a colour not a smell at all: green, soft and deep. I'm already gasping before I see what he wants to show me. He doesn't need to tell me to stop here.

At the top of the rise is a picture window formed of bowed trunks and branches stretching one to the other, and it frames a pristine valley, above which sits a sheer escarpment. The rock is grey now, as the clouds pass over the sun, then tanned in the light again, then grey. I look up and around to try to imagine how this would look at dawn or dusk, whether it might flame like my rocks on my hills, but I don't know where I am and have no sense of direction at the best of times, even among the clear lines of town. I look into the window again, and finally see it: he hasn't brought me here to show me just a lovely view after all.

On the far top edge of the escarpment, set against the clouds, is the profile of a woman's face. She is looking out towards the distant blue of gum haze and her long hair of perching plants trails around the side of her face and down into the valley. Just when I think that this is a figment, he says: 'Her name's Calypso.'

Calypso? I could not be more astounded. Calypso: abandoned by Odysseus on her island of Ogygia, looking out to sea, bereft in acquiescence to his will and that of the gods, but secretly defiant. So taught to me by Sister Carmel at Our Lady, who was something of a radical educationalist when it came to Homer and Other Great Works of Classical Literature, if contemptuous of us all. I have no idea why Calypso was bereft and defiant, yet there indeed she is, on the escarpment.

'How did she come by that name?' I ask, still gawping.

'My mother, she's always called her that,' he says, but that's not an answer. 'She's a goddess or something — Calypso, not Mum.' He laughs.

'I know.' She's a nymph, daughter of some titan or other. But how does Mrs Ackerman know? As if I'm the only person in the world to have read a book or had a Sister Carmel, I chide myself.

'Mum says she waits there for justice that never comes.'

He says it mildly, but it jolts and I don't ask him what sort of justice she might mean. Instead I ask him, remembering the faint vestiges of somewhere-in-Europe in her accent: 'Where's your mother from?' This goddess of wisdom and obscure Homeric allusion.

86

'Germany. Dad too.'

'Ackerman doesn't sound German,' I blurt. As if I'd know; I've never met a German before. They all live in South Australia and make fine wine for my father, or import coffee. When they are in Germany, so say the newspapers, they have a big army, and want a bigger navy, which upsets Britannia for some reason or other. They're all Fritz and Schultz, or Albert if they were Queen Victoria's husband, and they have a kaiser. Sister Simon-Peter didn't get through much in The History of the World and Geography; she was more interested in penance. But I do remember that that von Bismarck character had a funny helmet and that the Teutonic Peoples live somewhere in the middle of the European Continent. I flush at everything I've not bothered with.

'It used to have two n's,' he explains into my wondering, 'but everyone kept dropping the second till it disappeared altogether. Suited Dad: he never bothered much with unnecessaries. Didn't see himself as German anyway. Just Australian.'

Australian. What is that? Except being here. Everyone comes here from somewhere else, except the native Aborigines, whom I also know little about. Australia is a photograph of the opening of the first Federal Parliament the same year that my mother died.

'Why did your parents come here?' I ask him, thinking about my own.

'Don't know, really.'

He shifts his shoulders and is quiet again. I should like to tell him we have something in common there, with mysterious transplantation, but I won't: his seems a sore point and mine is just a void that will stay that way. Certainly not going to tell him about Father's criminal past. Maybe he's thinking about his father's death; another thing we appear to have in common, sort of.

It's too beautiful here to let those thoughts take hold, so I say: 'Daniel.'

He looks at me. 'Hmn?'

'I just wanted to say your name,' I tell him, truly, for the first time, properly. Daniel. The Prophet. Daniel in the lions' den. God sent the angel to shut the lions' mouths so that they could not hurt him. It's old, Hebrew. And lovely on my tongue.

His face becomes the smile that seized me in the street, and at the back of his house, that fills me now.

He says: 'Francine. It suits you. It's unusual.'

He says so little, but whatever he says is what it is: sharp, intent and clear. Without ornamentation. He doesn't need it, believe me. I wonder if he thinks as concisely, or if, like me, his head is a sludgy mangle.

'I mean that as a compliment,' he adds. And I know; I heard it in the way he said it. My whole body is soft with the sound of it.

But there's so much that separates us, I can't imagine how we're going to broach … Is it really possible for us to …? Stop it, Francy. Choose a safe subject and get on with it.

'You never told me where you learned to whittle like that — I love my kookaburra; he sits and looks at me from my dressing table. You're really very good at it. Is it something German too?'

His face darkens; I've said the wrong thing. 'Don't know if it's German; it's something of Dad's,' he explains; the chasm gapes.

I want to touch him, tell him that has nothing to do with us; but it has everything to do with us. The arithmetic is painfully simple and ruinous.

But he saves us from it this time. 'Dad's pieces are pretty impressive. They're all over the house. The backs of the chairs, bedheads, trims round the table, the mirror in the hall, doors on the cupboards, on the handles of the cupboards. Everywhere.'

'Oh.' And I am impressed. I can see the kitchen cupboards in my mind, with their relief pannelling, a crosshatch pattern of leaves. That's what I was looking at when I nudged the kettle off the stove top. I had thought their furniture rather nice — like everything else, not as I expected — but I didn't consider who had made it that way.

'My pieces are all pretty useless. Like kookaburras,' he laughs, releasing me and returning me to him. 'Toys for my sister's kids, really.'

'Must be very pretty toys,' I say. 'Kookaburra's more like a sculpture than a carving.'

'What's the difference?'

'Well ...' Must be very careful to avoid suggesting that I think he is artistic and that his father wasn't. 'It's in the movement that you've captured.'

'Is it?' He's teasing me, because I am on the verge of embarrassing him, I think.

'Anyway, I love it.' Enough said on that. The clouds have thickened and fill the sky in the window, round grey puffs of cold. 'Maybe we should turn back now; I should get home to Father.'

'Mmn,' he says, and I wish he'd say more. I don't know what I want him to say; something to keep us here. Should I ask him about his sister? Perhaps I should cut short my babbling while I'm ahead. And I really should go. I've been out for hours now.

I turn the trap around and Hayseed takes us down and up again, our shoulders bumping all the way, and I don't want that to stop either. It's too short a distance back to his house.

'Shall I come back next Friday?' I ask, since I already seem to have that routine, though I'd like it to be tomorrow.

'Could you come out on Sunday, around midday?'

'Why Sunday?' Joy! I don't really care why, but maybe he has something particular in mind.

'There's a game on, rugby, at the paddock at the Wattle, that I should really turn up to, but I need a ride, if you could make it …'

What an invitation. Rugby! Didn't think working men played it. Though I've only ever been to one match — Joey's boys barrelling into St Ignatius boys one picnic day at Hunters Hill, the Marists in violent contest against the Jesuits: the sound of thumping, mud flying, inexplicable cheering and poor Iggy's boys getting a beating. But I'm hardly going to say no, am I. So: 'Of course.'

'Good-o,' he says, manoeuvring himself up and over and out. He stops there with his hand on the wheel to reach in for the crutches. 'See you Sunday then.'

I very much want to touch his hand, but it's gone. I say: 'Yes.' Then I'm gone too. I can feel him watching me go, everything unspoken trailing between us, but I don't look back to wave. The enormity of what I have just done is settling already.

DANIEL

If she's serious, well then she may as well see me as I am. All very well to go for a ride and look at each other and wonder what the other's thinking about the scenery; she may as well know, sooner rather than later. I still feel a bit guilty, though. She probably has no idea about rugby, not as it is with us at least, and she doesn't know anyone, and everyone from the Wattle will be there, curious about the Connollys' latest act of charity. But they won't twig that anything's going on: why would they?

Mum's not impressed; I've told her the sum total. The lot. She says: 'You'd better not be having a laugh at her expense now, Daniel.' And presses her lips tight, which is as close as she gets to a frown. 'She's out of the ordinary, but in a good way. If you upset her, I will be ashamed of you.'

'I won't.' Hopefully.

'What do you want from her?' she says, pinning me with her eyes.

'I want to know if I want to marry her.' There, stupid as that sounds, it's said.

Mum's not surprised. But: 'What will you do when you marry her?'

Like it's going to happen. Badly hopeful. But the answer is, I don't know. I'm avoiding the idea that marrying Francine — Francine Connolly. Jesus. Marrying her would practically make me an owner. That's just not a consideration, obviously. So I ignore it. The likelihood of all this ever happening is so remote that it's easy to ignore. So what am I doing mucking her about like this then? I can't answer that either. I just have to know first if that's what I want, and I reckon I do, and then if she *will*.

'Tell me why you went out today when you knew she'd come here,' I say. And it's the first time I've ever challenged my mother in my life.

She lets that lie there, and turns back to the stove. Because I know why: there is only one reason why you'd leave a bloke, even in my fairly arse-bound state, alone with a girl; well two, but Mum wasn't thinking of the second one. She sees this as a way for me not to go back in. That's not going to happen either; I still don't want to. So why am I going to the game then? When I see everyone, I know what's going to happen: I'll feel like I should go back in. I already feel like I *should*. How can I just say thanks for the payout for Dad, now I'll be off then? And to do what? I'm nearly twenty, locked into mining, and not qualified for anything but. Be a dock manager like Pete? I'm sure Francine would love to be married to a docker. No, a plumber. Start smoking a pipe and drinking whisky and pretend? Carve kookaburras for her? Well, I wouldn't mind carving all day — I've got used to doing little else lately — but, as Francine put it, it's just not reasonable.

I shouldn't have asked her to come on Sunday, I'm never going to ask her to marry me. I don't have the bottle to. I'm such an arse.

FRANCINE

Naturally, the Leprechaun hooted with delight when I told him of the rosebush incident, the jaunt, and subsequent plans for Sunday. He seems interested in little else but my Great Romance now that he has been through the workings of the trust accounts with me; it all seems fairly straightforward, even for someone as distracted as myself. And he's left copious written instructions anyway and reminded me a million times that Stanley and Bragg, the solicitors, will look after me. He's very tired, and says he'll only go out for a short time every day or two from now on, till he gets even more tired and then he won't go out at all. He needs to check on his Lavatory and Washing Facility, which he is having built so that the men may be able at least to wash their hands and faces properly before heading home after work. They laid the first brick on Friday, while I was out romancing. I still can't believe Father is dying, though I am surely watching it: he must have lost a stone this week and I'd prefer to believe he's looking rather fit for it. I simply can't believe it. Prefer to dwell on disbelief that there is no toilet at the mine. It's not even going to cost all that much to build; it's only very basic, for a very basic need. More appalling still is that, Father told me, no other mines have these facilities either. Why not? They can wash the coal for market but not the men? And it's personal now: Daniel would work every day down a dark hole, risking life and limb for the company, and could not so much as go to the toot

93

in any dignity at the end of the day. Could not wash his face; no wonder he was filthy.

And the toot is of small concern in the scheme of general unfairness. Father has also told me that the miners have to pay for the repair of their own tools, which they have to buy themselves; that they pay for the gunpowder to blow apart the coal, and the fuel to light their lamps; and that they even have to employ their own man to check the weighing of the coal they dig up to make sure they are duly paid. Then out of their pay come union fees, doctor's fund, mutual protective association fund … The ponies that wheel the skips fare better: free food, lodging and equipment, and a well-aimed bullet when they've had it. What do miners get above pay? A free bag of coal to take home at the end of the week, and, if they're lucky, subsidised rent — in a cottage if they're married, in a shack near the works if they're not — which they pay, naturally, to the company. Impressive. My eyes used to blur over any article in the newspapers about strikes and union claims and unfair business practices. They don't any more. I read yesterday that the wages of labourers, seamstresses and young public school teachers do not meet the ordinary expenses of living; the article was suggesting that the teachers should be paid more, regardless that so many are women, but why should anyone do a day's work and not be able to live off their income? That's not a tangle, it's a face-slapping travesty. While the disgrace makes me want to sell the mine and go back to forgetting such things exist, I can't do that till I'm twenty-one — three years from now. Till then, I'll do as Father asks, the little that Father asks; it seems so terribly little, but he's also made it plain that's the extent of what can be done from this small quarter, and that Mr Drummond is never going to be easy with any of it. And that Mr Drummond was right about the mine enquiry thing too: it took the coroner twenty minutes to decide that the cave-in was *a most unfortunate calamity*; Mr Lewis thanked him on behalf of the dead for nothing, and Mr Drummond thanked him and smiled.

Still, all this gloom makes an afternoon at the rugby look appealing at least. Besides, after forty-eight hours, I am fairly dying to see Daniel again. Not only for the obvious reasons; it's taken on crusade proportions now: I'm not going to let him go back inside that hideous hole. If I have to I will ask him to marry me and cart him off, against his will if necessary. I'm one of the bosses — I'll force him, or break his other leg.

Father comes in now as I'm getting ready to go. 'You're a picture,' he says, standing in the doorway of my room. I can see him in the mirror of my dressing table; I've been inspecting the two-inch scratch on my cheek; it's not too bad, and there's nothing I can do about it anyway. I turn to look at him properly for a moment; his eyes are wet and he's grinning like the devil. I grin back, and fix the last pin into my hair, for what that's worth, since it'll fall out again in five minutes, my hair's so straight and slippery, then I gather up my winter coat. Every moment we are together now he does not take his eyes off me, and I embrace him ten times a day, as I am doing right now, imprinting his warmth into me, and making myself promise again that he will not see me cry, not once, he will not see my heart breaking, only feel it beating against his. He will not hear it whispering: *Maybe if I refuse to believe it, it will not happen.*

'Get off then, girl, you'll be late,' he says, but his arms are slow to let me go. And yet that is exactly what he wants me to do. As far as I know it's unheard of for a father to send his daughter out alone with a young man she barely knows, into strange company, for the purposes of allowing her to follow her impulses, while at the same time preparing her for a morally responsible career in business. Stranger still is that my head is not spinning with it now. It seems that my part in his atonement goes very deep, and gratitude matches my fear. With one last glance for luck at Kookaburra, to the rugby I shall go.

But luck is not happy this afternoon: Daniel utters nothing but directions as we head out to this paddock place; he barely even looks at me. I am the cabman apparently, with a moody, broody passenger. I try to make conversation — 'Goodness, it's chilly, isn't it?'; 'I've brought a little picnic'; 'I hope it doesn't rain'; 'Here, take the blanket, your toes will fall off' — and the monosyllabic responses wear me down. Eventually, impatience roils and I pull Hayseed up by the side of the road somewhere in the labyrinth of dusty tracks beyond town. 'Are you going to talk at all today? Because if you're not, I'm going to turn this trap around right now.'

That makes him look at me, fierce, then frown, then sigh: 'You were right, Francine, this isn't reasonable.'

'Oh.' I sink through the seat of the trap and into the dirt below.

'I want it to be,' he adds.

Say more, I demand with my eyes, and stop frowning at me like it's my fault, even if it is.

'I can't think about anything else other than how much I want it to be, but it doesn't help. We're too different, aren't we.'

He's not getting away with leaving it at that. I keep staring.

Half sigh of exasperation, half grunt: 'I mean it's a bit of a Romeo and Juliet, isn't it — a make-believe that didn't end too well.'

Astonishment at literary reference, but still staring.

'Stop blinking at me!'

He smiles; I blink again: I've won. We've won.

'It'll end in tears,' he says, deadpan. I love him.

'You only live once,' I say, and that hangs there fat with meaning for a moment. 'So do you want me to take you to this rugby thing or not?'

'It won't be like anything you're used to.' Last grasp.

'I'm not like anything I'm used to any more. Just try to shock me.'

'All right,' he says, proper smile this time. 'Let's see what we can do for you.'

It doesn't look like a hideous hole in the ground as we pass it. Beyond the small office building and some big sheds and machinery things, and further on, presumably, the foundations of Father's Lavatory and Washing Facility, is a rather grand portal arch set into the side of the hill proclaiming that this is *The Wattle Dell Colliery, 1902*. The irony is awful: fabulous façade, but, sorry, no toot. And the wattle, scraggy and olive-dull this time of year, is prolific; come winter's end, when the fuzzy blooms cover the hillside with bobbing yellow, it'll look like the entrance of a tourist retreat. Except for all the sets of rail tracks, especially the ones that disappear beneath the arch. They fade abruptly to black. And I don't let my eyes linger too long; I don't want him to see me staring at that. I look at him instead and he says: 'Keep going round, past the stables.'

And way round the other side of the hump of bounty and degradation, and past another couple of holes in the ground, one of which is called 'Stables', lies a paddock. It is a natural grassy flat, upon which tall poles and crossbars have been erected at either end; I do recognise them as the things through which odd-shaped balls are kicked. Chalk lines mark out the playing field, and a few dozen men are spreading themselves out across it. Looks just like a football match is about to start, except there are no stripy jerseys in sight: they all wear work boots and various utilitarian shades of navy and grey. There's a gathering of other men and boys, and women and children ranged along this near edge, with picnic rugs spread out and treats laid on; very civilised.

It seems the other edge of the field drops off sharply, gums dangling their branches up and over on that side, and I wonder how many times the ball goes over it. Altogether there must be around two hundred people here, and almost the same number of ponies it seems when I look across at the other end of the field again.

'They're the pit ponies,' Daniel explains when I comment on how lovely they are, standing in such easy formation. 'They never miss a match. Keep the grass short for us too.'

I look across the whole scene again; they are all facing the field: people and ponies. None looking at us, though, as we slowly wheel in; more important things afoot.

Daniel says: 'Stop here.' He's so abrupt I pull Hayseed up with a bump, and here we are on the sideline close to the nearest of the posts, conspicuous as we could possibly be. But still no one shows interest in us; a whistle blows, the ball goes up and the game begins.

'Who's playing who?' I ask, daring the obvious.

'Caps and no caps. See?' Not looking at me.

'Everyone here is from the Wattle?'

'Yes.'

'How do you know who's on which team?'

'By the caps.' He drags his eyes from the field and looks stunned by my stupidity.

'No, I mean how do you decide who gets a cap and who doesn't?'

'It's a cavil.'

'What's that?'

'A lottery — pick the names out of a hat, before the game.'

There you go; don't ask what happens if caps fall off. Stop blathering on anyway; he's half off the seat of the trap now, and muttering something unintelligible at whatever's going on out

98

there. I haven't a clue, but watch too, thinking: so you all work together then smash into each other on Sundays for fun, at random. Hmn.

'Yes. Yes. *Yes,*' he's calling out and I look from the field to him, and back to the field: clearly not the time for inane questions from the ignorant. It seems half of the players are charging straight for us, till the one with the ball gets thumped down and then they all appear to jump on top of each other indiscriminately. Another one emerges from the scrap with the ball and breaks away from the mob, and he really is charging at us, full tilt. Hayseed stomps and nickers, not in fright, I don't think, but in a merry excitement. Good heavens. And the man throws himself over the chalk line, just a few yards away.

Daniel explodes: 'Robby!'

And this Robby fellow picks himself up to the claps and cheers of all, runs over, jumps up to punch Daniel on the shoulder, says, 'You beaut,' then runs off again.

Baffling stuff but so joyous it's hard not to be swept into the enthusiasm. Daring again I ask: 'What happened just then?'

With a look of the most delightful forbearance, he says: 'That, Francine, was a try, scored by my good mate Robby Cullen.'

'Oh. Good,' I say, and still daring I have to ask: 'How do you know who to cheer for? I mean, which team?'

'Whoever you like,' he grins and that's all the explanation I'm going to get since he's watching the game again. One of the players sends the ball sailing over the posts from about twenty yards off, and Daniel leans down to say: 'And that was an excellent goal.'

Terrible need to fan my face after the sensation of his breath on my ear. Oh goodness. Calm down, Francy. I watch the crowd and notice that they've started to make glances at us; how could they not? I suppose they all know who I am and are wondering

what I'm doing here; and there's that tough-as-nails-looking Mr
Lewis, in the middle of the players with the whistle: he certainly
knows who I am. Oh, I hope he doesn't recognise the trap from
the other day when I was hiding in the rosebush. I've already
decided to play the happy cabman, but now I am nervous. It
seems important that I have the approval of these people, not for
being here with Daniel — I'm not sure I want to know what
they'd think of that — but simply for being.

Thoughts are a mire of ifs and buts until the whistle blows
again, for the break in the game, and when the players leave the
field, people start coming over to us. It's a blur of:

'Danny, mate, it's good to see you.' Back slap, handshake.

'Miss Connolly.' Doff cap or nod, pretend not to stare.

'Danny, come on second half, why don't you.'

'Miss Connolly.'

'Danny, you loafer. When are you back?'

'Miss Connolly.'

I want to know who this Danny is, this beloved Danny.
Untouched by myriad unmentionables.

I feel a gentle tap on my arm, my side of the trap. A woman
stands there; she's perhaps about thirty, but it's hard to tell, since
her forehead is deeply lined. I smile my happy cabman smile and
she says: 'Miss Connolly, how do you do, I'm Moira Jones.'

'How do you do.'

'Better than I should be doing, thanks to your father. He
should be sainted, if only for what that money means for my
children. I just wanted to tell you that.'

Saint Francis, of course; a company of sulphur-crested
cockatoos rises out of the wattle behind her as if to confirm it.
And this must be *the* Mrs Jones. I'm so moved by her directness
I don't know what to say.

She adds: 'And you must be a kind girl too, bringing Danny

out today.' The whistle blows for the game to start up again and she says: 'Well, I just wanted you to know that we appreciate it. Good day, then.'

'Good day to you too, and thank you for telling me.' I barely breathe the words out.

She looks softly into my embarrassment, then walks away. She glances back at me once, and then I see: she knows, or thinks she does. Of course, most likely everyone knows. This town is a heaving bustle, but it's not that big, certainly not round this side. She probably lives in Dell Street too, has seen me and Hayseed traipsing up and down. That's not a difficult two and two, is it, not for a woman with an imagination at least. Opinion is inscrutable, though: was I being reminded of my place and to be kind, or being given approval? Does it matter? No: it only feels like it matters because I've been conditioned to think it *should* matter. Facts are, kind is not the word for what I feel and I have my own approval. That'll have to do. At least they don't appear to hate me.

Daniel's bellowing out something or other again at whatever's going on in the field; I can't even pretend to watch: I'm too busy grabbing glances at him. And I feel like bellowing too. We're different, but there's nothing impossible about us. I must be staring shamelessly now, because he turns to stare back. Good. Except he keeps on looking at me, till I can't bear it any more. I look into the sky, into the grey cold clouds; take deep, steady breaths. And see the ball, high in the air, spinning end over end; rather like my brain, I think, as it descends. And descends. And descends, landing with a filthy thump in my lap, stinging my thighs.

'Oh!' I squawk, but I stand straightaway in the trap and throw it at the nearest man on the field. A cheer roars up at that and I feel ten feet tall. I'm Francine Connolly and that'll have to do!

'Good pass.' Daniel's looking up at me in that way, like I am a lunatic. 'They should have you on side.'

'Just an accident, I'm sure,' I say, sitting down again; the cat that ate the cream.

He's still looking at me. He says: 'I might have to accidentally marry you one day.'

'I'm still not shocked,' I say, and my heart is charging like a train.

'Well, I'll have to make it deliberate then. Would you? Consider it?'

'Yes.' As if I was ever going to say no.

No caps win and it starts to snow. We don't stay to picnic. I've never seen snow before and I am positively weepy with ecstasy, watching it fall upon his dark hair. Driving back to Dell Street is bliss itself, flakes zinging on my cheeks, a beautiful silence of possibility between us. When we pull up at his house we just sit there in the trap. Didn't expect all that, did we.

DANIEL

I don't want to say a thing, but I want to make it real. Make sure I did actually ask her and that she did actually say yes. She didn't hesitate for a second, did she. Flaming hell. So I say: 'We should probably wait a while, so at least it looks halfway reasonable, don't you think?'

I can't tell you what she looks like right now, I just can't. But we have to wait: Dad's barely cold, and although I reckon he'd see the brutal humour in this, it's just not appropriate. And the rest.

She nods, and after a while she says: 'You'd better ask my father sooner rather than later, though.'

I meant wait a while before we start stepping out, not asking her father, but she's got a point. 'Yes, when I get this thing off my leg.'

'How long will that be?'

'A month maybe; Nichols said about eight weeks, and it's been just over three.' Very long and now very eventful ones.

'That might be too long,' she says; that's too real. I want to hold her to me but I'm not sure if she'd want me to. Not only because we're out here in the street, but because she is who she is. I don't want to do anything to make her think twice.

'Well, should I do it tomorrow then?' I can't do it right now — I have to tell Mum first, then have a bit of a long moment with myself.

'Yes, but we can keep it quiet after that for a while. That's sensible. We'll need time to work everything out anyway.'

Too right. 'I suppose you'll have to come and get me, though. It doesn't seem right. But I can't very well ask any of my mates, can I, without making it obvious. Maybe I could ask Mum to give me a double on my bike.'

She laughs her head off at that. 'How about Mr McNally comes to get you?'

Forgot she had servants; poor old McNally. He used to be a miner, uncle of Fred's, I think; had some sort of mental problem years ago when I was a kid. Which makes me think of Fred, who died with Dad … this is going to trip us up everywhere we turn. But I've done it now, haven't I. And I'm not giving her up for anything now anyway — there is only one Francine Connolly and I've got her, thank you very much. I've already got a bit of a plan forming too. When I'm fit, I'll go back in for the rest of the quarter, just to prove the point that I haven't choked on them, and then we can get married, and then I'll … don't know. It'll come.

'All right,' I say and then I can't stand it any more. I just have to do what I've been wanting to do every second since Friday afternoon. 'Well, I'll see you tomorrow, I suppose,' I say, then I lean in and kiss her. Just on the cheek, quickly. Any more than that and I'd be dangerous. She blinks at me then — and I've definitely got to go. She touches my hand on the trap wheel as I get out, just lightly, but it's enough to make me feel like I'm going to fall over.

FRANCINE

Father is only holding up by a thread, but so determinedly incorrigible: he pretended shock and outrage at first with Daniel; I know because I listened at the parlour door, of course. 'YOU WHAT!' he began, but I couldn't hear much after that. Polly actually laughed at me when she saw; she's much nicer these days, I've found, possibly because I am less of a morose horror to deal with. Another easy equation. So I had to tell her, and swear her to secrecy until we're ready to announce. Daniel looked as though he'd been through the Inquisition when he hobbled out, but when he saw me sitting on the stairs he pointed and said: 'You're sold, if you're still keen on the buyer.' Father guffawed and offered him a malt, but Daniel doesn't drink — 'What, not a drop?' 'No.' — *Deo gratias*.

We've stuck to our Friday rendezvous, my weekly kiss, my fix of joy, except when I can't bear it and have to sneak round for extras, and Mrs Ackerman, goddess of wisdom, is as sweet to me as I could ever have hoped. She makes the most delicious cinnamon cake, I wonder if I'd go there for that alone, and has filled me in on the extent of the clan. There's Peter and his wife Violet in Newcastle, whom she hopes to get up to see as soon as Daniel is on his feet. Then there's Miriam and her husband Roy McKinnon and seven little ones, all of them naughty, she says, and clearly adored by her. She'll go off to stay with them in Bathurst for a while too, and help Miriam with her brood. She's a lovely, soft-spoken woman, so delicately made that I find it hard to fathom how she has a son as large as Daniel. I'd love to ask her about Calypso, and about the bookmarked copy of a French tome entitled *Les Arcs d'Amour* that sits on the side table by the little sofa, but something about her tells me not to pry, to let her do the talking and the asking. I'd love to hear the little upright against the far wall being played, too, but I don't dare ask that; this house, I must presume, is still in mourning. For now, I can only imagine Daniel playing it — I just bet he does. And I bet he's better than me — wouldn't be hard: I'm all fumbles with that.

I am so very happy, I mean inside my bones happy. I tingle with it, it ripples even through the knowledge now that mourning is not long away for me; it sings to me: your father gave all this to you, how can you not be joyful? The Lord giveth and the Lord taketh away, but Father has the trumps on that: Go forth and be in love, Francy. And I am. Oh, I am. So, miraculously so, I can hide my tears for him inside it, entertain him instead with tales of lovers not getting around to much working out of dull details. We've been too busy, Daniel and I, doing what is conventionally done *before* a marriage proposal: getting to know each other, and everything I'm getting to know makes me adore him more and more, from his preference for lemon in his tea, to the fact that he actually used the word *proletariat* in conversation the other week and I wasn't certain of what it meant. He's also intriguingly neat: no slurping or crumb-dropping or staining of napkins; he makes me feel deliriously unkempt. Even this waiting is sublime, though Daniel's kisses get a little longer each time, and he has expressed some impatience: 'You are a torture.' Good. We're even. He calls me France, says he'll have this *bourgeois* princess conquered by spring; I tell him the Kaiser wouldn't dare. I'm such a tease! Where do I get that from? I can guess the answer to that easily enough.

Then three things happen in the last two weeks of July:
Daniel is released from The Thing.
The Kaiser, it seems, will dare, and Europe braces for war.
Father takes to his bed, and he won't be getting up again.

TWO

JULY 1914 – SEPTEMBER 1915

DANIEL

Francine is unimpressed when I ride up to her house on Sunday morning to tell her. But I'm not moving on this; besides, I'm fat from loafing and my left leg looks like a sick twig — it took me a week to get it going at all. France's not marrying that; two months back in will fix me up.

She's standing with one hand gripping the side of the mantel, tiny in her huge sitting room, glaring at me after the surprise. 'So is this a once a miner always a miner sort of thing? Like once a Catholic always a Catholic? If so, that's ludicrous. Look at Joe Cook — he doesn't seem to need a *spell in the pit* these days. He's the Prime Minister.'

What? 'That liberal, Free Trader, capitalist arse?' I say. 'Cream rises to the top and has a vested interest in staying there, is all he's about. Took him five minutes to see what side he'd butter his bread on and forget there ever was another side. They kicked him out of the Labor Party for it before I was born. He's got nothing to do with me. And I've got a commitment to finish the quarter.'

'No you don't,' she says, and that's true enough. 'And don't be crude.' Sometimes, even looking at her, I forget that she's a woman — and that she's only eighteen, for Christ's sake: who made her? — and let the language slip out.

'Well, I want to finish the quarter, then,' I tell her. 'I don't want all this to change who I am, how I live, just like that.'

'You sound like some bleater from *Australian Worker*,' she says, for all our previous agreement on the issues, for all that she's read every red rag in my house. 'No.' She's changed her mind. 'You sound like a gaga Wobbly from *Direct Action* — except you're not planning industrial sabotage: you're planning to sabotage yourself. Is that who you are?'

'I'm a miner so far, is all.'

This is not going too well.

Then she says: 'I don't want to be married to a miner — and I don't want to be your *employer*!'

'Then don't marry me.' Out before I could stop it, and it stops her. 'I didn't mean that,' I say.

She stares: 'You're an arse.' And keeps staring, wanting me to roll, and stares some more, until it's just dippy, her own *crudity* hanging there like she's holding a sign.

'Don't laugh, will you,' I say, stoking it, and she nearly cracks. But doesn't. Instead she says: 'Well, if you get hurt again, don't expect any sympathy from me.'

Didn't think I got lashings of it this time around, and that only proves her more, but I don't say that. 'It's not forever,' I tell her. And it won't be, just till I sort out what it is I am going to do. Write rubbish for the socialist papers? I can barely string two sentences together. What about carving? I'm a bit beyond that by now, though I've made France a beauty that I'll give to her after we say 'I do'. I love her so much I'd punch a hole through this wall to prove it, but she's not going to keep me, not while I'm sorting myself out, not ever. Anyway, if she's all for the worker, then she can know what it is to marry one for a bit, that it's more than just doing your own housework, it's … It'll do us both some good. I reckon Dad would be happy with that.

FRANCINE

I'm still furious, but there's no point in arguing about it. I suppose this is what is called a man's prerogative: to be irrationally stubborn when it's too hard to come up with a more sensible alternative. As if I am qualified to judge. So much for the crusade … Well, he can finish his *quarter* and then we can marry and when we're married, he'll have to give it away: it'd be too ridiculous after that, and possibly immoral since he'd be depriving someone else of job.

He comes around the other side of the sofa now — for heaven's sake he's still limping — and I know he's going to kiss me. And I know that I will vaporise happily at it too; it's glorious to do it standing up properly like this, on the tips of my toes, and he smells wonderful now — The Thing was beginning to stink a bit, but today he smells of Sunlight soap and clothes bleach and Daniel smell laced with wood and linseed oil. And I can sympathise, sort of: what *is* he going to do with himself? Can't he just love me and forget about the rest? We've broken almost every other rule … What's wrong with whittling useless pieces of art? There are worse things a man can do with his time.

Anyway, it's a good thing he came round, because Father wanted me to get The Lad over here today; he wants to see us both upstairs. And now it stabs that I've spent this time arguing and vaporising with Daniel. There is no more point to squabbling than there is to not spending every last second with the Leprechaun.

113

★

Father's propped up in bed: jaundiced and looking a hundred, while his indomitable cheerfulness winks through my shock at seeing his frailty anew every time I come back into the room. Methuselah says: 'Daniel, you must have heard me calling.' Then fakes a death cough, like there is something wrong with his lungs. 'Pour us a drink will you, son,' he adds, gesturing at the stand by the windows.

Daniel is supremely respectful with Father, but there is a look that comes across his face which betrays his utter bewilderment. He's wearing it now as he does as he's bid, and I swear his hand is a little unsteady as he gives Father the glass.

'Thank you, that's lovely. Now sit down, the pair of you.' He indicates either side of the bed. And we do.

He glances at me and says: 'For the moment you're decoration, so be quiet.' Then he trains his eyes on Daniel, who looks like a boy of twelve with his yes-sir ramrod-straight back. 'As I said to you, son, if you upset my daughter I'll come back to murder you, and don't think I don't have the power — I'm more religious and better connected than I let on. Now, having reminded you of that, I'll remind you that I am a betting man. I have a very sure tip for you: Britain will declare war on Germany by the end of the week, give or take a day, and we will all tag along for the ride. Jingo-jangle all the way. And with the call to arms will come heavy profit for heavy industry, which is always an outstanding but less publicised result of war — ah, if only I'd held off investing in aeronautics till now; but there's no sense in regret. I will offer only one piece of advice: try not to do anything rash, nor anything you don't want to do. But having said that, war does strange things to people. So, having a bet each way, I give you this.'

He hands Daniel a thick, large envelope from the bedside table; I see a pile of smaller envelopes behind the lamp. I lean across to look at this big one as it trembles ever so slightly in Daniel's fingers: on the face Father's written *INSURANCE* in determined but scratchy letters.

'Don't open it now,' Father says, though Daniel's too transfixed to do anything of the sort anyway. 'Open it outside, in the drive. Now off you go, the pair of you. Leave me alone, I'm feeling poorly.'

I say: 'Father, what's —'

'I thought I told you to be quiet.' Wink, reaching for his pipe. 'Don't worry, I'm not going to die this afternoon. Polly will fuss about me while you're out. And Mrs Moran is coming in a little while. I'll be well entertained.' Daniel bends his head and smirks under his hair at that in shared experience.

Father says to me, 'Better give me a kiss, just in case.' I do, then Daniel stands, gigantic over Father, and shakes his hand, saying, 'Whatever it is, I'm sure I don't deserve it.'

'Make sure you will then.' Daniel wants to say something more, but Father won't let him. 'Now go!'

One last death cough for us and an impatient wave, then we head for the stairs — and bolt down and out to the drive.

It's a title transfer, from one Colin McLaughlin, whoever he is, to Daniel Ackerman. There's a little note pinned to the top which says: *Sign in the obvious places, if you like it. All property is theft — blah, blah, blah — but there are some things you can't help thieving, and not an innocent among us. FPC.* There's a map below, showing the way to *Josie's Place*, and I'm already crying: Josephine was my mother's name.

Daniel pushes the hair away from my face and holds his hand there against my cheek, and I can't move for a minute. Then I say: 'Quick as you can — you drive.'

Poor Hayseed, in a canter all the way, through rough short cuts down to town and across Main, and away out of town, then along the length of Dell. Daniel knows exactly where he's going, right past his house. He slows as we hit the ruts leading into the gully, but so soon there she is: Calypso in the window, and then she's gone, behind us as we wend and wend to the left, and down, and then up again to a sharp plateau, and Josie's Place. The sign on the fence is new, and small, one lavender-blue hyacinth and one golden wattle sprig behind the name. The house is a marvellous abandoned wreck of peeling boards and smeary windows which look directly at the escarpment, at Calyspo, except you can't see her face from here, but the V of the true shape of the precipice, like a massive prow.

And as if this is not enough to do me in, beside the house lies an orchard. I can see what they are now: apple trees. Of course that's what they look like, now I see them in a bunch, fruit scattered all over the ground beneath them. I snagged my sleeve on the one by the side of Daniel's house and couldn't see it for looking. And I've dropped to my knees inside the gate and I can't feel anything except Daniel's arm around my back and I weep and I laugh like the ground's surging up through me.

'You like it then,' Daniel says when I calm.

I can't speak. And I don't need to.

Daniel folds me into his chest, and I know that this is what Paradise is. It's just here. Right here in front of your nose. If I didn't know better, I'd suspect Saint Francis himself.

True to his punt, Methuselah is not dead when we get back at dusk. Daniel stays down in the parlour while I go up to see if Father's awake; Mrs Ackerman has gone up to Newcastle for the week and won't be back till Wednesday, so Daniel's decided to stay for dinner anyway, rather than go to his workers' club for a *feed*; and as I climb the stairs I'm almost tempted to decide that he should stay the entire night so that I can whisper all my wishes into him and … Stop there, Francy.

Father's alive enough for me to kiss him all over his face, then lie down next to him and cuddle him. 'Thought you'd like it,' he chuckles softly, then his eyes spring open at me, twinkling even in this dim light. 'You two had better move swiftly, though, my girl, because I've sold this house to pay for it.'

No more surprises, hmm. And I know he's planned this so I don't have time to mourn him — I've come to suspect that his every word and deed over the past few months has been calculated down to the second: *It's far more indulgent than that,* chortle, chortle.

He says for the hundredth time: 'Is the lad gentle with you?'

I say: 'Yes and no.'

He says, 'Good,' and asks me: 'What is his gentlest?'

'When he touches me.' I can feel Daniel's hand on my shoulder now, reaching up through the floorboards.

'What's his worst?'

'I don't know.' I don't know what Father is asking any more when he says this. I've said Daniel's kiss is the best and his surly scowl is the worst, and described both in rapturous detail for his pleasure; that the rasp in his laugh is the best and … I don't know what is worst. The calluses on his hands? 'What should I know — tell me.'

Father closes his eyes and whispers: 'Nothing's more important than his gentleness — keep an eye on your own too.'

'My gentleness?'

But he doesn't answer.

He sighs into sleep, but it's not sleep. I can't say how long I watch him for, before I pull myself up to call Polly through the dark. She sends McNally out to get Doctor Nichols, but Father's already stopped breathing. I know. I know. I've pushed him and even slapped him and he's gone. And there's a sound that comes out of me that cracks the world in two.

As Daniel might say: like you wouldn't believe. And he is here now, pulling me away, just as my Leprechaun intended.

DANIEL

She cries so hard and loud it hurts to hear it. And there's nothing I can do but hold her against it. I know what she means, but that doesn't help. A few of my own tears fall into her hair, for all of it, as we stand here on the landing.

Polly puts on the light in Francine's room and comes over to us. She presses a little bottle into my hand and says: 'Make her have a good swig.'

I don't want to go into the light; I want to stand here in the dark with her. I want to hear her yell out everything I can't. Polly's pushing me towards the room and I get my sense back somehow. 'Come on, France.'

It's too bright in here; I leave her and put the lamp on and spin about looking for the bloody cord to turn the bulb off. She's quieter now, but I make her drink some of whatever quack's stuff this is. Probably just opium and brandy. It'll do.

I don't want her to cry any more. I don't ever want to hear that sound again.

I stay in the spare room, while France goes in with Polly to wash her father's body, and in the morning the undertaker will come. It'll be full Mick honours for him on Tuesday. I never thanked him; never knew what to say to him. What could I say? Thanks for your daughter. Oh, and the house on that old orchard and the half-share in the mine, and the rest to keep us going, and the compensation fund and the lav. This isn't the way things go: it's beyond my principles, and my understanding of the way things are. I don't think even Dad could come up with a good line for this. It's clear by anyone's principles that if all of us behaved as Francis Patrick Connolly did, then there'd be no rubbish. But maybe it was just death coming that made him do it. I'm not going to knock it back, but maybe it's not real either; just an old man's fancy. Blind luck. I remember the first time I saw this room, when Francine tried to wash my face and I thought I was dreaming again, and I hated her. I don't like what that says about me, and I don't sleep at all, tossing it all around and getting nowhere with it.

Francine would look good in a sugar bag, especially, but black and grief make her look fragile when she comes into the kitchen just on dawn while I'm looking for a cup to get a drink. She says: 'Well.' She's holding a bunch of envelopes, drops them on the bench. They're marked *Polly Rogers, Herbert McNally, Goods and Chattels, Orcharding, Fr Hurley — Wedding, One Last Word* and *Read This First*.

'Can you do it?' she asks me, staring at them. 'I don't think I could make my eyes focus even if I wanted to.'

Neither can I but I do. *Read This First* says that France'll need to leave this house by the sixth of August, since it's been sold — that's eleven days away. There are 'healthy' cheques for Polly and McNally, since he's assumed she won't want to take *the old folk* with her. I can guess what he's put in for them and it won't be very stingy. There's also a cheque for the Catholic priest, Hurley, that's already been promised to him *on the occasion of your wedding on the fifth, because it's a Wednesday and the middle of the week gives the best view of things.* Bloody hell — that's only ten days away. Keep reading: the contents of the house and all other effects are to be removed to Josie's Place, itemised list provided, and he's arranged for a Mr George Mellish to do it all. Basic instructions for apple cultivation are also provided.

That's the practicalities dealt with and France nods at the bench as if it's all in order, everything as expected.

'Do you want me to keep going? We could leave this for a bit,' I say.

She shakes her head. 'Read *One Last Word*, please.'

So I do: *GOOD LUCK! Remember to laugh at every opportunity. All other enquiries direct to Stanley and Bragg, Macquarie Street, Sydney.*

She looks at me, finally, and says: 'You can say no now, and that'll be the end of it. You can keep the apples. I'll get it sorted out.'

'What?' I'm reeling as it is, and she's having second thoughts? But I know she must be having a hundred thoughts a second right now, and she's just airing one of the worst ones: that all this is too much.

'I didn't mean that,' she says. 'I'm going to go to bed for the rest of today.'

Fair enough.

And I'll go and talk to Evan, tell him the lot: that I'll take a few more days before I come back to work, that Frank Connolly's dead, and that I'm in need of a best man.

FRANCINE

I'd forgotten Mr Drummond existed: now here he is in the parlour, looking from me to Daniel and back to me in some understandable forehead-creviced confusion. He's come to take me to the service for Father, because no doubt he assumes that there is no one else to take me. I only remember now that Doctor Nichols said he'd go and break the news to him for me. I want him to go away; Daniel's taking me. Father's last words to me on Mr Drummond were: 'He's not really as dark as he seems — but he's the worst sort of Catholic: an English pious one, for whom hypocrisy is an inborn way of life. He might frown and bluster, but just ignore him: he doesn't know any better. Stand firm and he'll give in to you as far as he can bring himself.' Father chuckled and added: 'He won't know what to do with you, my girl.'

I put him out of his present wonder quickly: 'Thank you for offering, Mr Drummond, but Mr Ackerman is taking me. We are recently engaged, you see. But we shall all stand together, yes?'

Rumbling silence. I feel a little sorry for his flummoxing now. But dignity and propriety, skewed as they are for me these days, are paramount. 'Of course,' he says. 'But may I have a brief word with you alone first, Francine?'

He looks to Daniel again now, who's all poured into his dark grey suit and seeming more the broader for it; he's holding Mr Drummond's gaze and for one very uncomfortable moment I wonder what he's going to do. He's virtually twice the size of The Boss and a third his age. Much as Father might think it a hoot for a punch-up to occur at this juncture, it might cause in me a very swift nervous collapse. But of course Daniel wouldn't do any such thing; he's not a thug. He only says, 'Certainly,' a breath away from impolite, and leaves the room, not closing the door behind him.

Mr Drummond doesn't bother closing it either, and gets straight to it: 'Was your father aware of this *engagement*?' Contempt, undisguised.

'Yes.' I feign horror at the scandalous allegation behind the question. 'I trust you shan't do anything so rude, but you might care to read Father's final instructions to us, or contact Stanley and Bragg regarding his will, if you have cause to query further.'

'Ah, naturally.' Mr Drummond presses his pale lips together, no doubt thinking upon the idiosyncrasies of his departed financier, and the implications my marriage presents for the future. I can fairly hear the wheels turning in his head.

To rub it in I say: 'In future, anything you have to say to me can be said to Mr Ackerman as well, since we shall be married on the fifth of August anyway, as Father wished. I would appreciate it if, under the circumstances of my grieving, you might direct any business matters to Mr Ackerman for our consideration.' I can feel Daniel's ears burning at that, but he may as well get used to it.

'And what is Mr Ackerman's role in the company to be?' Patronising prig.

I'm well riled now and I can hear Father guffawing with glee as I reply, seeming stunned: 'He's a miner, of course.' And say no more. This flummoxing is too agreeable to the circumstances of my grieving. I add: 'So, we shall see you at the church, then. Thank you again for your kind offer to escort me.'

He nods, under his black-bellied cloud, and strides out.

I'm still shaking after the rush of blood when I hear Daniel say: 'Who the hell made you?' And we laugh, or *crack silly* as Daniel would say, and I am light again: it's all right, everything is all right, for now.

Yes it is. It's an almost joyous day, despite the absence of a eulogy from Drummond — I've dropped the Mr now — despite Father Hurley's ramble upon thanksgiving and charity and a man he barely knew, despite being surrounded on every side by parishioners who've kindly turned out to make up the numbers in the church, despite Daniel looking like a fish out of water amid all this Catholic mumbo-jumbo. For inside this place of prayers and cool, damp bricks, scores from the Wattle have turned out too, and it's miners who carry my father to the cemetery. That they will not be paid today is a fact not lost on me; it bruises and embraces at once. And there is singing all the way, hymns I don't know, and even one sung in Welsh I think, but which sound more apt than anything I could have imagined. Apparently Evan Lewis arranged all this with Daniel and Father Hurley yesterday; and now here at the burial, Drummond is nowhere to be seen, the Lithgow conspiracy has done him in today. I weep and weep and not only because my father is gone, but because I know he would have loved this show and this enveloping of me, safe in all this strangeness.

The sun blazes down through the cold air; there is talk of carrying on to the Workers' — their club — and I cry some more for the cruelty that Father is not here to lay on the drinks. Then Daniel and I are alone by the grave, but for Father Hurley, who says as he makes to leave: 'So I shall see you two again on the fifth.' And I don't think Father's generous donation for *the occasion of your wedding* has put the gentle smile into his tired priestly eyes today. He will overlook my lapsed state and Daniel's atheism and our poor timing for some other reason; perhaps a higher thought of his own. I could kiss him for everything he does not ask, for everything he will do for us that he doesn't have to, and by canon law probably shouldn't. 'Around three, would that do well?'

'Of course.' I don't care; right now would do well.

I look up at Daniel as we make our way back to the trap outside the church, and all I can think of is that I wish he hadn't put his hat back on so I could see his hair. As Hayseed begins the journey home, I grab the brim and pull it off. Yes, this is my home, in Daniel's you're-a-lunatic look, and in the land that contains our fathers' bodies and their spirits, drifting up from the smokestacks, swirling between the sleeping hills, the dreaming women.

I wonder vaguely if the war's begun yet, papers are full of talk of it, but I can't catch hold of that thought. The rest of the world is a universe away.

DANIEL

'How'd you manage that?' Robby says first thing on my first day back at work, when I've told him, yes, I'm getting married. To Miss Francine Connolly. He's referring to the wonder of how we'd kept it on the shush; he'd heard a rumour, saw me with her that day at the paddock, but ... And now he's looking at me as if I've just told him I've robbed a bank. From his point of view I have, I suppose.

I don't know what to say; his wife, Cass, had their second one a few weeks ago and it's written all over him: not exactly a good advertisement for marriage or the state of the working poor.

But he says: 'You lucky, lucky bastard.'

'Don't carry on,' I tell him. 'Haven't you got work to do?'

'Fuck off. Boss already, are you?'

'You fuck off.'

What sort of a goose do I sound like? One that should fuck off and let Robby get on.

Mum's a fair bit less than impressed with me when I come home. She'd have come in from the train, expecting me to be here, but probably thinking I'm with Francine. What she sees is me stripping off round the back as she puts her head out the door. She doesn't ask, doesn't say anything, and she's not going to put on any hot water for me; she disappears into the house and there's silence. If she's not been inclined to show her disappointment

with me in the past, she's making up for that now. So I just fill
the tub with cold water out here and do the job at lightning
speed as a sleety wind comes up through the gully.

Inside, she's starting tea, with her back to me, and I give her
the rundown of what's been going on while she's been in
Newcastle. She doesn't respond, just a sad sigh when I tell her
about Frank Connolly, nothing else, not even when I laugh:
'You'll have to talk to me, if you're coming to the wedding.'

Eventually, she stops clattering about at the stove and goes into
her room; comes out a minute later, holding one of Dad's boxes.
His records. Then she whacks them on the table and says: 'You
should bother to read at least these one day.'

I have read them, though, a few times in the last month when
she's gone out. I was looking for mention of old Herb McNally,
to see what his problem was, but there's nothing in there —
obviously Dad considered it *no one else's business.* But I know
better than to say that I was looking at all. I don't want to talk
about Dad right now; and not with Mum. What would he say?
What's for tea, Sarah? Sa-hra, he said it.

She says, and she's gripping the string around the top stack of
pages: 'You don't owe anyone anything.'

I owe everyone for everything is how I feel. But, again, I don't
say it. I'm still hearing *Sa-hra,* like I'm watching him looking at
her.

'What are you trying to prove?' she says.

That I can work things out my own way and get up
Drummond's nose for a bit while I'm at it. France is at least keen
for that now. But I say: 'It won't be forever, just till the end of the
quarter.'

'So you can say you're still *true blue* with some more weight to
it? Why don't you use your brain for a change and accept the
challenge you've been given. This is not a game about who you

think you should be, Daniel — you are who you are, so go and learn how to be a good boss.'

I'm never going to be a boss. But even that thought is dippy in my head: I will be come next Wednesday, sort of, and in three years' time we will be definitely; what will we do then? It's too far away and it's easy to ignore for now.

'Or you could go back to school and learn something else!' Mum says, and she's yelled at me. She's never done that before, except when I was a kid and doing something dangerous.

What would I do at school, though? I'm too old anyway, except for technical college, and what would I do there? Learn how to type? Bookkeeping? So that's all easy to ignore too, and I say instead: 'France and I *are* going to do something else. She's giving up her bourgeois rubbish and she's going to grow apples. She doesn't even know how to cook, can't even fry an egg, but she's going to learn to. We're going to see what happens, all round,' I say. 'You've got to admit that's going to be interesting …'

'Sure.' And Mum cracks, finally, smiling as she shakes her head at me. Probably because I've only admitted that France is keener for a challenge than I am.

Time to change the subject: 'So how's Pete then?'

Now she laughs, but sad with it: 'Do you care?'

Not really, but I have to say: 'Course I do.'

'Your brother is very well,' she says and I say, 'Good,' and that's the end of that chat too.

Later, when she's cleaning up after tea, she says: 'I bet your leg is hurting.'

Too right. I hated every minute of today, but I shrug.

She says: 'Good. I hope it keeps you awake all night thinking.'

It doesn't. I'm out like a light as soon as I hit the pillow, I'm that buggered. Every day, through to Saturday, and Sunday I sleep till midday, then ride up to see Francine. She's got everything organised; the house is empty, no Polly or McNally, just France.

'Is everything gone?' I ask her.

'Yes, absolutely gone,' she says proud as punch. 'Last load just left. And I slept on the floor last night.' She points into the sitting room, where there's a pillow and a blanket folded near the hearth with a couple of her Sydney *Herald*s and a Lithgow *Mercury*. 'Doing penance for my sins, so that you'll have me pure. Nothing here but me. Now you have to go away — I can't bear to see you and I have far too much to do by way of setting up nest. Go on. Shoo. Go away till Wednesday.'

All right. A kiss and I'm off. Mum's horrified when I tell her France is alone. She takes off round to the orchard with her when Francine passes in the trap. Another kiss, and now I'm alone. I'm getting married in three days' time. Mum doesn't come home, she stays with France, and I'm the happiest bloke that ever lived. I even hit the piano. Christ, I even sing.

I turn up early, so close-shaved my face is still stinging from the ride, and I stand there in the church, having a quiet word with Dad about everything except what I should be thinking about; he's ragging: *You're making a bad habit of Roman Catholicism lately, boy. Leave it alone — you're unattractive enough as it is.* While I'm trying not to think about how much it cuts that he's not here, and reminding myself he is here so long as I am, then startling myself again with the fact of me being here, and hearing Dad say: *Settle down — anyone would think you were getting married today,* Hurley, the priest, pops up from nowhere and just about tears the skin from me with his 'Hello there, lad'. But Evan's popped up from some other nowhere too, to say hello back. They have more in common in this place, and they talk about the weather, which is about to piss down.

And then I hear the trap; she comes in, with Mum behind her. I can't tell you, except that I see the flowers wound through her hair, white against her hair and her face. It's mercifully quick, and I can't hear much for the rain. I'm too busy; busier as I'm trying to move the Holy Host's piece of cardboard off the roof of my mouth with my first taste of wine, knowing Hurley's given it to me against the rules, and wishing he'd given me dispensation from this as well. Still trying to swallow as he's talking me through the I wills and the haves and to holds and I dos, and I give France the ring that I only bought yesterday, which is too big but pretty on her finger because it's there, because she's thrilled with it, and we're all nearly laughing when I kiss her, except for Hurley, who's only trying harder not to.

And then we sign the papers. Her middle name's Veronica. It's all over, we're legal, and I'm wondering what I'll do with my bike when Evan says, 'Well, get going then,' and Mum's giving Francine her cardigan and waving us off.

It's teeming bullets and it's perfect; her little Hayseed is just about knackered when we get to Josie's Place, our place — I don't know whose heart is pumping fastest. I pick France up out of the trap and just the smell of her makes me think I'm going to drop her, but I wouldn't. These hands aren't going to let go for anything. She's soaked through, the flowers have slipped every which way down her hair and she is mine. I push the front door open with my foot, thankful it's off the latch so that I don't have to put her down, and I don't clock my head on the door frame, and I walk through our dark and dusty falling-down house which is stuffed full of fat heavy furniture and packing boxes, with food laid out on the table in the back room next to the kitchen. I don't know where to set her down in all this, but here'll do. And still I don't let go. I kiss her, properly forever now, for the first time, and I don't know what I was so wound up

130

about; I've got no idea what I'm doing and it doesn't matter. I'm still kissing her even as we're taking off our clothes.

I'm not game to look at her, for obvious reasons: it'll all be over in a second if I do. So I stop everything and just hold her for a long moment, till it's too bloody freezing and I have to chase her to the bedroom. She dives under the covers and looks at me now, wide-eyed and so am I. The luckiest bloke in the world having the best day of his life.

I'm shivering with holding back now as I climb in with her, and I just have to kiss her and kiss her to rein myself in. She is so soft, everywhere, pale and smooth as willow. She whispers, 'Oh my goodness,' and arches her back when I touch her breasts, and I kiss her there too. I can't wait any longer, and somehow I find her, but I'm too scared to push, that I'll hurt her. But she pushes up to me, and she cries out then. I stop. Jesus, I have hurt her. She cups her hands around my face, blinks up at me and smiles. And then it really is all over, for now at least.

I roll around next to her and she winds herself around me. Don't know what I was so wound up about, there should be a law making this compulsory.

FRANCINE

No bridesmaids, no carriage, not even a special wedding dress, and my mother-in-law gave me away; but I have *this*. There is no word for this. I'm not even going to try. This is not something for thoughts but for our skin, as much of my skin as physically possible touching his. I am a limpet on a rock, and I'll have to be prised off. Daniel doesn't mind; in fact he's fallen into a doze. I should get up, though, and stable poor Hayseed, give him a feed of the grains from the sack that McNally made up for him before he left, then bring in something for us to eat for dinner. Daniel has to be up at five in the morning; well, he doesn't have to, but he's going to; and Mrs Ackerman, or Sarah now, has given me a very short course in the daily routine, and some of her recipes, and her paper patterns for Daniel's underwear. *Oh?* But she's an angel of rescue; she told me she'd been in a similar position once herself, not knowing what to do and how; again I wanted to ask her about herself, but she makes it so plain when she's said all she wants to say, I daren't ask. Too grateful to push my luck anyway. When I crumpled into the mirror this morning, she held my shoulders and said, 'Now, now, stop that. I'm sure your father would want you to be your prettiest today,' and there was something firm and tender and all-knowing about the way she said it that stoppered up the flow; something in the way she said, 'Not that Daniel would notice of course,' that made me giggle; more so, and with a jolt, when she added: 'Blind as a boot, he is. And such a kind, sweet girl you are to take him off my hands.'

She hasn't said anything more direct than that, but I don't think she approves of him going back to work. Why on earth would she? Neither do I, but perhaps there is something in Daniel's rationale, at least where I'm concerned: to really understand something, you should experience at least a bit of it, otherwise you're just barking into the wind. I'm sure Father would endorse this *knowing what it means* exercise, and it's only for a little while. Still, I don't want him to go, and it's not just because I am a limpet. My stomach turns over every time I think of him going into that hole in the hill. But perhaps Father would say that's worth my knowing too. And besides, when I think of Drummond's contempt, I want him to have to deal with Daniel at the mine, I want him to see what it means too; even if he is as dense as Father said, then at least I'll feel we made some attempt at making a point, making sense of Father's last wishes and all that. Daniel's told me the other miners think it's hilarious too. And besides, this is what Daniel has decided to do; I can't stop him, short of having him sacked. And besides, besides, lightning doesn't strike twice, does it; not in so short a time. But it has, hasn't it: we've lost our fathers within three months of each other. I limpet-cling a little tighter; surely, lightning doesn't strike thrice, then? He doesn't wake. Tell myself there's more chance of him being attacked and eaten by a mob of savage wallabies out here in the backblocks.

And so, fully rationalised, I slip quietly out of the bed, don my nightdress and garden boots to risk the wallabies myself as I tend to my faithful but by now impatient pony — very quickly. It's so cold! Then I run back inside and set up a tray of the wonderful food that Sarah has made, and wake him: my husband, with my hand on his chest, my lips on his cheek. He only eats a little and we're back to it again. Oh my goodness.

★

'How do you know when it's time to get up?' I ask him, bleary in the dark as he's creaking around on the draughty floorboards hunting for his work clothes, which Sarah hung over the chair by the wardrobe yesterday morning.

'You didn't hear the whistle?' he says.

'No.' Gaping yawn. Good God, this hour of the day should be banned. And if I thought it was cold yesterday …

'I suppose it's quieter round here, and I half listen for it in my sleep. I'd probably hear it in the grave,' he says, pulling on trousers.

Not funny, I glare into the blackness.

'Don't get up, not today,' he says. 'I've eaten what was there.' He lights my little oil lamp and kneels by the bed to kiss me. 'I've put the stove on, be a bit warmer in a minute, in the kitchen at least.' Laughing at me. Another kiss. 'I'll have to take the trap in too, pick up my bike at Evan's. You don't need anything in town, do you?'

'No.' I hug him: stay here, we've already made enough of a point.

'Be back around five,' he says, extricating himself, stuffing cap in back pocket.

'Five? I thought Lithgow was a strictly eight-hours town.'

'It is.' Just one more kiss and big black boots stomp out into the world.

So I do lie in, languishing in very, very last grasp of former reality, and listen to the trap wheels fade back into silence, while I try to fathom how eight hours becomes twelve, and fail; even with travel time, from the furthest reaches, it seems impossible. I stare at a mouldy patch in the far corner of the ceiling, stricken with the even more impossible contemplation of my aloneness.

As much as I enjoy my own company, I wonder how I'll go at this much aloneness, this kind of aloneness. Mould goes drippy with tears as I wonder if Father is with Josie now; I wonder if they are watching me. I don't think I believe in heaven, but I hope he's with her, I dearly hope he is, sparkling at her. I wonder what they think of me lolling lugubrious in bed, if his Josie's saying to him, 'Good gracious, look at the girl you raised, Frank.' Whimper now: Father's voice is so fresh in me, but what did Josie sound like? How would she have said *Frank*? What did I call her? Mother? It doesn't sound right. Neither does the sound of me whimpering as if I'm the only orphan in the world.

Get up, Francy.

You've plenty to do today. Plenty to be too busy with along the lines of general drudgery and culinary experimentation. While husband of thirty seconds has gone down that wretched, hideous, stinking, putrid coal mine when there's absolutely naught that says he must. So get up, Francy, and just get on with it. Isn't this what Father wanted too? And you *agreed* to this *temporary* arrangement with steely boned resolve, so you will now do a proper job of it. Learn essential skills and build character. Be a good Socialist. Be a good Wife. Without a honeymoon, without a lazy breakfast over which we should be gazing into each other's eyes over the unopened newspaper that contains a paragraph on our swish reception and gift list, without even a door on the toot out the back. Without rolling congratulations everywhere I turn; only proof that there must have been a hundred girls in love with him if some of the sly glares I received in town on Monday were anything to go by: look at her — her father's only dead thirty seconds and now she's wedding Our Lad. Who does she think she is? Wife without household help is who I am today, and as much as *help* in principle does seem unnecessary, this morning its absence is … daunting.

Oh, enough *whining*.

I whip back the covers and I'm up and out, to see the small blood splotch on the sheet. Of course. Though I can attest now that there was a great deal that Sister Terrence did not tell motherless me about Marriage, she did manage to impart in a steady whisper that such an occurrence of Stain on the Wedding Night is a commonly Good Thing and not usually cause for alarm. I'm not alarmed, no, it's just another thing I have to keep me busy today: washing.

Sarah has advised a foolproof recipe to start with, a flavoursome stovetop one-pot thingumy that's so quick and easy you just throw everything in and stir occasionally. She even provided most of the ingredients for me. But I'm muddled after a day of sweeping and cobweb snatching and window washing and wrestling sheets through the wringer and cursing whoever decided they needed to be pressed, and having to make the fire in the stove again because I let it go out — twice. This valiant worker's fist is pleased with all the effort, but limp. And I think I've left my brain inside the stove. Flavoursome is not quite the word for my thingumy. It's bitter and tastes vaguely of a dash of borax. I don't know how to save it, or if it can even be saved at all, and Sarah's too far away to ask right now. Daniel will be home any minute. I check the *jacket* potatoes in the oven part, remembering that Sarah said to prick them with a fork before putting them in, and hope it's not too late to do it now. None of them have exploded yet, so I chase them round with the fork and burn the back of my hand on the top of the oven, and yell out my worst word: 'Arse!' just as I hear the trap pull inside the gate. I run my hand under the tap and fan my face and wait for him, wondering what else we might have with the potatoes. Bread and honey? Some leftover cinnamon cake?

Daniel looks like thunder when he finally walks round to the back door, and I'm sure it's not just because he's covered in coal. Perhaps he smelled dinner while he was stabling Hayseed. My God: I remember I haven't put the hot water on! Mad scramble with big heavy pot and tap, and abject apology for idiocy. He laughs as he kicks off his boots on the back verandah and says, 'Don't worry about it,' grabs the tub from against the wall, fills it and starts stripping off right here by the stove.

It's not hard to smile as I watch him wash, with relief and delight in watching him; he should never be allowed to be clothed; and of course he's not going to be fussed on my first day on the job. He flicks the wet flannel at me in fun to make that clear.

'You looked so fierce just now,' I say, 'I thought you were angry.'

'No.' Splash, splash, the water turns grey, but there is something the matter in the surly way he's scraping his arms clean; he just doesn't want to say it. 'I'm knackered is all. And starving. What's for tea?' He looks up and grins and that does me in. Tears sting, but I'm not going to cry. Too late, he's seen. 'What's wrong?'

Blather: 'I'm tired too, and I've mucked up dinner, and I burned my hand — see?'

He really belts out a laugh then, but pretends to inspect my hand seriously. It's such a tiny mark, not even a blister. He kisses it and says: 'You'll live. And whatever you've cooked, don't worry I'll eat it, as long as it's food. It can't be that bad.'

Oh but it is. I hold my breath as he stands, wraps the towel around his waist and tastes a mouthful of my bubbling disaster.

'Nothing wrong with that, it's just like Mum's, nearly,' he says: you're a lunatic.

'Really?' He's just being lovely about it. 'It seems a bit bitter to me,' I fish but don't mention the borax, just in case I accidentally did put some in.

'Maybe you put in too much tarragon,' he says, around another mouthful. 'Add some cream to smooth it out — that's what Mum does. Stop worrying. It's good.'

Must be. I blob in a dash of cream and there's nothing left in the end. I've never seen someone eat so much; we'll need the profits from the mine just to feed him, I'll have to cultivate potatoes. It doesn't hurt to eat a bit of borax, does it, I tell myself. Or maybe I'm simply not used to tarragon, whatever that is — the little jar of dried dust-coloured leafy stuff Sarah gave me along with the rest. But there's still something wrong here: moody, broody hand on fist as he looks at me above the carnage. What do I ask him? *How was the coal today, dear?* Hmn. Maybe it's not so hilarious being married to The Boss after all, and he's got a ribbing now it's done. Or maybe Drummond has done something insulting already. Or maybe he really is just tired. As if he wouldn't be. I'd really rather contemplate the circumference of his forearm, the shape of the bone there at the wrist, and ignore the fresh graze that runs across the top of his knuckles.

'Your father was right,' he says, sardonic. 'Australia's declared war on Germany too.'

War? That's right, there's a war on. In Europe. Germany's invaded Belgium or something. I didn't get a paper today, obviously; barely glanced at yesterday's *Mercury*, naturally.

I say: 'Yes. Of course. Well, we would, wouldn't we.'

DANIEL

'Doesn't matter that it was inevitable,' I tell her; everyone knows that; doesn't make me any less shitted about it. It's the point-proving matter of arse-end Australia trying to be large as it feels. 'We're Mother England's best little kid, aren't we. But it's, I don't know, embarrassing.'

'Because you're German?' she says, and she's woken herself up out of her dippy-headed fuss over tea to join me at last.

'No. And I'm not. It's because this shouldn't be anything to do with us; we shouldn't be *tagging* along. We're supposed to be an independent country, but tagging along is a forgone conclusion. Worse, when I came out today, Robby was in a lather for empire about it, and so were a dozen others, like Britannia cares what they think.'

'Father's been known for a poor punt — it probably won't amount to much,' she says, unconvincingly. I haven't even thought about it properly yet, been otherwise occupied over the last little while, but it's taken five seconds to work out that this isn't going to be any old stoush over some scrap of land that's not happy with colonisation, like that one in Africa when I was a little kid. This is a war *between* empires: Britain, France and Russia are going to crush Prussia and Austria, out of existence according to Robby, like that's something to yahoo about. All I know is that sounds like a lot of empires. Like she's picked up my thought, Francine adds: 'Or maybe they'll all decide it's far too unwieldy to manage and call it off.'

She's a lark ... if only everyone thought like her.

'They're already going for it,' I tell her. 'Some idiots started firing a cannon at a German freighter out of Melbourne the second they called it on yesterday and the ship's been impounded. If you can believe that, then you can believe this is fairly serious. It's some big skite that we've fired the first British shot of the war, and Cook's already promised to send Mother twenty thousand troops.'

'Twenty *thousand*?'

'Yep. While the *Mercury*'s saying we should all keep calm and prepare to be invaded shortly. Make sense of that, if they're going to send away defences that we don't have now.' Unless they'll look to compulsory school cadets, which I missed out on by a couple of years — they haven't started shaving yet. 'So where do you think Cook'll get his twenty thousand?'

Not hard to work out either. He'll get them from blokes like Robby. He's talking of joining up already. Evan says it's all a load of imperialist rubbish that we should keep well out of. Too right. But tell Robby that; I'm sure it's crossed his mind that the army might give him something better than the mine, too; soldier's pay might not be a fortune, but it's regular and all expenses paid. I'm not sure about the conditions, though. Whatever, there'll be no solidarity on this issue.

'Ah.' She can see why I'm so dark about it now. I'm sure Connolly was right that there'll be money made out of all this, but it's the working class that'll pay, with the ultimate if all the carry-on is anything to go by. She says: 'But maybe the election will change things? Cook can't hold on, all the papers have been saying so for months, couldn't run a raffle at a church fete, let alone a government. Good heavens ...' She stops to think some more: 'How could he make such an enormous promise knowing he's on the way out? That's ... that's ... Well, Mr Fisher will be returned and there'll be a Labor Government again soon. Perhaps that will calm things down.'

'That's not going to make a blind bit of difference, France,' I say, but you've got to wonder how many girls out there talk like she does. 'The Labor Party's not going to turn around and tell Mother they've changed their mind and rediscovered socialism. Or worked out what an independent country is. Fisher's already been careful to say that if the worst came to the worst then we'd be in it. And here we are. There won't be a vote on the war.' I'm parroting the *The Worker* with this, but it's true. Not that France and I could do anything about it: neither of us are old enough to vote. And what am I doing letting this rubbish into our house? We've only been married a day — there are more important issues we should be attending to.

But France is serious now. 'If it does really blow up, where will that leave you?'

I know what she's referring to: 'I'm not German. I was born at Mount Kembla.' I say that sharper than I mean to, but I have a flash of memory, of Kembla, after it blew, and the funerals, endless. Wollongong, going in to buy my first pair of boots, catch the train. I must have been about seven or so. That's where the other Daniel is buried too. And Dad is buried here, under the ridge below the paddock. 'I'm more Australian than the jokers that have put us up to this.'

But I haven't answered her question, because it doesn't have an answer, yet.

'Anyway,' I say to get a smile, 'I'm just German enough to be able to give the Kaiser directions straight to parliament if they do invade.'

That does the trick. 'You never told me you speak German,' she says to me, like it's a scandal.

'I don't. Not really. Just bits and pieces.'

'Say something to me in German,' she says, and I could grab her right now the way she's looking at me. She's got a little streak of soot on her forehead and she's still wearing her filthy apron; no idea and she's perfect.

'I'll do better than that,' I say, getting up. She follows me out to the front room, where her piano is, and I flip the lid. I can't see the stool anywhere for the packing cases so I stand and sing her 'Twinkle Twinkle Little Star', which in Deutsch is too hilarious to ever forget:

Funkel, funkel kleiner Stern,
Was du bist, das wüßt ich gern.
Stehst hoch über aller Welt,
Ein Diamant am Himmelszelt.
Funkel, funkel kleiner Stern,
Was du bist, das wüßt ich gern.

Those bells of hers bounce round the room at that and we're the only two people on earth again as I kiss her and hold her to me.

But it's then I remember the present I made her weeks ago; I picked it up from Mum's at sparrow's this morning when I was heading in, seems like a hundred years ago. It's still sitting in the bottom of the trap wrapped in an old tea towel; can't believe I just left it there.

'Wait here,' I tell her, pulling away, 'and close your eyes.'

I've gone out and grabbed it and I go to unwrap the tea towel on my way back in, then think, no, she'll like it better just as it is.

'You can open them now.'

She is priceless the way she looks at it, frowning then excited like a kid. She makes that sound like a kitten as she unwraps it and sees what it is: it's her. Just her face, about to blink, framed by her hair, which was dead easy since it's so straight. Even I was impressed

142

when I finished it; she's let out another little squeak as she turns it around in her hands. She sets it down on top of the piano, then she folds around me and the shape of her fits against me everywhere.

All through the day I'm thinking about her so much I'm dangerous. We should have gone away somewhere, or at least stayed at home for a few days. Any kind of honeymoon or celebration didn't seem appropriate a week ago, but today … I reckon they should give you a month off after a wedding to give you time to get over it. Paid leave, if such a thing existed, for your contribution to the country's general state of happiness.

'Danny!' Evan yells at me. I've knocked my belt sideways getting up from packing under the cut and I'm spilling shot all down the front of myself without noticing, about to blow apart my happiness. 'You're having a good time, then,' he says as I'm cleaning myself up. Like you wouldn't believe, though he looks like he knows very well.

Later on, as we're walking back up the drift at the end of shift, he says: 'Thought about what you're going to do? You've had your laugh now, and you can't stay down here indefinitely. You're not union any more, strictly speaking.'

Here: I let the way he says that word hang about in my head for a bit; he says it *yur*.

'Daniel?' he says, laughing at me like he knows what I'm thinking about.

'I heard you,' I say.

'It would be good if you were managing the place, don't you think?' He's out with it.

I've thought about it, obviously. But there are two things against it. First, the place already has a manager in Stevens, useless arse that he is; for all his School of Mines and Industries Certificate on the wall, he's more paymaster than manager, and

Drummond's not going to want to replace him with me for any reason. Second, I'm not sure I want the responsibility; a manager *should* be responsible for answering concerns from the pit, and making decisions about safety and such. Despite the seniority of the work I already do, I'm still the youngest at the face; I'm younger than most of the wheelers; it doesn't seem right.

Evan says: 'You wouldn't be on your own, boyo; we'd work in together. You'd only be in a position to do what your dad always did anyway on fixing and such, except officially, and without breaking your own back; you might even teach the Premier something about it while you're there.' Gives me a nudge; the Premier is Holman who for us is not the poncy fat-headed State Labor leader, but the manager's deputy, and for all that he's a nice bloke and spends all day underground, no one's quite sure what it is he does apart from headcounts; gives me a laugh as he says: 'It makes sense, don't you think?'

It does, but: 'Drummond's not likely to agree.' And I'm not likely to push the issue. I don't know how to deal with him; never had to, don't want to. Evan's aware of that.

'We'll agitate for Stevens to be sacked — and there's your vacancy.' Just like that. 'Well, he's not exactly competent, is he. He can't think without Drummond's say-so. Wouldn't listen to me a few weeks back with the ventilation, told me to have the men keep on till he came down to check the air himself — meaning that the boss wasn't about so he could ask him. I wasn't going to wait for a few more to give way to the lack of it while he was dithering, was I, so I had to ignore him and bring everyone up. What's the point in him? He's got no idea. I don't have to tell you that.'

'But —'

'And *we'll* demand that you replace him. Everyone'll be onside for it. And you're entitled to it, in all ways of looking at it. So?'

'I'll think about it,' I say; I've got to, properly.

'You're a puzzle, Danny,' he says. 'You get married after five minutes, but if you were any slower on this I'd say you were backward.'

He shakes his head, but I'm not committing yet. France, once I saw her properly, seemed like she'd always been there waiting for me to catch on, but this is a big shift in thinking. I always expected to get married; I never expected I'd manage a mine; and neither of them at nineteen. Never expected I'd have money, either, and so far I haven't felt the effect of that, but I know I will soon. It is time to be reasonable about it.

More than time, it seems, when we come into the lamp room and Stevens is there waiting. He says, in front of the others, 'Something for your wife from Mr Drummond, Ackerman,' hands me an envelope and walks back towards the office.

That's it; decision's made. I pull him back by his runty shoulder and tell him: 'Mr Ackerman, thank you.'

He tries for an eyeball but he knows; I crack with laughing, at him, and so does everyone in the room. I'd very much like to take him round the paddock and belt him for extra clarity, but he's too small. And I've had my fun.

It's an offer to buy out her share of the mine. France throws it on the fire. She couldn't sell even if she wanted to; not till she's twenty-one, but she's not going to tell Drummond that. Leave him to wonder. See why I love her?

She says of my decision: 'So that'll mean you don't go down that hideous — into the pit?'

'Not that often. No.' Not all day every day.

She's so happy she's almost dancing around the tub and trying not to. And then we're all over each other again. *Dinner* does get ruined this time, but it's my fault she left it burning on the stove.

FRANCINE

Not a peep to me from Drummond, not even when the men down tools and win their coup. Daniel tells me all about it, not that there's much to tell: it was over quickly, since the Wattle has just received a massively extended contract from the railways — Drummond didn't tell me about that, of course; Daniel did. Drummond had no choice but to cave in to them, so they'd get back to work. It's only the end of week two of this preposterous war and it appears that the lift in heavy industry is already well under way, in accordance with Father's prediction, and I imagine my business partner is busy counting pennies in advance. I feel a little sorry for this hapless Stevens fellow, though, but Daniel tells me not to.

'Save your sorrow for Robby.'

'Why?'

'He went to Sydney and joined up today.'

Oh dear. Daniel knew he would, but the fact of it has clearly shocked him. If you read the papers, this *joining up* with the Australian Imperial Forces business seems to be spreading like a disease. There'll be no trouble whatsoever filling the quota of twenty thousand. Despite plenty of loud dissent from the trade unions and the Irish generally, decrying, rather compellingly at times, Britannia as mistress of tyranny, ordinary men are lining up in droves across the country to volunteer to defend the Glorious Empire, the Realm and Dominions of King George V, whoever he is. All comers considered for service, except for Asiatics and the native Aborigines, who've been officially banned from the AIF under the new Defence Act. Why? Because, as the *Bulletin* portrays them, Chinamen are all treacherous and Jacky-Jacky's a raggedy drunk? I don't know anything about Chinese, except that they can grow vegetables anywhere, and that they get addicted to opium while they're stealing White jobs; knowledge of Aborigines even scantier still, beyond consensus on their moral and intellectual inferiority; comprehension of Robby Cullen's decision almost as slim, and there's a tug upon my ignorance of tyranny, like a small hand belonging to a child I can't see.

'He won't be the last from the Wattle, either,' Daniel adds, staring out at the apple trees, grey shapes in the darkness.

It's hard to imagine all this going on beyond our little world, where, when I'm not diligently drudging, I'm perusing *Common Diseases of the Apple* which I've borrowed from the library, and bursting for Daniel to come home, reasonably coal-free from now on. Hooray for us. The Leprechaun's power resonates. And I know Daniel will never join up; never been so chuffed at being wedded to a socialist German, even if he denies the latter. I had been worried that there'd be some big brouhaha against German Australians, but there doesn't seem to have been much so far. Apart from a few silly incidents reported in the cities, mostly involving overzealous patriots and bricks through windows, German nationals are simply being asked to go home in a calm and orderly manner or be politely interned for the duration. Nothing like that going on in Lithgow: there aren't any *German* Germans here; there's a pony breeder called Keffler outside Wallerawang, apparently, but he's really 'Aussie'. Perhaps Daniel's right: if you're Australian, you're Australian, no matter where you came from before that. So many seem to be taking that sentiment deeply seriously, though, and wedding it to Motherland pride.

Preparing to stake their lives for it: we'll show Blighty what we're made of! It's not helped by the jingo-jangle in the press: one super-excitable journalist even used the metaphor of Achilles to describe our projected manly might in the forthcoming tussle: *Handsomest of All!* Ha! Achilles: I've got him right here, if you please, and he won't be going off to war.

'It won't be so many from here, surely,' I say to Daniel now. Lithgow is, after all, a workers' town and the opinion of the union leaders must count for something.

But he doesn't want to talk about it any more. We're celebrating our own victory tonight and Daniel *hits* the piano. No singing, though I'd love him to; he doesn't ever quite sing as such but rather talks to the music: '*You made me love you. I didn't want to do it, I didn't want to do it. You made me want you, and all the time you knew it. I guess you always knew it*'; hardly Al Jolson but I adore the sound of his voice — I'm unashamedly biased and most disinclined to ever hear that phonograph disc again. Now he plays his *bit of Beethoven*, the sonata *Pathetique*, and I think I know why. He played it last night and it turned me to vapour: *très* pathetic. He's a ceaseless wonder; he says he can't even read music much — 'Mum taught me.' Sure. Some things can't be taught; they just are what they are, as they come. Not exactly the world's most difficult piece, and he avoids any tricky embellishment, but I can't play it so well, and when he comes to the final bars I hear that he's not just playing for me: tonight it fades with love and sadness. It sounds older than him, us, Beethoven too.

We'll see the fever in the flesh, I suppose, when we travel to Sydney at the end of September. We, or rather I, have to sign some papers saying that I agree to the terms of Father's will; it's only a silly formality, since it was all signed, sealed and delivered months ago, and I'm not of an age to be signing anything instead of my *husband*, but it needs to be done, and we may as well meet this Stanley and Bragg lot, quiet keepers of our universe as they are. Daniel's *skived* off for the day — who's going to say he can't? He's the manager and my *husband*. Father hoots as I futilely pin my hair getting ready to go, but it's Daniel watching me in the soft dawn light. He's wearing that dark suit, filling it and the mirror as he stands behind me. There are other things we could do today, and I half want to stay here and luxuriate in this weekday off, continue with the all-day-Sunday attention I lavished upon him as his twentieth birthday present. It's a wrench to leave, and not just for *that*, but the buds on the apples are beginning to sprout and our secret valley beyond the fat cigars is at last warming up so I can sit outside and draw and dabble with my paints when I'm not drudging.

Still, I'm interested to see what I've been missing out on in the city, and not a little thrilled to be stepping out with husband, even at this hour: I am Mrs Daniel Ackerman, look at me! No sly glares now: I am respectability itself. And I imagine that in no small part this is a result of Daniel's *I don't want all this to change who I am* intransigence: it's proven I'm no snooty toff either, despite my rounded vowels: I scrub my own pots and pans. Oh, but I was once, wasn't I, a snooty horror. I can hear Sister Simon-Peter bellowing: 'Pride Cometh!', never adding the 'Before a Fall', only pointing at the floor for me to kneel and receive standard three lashes across left shoulder. Grinning high above that memory: I've fallen rather well this time, I think.

Five months ago I came up over the mountains and down into Lithgow by Father's motor car, since gone to God, or rather to Mr Colin McLaughlin, previous owner of our hearth and home, who had the Austin thrown in with the deal. Father really did think of everything: I hated that contraption, and every divot and bend in the road had my fingernails, long since also gone to God, digging in the leather of the seat. So Daniel and I go up by train today, *tooooot tooooot*, engine puffing, probably with our Wattle coal, through the Ten Tunnels, black and like I can see the hands that made them, then above the sandstone curtain to Mount Victoria and Blackheath at the very top, *tooooot tooooot*, on and steadily down through Medlow Bath, with its Hydro Majestic resort, then Katoomba, with its swish Carrington Hotel, then Leura, then Wentworth Falls, where Father and I holidayed for several summers, all pretty little weatherboard towns between the tracts, no, oceans of gums and gums and gums sizzling blue beyond the weepy shades of brown and olive.

Our carriage is full of men now. I hope they're all off to work today, but suspect that at least some of them are heading for Victoria Barracks in the city. I clasp Daniel's arm a little tighter and he smiles at me, then looks back out at the view over Woodford. He hasn't been to Sydney since he was a little boy, when they moved from Kembla, so he's taking in everything: the mountain range from this vantage really is something to look at.

Then Sydney appears, briefly, at Faulconbridge, a great grey clumpy blotch on the horizon. Sydney: the Lions' Den, or maybe Babel. The descent ends abruptly with the Lapstone tunnel and a sweep down to Emu Plains, where the broad spread of pasture land begins. This is the worst part of the trip for its monotony, but the men on the train chat faster and more and more cheerily the closer we get, and I block my ears to it. Seems most of them have decided to respond to the call for arms. Daniel whispers, still incredulous: 'They're all bloody mad.'

And I nod. 'Do you know any of them?' I whisper back.

'Not really,' he says. 'But that bloke at the very back, no coat, fair hair, he's the younger brother of a bloke I went to school with, Templeton — already joined.'

Despite my aversion, I turn around quickly to look at him. Good God, younger brother? He's so baby-faced he looks like he should still be at school. 'They won't let him in, surely? He won't pass for twenty-one.' And surely he can't have his parents' consent.

'Why not? They let his brother in and he's a few months younger than me. For nothing you can buy a brand-new birth certificate.'

I do the arithmetic: that boy must be about the same age as me. I'm going to sign meaningless bits of paper that say I'm a fairly comfortable lass today; he's about to sign his life over to the army. This is too awful.

And it gets worse. We lose the eager lambs when we take the tram from the Sydney Terminus to Hyde Park, since I thought Daniel would enjoy the walk from there down to Macquarie Street, but the park is teeming with men already snared. Let out from the slaughterhouse for the day. Wearing their straight-from-the-Lithgow-mills uniforms. That government contract must be worth a fortune. Cheap, no-fuss mass-produced gum leaves swirling beneath the feet of Captain Cook is what they look like. The Captain, up there on his plinth, always appears as if he's about to burst out in Gilbert and Sullivan, but today he exceeds himself in absurdity.

Daniel's wearing his fierce look, he's had enough of this now, no doubt thinking of his friend Robby, and the others whose names have fallen across our dinner table these past weeks. I don't know these people, but Daniel does. He hasn't challenged the decisions of his friends, says there's nothing he could say — and it would be a little awkward given his new position, I presume; but he looks now as if he'd like to take a few of these strangers *round the paddock*.

Seems he was right about the politics too: any dissent sounds like barking into the wind, or treason, if you believe the papers.

Fisher has won for the Labor Party, and it's provided no calming influence: Fisher has won over Cook's *if the Armageddon is to come, then you and I shall be in it* by his own febrile claim that we will defend Britain *to our last man and our last shilling*. Shillings are going to pour in for Daniel and I at the end of next quarter, that's for certain; but our 'overwhelming' Labor majority government is standing firm for its workers against exploitation by sending them off to fight a foreign foe on behalf of a foreign power. A small force has already been sent, to the tiny German colony in New Guinea, which it overran in a week, yet still we're told to brace for invasion. From whom? From where? And I thought I was prone to moments of overstrung farce. I'm now prone to moments of intense nationalism too: how dare they do this, all of this.

I'm not likely to refuse our shillings, though. Comfortable as we are, or will be, there's not too much left in the bank for Daniel and I at present; Father wasn't joking when he said he had to sell the house to pay for our new life. And Daniel, *on principle*, is not drawing a wage from the company. We can't live on principles alone, not the way he eats, and today's errand will enable our share from this last quarter to come through, which will contain half his forgone wage anyway.

I'm still trapped in this moral conundrum, stepping up our pace through the park, when I hear: 'Francy! Francy!'

It's Anne O'Dare, from school days, waving at me, dead ahead, from the arm of one of the snared: he's a Joey's boy under the drab khaki wool and the tidy puttees, but I can't remember his name. He's wearing one of those hats with the half-pinned-up brim that's presently causing some controversy as being undignified; it rather suits him. But good God again, the picture sends me fairly reeling: we're all Irish and Catholic and I can't imagine they have consent from their parents, for any of this. If they do, I'm not sure I want to know the answer to that conundrum: as Sister Simon-Peter would conclude at all mentions of Great Britain: 'And know that they are up to Great Nasty, Heathen Shenanigans as we speak! Pray for your brothers and sisters now!' But there is some sort of nastiness going on in the Old Country, something to do with the stymieing of the Dublin parliament because of the war, as we speak, or will speak, since there's no avoiding Anne O'Dare now.

'Anne,' I say; can't say *good to see you* since I couldn't abide her at school.

Introductions, pleasant smiles and handshakes, and a gushy: 'Oh, you don't know? We're engaged. Daddy's throwing us a party — must send you an invitation — be wonderful.' Big Fib, I'm sure: if memory serves, her Daddy is somehow associated with Sinn Fein and Father described him once as a *card-carrying mongrel*; she also wouldn't invite me anywhere. And The Fiancé's looking a little confused. I glance at Daniel, who's looking dangerously close to touching his plain black brim and walking away; but he won't: he'd never be quite that rude. But Anne is.

'So this is your famous miner,' she chimes, looking Daniel up and down as if he's on exhibit. She is as imbecilic as they come, but I could still slap her, as I did once when we were about thirteen for some similar act of scalding stupidity. Not surprising she knows, though: Australia may be a vast land, but no woman would ever let that get in the way of the serious business of transmitting good gossip as rapidly as possible, not any bred from Our Lady at least. I remember now why I never made lasting connections there. She adds, so unnecessarily: 'We've heard all about it.'

'Well,' says Daniel, very slowly, and I hold my breath, 'you'll know then that we're in a bit of a hurry.' Touch to the brim and he's off, fairly dragging me. I wave silently at her as my rescuer resumes his pace.

But the lark doesn't cheer beyond the moment. I've already forgotten that Jo boy's name, if I was even listening in the first place. That doesn't feel very righteous under the circumstances. I feel like running back to wish him luck. I won't, of course, and anyway Daniel's a juggernaut now, so sprung I can feel the muscle tight under his coat sleeve.

And it doesn't get any better when we finally meet the surprisingly elderly Messrs Stanley and Bragg, even though they are genuinely friendly and more avuncular than polite in the way they handle the matter — efficiently and with firm assurances — of course they would be, they were associates of Father's. But after I've signed here, here and here, the younger of the two, Mr Stanley, extends his hand to Daniel for farewell and says: 'So have you come in to join up too?'

Oh dear, oh dear. It was said just as an enquiry, because I suppose that is what Mr Stanley has been seeing and hearing every day, and Daniel does look as if he's stepped off a recruitment poster: *FIT MEN WANTED!* Daniel drops the handshake and the silence is terrible: it goes on and on and on, until he finally says: 'No.'

I'm waiting for him to add a curt 'Are you?' But Mr Bragg, with his scratchy old voice provides a small mercy: 'Good lad,' he says, with a wink.

'Quite,' says Mr Stanley, nodding sagely.

But it does little to ease the awkwardness.

Daniel does not reply, and neither can I beyond: 'Thank you, for everything.' The return train to Lithgow doesn't leave till three, and it's only half past one; we were going to have lunch in one of the tearooms down by the harbour, but not even Daniel is hungry now, so we'll go and sit on the platform and wait. I buy a bag of green grapes from the fruit stall. We won't be returning to Sydney in a hurry, I don't think.

★

Halfway home I can still feel the anger steaming from him as the train pulls up with the extra engine from Faulconbridge. He's hardly said a word for hours. It frightens me, until I say into his blankness my worst fear: 'You aren't going to change your mind, are you?'

He looks at me with the worst blackness. 'What sort of a question is that, France?' He snaps out the words and doesn't care who hears.

Quite. It's ridiculous: he's German, for heaven's sake, even if no one thinks he is, least of all him. Rub my wedding band with my thumb: not too big now I've had it cut to fit. Perhaps I should learn better when not to express myself.

But then he softens just as quickly and whispers into my blind shock: '*Never.*'

'I'm sorry,' I say. 'I just needed to hear it again.'

'I know,' he says, closing his hand over mine. 'I shouldn't have spoken to you like that. I'm wound up about it is all.' He tries for a joke: 'You know, only *Direct Action* is coming out hard against it now, and we all know they're barking.' He looks as if to say: so what does that make me?

I want to tell him that it's nothing to do with him and his admirable principles, but that's not going to help. It's so clearly everything to do with all of us, and in so many ways. I put my head on his shoulder and squeeze his hand, as if that will make a blind bit of difference.

On November the first, troopships carrying twelve thousand of Our Boys left from Albany in Western Australia bound for jolly old England, to join with New Zealand's, possibly for service in Belgium's blood shop. And they knocked out a German cruiser in the Cocos Islands on the way. I can still hear the hoopla all across the continent as I read today that they haven't quite reached the Motherland. Turkey has entered this glorious war now too, so Our ANZAC Boys will be fighting Allah and his Ottoman Empire, not Fritz, and they'll be defending the Russian tsar's interests in that part of the world full of Biblical and Homeric names when the call from Britannia comes. Achilles really is off to Troy, and I've completely lost my grasp on this behemoth. How could a squabble between Austria and Serbia over some mad rebel shooting some duke and his duchess lead to all this? I haven't the foggiest idea where Serbia is, and it's a silly question anyway: it's all happened so quickly it seems the world was just waiting for an excuse to set this going. Why is it happening? No one's addressing that: except to say that it's all Fritz's fault.

As I watch the apple blossoms going about their business out the back, or stare into the escarpment's prow from the front steps, I see the faces of those boys on the train and in Hyde Park and contemplate that this is all beyond sinful. Seems I've taken up prayer again. Daniel's taken up painting the house, patching the ceiling and replacing weatherboards, the toot door and window frames every spare moment he's not at the mine, and walking off by himself through the bush: says he's getting fat without the hewing. I can't see it, but then there's a fair bit of him to cover. He's also sworn off newspapers and refuses to talk about anything to do with the war.

Christmas is a quiet affair with Sarah: only Evan Lewis pops in on the day to say hello with his three little granddaughters, and no talk about It then either — just loads of cake and biscuits that Sarah seems to be able to pull out of the air, and gentle joking about wages going up the same rate as the price of everything else, while we watch Evan's *sweet wonders* skipping about in the yard and taking rides on Daniel's back for an hour or so. Not quite yuletide as I remember it: slap-up dinner and sloppy carols getting sloppier the more enthusiastic Father became with the malt. The shift in tone is hardly surprising, given Daniel and Sarah are quietly atheist, but once Evan and the children leave, Daniel seems sombre, morose. I ask him if there's anything the matter; he says he's only eaten too much. Then he spends the rest of the day eating; can't really blame him there: his mother's cooking is too delicious. I spend the entire holiday practising my culinary skills on him and asking God for a baby of our own.

New Year brings Miriam and her brood up from Bathurst and Sarah's tiny cottage is filled with smiley noise, belated congratulations on nuptials and a dreamy-eyed proclamation from Big Sister, who's only a smidgen taller than her dainty mother: 'Aw, but wouldn't Dad just have loved Francine. It's not fair, is it, Mum.' And Sarah says through the cacophony, 'It's less fair that all your children were born deaf,' hands on her ears as she gazes over all the seven dark-haired imps, shooing them outside, obviously tickled by their antics, naughty and adorable every one — even the baby has a glint. And Daniel's so thrilled to see the children he has to be called in for lunch along with them, Miriam dragging him by the sleeve, saying to me: 'I do hope you're fond of kids — you've married one, you realise.' Daniel pretends to cringe.

But Miriam has also brought a bomb to the table: Roy, her husband, cannot stay tonight, as he's going on to Sydney to present himself for AIF consideration first thing in the morning. He's a peach-faced, impossibly jovial carpenter of thirty-odd, who says: 'Anything to escape this lot.' After so many children, he says, Mim could do without him for a time, and since his joinery business could run itself blindfolded, he wants an adventure before he settles down too far — and he'd better hurry so as not to miss the boat: the war won't last long. He's also built like Fort Denison: the AIF is unlikely to say no. Miriam, who's likewise impossibly jovial about it, jokes that there were a few arguments between Fritz and Brits, but that Brits won this round by a whisker. Sarah chides her for poor taste but laughs with them anyway. I make a weak uncertain sound, looking at Sarah for further cues, and she's looking at Daniel, who's not reacted at all: he's biting into a piece of thickly buttered bread and staring out the back door, communing with Beatrice the cow. He says goodbye to Roy, just; lost in the shrieks of 'Byebye, Daddy!'

We walk home, and his hand is not really holding mine, and then at the gate he says he'll go for a walk. I say, 'I'll come with you,' and he smiles: 'I mean a proper walk.' I smile back: I can't match his stride. I lie awake thinking, I fall asleep waiting, and when I wake up, he's already gone to work.

A few weeks later I read that the German Club in Broken Hill has been burned down after a bizarre attack on a train by two mad Turks wanting to wage their own little war on a bunch of defenceless picnickers. I wonder if it's weirdly wrought propaganda, the mad Turk part at least, and want to talk to Daniel about it, maybe for a laugh, but he virtually ignores me. Grunt. He's just not here. Not carving, not hitting the piano, not here. Even eating, not here, but he's eating so much it's a wonder he's not fat as a house. Hmn.

The only time he's with me, really, is in our bed. Which is my favourite place to meet him, but I want to know where his mind and body have gone the rest of the time. Please God, I want a baby, to give us something safe to talk about as much as to fulfil my growing yearning. I'll even raise it Catholic. But no baby comes so far.

Just lots more shillings — the mine can barely meet the demands of the contract, which has been increased again. But of course we can't talk about the knotty issue of our profits either; never have done. Can't talk about his work at all: I think he hates being the manager, one of the bosses, but I don't know why.

Seems this war has taken him away from me after all: *does strange things to people* ... Not sure what sort of insurance the orchard might provide against this event. Another worst fear: maybe he wasn't meant for me after all. Can't think of that; won't.

February is stinking, blindingly blue hot; our valley hums relentlessly with it, and Sarah's back in Bathurst, Drummond's still avoiding me like the plague, and I'll have to resort to talking to myself or perhaps Father Hurley — don't know who'd be more entertaining right now. I've even contemplated hiring help in the house, just for company, or maybe to start an argument between us, but he'd probably only shrug, grunt and ignore her too. I'd go fight Fritz myself if it'd mean I could have Daniel back. I can't fight his surly silence, though; two and two, at last: he's having one, or possibly several arguments with himself.

I want to ask Father precisely which horses he put his final each-way bet on.

DANIEL

I've never felt so useless, well, I have, but not with no end in sight and not with so much on my mind. I go in and fire shot and hew when there's not enough men on, which is fairly often, just for something to do, and for something to lay into, and I don't care if the union has a problem with that. Don't tell France though; I wash before I ride home, since I can now. We don't need to have that conversation.

Or the one about Drummond's little digs he has to have every time he pops his head in: every time someone leaves, he says, 'Good thing we have you to rely on, Ackerman,' or 'Thank heavens for you die-hard socialists — someone's got to keep the wheels turning while our boys are away'; or his constant amazement at how quick I finish the books, like it's hard to count to twenty, like you wouldn't want to get it over and done with, it's that boring. I don't bite, but if he was younger … I wish I knew what Dad had held over him, that *no one else's business* that got us the lamps all those years ago; I wish I had it in me to make him think I know what it is, to make him fuck off. He's not had a shot at the other obvious target of my background, because I'm certain even he knows that could lead to violence. Someone at the club last Saturday evening, a filthy arsewipe blow-in who's only been in town five minutes, said to me he'd heard my mother was a Kraut. He was having a smart-mouth go at The Manager of the Wattle who by his great opinion has no place at the Workers'; he didn't say it nicely, and I stood up, watched him shit himself, before taking him outside. Those who joined us weren't standing behind him; I didn't hurt him, much, just enough to make it plain. Evan says I shouldn't have bothered at all, and he's right: I'm not in any position to start making trouble, with anyone. I won't go back to the club. Evan hasn't mentioned the hewing, though, so no one's made a complaint against my non-union labour; I think he knows that's all that's keeping my temper.

Evan's the real boss here, not me, and we're making so much money that I don't even have to check the weights; our weighman, Tanner, joined up and so I put old McNally on the bridge, to give him something to do, but he's only there for appearances and I pay him out of the cash tin in the office, half to spare the cost to the miners, and half to shit-off Drummond for the weekly two and nine I call *Maintenance*. I write up everyone else's pay before McNally's totals are even in. And Holman, the deputy, he's joined up too, taken a clerical position in the Department of Army; and Drummond's not going to bother replacing him with a real deputy, because we don't really need one; we have a Night Deputy, Campbell, and there's me on days, overseeing a hundred and thirty, give or take, who all know what they're doing. Even the coal is easy everywhere at the moment, there's never much for me to fix, except for that bastard pinch in three, and Evan won't let me near it; I don't want to go down there anyway, not yet.

Which all leaves me with too much time for thinking about what's going on with the others who've left. I don't want to know about it and the effort it takes not thinking about it is almost as buggering as the coal.

I walk down through the bottom of our valley, under Calypso, and around into the next gully up to the ridge below the paddock. It's where I usually go, on Sundays, when I can't just hang about with France watching her paint wallabies or apples or lizards. Sometimes I run, just to have a run. I feel guilty about the way I'm leaving her out of things so much, about the questions she's not asking and wanting to all the time, but I feel guiltier about other things. About not having the power to change anything. And everything's changed around me.

There's no rugby round here any more, not enough for two teams, and the new blokes have no idea of the game — if they play at all they play club league in town. Stop-start ring-a-rosy, Evan calls that code. Anyway, if I put myself in the cavil for it now, I'm sure it'd only give some of them another reason to think I'm properly on myself, just for playing union rules. Because it's a 'gentleman's' game, except in Wales apparently, where it's a working man's obligation to strive for a red Cymru jersey just for the chance to belt an Englishman legally; or in New Zealand, where we all know they're so egalitarian anyone who doesn't play gets called Nancy. And at the Wattle, where it was … just what it was. Evan set it going when he first came here more than ten years ago, because it's good for your heart, and as a way of keeping things steady among the younger blokes, getting it out of your system without things leading to a brawl. And because the women and the kids always came, there had to be a certain amount of decency. He's a clever bloke, Evan. A few of us did kick the ball around for a while, but lost interest after New Year's. Just picnics now, to Mount Vic or somewhere, and I'm never in the mood; don't really feel invited, even though I am: the new blokes don't say anything outright, but some of the looks I get in-pit say who the fuck are you, and I wouldn't blame them for thinking that the kid-manager who thinks he's a collier should keep clear of Sundays at least.

Staying at home seems to suit France all right, she'd rather be shy of get-togethers too; at least we still have that in common. As well as bed, when I let my body tell her that I love her. I want to give her more than that; but for now it'll have to do.

Dad's still noncommittal about the question I keep asking when I come here. He says it'll come.

Evan knows I'm stewing, badly, but he doesn't want to ask. I think he knows.

Today it comes. Cass Cullen, Robby's wife, turns up with her kids at the Wattle, comes into the office, and I'm in there today, doing the flaming books, and she's distraught. She's a Brit and barely literate, and she wants me to read this telegram for her, which the reverend from St Paul's brought her, and he's already told her, but she needs to be sure. Of its shortness, its bullshit and its brutality.

It's pink, marked urgent, and it says that on the twenty-fifth of April, 1915, Pt RT Cullen was killed in action at Gallipoli. It then conveys to Mrs Cullen, care of the post office: *deep regret and sympathy of their majesties the King and Queen and Commonwealth Government in loss that she and army have sustained by death.*

Sure.

It doesn't say plainly and directly to her what she urgently needs to hear: *We are very, very fucking sorry we killed your Robert Timothy and we promise to burn in Hell for this.* Bastards.

Robby is dead. First day on the proper job.

Cass's just sitting there nodding, trying to keep it from screaming out of her, baby boy on her lap, little curly-haired girl hanging onto a fistful of her mother's skirt and looking at me like she knows too. I tell Cass we'll look after her in some way, France'll work something out with the fund, on top of whatever pension the government might come up with. But it's not enough. She can't hear me, not really. She's thinking about no more Robby, and so am I. It's a different kind of anger: I know what I'm going to do.

★

Still, it takes me a few weeks to get the bottle up. A few weeks of being a cranky bastard with Francine; I can hardly look at her. I know it's her birthday this month, but I've forgotten the date, and I can't even ask her that. Can't ask Mum either; can't look at her at all. A few weeks of laying into the coal like a maniac, whether or not there's enough men come in now, and not looking at anyone.

Then, when I do do it, I do it like a coward. Not a good start. But at least I'm firm about it.

I leave Francine in the morning, early so she's still asleep, and I kiss her as I always do, but I go on into town and catch the train to Sydney. Not like the Wattle won't turn around without me for a day, is it. It's not hard to get where I'm going, it's practically signposted the whole way to the barracks. The bloke at the front desk of the enrolling office hands me a form along with the rest, but I tell him: 'I don't want to fill in a form, I want to speak with someone first.'

He raises an eyebrow, about to tell me to piss off, but looks at me again and says: 'Take a seat.' Spanner in the works that I am.

So I take a seat and wait, while twenty or so blokes fill out forms.

After ten years and twenty more blokes filling out forms, I'm looking at the floorboards when a pair of boots shows up, very small boots it seems when I look up and see the extent of the bloke standing over me saying, 'You want to speak to someone?' He must be as tall as me, and the first thing I want to ask him is how he stands up on those tiny feet. But I say, 'Yes,' as I stand up; and he's not quite as tall, but he's older than me by a good few years.

He's got this look on his face like I'm wasting his time already, poor bloke on spanner duty today as he is, so I get to the point: 'I want to join up but I'm not interested in killing anyone. I want to do something useful, if I can. But I've got no idea.'

He laughs and I think, well, that's it then. But then I hear something in it like he knows what I mean.

'Come on then,' he says, cocking his head for me to follow him behind a partition where there's a desk and two chairs, one on either side. He says as he sits down on the one behind: 'Captain Duncan is my name. And who might you be?'

'Daniel Ackerman,' I say sitting down too, and suddenly I'm all wound up and don't know what to say next.

But he solves that quickly; he's the one asking the questions.

'How old are you?'

'Twenty — twenty-one in September.'

'Do you have parental consent?'

'No.'

He has another chuckle at that, a gentleman's sort of lazy chuckle, but I'm starting to like this bloke already. He doesn't mind not getting bullshit.

'What's your current occupation?'

Good question. I stumble around it: 'I manage a mine, coal, the Wattle, out of Lithgow,' like I'm ashamed of the fact and add: 'But I'm a miner, really.'

He squints at me and says: 'What did you say your name was again?'

'Ackerman, Daniel.'

'You're that chap who married Frank Connolly's daughter, aren't you?'

Jesus; I nearly jump out of my seat. 'How do you know that?'

'My father and Connolly used to meet at the track — hard not to follow the life and times of an eccentric such as Mr Connolly, eh?'

Not sure I like the sound of that; I feel a bit protective of the old ghost, who might well have to come back to murder me for what I am doing today. This Duncan *chap* sees, though, and says: 'Besides, I'm a government engineer, roads and bridges, for the railways mostly, when I'm not doing this, and news travels round our industries, you know what it's like.'

No.

'Sounds like he was a good sort, Connolly,' he adds.

'Yes.' Now shut up about it, and thankfully he does.

'So, you're a miner,' he says. 'Well, I have another coincidence for you.'

What next?

'It so happens we're looking for men who can handle explosives and tunnel and work with their eyes closed and one hand tied behind their back and not panic for anything. And I haven't seen a soul today who doesn't want to join the artillery or light horse, or who's only good for it. Higgins, out the front, thought he was having a good laugh getting me to look at you, but sapper might suit you.'

I know I'm a joke but I don't know what sapper means. 'I don't want to blow anyone up,' I say.

'No. Why would you? We need men for fieldworks, building and maintaining trench lines, bunkers, supply routes, bridges, that sort of thing, supporting the infantry et cetera, chaps who can get a job done quickly and regardless. But you'll have to learn how to shoot people regardless too. It's a hazard of the job, I'm afraid. Most men, when being shot at, will feel inclined to want to shoot back and live; best to know how to use a rifle in those circumstances, eh? Besides, you'll do as you're told when you're told. Are you still interested?'

'Yes,' I tell him; can't believe I'm going through with this, so I have to tell him something else first to see if he'll still be interested. 'You should probably know that my parents were born in Germany, in case that's an issue for you.'

He pulls his head back in surprise. 'Good God, you are a bit special, aren't you. I think the question is, is it an issue for you? Is that why you don't want to kill anyone?'

'No.' Dad would have no problem with the issue of my nationality. Mum, on the other hand, is going to be very unimpressed, but not, I don't think, for any lingering allegiance to Deutschland. She's just going to want to kill me. France, well, don't think about that now. 'Not at all,' I say. 'I wasn't brought up German.' Wasn't brought up a subject of the realm either.

'You'll have to kill Germans if you're told to, or we might be obliged to shoot you,' he says and means it, then squints at me again: 'You don't speak the language?'

'No, just bits and pieces.'

I can say to myself right now: *Du mußt doch total blöde sein*: You must be right out of your mind.

'Hmm,' he says, 'could have been useful if you had — though a chap like you will be useful anyway.'

A chap like me: what's he when he's at home? Not sure I like this bloke too much any more; he thinks he has me pegged so easily.

He's still eyeing me, thinking. 'Why do you want to do this?'

I tell him about Robby and the rest somewhere in Turkey; he says: 'But you don't want revenge?'

'No. I just don't want to leave it to the others.'

'You're not doing this for King and Country either, are you?'

'No.'

And he laughs again, leans in and says: 'Neither am I.'

I want to know what his story is, but the interview's over. 'Unless you'd prefer to wait until you're of age, get a form, and get a new birth certificate. It'd be a good idea to get a new birth certificate anyway, without parents' place of birth and without the extra "n". A fair few good old Aussie German lads have been fiddling the facts to join up, or not, as they choose, no real law against it, but I'd say it's best not to advertise it, eh. If you want to sign today, come back with your papers and ask for me.'

If I think about it any more, my head's going to fall off my shoulders, so I do sign today, for the duration. It's all done in half an hour: I tell the bloke at the pub up the road that I'll write up the certificate myself thank you and the twenty-fifth of September is changed to the twenty-fifth of April and parents' place of birth, Dresden, Germany, is changed to Lithgow, New South Wales. Too easy all round. It occurs to me that I don't know a thing about Dresden or even really where it is, and I couldn't give a rat's; that's how much it matters to me now, and how much it mattered to Mum and Dad to tell me.

Captain Duncan says as I hand them over: 'We'll see you on Friday, then, for your physical checks and balances, but I'd say you're well in. Go home and spread the happy word. Good luck.'

Hmn.

'Where am I going to be sent?' I ask him, for what it's worth; I don't really care above the pounding in my head at what I've just done.

He says, dry as dust: 'Where you're told to go.' As in: does it matter?

That'd be right. I nod.

'Welcome to the worst job the army has to offer, Ackerman. And you can start calling me sir.' Yep, and he means it. And he's a nut.

And I think I might be a bit of a fully British subject now.

FRANCINE

The casualty figures thus far for the Gallipoli campaign are mysteriously absent from the newspaper reports; call me suspicious but perhaps that means it's likely to be a terrible number. The handful of sad, brief little notices in the local paper telling of sons and husbands lost say more. I didn't miss the one for RT Cullen; I'm sure Daniel knows, he must, and his silence says more than anything at all. Jingo-jangle higher than ever, though, for Our Brave Aussie Tribe of Achilles and his Kiwi-Polished Mates. It's a glorious proof of nationhood, a moral victory for courage and *great manhood*, apparently. Seems it'd have to be, since from the start they were dropped off in rowboats at some impossible place to face immediate fire from a waiting enemy and didn't mutiny. Even I can glean that there must have been some sort of strategic error there. But it hasn't caused a mutiny here at home, either: recruitment is higher than ever, must be well past the quota now; does our Labor Government even have a quota any more? I pray every day for it to stop, as I pray every day for a baby. Prayers are the last resort of the hopeless, though, aren't they.

I cut up the newspapers for the toot, as I've been doing before Daniel comes back every day, though he's not home yet. Lamb and potatoes roasting happily with their sprinkling of the rosemary I've grown myself, and I take my sketchbook and pencil box outside onto the back verandah while I wait, but I don't know what to do with it today. Sick of apples, that's for sure: they're beginning to bobble all over the place. Too busy with hopeless prayer, anyway, and low thoughts of all kinds about sad state of the world and my marriage. Telling myself over again that there's no point me becoming morose too: chipper up, girl. Doesn't matter that he forgot your birthday; you were never overly fond of birthdays anyway. Celebrations are only for the frivolous, aren't they.

Just on sunset I hear the wheels of his bike scrape up the dirt inside the gate. There's a magnificent feathery purple and orange arc above the hill behind the orchard and I stay here to watch it as he clumps through the house, amusing myself with the thought that it might only be the pollution in the valley beyond that makes the sunset appear so beautiful this evening. So said a recent science article in one of the papers, so it must be true: I'm seeing the colours refracting off the smoky fuzz of carbon something or other and other such gases that are no good for you in concentrated doses; just as well they are happily dispersing then: hmn, very chipper.

He comes outside and sits down on the boards next to me, his legs stretched out to the verandah edge. 'Lovely,' he says.

'Isn't it.' Though lovely's not a very Daniel sort of a word.

'I meant you too,' he says, and that makes me turn around.

He has an odd look on his face; I couldn't pick what he was thinking if you gave me the word to describe his expression; I can't ever pick what he's thinking anyway. He takes my book from me and takes a piece of charcoal from my pencil box, and scribbles something on the paper; I can't see it over his knees. He scribbles some more. He's drawing something; I've never seen him do this before.

He hands it back to me. 'There you are, Francine at nineteen. When exactly is your birthday?'

I think I say, 'It was on the third,' but I can't be sure of that, because … it is me, a sketch of me, looking out at the orchard, though there's no orchard in the picture. There are only a handful of lines. But it's me all right. The image makes me shiver. I couldn't ever draw anything so plain and clear; and I couldn't ever draw him … not like this. I want to say: *Why are you working at a mine at all? You should be doing* this, *you should be studying somewhere.* But I begin to cry, and it quickly becomes big heaving crying. I can't help it. This is such a tangled mess and I don't know what to do to get us out of it.

He says: 'Don't cry. Please.' But when I look at him, he is teary too. I have never seen him do this before either.

'What's happened?' I ask him, hoping we're thinking the same thing, but somehow knowing that we're not.

'I didn't go to work today.' A droplet slides halfway down his face and stops there but his voice is steady as ever. Blood drains away. 'I went to Sydney and joined up.'

You what?

Stare.

Stare.

Stare.

He shoves away the tear and says: 'I have to do this.'

No you don't, not for any reason. 'I don't believe you.' But I do, terribly.

'Well, that's what's happened.'

'No.'

'Yes.'

He says something about Robby and his wife Cass but I'm not really listening. I say, last grasp of many to come: 'So Robby decided to jump off a cliff and now you have to follow?'

'It's not as simple as that, it's —'

'Yes it is.' Hysteria: thank God we have no neighbours. I am a feral cat on my hands and knees on the verandah. His drawing slides across the boards back at him.

'It's not.' Fierce.

Don't care: 'I'll go to the post office and telephone the barracks tomorrow and tell them you're not twenty-one. I'll tell them you're a German spy.'

'No you won't.'

That's true, wouldn't want him to be carted off to Darlinghurst Gaol for interrogation, but: 'You've betrayed me. You said *never.*'

'That was before —'

'Before what? Before devotion to misguided mates became more important than devotion to wife? You don't even love me any more, do you.' Oh, did I really say that? But I can do a lot better: 'I'll never forgive you.'

'I'll talk to you when you've calmed down.' He stands up and starts to walk away inside.

I spring up and grab him by the shoulder, push him hard in the chest. 'You'll damn well talk to me now! You've barely spoken to me for months and months! You can't do this!'

'I have and I am.' He's holding me by the wrists, so easily, gently, hands too big for my bones.

'No!'

'Yes.'

Stare.

Stare.

Stare.

Still holding my wrists: 'I'm going on the early train Friday morning.'

Yes. 'You can let me go now.' He does. I sink back to the boards. Unbridled self-expression complete. Just shock. One whole day left.

'Not *going* going obviously.' He sits down behind me. It's dark, and cold now.

That's right, I think, you'll have to pass a medical examination and do your short course on how to kill and be killed first, to make sure you fit the mould. Unsocialise yourself and join the greatest union in the land. But I can't say any of that. Most of what I am thinking I can no longer say, maybe even to myself. I want to moan: *Why? Why? Why?* But I do know why.

As his arms encircle me I become so very small. I'm still crying, but quietly, until the tears seem to be doing what they do without my participation.

I can hear myself ask him about Cass Cullen. During my fit he'd said something about helping her out: 'What do you want me to do?'

'You can arrange something through the compensation fund, can't you? Those lawyers will do whatever you ask them to, regards that money.'

That's true. There's nothing to say I have to provide any proof of employment or documentation of any kind. I can just tell them to pay out for Robby and no one will be any the wiser. 'Yes. I'll organise it for her,' I tell the apple shadows, then calculations needle through anguish: if there are too many Robbys from the Wattle, we'll run down the fund; but then the longer the war goes on, the more money we stand to make. I'll have to ask Stanley and Bragg to increase the profit percentage going to the fund, just in case.

It's not like I need the money; I'm swimming in it. No one to spend it on but me soon, or Sarah if she needs anything, and she never does; she says since Peter's been doing so well for himself lately in Newcastle, it's hard enough trying to stop him from sending her money she doesn't want. And now Daniel will be earning a wage again too: a grand six shillings a day, and being fed by the AIF, whether he likes it or not, while English Boys only get one shilling. One shilling? Massive calculations scream at me, and I want to scream back at them: *No*!

Instead I say: 'I've heard army food's appalling.'

He says: 'Couldn't be worse than yours.'

I turn around and hit him in the chest again, for being back, for five minutes, and now going away.

'I'm an excellent cook, thank you.'

He squeezes me tighter. 'You're an excellent everything.'

Don't you dare start the weeping again, Francy.

'What on earth could the AIF possibly want with the likes of you?' I ask him.

'Digging holes, by the sounds of it; what else? Engineers, I think. Once I've learned how to shoot and stand to attention. They might decide against me after a week.' They won't. He adds: 'A bloke who knew of your father recruited me.'

'Who?'

'A Captain Duncan, says his father knew him from the track.'

The Leprechaun lives. Never heard of this Captain Duncan but he'll do.

'Strange bloke,' Daniel clarifies. Strangeness seems apt, while we're shifting realities again.

I have every kind of emotion bursting as I kiss Daniel all over his face. 'I'm sorry.' For everything. Oh Daniel.

DANIEL

'One day you'll do something surprising, Daniel.'

Mum's not angry when I ride round in the morning and tell her. She's beyond disappointment with me, and she's been talking to Evan. They were expecting it. Good thing everyone else knows what I'm about. She tells me: 'Roy's with the Engineers too, he's just arrived in Turkey. He says it's wonderful weather.'

My mother can put on sarcasm far too well. There's nothing *wonderful* about any of this. And I'm scared already, but who wouldn't be? Those that aren't must be idiots. I don't know the first thing about it yet, but I write that down as rule number one from today.

Mum says: 'Your father would agree with this commitment to your country.'

I nearly lose it.

But she adds: 'And he would agree with me that you're an idiot. *Ein totaler Idiot.*'

She goes to fill the kettle and when she turns back round to me she says: 'You don't owe anyone anything. If there is one thing I want you to get through your thick head before you die, it is that.'

She's taking cups from the cupboard, but I can't stay long. France wants a baby, and I'm not sure when I'll get another chance. I'm not going to die. Thanks a lot, Mum.

FRANCINE

He's being let out from imperial death practice for a whole day. I'll meet him at the station tomorrow morning, me and Hayseed, come for Our Boy in Our Drab Khaki. I've never been so excited in my life. It's been six long weeks and Miss Frankston at the library is sick of seeing my face: I've read every rubbishy novel in the place, and half of a compendium of Henry Lawson's stories: I stopped at 'The Drover's Wife' after it gave me dreams of snakes under the bed; I've read *Bituminous Coal in the Western and Illawarra Fields*, and the equally obscure *Expressionism: Continental Art or Arrogance?*, neither of which I understood much of, and I'm now working my way through *A Critical Study of the Iliad & the Odyssey*, and I can recommend that it is vastly more tedious than Homer himself. I'll give it away, after it puts me to sleep tonight. I've given all our apples away too, a sack for every man and boy at the Wattle; it was snowing a bit, Christmassy, sort of, seemed appropriate. Mr McNally had dropped in with some more feed for Hayseed and agreed to help me bag them, after Sarah and Miriam and the seven imps had come round the day before to help in the emergency of picking them and eating some of them, but he wouldn't take anything for it, or for carting them for me. Said: 'Fact of 'em all's too entertaining,' whatever that means; he's a very odd man: he has wrinkles so deep they look like blue tattoos, etching a scowl over his kindness, and his gruff, grumbly: 'Good girl, Missus.' My goodness wasn't much more than a small thought: the orchard is so small, you couldn't make a living from its twenty-nine trees yielding approximately two thousand seven hundred and forty-two fruits so far, give or take an apple. But dear God, has it been insurance in its provision of a little time-consumption.

Can't read, can't sleep, can't count apples now, though; convinced that the trains won't be running, so I arrive at the station an hour early, to check with the stationmaster. Yes, it's coming, barring a blizzard or a bushfire; as if anything short of Armageddon would stop the coal trains steaming up and back. Wait, wait, wait. Avoid pacing, stop jiggling. But have I got the right day? I didn't bring his note with me to check. It said the fifth, didn't it; or could it have been the sixth? His handwriting is so scrawly, maybe I have got it wrong. Oh stop it, Francy! What am I going to be like when he goes *away* away? When we'll have only notes. Not even the stupid telephone: a couple of weeks ago we said a few words to each other down the line at the post office after Mr Symes sent a boy around to tell me Daniel had booked a call. Daniel said, 'Hello'; I said, 'Hello'; he said, 'I just wanted to hear your voice.'; I said, 'What did you say?'; he said, 'Can you hear me?'; yes I could, but it didn't even sound like him, and then the line went off, or whatever it does when it stops connecting. Everyone who's anyone is getting a telephone installed these days. Not me. I want Daniel. Here.

Oh heavens, I can hear the train coming now. Here it is. And I run along the platform when I see him, he's not hard to spot, I run with everything. And I kiss him all over his face, and I don't care if that's indecorous. I can't say anything, I just kiss him.

We don't even make it home, only so far as Calypso's window on the rise along the track. The fresh dusting of snow crunches against the heels of my boots as we melt together.

When we've fallen back into the ferns on the embankment, he says: 'Hello.'

I'm just so terrified, even through this pulsing delirium, with him, within me.

I look at him properly now. His hat chucked back in the trap, my hands on the shoulders of the wool of his tunic, his eyes greener for its dry gum-leaf hue. He's cut his hair so short round the back and sides it's like sandpaper under my fingers. He says it's just too hot against the collar; it'll grow back. Collar: pinned with two spiky brass rising suns containing tiny crowns and even tinier Australias.

I want to weep, but there's no way in the world I'm going to.

'And I still can't shoot straight,' he says. 'The only thing of sense I *have* learned so far is that I'm six feet six and a half inches tall and that's just shy of two metres metric — which means my feet overshoot an army issue cot by about twenty centimetres. Which is roughly ten per cent of fifteen stone not accounted for, which is nearly ten kilograms if you're a Frenchman.'

'You overshoot this bed too,' I say, looking at his feet. We've just made love again, barely in the front door and I didn't think we'd even make it to the bedroom.

'True.' He wriggles his toes. 'But this bed isn't nearly so comfortable.'

And it is funny after every shambles he's described about the barracks and the camp on the sportsground and the training drills. The lot he's with are not really much chop as soldiers, he says. But that's what they are and I want him to shoot straight. I want him to hew coal instead. No I don't. I just want the angel to come to still the lions' mouths.

Sarah's back in Bathurst again, so we don't stop by her house, but we do have to go and have some photographs taken in town. We don't even have a wedding picture, but it seems we need something now. Daniel says he'll be back on proper leave sometime before their ship departs. Whack. So I can give him his photograph of me then.

I don't make a show, of anything, on the platform as I wave goodbye to Sapper Ackerman. Who'll be going off to war to dig holes somewhere, sometime. Who can clean a rifle in his sleep but can't use it with any confidence. Who's so fit he's dangerous. Who has difficulty with the word 'sir' but whose captain is trying to help him with his attitude by the judicious application of full pack drill and a lap or several around Moore Park. I still have difficulty believing all this, but it's real. All around me, as Lithgow gives up its rocks, and metals, and rifles from the factory across town, its acres of khaki wool and Daniel.

Who has no idea at all where his ship will take him.

DANIEL

Rule number two: most men are disgusting. Working together is one thing, but living together … should be banned. There are some things you don't want to know about another bloke. And most men talk rubbish, just for the sake of filling the spaces between each other. Strangely enough I'm called Noisy here; after it became apparent that I don't answer to Lanky, Shorty, Stretch or the like. I'm so used to my own ways, I suppose; don't have to wonder where I get that from, but it does set me apart a bit, as usual, except with the hardline Methodists, and I haven't met any of them here. I don't drink, smoke, gamble or whore, and I don't fart or belch or brawl unless there is a need to, and I clean my bloody teeth. Women should have a secret viewing window so they can see what their dearest are really like; I know Francine would be *morbidly fascinated*.

Most fascinating, though, is church parade on Sundays: half of those who feel the need to attend wouldn't know God if He spat on them. Neither would I, but at least I have an excuse: I'm hidden from His Sight. Even if it now says I'm RC on the embarkation roll, because I was told I had to put something on the form. You can't put N/A, the clerk said, and he was getting upset about the blank space. Mum and Dad must have had some religion back there somewhere; suppose it might have been Lutheran and I couldn't put that there, could I. Thought I might put down Jew for a second, because I'd overheard some bloke

180

talking about the lack of a rabbi chaplain for him and his like, before I realised I've got no idea what they believe in, apart from circumcision, which could be very embarrassing in the event of being caught out. So I put Catholic, a quiet one for France and a laugh for Dad maybe, and for convenience: no one looks sideways at a Mick who doesn't attend Mass; it's practically standard issue: you get the impression that the majority of Catholics here joined up to avoid it.

Micks or otherwise, not all of them are disgusting, obviously. In fact, most of the Engineers I'm with are respectable neat-and-tidies-church-on-Sundays from Sydney: carpenters, builders, masons, plumbers, even a mathematics teacher from some private school. I'm the youngest of this lot, and mostly we're apart from the rest, tented out the back of the barracks so we're handy for spot examinations to test that we really do know what a right angle is and which way is north. It's the infantry recruits at Kensington sportsground that are the worst offenders with filthy behaviour, and have an average age of eighteen and a mental age of twelve; no, that's not quite true: we had to go out to Casula last week, on foot, for entrenching exercises with a pack of light horse, and one had trained his intelligent friend to backfill on command: ten points for hitting sapper in the face with a good hoof-load of dirt, a hundred with manure. Strange for me: a man with a pony is a peg down from a man with a shovel where I come from, and I wouldn't hit anyone with a shovel, least of all a man with a pony, no matter how much you might want to if he's a smart-arse. But then, part of all that's the boredom of not really doing anything, isn't it, and the other part would be letting off steam. Turkey's dragging on and on and no one says anything outright, but it doesn't look too good. Laughs are harder, but the fun's worn off, and the desire to kick heads has kicked in — each other's as much as the enemy's, whoever that'll be. We've been training to reinforce the 1st Division's failing effort. Can't say I'm thrilled to be here, but it still does seem the right thing to do, most of the time.

Even when Duncan's pulling me up for every little thing in barracks — pays me that much bloody attention I've wondered a few times if he might be a bit queer. Drill sergeant's had it with me for shooting like a girl, but Duncan's telling me later: 'Pity you've not got a better sense of discipline and respect, Ackerman. I'd like to be able to rely on you to take a bit of charge if necessary when we get to where we're going.' By *discipline and respect* he means this yes-sir no-sir saluting business, I think, since I am disciplined and respectful, ten miles more than most, but I still get stuck on the 'sir', not just because it's against my religion, but how can you call a man with feet that small 'sir'? I'm too busy trying not to crack. Anyway, I don't think it makes a blind bit of difference what you call someone, it's what you know and how you act that makes you in charge, and properly in charge should be obvious to everybody at the time, not forced. *If necessary*, I can't see I'd have a problem with the neat-and-tidies, if not the rabble, who wouldn't salute to save themselves; I already know the importance of being certain everyone knows what it is they're supposed to be doing: I started in that particular school quite a while ago. The neat-and-tidies do as they're told anyway. They're all right; *bunch of pleasant chaps* I think you'd call this unit of sappers, not many stand-outs, but I suppose we'll see about that when we get to where we're going.

Which Captain Duncan, sir, tells us now, at long last, is Egypt.

To do what?

Don't know.

We will be told.

To go where afterwards?

We will be told.

Glad we got that sorted out.

Can't sleep tonight and that's not just because Anderson, the pleasant plumber next to me, is snoring to prove he can. I'm thinking about France. And for the first time in weeks I'm having second thoughts. Very big second thoughts. Too late to do anything about that now. And how much of an arse would I feel if I choked and went home at this point? Crawl back to the Wattle? I'll have been replaced by now, and whoever he is, I hope he's not a prick. Not that I could do anything about it if he is, and even if I wanted to. I can't go back, unless I want to sit out this duration in His Majesty's prison. I try to imagine where I'll be and what I'll see, but I can't; so far my world-travelling experience ranges not much beyond Wollongong through to Bathurst and this spell in Sydney. The other blokes, mainly the rabble, were getting excited today, ready to be off on their big head-kicking adventure, but this doesn't feel like an adventure to me right now, and it never did; I'm here for only one reason and that is I couldn't not go. And it feels like betrayal, in so many ways. So I have to focus on her face, her blinking eyes, till I finally pass out.

FRANCINE

Will it be Gallipoli or the Western Front, I wonder when he tells me it's destination Egypt, otherwise unknown. There's talk that Britain will pull out of Turkey altogether because the peninsular is unwinnable, but Europe doesn't sound as though it's any more winnable. A victory there seems to entail the loss of a thousand men for every yard's advance upon Fritz, followed by two thousand lost for every yard backwards, to quote a Socialist Party pamphlet I picked up the other day outside the Cosmopolitan Hotel where one of the union leaders was thumping the balcony with fervour while I popped into the butchers. Can't say anything like that, can I. Besides, it's his birthday today. Twenty-one today. Eligible for everything now except clear directions. Be chipper now, Francy. Give him your photograph.

I can't look at his. It's too perfectly him. When I brought the prints home I put his in the bottom drawer of the wardrobe. Then had to take it out again when I realised that's where the picture of my mother lives, has done since, at the age of twelve, I decided that Father might not miss her so much if I hid it there. Didn't work, did it; but there she has stayed, face down over my Certificates of Baptism, Holy Communion and Confirmation, and under the box containing her amethyst rosary beads: wedged between the evidence of my blessedness and hers. I'm too superstitious for my own good. Damn persistent *Mick* that I am. Daniel couldn't live in my forgetting place, not ever. So he sits on my dressing table, with Kookaburra; they look at me, but I don't look at them.

The flesh of him is sprawled across the sofa at present. Very easy to look at. He's wearing a laundered-soft white vest, and every stitch in it is mine, and a pair of old trousers. He's just had a wash and he's half asleep, looking at me. We only got out of bed an hour ago, and already I want him again. Maybe I could make him unfit for service myself with my passion. I've got three days.

And that's fairly much all we do. But it doesn't work. He's fitter than dangerous and has to go. I give him the stupid photo at dawn: it doesn't even look like me. He loves it, though, in its little red leather frame with a cover to keep it safe. Puts it in the top pocket of his tunic. We drive to the station in the trap. One last kiss. No, just one more. Nuther quick one. *Tooot tooot*. He's gone.

And then, as Daniel might say, I lose it like a girl. All the way home. For the rest of the day.

I won't be going to Sydney to wave at the ship. He didn't ask and I didn't offer. I'm sure there'll be bands and streamers and such and I just would not cope. Sarah certainly won't be going. She barely said two words to him yesterday when we walked round for lunch. I didn't dare ask, either of them. But when she hugged him goodbye I could see the devastation on her face, only a glimpse before she pulled away from it and said: 'Have a good war then.' She speaks so evenly and beautifully it's always a jolt to hear that wryness. I'll have lots of time to get to know her better now, when she's here. She spends so much time in Bathurst, though, or going up to Newcastle since Peter's wife's just had her first baby. Where's my baby? Peter's not going to war: he has a well-paying job doing something on the wharves, and a wife and a child. Why is Daniel going? Wasn't I enough to stay at home for? I know that's not true, but my loneliness is shrinking me already. No one to have to be chipper with here on my bed alone, so I'll let it go and be misery itself. And the Leprechaun can watch me from wherever he's hiding and tell me what there is to laugh about here.

THREE

OCTOBER 1915 – AUGUST 1916

DANIEL

Can't say too much about the voyage, spent most of the time chucking my guts up, to the amusement of all and sundry. Noisy takes on another meaning. All the way from Sydney to the Suez Canal. Well, not really, but just about up to the Red Sea, kept me busy, enough that on one alert I would have asked to be the first to be drowned had it come to anything. And I'd like to meet the bloke who invented the hammock and tell him what a shithouse idea that was. Still, for the last thirty-three days it's provided for a decent share of natter over whether Noisy's a champion malingerer or so patriotic he wants his face to match his uniform. Either way, I'm almost looking thin by the time we set foot on land again. Who'd be a sailor anyway; there's nothing to look at out there on the ocean. The emptiness, the grinding on of the engines, only shows how far into nowhere and away from home I am, and the constant smell of coal is not a comfort. I didn't say hooroo to anyone except France and Mum; that was bad enough. Didn't have time to say goodbye to Mim and the kids; sent her note: *See you when I'm looking at you.* I'll say hello to Evan and the rest when I come home. I'm not being an idiot about it, but denial has its purpose.

We're not stopping at Port Suez for long, just to stretch legs, trying not to fall over, among the camels and the locals who are small, brown and scrappy and make us feel ten feet tall, until I notice how the Brits lay into the Gippos they have working for them round the docks: I knew this land had slaves, but I thought that was a few thousand years ago. Don't think about it; find a postcard for France instead. I buy one with a picture of camels on the front and scribble a few lines about unseaworthiness. Then it's back in the tin can again. We stop at Port Said in the middle of the night, where I'm fairly ropeable at not being allowed to get off, and almost follow the few absconders prepared to risk it. Should have; they got away with it. Then we finally arrive in Alexandria, unload everything and take off as much uniform as possible as we go, it's that hot, pile it all onto the train, cram in shoulder to shoulder and it's welcome to Egypt all the way to Cairo, and on to a huge camp at a place called Mena. Where we wait. And wait. We're not where we're going yet. The top brass, our General Birdwood and Blighty's General Haig, don't know what to do with us. And there are an awful lot of us and we keep coming. About fifty thousand here and in another camp at Tel el Kabir, and that's not including those coming back from Turkey. They reckon there'll be a hundred thousand of us by the time everyone's here. That's something to think about. Who's left at home?

There's that many faces, you couldn't count them, and I have to wonder how many good old Aussie Germans there are among us, but we're not likely to put up our hands, are we. *Best not to advertise it, eh?* One bloke by the name of Zwiebelkopf copping a ragging the other day for being a Kraut, says his parents are Belgian. Sure. *Zwiebelkopf* means 'onion head' in German; but maybe that's embarrassing enough to want to keep it on the shush. Doesn't matter anyway, when we're all having such a marvellous time.

You go and look around the pyramids and say that's impressive, and then you go back to drills and drills and drills, and some more drills, and play endless bloody games of cricket, a sport that's so dead boring I'd rather have a lie-down or put my hand up for latrines fatigue. You can get a pass to go into Cairo, but I don't that often, because the things that go on there are making me begin to question the issue of my nationality, especially when the blokes from Gallipoli start turning up in numbers. They're all fifty years older than me, and more than a bit relieved or badly wanting to be relieved; rough as. Things get a bit silly and for obvious reasons disciplinary measures are not as liberally applied as lectures and inspections for venereal diseases. Anyway, I reckon if I stay put in camp I've less chance of running into anyone I know. The longer this waiting goes on, the more I reckon I prefer it that way; I don't want to meet anyone I'm going to need to have to say hooroo to when we begin our European tour, which seems the only place we can be going, once they've sorted us out: we've not been issued with short pants. And I don't want to know what any of my old mates are like now, or Mim's Roy, or anyone I might recognise, who's been through the mill, or who hasn't come out the other side. That sounds a bit rough, but a dose of reality has its purpose too: we're not going to sit here in the desert forever, are we? Thanks for coming, you can all go home.

I've taken up carving again, whatever I can get my hands on, and sending it back to Francine. But despite the fact that I'm minding my own business, as much as you can with one hundred thousand mates, and despite the fact that everyone's been tossed around in a cavil to sort the veterans among the new arrivals, which sees half of us sent off as attachments in this other field company or that, seems I'm stuck with Duncan like a bee in my ear. This evening he stands over me as I'm sitting here outside the tent carving, alone for a change, and says: 'Get up, Ackerman.'

I do, slowly. What now? Like I've got something better to do. Well, I do actually.

'Where's the button on your left-hand top pocket?'

I'm not even wearing my tunic and there's no reason why I should be. 'In the pocket. Sir.' It keeps falling off, because that's where France's picture is. He must have seen the offending absence of button on parade this morning. Jesus. And why leave it till now? It's hardly his business anyway, and hardly relevant to anything at all. He's having a special private moment with me.

'Why is it there?' he asks.

I very much want to tell him to fuck off, but I say: 'Because I haven't sewn it back on yet.'

He lets the 'sir' go now, there's not much call for it in these parts at the moment. 'Why not?'

Well, to tell the truth, I couldn't be arsed; the buttonhole's too big for the button anyway and it always slips. Why are we having this conversation? But I say: 'I forgot to.'

He says: 'Don't forget. It's the details that count. When we get where we're going I won't care a fig about your buttons, but here, practise concentrating on the details you have, will you?'

I do concentrate. He can't fault me, except with a rifle, and I'm not that bad at it any more; not as bad as some of the blokes just in at Tel el Kabir who'd not even touched a rifle till they set foot in Egypt because the factory back home couldn't keep up with demand — good on you, Lithgow. And that's all good enough for the AIF. What's Duncan's bloody problem? I don't answer him, just look.

He says: 'And you don't want to lose that photograph either. Do it now.' And he walks off, on his tiny feet. He's a fucking nut.

But I sew it on anyway.

Next morning, here he is again, and I think he's come to check on the button. I am going to tell him to back off, and bugger the consequences.

Except that he says: 'Get up, Ackerman, and come with me.' Like I'm really in the shit for something. Well, whoever did it, it wasn't me. I don't say anything, just follow, quietly fuming. He says: 'Don't salute, and let me do the talking.'

And he's got me hauled inside the well-kitted digs of this Tommy major I've never seen before, who's a good foot shorter and still manages to stare down his nose as he looks me over. He's holding a riding crop under his arm, as they do, all polished brass and spotless Royal Engineers red tunic ready for the ball. I don't salute, as if I would, and he doesn't blink; clearly he's been involved with the AIF for a while. He ignores Duncan, whose hand is still falling from his own salute, and says: 'So, Sapper, you're rather good at blowing things up, are you?'

How to answer that without talking. Well, yes, but whatever's blown up recently, I didn't do it. But I've had a lot of practice. Sir. Strangely enough it's one of the things I am best at, and I would never lark about with it. Best to obey captain and keep my mouth shut, I think.

Duncan says to him: 'Yes sir, he is indeed, but he doesn't know his arse from his elbow.'

Don't I? Apparently not. I'm looking at Duncan, who's ignoring me.

He says, shaking his head: 'As I've told you, sir, he's a bit dim.'

Thanks very much. What the fuck is going on?

The major's still looking at me. Best to look dim? I'm certainly confused.

Major looks a little further down that nose and says: 'Hmmmm. I see. Oh well, off you go then.'

Just try to stop me. Sir.

Outside, Duncan says, quietly: 'Sorry about that, but I don't want you pinched.'

Meaning?

End of conversation. And off he goes; don't know whether I want to thank him or deck him. One clear lesson here, as if it needed clarity: my opinion, much less my question, does not count.

★

Still not gone anywhere and I'm not thin any more. I'm practically skinny. There's just not enough to eat, not for me, and I'm sure I sweat it all out before it touches the sides anyway. Mining is hot work, but you do get to go outside afterwards. Here it's not just hot but dry as Tommy's washtub, every day, and it's supposed to be winter, which we get after dark, when it's that freezing I have to wear a jumper and two pairs of socks to get to sleep. Come midday, though, and I don't know what I want more: food or rain. I like the sun, but not this much of it, especially in full kit on parade. At least in the mine you strip off while you're actually working at something, down to your undies when you have to — and you're not marching for miles to dig pointless, endless trenches and fill them back in again like you're going to have trouble remembering how to do it on the day, or getting excited about going out to mend a bit of road or drainage duct. We strip off here, of course, to what's decent, which only gives the Tommy officers another reason to think we're uncouth. Fuck them. They must be skeletons under all their gear. I'm so hungry I get myself on kitchen fatigue whenever it's available, do anything for a sly sausage roll, and I go into Cairo for extras when I can, just straight in and out, and if I eat another date I'll be sick. The AIF should have height restrictions that go the other way.

But today, when I come back with my sack of oranges and my two loaves of bread, there's a letter for me. Francine's first. And what she says spins me round three times and backwards.

FRANCINE

I'll never forgive you … my mad and dangerous and unforgivable words seep out from where the mould splotch used to be, before he fixed it. Shame bites deeper and louder than the screeching headache I've provoked in myself by weeping till dark, as I make my decision now to embark upon some sort of radical course of action to make up for it. Make up for our famous last words too, or at least mine: I think the last full sentences I uttered to him were when I asked if he'd heard that the editor of *Direct Action* had been arrested for anti-war propaganda. *To arms! Capitalists, parsons, politicians, land lords, newspaper editors and other stay-at-home patriots. Your country needs you in the trenches! Workers, follow your Masters!* said the poster that an army of Industrial Workers of the World Wobblies had plastered all over Sydney. I said: 'Didn't know being cheeky with the truth was a crime.' As soon as I'd said it, I knew it was the wrong thing to say; and a selfish thing to say. I'd just wanted one last laugh, and it wasn't funny; I could see that in his eyes, though he gave me his raspy chuckle anyway: 'Probably about time someone shut him up, the IWW only give the working class a bad name. But something's got to give, hasn't it. The revolution'll just have to sit it out till it's ended.' Mmn.

And it's him who's giving. So many hims. And quite a few hers, too, going abroad as nurses and drivers and doing extraordinary technical sorts of things with telegraphy and such. While I'm sitting on my bed …

195

Grand Plan for Radical Change doesn't go much further than resolve to stop blubbering, resume eating, and start spring-beating the carpets; then it takes off very ambitiously with a decision to go to Sydney University to study law, prompted by the first thing Drummond does as soon as he's aware Daniel is out of the country.

He drives round in his big black Buick to see me; he's done his own contacting of Messrs Stanley and Bragg, probably a year ago, and now he's saying on my front doorstep: 'Francine, surely you don't need the worry and responsibility of the mine now?' Meaning so I have more time for pining and prayer? 'There is a loophole I've found that will get you out of it if you want to. I'm prepared to buy you out under very generous terms.'

Meaning he wants to get rid of me because I have just this minute refused to agree to relax the shift regulations to accommodate the demands brought about by the war and his desire to make even more from it. He's said that he'll pay the men well, and that the new manager, a Mr Robbenham, has a good deal of experience in implementing such things smoothly and amicably, but I've said no: Robbenham sounds very much like smoothly and amicably robbin' 'em to me, and it's dangerous enough as it is down the hideous hole without falling asleep on the job. I know that the ten-hour days he wants will translate into fourteen, as eight translates as twelve, and that's just not acceptable. I'm sure that Daniel would agree, and that Evan Lewis would too, at least I think I'm sure: it makes sense that most men would jump at the extra money, but it can't be safe, and I believe it's unfair. It's probably against union agreements and whatnot too. I'm too angry to bother with consultation; too angry that the man in front of me has just tried to bully me, in the nicest possible way. Well, this relaxation of regulation is not going to happen while I have a say, and thankfully I do on this matter. As an equal partner such a change would require my signature on a new agreement, via my elderly legal angels in Macquarie Street, and Drummond's not going to get it.

I say: 'Mr Drummond, I'm very happy with the way things are, but thank you for your consideration. Must rush, I have a very busy day today.' And close the door on his open mouth. Listen to his engine splutter away, hope he gets a wheel stuck in the ruts just to rub it in.

But I don't have a busy day, and I spend part of it pacing round the house muttering to myself, wishing I knew more about industrial laws so that I could have told him his plan was illegal instead of sounding like a petulant little girl. I don't know if it is illegal or not, but it probably should be. And to come here, after all this time, when I am alone — he is despicable. But Father was right: Drummond is blinkered. He thinks it's canny business practice. Everybody wins.

Grand Plan stalls as I exhaust myself with it and reality returns. I can find out more about the law easily enough, but I'm not about to go off to Sydney to study it. A few women have, but they're not permitted to practise. What's the point of gaining knowledge you don't have the power to use? Besides, to use a Danielism, I don't have the bottle to do any such thing. I couldn't bear to leave Josie's Place and Calypso anyway, even if I passed the entrance requirements, even if they overlooked the fact that I am *married* and therefore unsuitable for anything that might require use of a brain. Fact is, I am pining and praying. And becoming frustrated with myself because of it. Back to beating the devil out of the hall carpet.

What are the alternatives? I can't join a gaggle of women knitting socks and pining and praying together. Bolstering each other with talk of proud sacrifice. I don't think I'd trust myself to keep my composure; I'll do my bit for the Sock Fund on my own, where I can bolster myself with the private confabulation that I can knit lucky socks. And I'm not about to head off overseas to be a nurse or other extraordinary sort of thing. I'm not adventurous enough, don't have the stomach let alone the bottle, and they probably don't want married women either. What about joining the Wobblies, or the Socialist Party, or even the Feminists — that Women's Peace Army in Melbourne that's been in the papers lately for their more genteel call to destroy militarism with their *War Against War*? Same problem: too little bottle. And I think you'd have to be a devout spinster in the mould of their leader, Formidable Miss Vida Goldstein, to join that club anyway. Not to mention the added conundrum my marriage presents there: husband in voluntary service overseas: how would that look? Not very supportive of My Boy.

So, come Sunday I go to Mass, for the first time in more than a year. I am that desperate for a higher thought. I won't take communion of course, I'm too brimming with sin; I'm just here looking for signs, smelling the damp bricks. But Father Hurley's sermon hurtles through me past the Latin: he's so fired-up he's almost violent as he speaks of false sacrifice and the tyranny of men who will play God. Sounds like he's been studying that mad Melbourne bishop, Doctor Mannix, who's pitted himself against the government, the *colonial trade war* and, in particular, British imperialism — papers can't get enough of the scandal. How dare he make such a terrible traitorous hullabaloo. Scandal indeed: this humble parish priest reads the roll of those recently sacrificed from the region and reminds us that the same self-appointed British gods are mercilessly oppressing the Irish as they are failing to liberate Europe from a foe which they, by their imperial conceitedness and greed, created, sending our boys to their senseless deaths, consuming youth and justice till there will be none left to defend.

Too damn right! I want to bang my fist down on the back of the pew in front of me, but I'm too busy quaking all over, oblivious to the Eucharist. This wasn't a good idea.

I can't move when everybody wanders out, back to the real world; can't even look over my shoulder to see if Drummond was here to ignore the condemnation. I just kneel and cry, and Father Hurley, gentle and wearied again, sits down next to me and rubs my back, willing peace into me.

'Shhhh. We'll have to find something to keep you from your idleness now, won't we, Francine?'

Yes please. When I've finished being pathetic.

After a while he says: 'Can you drive a motor car?'

'No.' Sniff sniff; I look up at him as if he's just asked if I can fly. 'Why?'

'There are a few lads come back from Turkey, in a bad way, and it's difficult for them to get about. I'm looking for someone to help them with transport, a particular sort of person.'

'Me?'

'I thought it might suit you, but you don't drive, of course you don't, so we'll think of something else.'

Divine intervention shakes the roof and I say: 'No, I'll do it. I'll buy a vehicle and learn to drive it.' And I can buy a vehicle too, it's not like I don't have the money, and it seems a good way to start tearing down this wall of fear in front of me. I'm terrified of motoring and I'm terrified at the prospect of meeting the casualties of war. Perfect.

I don't tell Daniel any of this when I finally write to him, and I have been putting off writing because I just didn't know what to say. Beyond I love you, please come home; not very chippering stuff and too much of a temptation for fate. When I put pen to paper now, I don't tell him about the mine or Drummond, or the great thumping green all-American-made Cadillac I've acquired, which is twice the size of Father's little old Austin and has an electric self-starting thingumy for the engine suitable for 'the lady-driver', all arranged for me by my elderly angels in Babel — quick sale and a bargain: a fair few orders not picked up, due to young male drivers heading overseas — or the fact that my terror actually makes me a fair chop at driving, for this job. Young Mr Christopher Templeton and his mother like me driving slowly and carefully, since Chris's spine is damaged somehow from a bullet so that he's in constant awful pain and he can barely walk. They also like that my reined-in dread means I don't pry or chatter on our first trip out, to the hospital for a check-over, but we get to know each other well enough for me to work out that he's the elder brother of Baby Face from the train. Daniel certainly doesn't need to know that. And neither do I tell him I've had to cut my hair short since no matter how I pinned or plaited it, it kept blowing around in my face too much when I was learning to drive, under the instruction of Doctor Nichols who kindly offered to lose a few hairs of his own till I got the hang of it, and that I now look like a five-year-old playing dress-ups, or Joan of Lithgow, as Father Hurley has taken to calling me. Daniel doesn't need to know that I really do need to see an optician, and that I've made an appointment for tomorrow: I have no trouble whatsoever seeing close up, but my distance vision is appalling I have discovered, now that I have the responsibility of operating heavy machinery carrying delicate cargo. No, I have different news for Daniel. Very, very different news.

DANIEL

'Oi,' says Anderson, the pleasant plumber and faithful snorer. 'Noisy's happy today — look, he's smiling.'

I am too, now I've got over the shock, a bit.

My darling husband Daniel, she begins and she's having fun with me, *I do hope that you are able to down tools for a moment and find yourself a comfortable place to sit or fall over. Apologies if that's bad taste in present circumstances, but it is good advice. It appears you have shot straight at least once in your life — for I am with child. How about that!!!!!!!! Our timing, as ever, is impeccable. Can't say any more than that for now — if I did I'd have to do nothing but touch wood for the duration, you know what I mean — still a superstitious Catholic despite all your good influence. But I can say that I am thrilled to the marrow, obviously, and fairly floating on love for you. Have been since forever and I always will.*

Your obedient and dutiful and fruitful wife, France.

I even laugh; not very hard to, she's a lark.

'Good news?' says Anderson.

'My wife. She's going to have a baby.' Yes she is. She's going to have a baby. Our baby. That's what she said. You beaut.

'Congrats, mate. First one?' He's genuinely excited for me; he's got two little sons of his own.

'Yep.'

'Well, come on, let's go and get you good and plastered, then, ay,' says this bloke Stratho who's one of the new in with us after

201

the reshuffle and another plumber. He's not new, though: he's been here from the start, joined up in September 1914, and has taken on cracking me as his personal responsibility. Likes to call me the DT, the Deepest Thinker, in reference to the not very friendly term applied to anyone who joined up after April 1915.

'Pity I don't drink,' I tell him for the third time since I've met him. And the reason I don't is plain: it tastes disgusting and makes me chuck. Not that I go to the trouble of telling Stratho that — let him wonder if I'm a wowser or not; got to have some amusement round here.

'Oh, come off it — I don't drink very often either, but this is an occasion,' says Anderson.

'I don't fucking drink — you two go and have one for me.'

'You're an odd cunt, Ackerman,' says Stratho, getting up.

'Yep,' I tell him: 'you've picked me in one. Must be all those deep thoughts of mine.'

Only one thought going on right now: Francine's going to have a baby, and I'm going to sit here quietly and plough through my bread and oranges loving every mouthful. Can't take the smile off my face.

Smile's still there on the ship to Marseilles, every time I think about her. The Mediterranean is kinder to me, but maybe I've just relaxed a bit. It's all going to be on from here for old and new hands, but it's a relief to get going somewhere. Not me gut-chucking this time; plenty of it going on, though: the amount of grog downed on this ship would make Fritz think we're giving him an advantage; but he'd be wrong I think. A large majority of the Gallipoli blokes are raring and roaring, not keen to get back in but keen to even the score, and it's contagious. I don't rattle easily, but there's barely contained savagery in them that's something to give a wide berth to; we pass a destroyer on the lookout for submarines and I think: just let this lot in the water. They've all been warned, though: soon as we're off this ship there'll be order. Apparently the top brass is nervous that lack of discipline will become a problem; can't see it myself: I wouldn't take any of them on.

And when they're not busy drinking they're busy trying to learn a bit of French; don't know which is more hilarious or frightening. Not that I'd do better, but I do have a clue as to what it's supposed to sound like. Which makes me think I should probably write to Mum at some stage, for what it'd be worth. But decide against it again; she won't want to know and France can tell her I'm still around. And that I'm a bit more than an idiot. *Totaler Idiot.*

When we dock I scribble a few lines for France, my France, about having taken the long way round the block to reach her this time; it's pissing down and freezing and I breathe in the cold wet air like I've been holding my breath all these months. There's young women everywhere in the Marseilles welcoming committee and I see why the blokes were so eager to learn the language. Things must be grim here, though: they're all so bloody happy to see us. But there's no time for anyone to exploit the goodwill among the *mademoiselles*, because we're straight on the train again heading north.

I get lost in the green outside the windows, trying to imagine I'm home for a bit, but the colours are sharper, darker here, although the sky's dull, washed out whether there's clouds or not. The train steams on forever, and it'd be good if it would really, but eventually we pile out at a village with the name of Ebblinghem, as if the person who named it knew that one day we'd be passing through and wanted to be sure we'd feel at home with an easy pronunciation. And we're dossing in an empty brewery of all places. Someone's got a sense of humour.

I'm outside having a piss in the dark when Duncan stalks up behind me for another private moment. He's left me alone for weeks now but I knew he'd be back sometime.

He says: 'Ackerman, we've almost got to where we're going, and things might start to fray from here. Time to forget your buttons and start looking at the men.'

What the fuck does that mean? I don't know why I choose this moment, maybe I'm jumpy and tired, maybe it's because I'm sure he's queer, but at this point I completely forget myself with him and I crack silly as.

When I've worn myself out and put myself away he says: 'Now that you've got that out of your system, let me tell you how I'd like to exploit you from now on.' Chuckle: 'And it's not for your soldiering or your shovelling technique. I want you to keep an eye on the men generally and let me know who you think's not bearing up.'

'How would I know that?' There are more experienced men here than me, and I'm bottom rank.

'Because you're a *miner, really*, aren't you.' Smart-arse, slinging my words back at me. 'Somewhat conditioned to difficult circumstances and the suppression of fear. Panic: I think you'll be able to spot it quickly in others, don't you? You are also perversely honest and aloof and won't give a second thought to telling me who needs a rest, or taking a bit of charge if necessary.'

'What makes you think I won't panic — I've never done this before.'

'I don't believe you will.'

I have to ask him: 'You've got so much faith in my abilities, what was all the round the clock "sir" bullshit back home about then? Especially since I *don't know my arse from my elbow.*'

Chuckle, chuckle, chuckle, and all he says is: 'You have to understand the way authority works in order to circumvent it; at least appear to play along. It's called *diplomatic* insubordination. Grossly undervalued skill. Should be part of military training, for Australians. Tommy simply copes better when he hears "yes sir". Besides, I enjoyed seeing how far I could stretch your self-control. Outstanding nerve, you have.'

Is that right? Good thing you're so sure. Prick.

He adds: 'And I've seen the way you look at that photograph. You won't give in in a hurry.'

That's probably true, but it's a bit unsettling that he's been looking close enough to have an opinion on that too. Maybe he's not queer. I ask him. 'Are you married?'

'Divorced.' And he makes it clear that that's the end of that enquiry; not surprised: I've never met anyone who's divorced.

But I have to ask him while we're being chatty: 'Why are you here?'

'Same reason you are.' And that's the end of that enquiry too.

I want to ask him why field engineering is the worst job in the army, apart from the obvious of being walking targets weighted down with all our gear along the front, or being buried underground tunnelling, but I don't think it would be a help to hear it tonight. It'll come soon enough. And he's already walked off anyway. Not all that sure what he's just asked me to do, either, but I suppose that'll come too. It occurs to me that he's never seen any action before, so what would he know, but he talks as if he has — but then he's a commissioned officer: he'd know more by the company he keeps when he's not with us.

Everyone knows it's not going to be a picnic. Still, we've all got helmets and gasmasks now. More protection than I ever had at the Wattle, or that they had at Gallipoli. Maybe they've got it better planned this time. Whatever, I do know it will be like nothing I've ever seen. And I'll be sticking with rule number one: I will be scared. I am scared. And Duncan doesn't need to tell me I'll be doing my best not to panic, like you wouldn't be trying very, very hard not to. It'd be the same reflex that'd make you shoot: you just don't let it get you. But what would I know? I'm not going to think any more about it till it happens.

It's pitch-black inside the brewery with no beer so I rootle around in my kitbag for a piece of paper and pencil and take it back outside, but it's clouded over again and it's just as dark out here, as if I could have seen anyway. I want to tell France that I love her. I know she knows, but I've never said it outright. Half the blokes inside write up their diaries and spend ages writing letters home, to their families, their wives, their sweethearts, the fucking postman, as we've all been encouraged to. What do they write about? Buggered if I know. What could I tell France apart from that I love her, that I want to see her belly growing, with us, but tough luck that I can't. Luck? The way I closed her out and then just left, left her alone, makes me feel, as they say in dinkum Gallipolese, like a fucked-up cunt. I've done this to myself, to us both, and my language has deteriorated further; France would be appalled and look at me and blink.

I focus on that as I draw in the dark anyway, then I find my way back in, and lie down and do it quietly so I pass out. There are plenty that do it louder than me tonight.

FRANCINE

First word from Daniel is a card with camels on the front and it says: *France, if they are ships, then I am a sailor, I reckon. Don't wish you were here — very unattractive, me and the camels. Still, I do, every moment. And the rest, x Daniel.* And there's a tiny sketch beneath showing a soldier leaning over the rails of a ship. So few lines, but somehow I can feel the queasy sway in it. How does he do that? When his handwriting is so outrageously untidy. I've never really noticed that contradiction before, and now here it is, another wonder.

Our notes must have crossed. I want to know what he thinks of my tardily fruitful womb, whether he laughed at my jokes, as if he's just gone off on a lengthy jaunt somewhere, as if he does that regularly. I look at his photograph now, sometimes take it to bed; I've even taken to wearing his old clothes to bed too. Must be a maternal derangement. Good thing I live alone. But then again, I'm a serviceman's wife, aren't I: it's my duty to perform ritual longing, so long as I'm keeping this little home fire burning. I want to know if he's still in Egypt, even though he must be. The news is, Britannia doesn't want to let the AIF be its own big army in charge of itself, but wants it to stay broken up into smaller corps or something, under British Expeditionary Force direction. Seems Australia is not quite grown up enough to go into bat on its own behalf, but there's been a crisis in finding enough British officers to lead these separate corps, so it's all stalled in the desert for Our

Boys while they sort it out. I still want to be told that they've become fed up with the mess and called it a draw. But they haven't: Achilles is going to team up with Sisyphus on the Western Front, inevitably. If only it were truly myth, Sister Carmel, and my interpretation *designed only to give the Good Lord cause to regret wasting a mind* on me: Sisyphus isn't rolling a boulder up a hill and watching it fall back down again in this tale: he's trying to cross a line, five hundred miles of it, across France and Belgium, and he needs rather a lot of help just to take a step.

I cry myself to sleep just about every night, diligent home-fire burner that I am. Sarah tells me when she sees my bleary eyes that it's not good for the baby to cry so much, and for the first time I want to shake her and scream at her: *Tell me if you think I can help it*. She's made of stone; no she's not, she's just wiser. I pull away from the hysteria: I remember her face when I told her my first suspicion of pregnancy: thrilled would be putting it mildly. We raced up to Mrs Moran in the Cadillac and I went too fast and nearly hit a dog, and I was Sarah's daughter as she said, 'Oh Francine, you need something more than spectacles,' then more so as she held my hand while Mrs Moran was extremely efficient about my body and while I laughed as I was embarrassed at her questions, and Sarah softly touched my face with the back of her fingers and laughed too as Mrs Moran proclaimed, 'Well, if you're not pregnant, you'll make me a liar.' But I went home, alone, because I wanted to be. I wanted to pretend that night that I was waiting for him to come home from the Wattle and I told him, over and over again, in the kitchen, at the door, at the table, in our bed. And Sarah probably knew that too; that she knows so much is not a help: for all my wanting to ask her questions, now I don't want to know. She's not my mother, she's Daniel's mother, and her pain must be larger than mine. I don't even really know what a mother is, and my eyes are raw with all that long-held and withheld wanting too, and the gnaw of barely thought questions: why did you call this house Josie's Place, Father? To keep close to my heart someone I can never ever possibly have? To place me inside a box of loss?

Mr Beckett appears to distract me from myself, however. He's the only person in town who's more insane. I've only known him and his wife Louise for two weeks, and have taken them twice to the large hospital in Bathurst, where Mr Beckett, her Paul, is a curiosity casualty. He knows exactly who I am, and he asks after Danny, and thinks he's going to the mine, where he used to work as wheeler with the ponies. The very quick verdict from the doctor is that nothing can be done for him. Louise tells me that he loves riding in the motor car, that it's the calmest he is ever, and we agree to make a weekly date, just to drive and pretend we're going to the mine to get Danny, for Louise really. I want to ask her what the army is going to do for her and Paul, but that would not help; the army is rather over-busy, and Louise, I think, would just like to drive and have a calm Paul, whatever that means. I find out when we run out of petrol on our first proper outing, thought we'd wend the very long way twenty miles round through to Hartley and back so we never get there, and Paul dives under the car when I say blast it and pull up the brake. Halfway round nowhere, not a house or a track in sight.

He won't come out. Louise says: 'Paul, we have to get you to work, you'll be late.' She's beside herself but you wouldn't know it unless you'd seen the look on her face when he scrambled out and under, unless you look at her fingernails, which are bitten down to the quick. We look at each other, as you do when you're absolutely bereft. I hear Father Hurley's endorsement of best-intention fibs and I kneel down and stick my head under and say: 'Beckett, Paul Beckett, you have to help me. Danny wants you to take me to Mrs Moran. I'm having a baby. Now!'

Paul's out in a hurry and he says: 'Danny? Where is he?'

'He's in-pit,' Louise says. 'It'll take him too long to get up, you have to help Francine. Now. We have to go to the hospital.'

'Well, let's get on then,' says Paul like we're holding up events; I tell him to get in the back and wait, for I need to catch my breath. Truly. But Paul just stands where he is, and watches intently as I flap about for the spare tin can, then spill half its contents on the road. 'Come on, Paul!' Louise yells as I turn the switch key and fumble for the clutch. He looks at the vehicle and smiles at us both, and gets in the back seat as if nothing had happened. Naturally, the motor then back fires as I accelerate up the hill, but Paul doesn't jump out again: instead he curls up on the floor behind us.

I say to Louise after my heart has stopped charging: 'You can't live like this.'

'No,' she says. 'But there's no other way, is there?'

'Why not?'

'The army doctor in Sydney said that Paul's condition might not have been brought about by, you know, said that it was probably just triggered by it, and would have happened at some time anyway. Said his nerves weren't strong enough, but the army can't be responsible for things they don't know about when the men sign up. Still, I'm hoping we'll get a little bit of pension for his service, from the government. That's something.'

Hoping? And I can't imagine a government pension will compensate for this *something*. I'd stop the motor now and tell her exactly that, but it won't help. I say, because it is the right and only thing to say: 'If you need anything, anything at all, come to me.' My ancient legal angels will slip it through the large loophole in Father's instructions called *Incapacitating Injuries* and I don't care if I run down the fund; I'll just raise the percentage again.

She answers: 'What I do need is to get Paul into a sanatorium or an asylum, but no one will take him, even if I could afford it, because he's either not mad enough or not normal enough, according to them, and I've taken him everywhere, in Sydney and the mountains. I've been told that since he shaves and dresses himself and generally does what he's told, he'll come good eventually. I don't believe that and I don't think you can help me there. No one wants to know us — Paul is just too much of a handful. People don't know what to say, even family, his family.'

'I want to know you,' I say.

She doesn't answer and we don't speak for the rest of the drive, but I am her friend. There is no charity in this: she has my admiration for life.

As we head back down the sweep into Lithgow, inequities slap harder than scars. How is it that Mr Andrew Fisher, our prime minister, could have resigned from office a few months ago, for reasons of ill health, exhausted by the war and his long and illustrious political career? Too tired to go on. Poor lamb. And, wouldn't you know it, he was a coalminer once too. Where's his bottle gone? Now Billy Hughes, the former attorney-general, has taken his place and is pushing for conscription. *Conscription?* He used to be some sort of a union man, didn't he? Cream rising to the top? Or curds? I can see his photograph: he looks like a wizened little troll and, call me flighty, but I doubt that he'll be asking the AIF to be careful to vet those with possible dodgy nerves. What does the war mean to him? Maybe it's just a matter of being the prime minister; of showing Blighty that we're made of even stronger stuff than the last prime minister showed. Of being too busy with all that to see the likes of Paul Beckett. I can see Paul Beckett, though, when I look behind me, and as he was standing just now by the car; I can even see a memory of him running round the paddock kicking a football around with

Daniel and the others: he's ordinary, not short, not tall, not fair, not dark, nobody, except Louise's Paul.

Nationalists sing 'Advance Australia Fair' but who's making things fair for those who can't advance? Those who can't have *wealth for toil*? How can it be left up to those who need help to help themselves when they're helpless and alone? And why should they be alone, when they did exactly what was asked of them: served their country? That's not a tangle: it's a fairly straightforward betrayal. *Australian sons* exchange *young and free* for nothing. I remember reading something recently about a returned serviceman's league being set up in Brisbane, to provide help for those who've come home to governmental abandonment. There's a circle: leave one union to go to war, then come home and have to start up another to try to help you find what you once had: a job. That's only if you're well enough to work, though. Even if there was a league like that here, what could they do for Paul Beckett?

He kills himself with his razor the following week, putting a full stop on that question and the wind up me. I write an angry diatribe to the *Herald*; it's not published. I write slightly less impassioned letters to the local member, the New South Wales premier, the prime minister and the leader of the opposition; I don't get a single reply. Not sure if it was my tone or the subject of suicide that put them off, but I've got a more important matter to attend to anyway: Louise.

She is not so much devastated as in a kind of deep, silent shock. Her hands tremble like a drunk's as she makes tea in the house near the top of Dell Street. She is quietly mad now too, and destitute: not so much in immediate financial terms since she and Paul had only got married just before he signed up, and they'd still been living with his parents, but because she has no place here any more and has no idea what to do next. Her mother-in-law behaves as though Louise herself has done this to her son, and wants her to leave. The black-clad crow says as she watches Louise: 'There are positions advertised at the mills.' Meaning setting the machines for the production of Our Khaki, which would earn Louise a tidy pittance, enough to move into a boarding house. Forget that for a bad joke. I say, 'I'm in need of domestic assistance, actually,' and stare hard at Louise. I mouth at her: 'Come and live with me.' We can be lunatics together.

She does, in a daze, and she doesn't care that I wear Daniel's trousers to bed and sleep with his photograph. This is all quite normal.

'These are lovely,' she says to me, looking at Daniel's carvings on the top of the piano. She's hardly said a word in these first few weeks but she looks now at least as if she's stopped holding her breath.

I say: 'Yes. They're Daniel's.'

There's the one of me, and then there's a tiny pyramid he carved in Egypt; it came a little while after the camel card, with a note saying: *Well, here it is, France. A wonder of the ancient world. No nasty surprises. But too b. hot for this slave and I am in terrible need of too much tarragon. Stop blinking at me or I'll go mad. I'm that bored. If you were running the shop, I wouldn't be. x Daniel. PS: Please send food, I really am starving.*

Then there's one of a tent, small too, and when I look at it I can feel the wind and sand against the part-opened flap. Note said: *Nothing has changed. Stop blinking at me. You'll have me sent home. Keep blinking. x Daniel.* No mention of the cake or silly love note and extra socks I sent him; maybe the package didn't get there. Still no idea if he even knows I'm pregnant.

My willow face looks at the pyramid and the tent in contemplation, as if I've just had a thought as to how to make sense of the objects in front of me.

I start to tear up and Louise gives me a hug. 'It's all right, you know. Don't hold back on my account. I might like to join you from time to time.' So we lose it like girls today, for a good long while.

Baby is a tight round bump in my tummy when I finally receive the note from Marseilles that says: *Took me a few moments to respond to your alarming news. Knocking on wood myself now, and I think your timing is just perfect. So, France at last — took the long way round the block to find you this time. I'll never do that again. But as they say, better late than never. Still, I didn't get crook the whole way across the Mediterranean — must suit me better round here. I'll take that as an omen, thank you. Enjoy getting fat, wish I could join you. Can you have another photograph done so that I can see what you look like? Missing you doesn't quite describe it.* There's a sketch on the next page: of me, *getting fat*; it's a simple nude, with a caption underneath saying *Vive la France.* And a PS right at the very bottom: *But you had better keep your kit on for the photo, I suppose.* Then a PPS: *Better send me something decent to eat too, or I might not be around to receive it.*

Good God: what do I look like? I peer into the mirror. I look like a very young bookkeeper with my short hair and my new spectacles. I take the specs off, but I can't do anything about my hair. I laugh, really laugh, for the first time in months. He loves my hair — I can't possibly let him know what I've done to it.

Takes my mind off the Western Front as Louise helps me solve the problem with a hairpiece that doesn't quite match the colour, but won't matter. It does the trick as I pose for Mr Grissom in town. Daniel will see that I've cut a fringe, that's all. And it is a peachy photo: my face is plump and I really do look as if I'm about to burst out in giggles.

I post it off to him saying: *Sorry about the fringe — it'll grow back. Been doing all sorts of odd experiments in your absence. You really shouldn't go away again — I shouldn't be left unsupervised. I've made a new friend though, her name is Louise and she's staying with me at Josie's, trying to keep me in check. Everyone's well, especially me. I'm fattening by the second. Don't worry about that! And I love you. I love you. I love you. Knock knock. More importantly, hope you get this cake. Might be a case of too much brandy in this instance, but I wanted to make sure it survives the trip.*

Crossed letters again and I really am a porker when another one arrives from him; there's no place name or date, it simply says:

My France,

Heading off on the long march to the proper job today. Please don't worry if you don't hear from me all that often — might be a bit busy and I'd rather not send you one of these field cards we have that look like an inoculation form and say 'I am quite well'. There is a fair bit more than that I want to say now, what I haven't said to you and should have. For a start I should never have left you, and I should not have compromised my beliefs to follow the sheep into this paddock. I can tell you now, not that you need to be told, that it won't be worth it, whatever happens, but since I am here I'll get on with it — no choice. While I don't believe any of us should be here (hope this gets past censoring) I still don't want to leave the others to it. Promises for you, for the future — I will never leave you out of it again, and I will never leave you again. I don't know how you put up with my behaviour — you should have whacked me harder. That you are my wife is a fact that still amazes me. How I feel about everything you are can't be called love. I set out to tell you today that I do love you, just because I've never told you plainly, but it doesn't even come close to say that. Every time I think about you, which is just about three times a second, the knowledge that you love me sustains me. I can do anything and I will do anything to get home in one piece, because I just have to, to see you, to hear your voice, that bell that comes out of you when you laugh, to smell you, to hold our baby, to touch you, and to behave myself for the rest of my life. Never let you or my beliefs go again. Well, that's about as much as I've ever put to paper in one go. Hope you appreciate the trouble I've gone to.

Your stupid husband,

x Daniel

There's another drawing behind the letter: a strange but no less beautiful one. Of me; one straight line of my long hair dissecting my face right down the middle, between my closed eyes. He says at the bottom: *PS: Did this in the dark a few weeks ago — thought you'd see the accidental point of it, in the circumstances. Says it all, really, doesn't it?*

It does: split emotions, tearing his heart and my heart in two. I'm so moved by the *trouble* that I can't move for a long time. There's a small package on my bed; it's from Daniel too. I can't bear to open it just now. Louise walks past my bedroom door with an armful of clean sheets that I was coming out to help her with before the post boy came; she says: 'What is it?'

I say: 'He's on his way to the front, I think.'

She says: 'Oh.'

Enough said. We press and fold the sheets and I start praying, harder. *Holy Mary, Mother of God,* the words don't need to be spoken or even thought; the lilac glitter of amethyst rosary comes to me from somewhere wrapped in long-ago fresh-linen perfume and I don't blink it away: *pray for us sinners now.* It's the end of May: I don't know how old the letter is, but he'd probably have moved all the way there by now.

I wonder if Sarah knows. I'm not even sure if Daniel's written to his mother, at all; if he has, she certainly hasn't ever mentioned it. Of course I haven't asked her directly. I usually drop round on Sarah going backwards and forwards with the motor, or she walks round to me with a load of cheese, which she insists is essential, or some delicious thing she's made to help me with my fatness, but we haven't talked about anything really other than baby business, and news from the naughty brood, and the other wicked one in Newcastle. On the few occasions I have mentioned Daniel, she's found some way to avoid talking, but that look of grief crosses her face before she pulls back from it to change the subject, or put the kettle on, or get home to milk Beatrice. So I've tried to avoid mentioning him. I should give her this news, though, but I'm not sure how to broach it with her. She'll be here sometime this afternoon, to watch over me, since Louise has to go out and I'm too fat now to be left on my own. Louise has taken over our little transport service because I am too much of an alarming sight behind the wheel and probably shouldn't be doing it anyway, and she is taking Chris Templeton out to Bathurst overnight. He needs to have more X-rays and tests, to see if he can have an operation to fix his spine a bit, fusing it or something, to stop the painful spasms that make walking difficult for him; Louise will bring Chris and his mother back in the morning. So Sarah and I will be alone together all evening. Whether or not she knows, I have to share this with her. How can I not?

The baby kicks, or rather seems to roll around like I'm carrying a trapped salmon inside me. It'll be all right. I can bear that look of hers I know I'm going to see. But I'm not going to grieve for him in silence with her. Pine, cry, dream, wallow: yes. Grief: no. He has to come home, and I've decided this minute that I'm not going to think of any other possibility. If I could, I'd bring him back by the force of my will alone. And maybe I can.

DANIEL

I have to expand my understanding of disgusting to account for the trenches. To think that I laughed back in Egypt when we were told that dentists would be touring with the military for the first time in history: bad breath is not an issue any more. You could follow your nose through the maze here and the stronger the smell of shit and rotting corpses becomes, the closer you know you are to the real picnic. Everyone wants to chuck on their first visit, but you try not to: you don't really want to add to it.

In this particular stretch, at the very front of the lines, the corpses are imbedded in the walls that have been rebuilt and rebuilt, grey bits of men, Fritz and Tommy together forever, sticking out of grey mud, and a river of shit banks up from the latrines when it's flooded. And in such a flood the walls widen and weaken at the bottom, so that when shells start hitting the ground above, the walls start to collapse or if you're unlucky, fall inwards on top of you. Which is why I'm here this, for once, fine morning, with my mates Foley and Anderson, to sheer back the forward wall a bit, and then try to encourage Tommy infantry to help sandbag it for more stability, as well as to cover up the stinking corpses. There's not a lot going on here at the minute, apart from our futile attempt and my horror at having to shovel through death and empty it into sandbags. Don't think I'm alone there. This shift of infantry have been sitting here for five days, propping themselves up with whatever they can find to keep out of the six or so inches of what I'm standing in above the duckboards; Stratho and others have already been through trying to drain the place: this is as far down as the shit level will go. You'd think the infantry would appreciate at least the gesture we're making, but they'd rather sit quietly in the sewer, I think, without this disturbance, before they have to look lively again. There's a lot of 'Watch where you're going', 'No, I'm not moving,' and good old-fashioned 'Fuck off' being voiced up and down the firing line. Rats and lice are very happy, though, as they ought to be in the circumstances. We'll leave them to it shortly and move on. Next job is to excavate some more kipping dugouts behind this line, in such a way that the sewage won't seep down the back of them when the floodwaters rise again. That'll be a feat of engineering. Especially if we can get it all done before Fritz wakes up, which will probably be about five o'clock this afternoon if he's sticking to the schedule.

Maybe I seem a bit too calm about all this, but it's not like there's a choice, and it's not like you don't get a few decent clues along the road to the hub of destruction either. As we marched beyond the village of Bac St Maur it was fairly clear that we were in a French place with little sense of humour in its shell craters, and here and there the wrecks of stone and plaster and metal that used to be people's homes, and the sound of very big guns going off in the distance, black clouds drifting up at the horizon, indicating that there's only one type of industry going on here. This is where we're billeted when we're away from the sewer: rank and file in an old mill, higher orders in a few farmhouses. I sleep in one of the farmhouses, the back half of which has been blown away. And I doss down with none other than my very best mate, Dunc, since I've been promoted to corporal and he needs me handy to have a word in my ear when he thinks to. No bumbrushing involved either; he doesn't have me running around as his dingbat. This is not normal, very not normal, but nothing about him is.

The new title doesn't mean much, and I've relaxed my understanding of authority a bit recently too, to account for the brutal equality that's going on here. Not among Tommies so much, who might well tell me to go jump but would ask one of their own corporals, how high, sir, can I jump for you and would you like a cup of tea while I'm at it? But with us, there's barely distinction between the lower ranks; just one distinction really: how much and how long you can make yourself believe you are not totally horrified and disgusted. Even the Australian infantry are appalled, and old hands have been known to say: 'If it rains again tomorrow I will send myself west.' But obviously the most brutal fact of it is that there's no distinction whatsoever when it comes to being killed, and without that fact there wouldn't have been a need for my promotion.

On our second trip in, a mile or so out from the lines, we got shot at out of the blue by an escaped Fritz who must have snavelled a rifle then set himself up behind the rubble of a house. Rain must have got to him too, for him to have decided at that exact moment that it was AIF engineers' day and open fire into the middle of us. Life might be a game of chance, but how chancy is that? At the time I was at the rear carrying a roll of wire with Foley, since he's about the same height as me, and he drops the pole the second he hears the shots. There's nothing quite like having a hundredweight of barbed wire smash into the side of you, but that had to wait a minute while I frigged around for my own rifle, shitting myself. I hadn't got there yet when Duncan, who was up the front, shot the self appointed sniper as he stood up like he wanted the bullet. Last stand maybe. Fritz fell down in a grey heap behind the rubble about fifty yards off, but not before he'd killed two of us and wounded another. The two that were killed were corps: Murchison, the private-school teacher, and a stonemason called Carter. Long way to come for a very short war, pleasant chaps pay today, and it woke me up to myself quick smart.

Everyone'd fallen out, all over the shop, while Duncan was shouting orders to get the bodies taken back and to help the wounded bloke who'd been shot in the neck and was screaming so we knew about it. Duncan was wearing half of Murchison's brain across the back of his overcoat as Watkins, the sergeant, behind him was yelling, 'Fall in! Fall in!' sounding a lot more rattled than I'd have preferred him to.

Foley was still on the ground, and for a moment I thought he must have been shot too, but he started to get up. Brown's bloody cows, everyone, and Duncan had started stalking off already. Very dark at our performance. I said to Foley: 'Fall in, you fucker.' And he did. But the blokes in between were moving so slow that we were going to lose Duncan before we got there. Great show turning up to spend the day looking for our CO. 'For Christ's sake, fall in!' the words were out of me and above their heads before I knew I'd said them; not very Noisy about it either. Stratho was further up the front and echoing me, with a few choicer words, and we caught up again.

We were nearly there when Foley saw the blood coming out of the rip on my shoulder, put two and two together and said: 'Sorry, mate.'

I said: 'You drop that frigging pole again and I will shoot you myself.' But I didn't mean it; didn't let him know I didn't mean it either: still too busy reining myself in. I'd marked him down for one who's not going to *bear up* too well, but since then he's been all right.

Anyway, that's how I got promoted; and Stratho got promoted too. Vacancies needing to be filled at very short notice. Hooray for us. Only consolation is we won't be going underground, for all my expertise; Tommy doesn't want this Australian rabble anywhere near his mine tunnels, which I can understand, in that Tommy actually does have whole companies of miners doing the job. There is one company of AIF miners out here somewhere and for five minutes I think I might ask if I can get in with them, just for some sort of familiarity; I look down at Shit River now, and up at the slimy, shattered state of no-man's land above the top of the trench and think better of it. I remember a very strange interview with a Tommy major back in Egypt and wonder, for five seconds, what he might have wanted to pinch me for and forget it: I don't want to blow anyone up and I don't want to drown in sewage. So for me, us, for now, the job is one of assisting *proper* soldiers in their attempts to live in this place. Flaming hell. I look at the miserable Tommies up and down the line: it'll be over the top and take your chances, lads, on a trench raid sometime tonight for them, a random raid; wouldn't put money on Fritz not knowing they're coming, sometime.

'Watch it!' one of them says as I splash past; as if another drop of shit is going to make a difference to the state of him.

'Right-o. Keep your hair on.' We're off.

Stratho and I get demoted again a few weeks later.

It's late, on a night off, in the mill that's become a temporary pub serving only one kind of drink: Instant Plastering Don't Ask What's In It But Thank God. I've wandered in, just for something to do; don't know where Dunc is, probably playing bridge somewhere with his own kind, and I can't sleep. The others are having a singalong and it's gone well beyond dreadful, one too many trips to Tipperary with Matilda and her Old Kit Bag, and one bloke starts singing 'Abide With Me'. Sergeant Watkins is so rotten on the snake juice, he's sliding down the back wall, slowly, and not attempting to stop. Jesus. I suppose it's one disadvantage of not being a drinker, that you get bored easily with others when they're at it. I've just received France's new photo too, and she looks so … I don't know, but I can't lie, sit or stand still. Not helped by the jumper she sent along with it: I can still smell her in it, even over the stench in here. Stratho's had a skinful, of course, probably assisted by the consumption of France's cake this afternoon. She wasn't joking about the brandy; it might have been able to survive a trip over the moon on a donkey, but I couldn't eat a crumb of it. When Stratho says: 'Oi, DT. Want a race on the bikes to the gas sign and back?' which is a decent distance up to the rear communication trenches at the front, I can only say: 'You're on.'

We're not supposed to take the bikes, obviously, since someone might need to use them for a better purpose. But they are for officer use only, and we're officers now, sort of, very noncommissioned ones, and there are a dozen of them, so who's going to miss two for an hour or so? And it's all fairly quiet out there, a big fat moon is shining and it's just too irresistible: proving to Stratho once and for all the major advantage of abstinence.

I win of course, since Stratho falls off, twice, the second time down the ditch that runs along the side of the road. And buggers his ankle. I don't need to be told that this was idiotic, but Duncan's waiting to tell us all about it as we walk the bikes back, slowly, on account of Stratho who's sobered up enough to feel it now.

Dunc doesn't raise his voice. 'Strathlyn, you are a disgrace. But, Ackerman, you've got no excuse.'

That's true, and that's the end of it. My one act of stupidity, one lapse of discipline. Out of my system.

Stratho's off for a week while I cart sandbags and ammunition, or run rations up to the shooting gallery, a job that cops you more verbal abuse than any other, for the quality and variety the infantry have come to expect of what could well be their last meal. But we're corporals again within five minutes because there's not a lot of choice for Dunc, who hands me his pistol and says to me now in another special private moment out the back of the billet: 'You can shoot yourself if you like, in the head, in the foot, however you'd like to leave us.' And looks at me.

I give him back the pistol; I've got the point. There's a piper playing somewhere, sending off today's dead, just in case I missed it.

'You have a responsibility to others before yourself from now on, Ackerman, and if you fail again on this issue I'll have you sent home with a brand on your fucking forehead to that effect. You don't want to end it like that, do you?'

'No.' Obviously not, but for Christ's sake it was only a bike ride and I'm not going to do it again.

He hasn't finished. 'Would you like your wife to know that you came all the way here to be killed skylarking about on a bicycle in the middle of the night, or would you prefer her to know that you were doing something a little more useful?'

I don't need to answer that. Wish that fucking piper would shut it off. He does.

Dunc still hasn't finished, though. 'You haven't seen anything yet. Think about how all those corpses in the trenches might have got there: that's just a fraction. Do you know how many are lying out there up and down between the lines? Hundreds and hundreds of thousands. We've just arrived and it's not going to stay nice and quiet like this forever. Are you frightened?'

'Yes.'

'Good.'

He sits down and starts unlacing his boots to clean them and dry out his lice-dipped socks; that's why I'm here too, so I do the same, not mourning the recent death of several colonies of vermin off the rest of me. While we're being so chatty, I just have to change the subject: 'You've got the smallest feet I've ever seen.'

He snorts and looks across at me. 'You've got more nerve than is good for you.'

'I meant for a big bloke, you know, like you were given the wrong pair.'

'They do the job,' he says, scraping out his toenails.

'I know — it's bloody amazing. From an engineering point of view.'

First proper laugh out of him, not that lazy chuckle, and we're back to normal. He says: 'So, how are we?'

He means how are we all today, or at least those I've been with and seen about. I say: 'Tiptop chaps we all are.' And we are, I think, for now. It occurs to me that whether I want to know these blokes or not, I should make more of an effort to not be so *aloof* while I'm telling people what to do, so maybe I'll be more useful when things get worse. Not sure how to go about that but, like everything else, I suppose it'll come.

Dunc says: 'Glad to hear it.'

I'm about to get up to go inside, to go to sleep. I'm that bloody tired. I haven't had a proper sleep for three days, but I can feel another little word about to come on, like my knees have picked it up before he's thought it.

He says: 'You haven't by any chance ...'

What.

'... ever played rugby?'

I think I might have. I say: 'What?' just at the question, throwing me.

He says: 'I didn't imagine so.'

I say: 'No, I've played rugby. But why are you asking?'

He says: 'Union? Thug's Rugby rugby rugger et cetera?'

Like I might not know the difference. I say: 'Very probably.'

Chuckle, chuckle: 'Of course, and I'd put you in the second row.'

'That'd be right.' What is it about me that even here, with a bloke who talks in riddles at me, it's assumed that I am second row: do I look as though I must enjoy having my head wedged between the arses of a front row?

'Excellent,' he says. 'Would you like to play for Australia tomorrow?'

What? No. I'd like to go to sleep and have my day off; I couldn't think of anything worse right now than running anywhere. But this is Rugby *rugby*, as in playing the gentlemen, with the gentlemen. I know I wouldn't be asked unless a spot for a big bloke needed filling, and unless Dunc could see an opportunity for his own amusement in it, but I might never get another opportunity to have a go at this, so: 'Who we playing?'

'Blighty.'

Twist my arm. Go on.

So these are the gentlemen's rules for today's friendly match between Australia and Great Britain. First, if you play for Australia and didn't go to King's, or Newington, or Brisbane Grammar, or Scots College, where Dunc went, you're an idiot: that's me. One and only. Hired help, making up a very small number in a spare blue-and-maroon that's too small, until they realise you can actually play. Except they don't tell you that; they just suddenly start letting you go for a run with the ball. Again, and again, and again. Very enjoyable for me up until confrontation with the second rule: if you play for Great Britain it's acceptable rucking behaviour, apparently, to lay the boot very hard and repeatedly into the kidneys of the opposition in full view of the referee, who happens to be a Kiwi, and either has a very confused sense of loyalty or is completely blind. The first time it happens you let it go — could have been unintentional. The second time it happens, you lose your temper. Well, I do: ring-in Wallaby goes right off at this particular Lion. And I get sent right off, ten minutes into the second half. Not that it matters: it's a walkover for Australia anyway, forty-two to six. But there's rule number three: hired help is not invited to the officers' mess for the celebration.

Dunc says: 'Come on in. No one's going to object.'

I tell him: 'Except me.'

He says, chuckle: 'Don't take it so hard. You played well, very well in fact — that's all that matters. Great show. You'll definitely be asked back.'

'And I'll definitely say no thanks.'

'Why?'

'I've had a very good lesson in authority. You were very right in saying that I would not want my wife to hear I was killed *skylarking* about on a bicycle, just as I would not want her to hear that I was kicked to death by a British officer.'

He says: 'It wasn't that bad a knock, surely?'

I lift up the back of the jersey to show him, mostly because I'm wondering why it still hurts to stand upright.

He says: 'Oh. You'd better get that seen to.'

Yes. I do. And I'm off for a few days pissing blood.

Not very useful at all.

Except in one way: the whole company finds it amusing. Not the damage to my kidneys, mind, but that I king-hit a BEF lieutenant colonel and got away with it.

Not laughing now.

Another letter from France, just before we move on again. She says:

Darlingest Daniel,

I'm not knocking on wood any more, but trusting that you will come home. You can be sure that every minute awake or asleep that is what I am thinking of. You should also know that without you I wouldn't be who I am. I shudder to think of how different I would be had I not stumbled around the back of your house that day and seen you sitting there carving. And the rest of you! How different things would be if Father had not brought you home that horrible day, had I stayed that rude, spoiled girl who couldn't say thank you to a miner in the street. Luck has been on our side from the first, well, almost, and there's no reason it should run out now. If luck does run out here, and this is the one and only time I am going to say or think it, then I want you to know now that we've already had the best. A lavish best. The rest just doesn't matter. No one on this earth could have given me the joy you already have. Except perhaps our baby, who is kicking me indignantly right now as a reminder.

I do understand your dilemma now, and more than that, I am proud to be married to someone who would do such a brave thing despite all his misgivings. I was angry and hysterical but that's only because I didn't want you to go. Fair enough, too. But since you've left I've done even more growing up. I won't bore you with the details; suffice to say that your 'stupid' decision hasn't been all bad at this end. Nothing with us is ever bad. The greatest gift you've given me is that in virtually everything you do you make me think harder and work harder. And that is what I will continue to do regardless.

You will come home, and you will behave yourself. I want you to do something different when you do; I want you to study, to sit on the verandah and carve and draw, do the things you need to do to bring you out of your state of 'stupidity'. And there's not going to be any argument about it. You've done your bit already, for everyone, and you deserve to know what it is you're really blessed with. For now, you can go back to shovelling dirt or whatever filthy thing it is you're doing, but you've been warned.

You are right: love's just not a word for us, it's more magical than that — and I'm not afraid to use its power. Baby should arrive in about a month's time — wish me, us, luck.

Your very wise, very beautiful, very demanding France.

Duncan walks in and catches me having a bit of a moment with myself and my France and wondering if the date makes me a father yet, and I'm just holding it in. If he wants a word with me right now, I'm going to job him and take my court martial all the way home. He sees, I think, and pisses off.

Things have got worse, did so to be sure I wouldn't miss it, and I'm just about feeling my luck has reached its limit. But I'm doing very well on my list of things I didn't want to do while I was here. Last night I lost three men in one go. There wasn't anything I could have done about it, or maybe there was. But it's … the worst. We were re-rigging entanglements one moment, we'd almost worked our way backwards to our line, me and Anderson up one end and two others, Smithy and Durban, at the other, not much more than a spit away, when Fritz decided to make a big move ahead of ours. The sky lit up like daylight and the wall of noise from both sides was enough to break bones, but it was all happening at least two hundred yards or so south, Fritz clearly determined to blast his way through the wire there, and there was a deep empty trench just a hop behind us so we tried to hurry it up and get it done before scarpering. No, not we, I yelled out to them and signalled to them to hurry it up, since we'd nearly finished anyway. Then a stray shell wiped out Smithy and Durban; I watched it hit them, where they were, whacking

229

in the last corkscrew on their side, and felt the wire rip across my hands as Anderson and I got knocked backwards into the trench, which I then scrambled over the back of as it began to collapse. I couldn't see Anderson: the whole thing had collapsed as far as I could see back that way. He should have been no more than five yards away from me. And then Fritz doesn't light any more flares, since he'd decided at that moment to finish his fireworks, so I couldn't see a fucking thing till my eyes adjusted to the dark again. I jumped back in anyway and started digging but I couldn't find him. Kept going till I did. And he was dead, the corkscrew he'd been holding rammed into his chest, propping him up in the hole I'd made around him.

Would it have mattered if we'd all hopped into the trench, which was the only place to go? Was it a stray shell or did I draw fire when I yelled out: 'Stay.' Couldn't have been that: Fritz is accurate, but not that accurate. I'll never know, though. There was that much noise and light. But still, I'll never know.

And then it got worse from there. I left Anderson where he was, had to, and belted back through the relative quiet, which consisted of intermittent machine-gun fire at who knows what from who knows where, and dived in with the infantry, just in time for Fritz to commence part two of his objective.

'Good of you to drop in,' said this Tommy corp, still dragging on his smoke, leaning back against the rear wall, like he'd just kipped through part one. Then he pushes himself up, leans forwards on his elbows to aim, as they all are down the line, and yells down at me as the shelling starts up from behind and the machine-gunners give it all either side: 'You could make yourself handy.'

I could. I couldn't have done anything else really, since the trench was clogged full of rifles, other than go over the back and make a decent target of myself, or wait for them to go right over the top so I could get past. Couldn't say *Sorry, mate, I'm not an assault pioneer, see this little purple patch on my shoulder, says I'm an engineer.* Couldn't just stand there like an idiot. So I got up with them like an idiot, and when I saw the shapes running out at us through the mad flashes of light, I can say that I had no trouble firing, and I doubt very much that I was shooting like a girl. No idea if I actually hit anyone, but it wouldn't have been for lack of trying.

What did Fritz achieve last night other than killing three Australian sappers in the wrong place at the wrong time, a handful of Tommy infantry and a ridiculous number of his own? Buggered if I know. And I realise, after all this time, that I can't remember Anderson's first name. Who's the best goose here? Me or Fritz?

Coming back to camp last night, alone … I can't tell you what that was like. Duncan just let me tell him what happened and then he said it was six of one and half-a-dozen of the other; what could I do? I had a responsibility first to getting the job done. Did I want to say anything else about it? No. Right, well I'd better get those hands seen to. Very attractive they were last night too: looked like I'd had a fight with a length of barbed wire, or tried to kill Fritz with my bare hands. Nothing a bit of iodine won't fix.

Now we're getting ready to head off for a camp outside a town called Albert; there's a big move planned for the village of Pozieres. A proper Australian assault it'll be, apparently. Can't wait to get there. Fritz is terrified, I've heard that's not a joke, and so am I. And I've been keeping to myself all morning. Now Duncan's back, and I'll have to speak to him. I'm not angry any more, I'm just … nothing.

He says: 'Which was worse? Losing the men or shooting at Germans?'

I say: 'Toss a coin.'

'It wouldn't hurt to let it show a bit, you know.'

'Show what?'

'That you're upset about it, the men.'

'I'm not in the habit of that.' Listen to some and you'd think this was stuff all.

'I'm aware of that. But you're not the only one who's upset about it.'

'Mmn.' Why don't you go and tell everyone how upset you are then, Dunc. Why don't you stop being so fucking *aloof* with everyone except me. I'm a bit busy right now not making sense of how it is I'm still alive.

'No one blames *you*.'

He looks like he's about to put a big-brotherly hand on my shoulder. Don't you fucking touch me. And he does. Of course. I lose it, not much, but enough.

'It's not a good idea to bottle some things. The mill's cleared — why don't you go in there and get it out of your system before we go?'

I do. I go into the empty space that stinks of dust and men and lice dip and endless farting and frustration, put my head against the back wall and let the weep go, quietly.

Stratho comes in and sees me at it; says, 'You big girlie cunt,' and jumps on me. It's not funny. He says, 'Mate,' holding onto the back of my collar, 'it happens. It's going to, isn't it. You think too much, DT. Everyone thinks you're champion, you know, getting in there and evening the score afterwards.'

'It didn't happen like that.'

'So?'

No answer.

Stratho says: 'How're you getting along with Dunc? He put the hard word on you yet? Ten quid says he's in love with you.'

'Fuck off.' He cracks me.

'How's that missus of yours? She had the baby yet?'

'Maybe. Don't know. Probably.' I want to steal one of those frigging bomb-shitting aeroplanes and fly home to her, if you really want to know. And he does know: he's not married but he's got a sweetheart in Sydney, poor girl.

He says: 'One more reason to push on, ay? Come on.'

Yep.

FRANCINE

'He's very clever with it,' Sarah says, almost dismissively. I opened Daniel's package just before she arrived: another carving. It's a kitten with its paw raised as if it's waving hello: pretty toy. The note says: *The Sphinx says g'day. That's about as interesting as it gets. x Daniel.* He must have sent this from Egypt, and it's taken months to get here. Kitten is very much more than clever and I want to say that to her but all my words are stuck: I'm preoccupied with the conflicting endeavours of trying not to dissolve and trying to convince myself that the arrival of the letter and the package on the exact same day must be a good omen. She adds, as if she's telling Kitten: 'Pity it's only him who doesn't seem to notice.'

I can agree with her there, but still I can't open my mouth. Beneath that wryness of hers she's unspeakably upset: blink and you'll miss it, there's that look. Perhaps now is not the time to give her the news of his whereabouts.

She returns Kitten to the side table and sits down next to me. Then she takes my hand. That's it for me: immediate blubbering. So much for willing him back with the magical force of my love.

'Oh Francine,' she says softly. 'Of course it hurts. Otherwise how would you truly know?'

'Know what?' Sniff, sniff.

'That you love. But you can't cry every time it hurts. If I did, that's all I'd do some days.'

That's fairly much all I do seem to have done some days, and she knows that very well, but she's not criticising me.

'You must think me very hard-hearted,' she says.

Sometimes. 'No,' I tell her. 'Just wiser.'

She laughs. 'I might have more experience but I'm not sure that makes me any wiser. I've learned to not want to know. Not very admirable, but necessary, for me.'

'Why?' I dare. How can you possibly not want to know?

'I've lost a son, and a husband, and —' She lets go of my hand.

'You haven't lost a son,' I say, desperately: please don't talk about him as if he's already dead.

She sighs. 'He hasn't told you.'

'Told me what?'

So she tells me. About her first Daniel. I hold my belly, my precious bump, as she speaks plainly about that loss. 'Just thirteen, so excited to start work, to be a man; then — bang — gone. On the seventh of September 1894.' I knew her pain was greater than mine, but I can't imagine this vastness, and how deep it goes, so deep that my Daniel hasn't ever told me he had this brother. She says, just as plainly: 'But I was pregnant at the time, very pregnant, and when he was born, I called him Daniel, and I remember promising myself that … I don't know, that I would do a better job with him, love him more, I suppose. That was *all* I thought about, for a very long time. Even when Peter followed his father in, even when the whole mine exploded.'

Peter was a miner too? *And whole mines can explode?*

She nods. 'Especially then. Ninety-six died that day, thirty-first of July, 1902. And they called that an accident too — all the fault of coal gas. Such accidental coal gas that the owners and their politicians could not be held responsible for all their lies about it, or forced to provide safety lamps to avoid another *unfortunate calamity*. And there was the implication, as there is always the implication, that the miners might have taken better care themselves, as if the joke is law: *Every miner is an owner — of his own risk.* We moved here after that.' She pauses again and I'm thinking they didn't mention anything like this in *Bituminous Coal in the Western and Illawarra Fields* or I'd have stayed awake, when she adds: 'I spent the next six years trying to make Daniel be good at school. I mean understand the point of it.' She raises an eyebrow: 'And you can see how successful I was there.'

But there's that flash of grief again, so much sharper for this, jabbing at me, and I want to refute the implication she's making against herself and tell her what a stupid, obstinate, abandoning son she has. Abandoning husband I have. I want to hold her, and I want her to hold me. She's got more wisdom to impart, though.

'Responsibility is a hazardous thing to contemplate. You can call something an accident, an unavoidable thing, you can say *What else could I have done?* and there's no truth to see your loss against anyway. This war is the same. Except there's more dignity, and more public excitement, in dying in battle, than dying at work. It's all the same to the dead, though, isn't it. And for me, it's better to try not to think about it at all.'

She takes my hand again and squeezes. 'I know you can't help thinking about it, Francine. I know you love my son and I am very glad of it, more than I could ever tell you. Something else experience has taught me is that true life, true love comes from the completeness of your union with your husband. No matter what a fool he is. Mine was just as bad, if not worse. I don't regret a moment of loving him; I still do. That's not something to admire either: it's a privilege, and a burden, of existence.'

Yes. Maybe that's all I need to know too. But I ask her, just to ask one of the thousands of questions I have about her, and how such a woman came to be … here: 'What made you choose your husband?'

She smiles, slowly, and laughs lightly. 'Heinrich. Ah. Well, I was sixteen and he, you know, looked just like Daniel, except he was blond and not quite so tall. I thought he must be a god. He was a conscript in the Saxon Guard, and that uniform only made him more of a heart-stopper. He hated it, he was eighteen, and impatient. We eloped — broke enough laws to have him hanged ten times. Very exciting then, to be such young fugitives, heads filled with more romance than sense.'

Good God: how many more questions does that make me want to ask. But, bizarrely, all I can think of in the wash is that this likely means that warrants for criminal rebelliousness remain outstanding on both sides of my baby's family. I try to blab out another question, but only manage: 'Wh...?'

'What's the truth?' In her skewed smile she is so delicate and so robust she is sixteen and something more than ancient. 'You'd laugh if you could really know it. Dresden is a very old city, a beautiful place, but one that can put big ideas into your head only to frown at you for thinking them. Heinrich was thinking about *Sozialismus*, not the revolutionary kind but the natural variety that was supposed to be springing up in the furthest corner of the earth. In Australia, so-called the Workingman's Paradise. He wanted to be something different, new, but he didn't know how to get there. So he shunned his compulsory military training instead, every boy over seventeen had do that training, but Heinrich didn't want to play soldiers in the woods, and so he earned himself a sentence of three years' active service. And if Bismarck didn't kill him, my father would have. Couldn't have my expensive education wasted on cannon fodder, and besides, I was already ...' She caresses my bump with a knuckle. 'He was born in Hamburg, just before we left, and I thought I was the cleverest thing; Heinrich joked that we were Joseph and Mary hiding from King Herod; I joked that I didn't think a good

Jewish girl like Mary would have stolen money from her father to do it. When we arrived in Sydney I saw the name Woolloomooloo on a sign and I thought it was the *funniest* thing. Almost as funny as the realisation that Kembla, where we were told to go by the port official since we had no contacts anywhere, had no *natural socialism*, no job for Harry but coalmining, and no house for us other than a sack-walled shack — I cooked on a fire outside with my baby on my back. I cried for the whole first year, I think. Harry didn't. Loved the place at first sight, all of it. Well, he was a natural *bloke* before anything else, so he was always going to love it here. Natural *liebling*, my baby, too: he'd take me out into bush, to try to cheer me up, and he'd say to me: *But look at the sun on the hills, Sarah — look at the colours on the water. Look. You can't get that in Deutschland, you can't get that anywhere but here.'*

Suddenly she frowns; I don't remember ever having seen her really frown before.

She says: 'And Daniel has run back in the opposite direction, a fugitive from himself. It hurts to think of how responsible I might be for that, but it's pointless to wonder about it. You can't tell Daniel what to do; you can't *make* him do anything. You know that already. He is his father's son, *this* land's son, except perhaps in one way: he's not nearly so tough. Couldn't shoot a sick pony. If he comes back from this European disgrace, I don't want to think about what will have been robbed from him.'

That falls like a stone into the room. I can't allow the thoughts of *if he does come back* and *what will be robbed*: Daniel will come home, and when he does, he will stop being Neanderthal Boy.

I ignore the threat and ask her instead: 'Did you teach him to draw too?'

'Draw? No. I didn't know he could.'

I get the drawings from my room and show her; she says: 'It doesn't surprise me. But look at that handwriting — terrible.'

She gets up then and leaves the room for a while. I don't follow her. I think I can guess what she's doing. Meanwhile, I sit and contemplate how complete my union is. I don't care if it's a maternal derangement; I focus on him, and he will come home.

And I keep focusing when the pains start. Unsurprisingly, given my track record, I don't do a good line in stoicism when it comes to labouring in childbirth: I scream for Armageddon. I scream for Daniel. I scream until he comes. And he does come. God knows how he does. It's a boy.

He is born in my bed, our bed, there is blood everywhere, I am shaking all over as I take him in my arms, hold his little lamb cries against my chest till he quietens. He is so very perfect I feel I'm never going to stop shaking and crying. Even Mrs Moran has a tear when she says, 'Well done,' and cuts the cord. Sarah touches his squashy pink face softly with the back of her fingers and kisses me on the head as she says: 'Let's clean him up. You too.' She takes him from me, and I really start up again then. No one needs to ask why I'm fairly wailing. Louise is holding me and she keeps a good hold of me till I get myself under control.

Calm again, all clean and soft and bruised and lovely and disbelieving of the miracle and believing that they must surely grow on trees, and here in my arms again. I call him Daniel. Just Daniel. Like his father. He has the hair to prove it. Sarah knew I would.

It's the fifth of July. Sisyphus wants a push across the River Somme and Achilles is most definitely there lending a hand. Little Danny is guzzling contentedly on me — couldn't give two hoots for any of it, least of all my wonder at the simple fact of his feeding — and I close my eyes, the better to feel the magic flow out through me, see it fly across the world to him. And when I open them again, it's snowing outside my window.

★

Second week of August and there are apples everywhere. Better get to bagging them before they spoil. Must do something after what I've just read: there's an estimate that twenty thousand Australians have been killed in France in the last month. *Twenty thousand?* For once I hope the journalist is lying. If he's not, must be some kind of a record, given the size of the force. That's possibly around a one in four or five chance, just of being killed. How many other casualties? No wonder it's referred to as a cauldron. I'm waiting for my missive from the AIF now, not from Daniel. I don't think magic can fight those sorts of odds.

Little Danny screws up his face at me as if to say, 'Nah, Mum, it'll be all right.'

Let's believe Baby Daniel is a prophet for the rest of the day, shall we.

More reasonable than putting any stock in reportage: that it'll all be all right because Fritz is copping it worse, because Our Boys, with odds against them, are rather formidable: noble savages. Anger jabs: I'm sure Fritz can cope — he has millions to sacrifice. Bite your tongue, Francine.

I can't really comprehend it. I feel as if I am drifting away from it. This can't be happening.

DANIEL

My identity tags slip across my chest as we settle in to camp and they've never felt more like cold meat tickets. I'd say I'm expanding my understanding of disgusting again, except I don't think it is possible to understand the scale of this. It's the most horrific shift changeover imaginable as thousands and thousands of Tommies head back from the front. It hasn't been going too well, obviously. They are ripped ragged, covered in mud and blood; a nod, a smile, a wave, got a smoke, tell a joke, dead eyes. The lot of them. There's that many walking wounded they must be turning anyone who's not at least half dead away from the casualty stations. One bloke who stops for a chat says: 'Me and Johnny here, we're the only ones left in our battalion.' And he laughs. Out of his mind. I don't see a single Tommy officer above a sergeant anywhere among these leftovers. Either they've all been killed or they're off having a port somewhere else after a bad day. Something makes me think it might be the latter. Duncan might be strange, but he wouldn't make himself scarce if we looked like that. And that's the difference between us and them I suppose.

So, now we'll go in with our own infantry, loaded up with enough wire to build a city, to advance on a tiny village. We've been drilled so hard that we're prepared for anything and everything. I can make and throw a jam-tin bomb these days as good as look at you, or any one and any number of the new

beaut grenades, and find my rifle under any circumstance, pull it
out sideways through a roll of wire if I have to. Of course us
engineers are not expected to join in the fun, just set up for the
get-together; but it is expected that a bit of that might be
inevitable, just to make sure that I don't leave here without doing
every last thing I didn't want to. A bit of something worse by the
looks of it too. Just when I think I couldn't be more excited than
I am right now, Duncan pulls me up wanting a word; very hard
one.

'Watkins is to shift to Transport,' he says, meaning Watkins has
had enough of the front; he's not been looking too hardy these
past few weeks and Dunc is culling a non-coper. 'So I want you
to take over as sergeant, see how you go.'

If I was a gambler I'd have put money on this.

'No,' I tell him. I don't want the responsibility of having to
account for so many. Don't want to see how I'll go, after my last
effort.

'No is not an answer, Ackerman. That's what you're doing
until I tell you otherwise.' And off he goes again.

First day in my new beaut position of authority is the day we
set out for the front. I'm at the head of the mob with Duncan,
though, once I've given orders to the parties that'll go out doing
this and that and everyone's had a good crack. I tell the bastards
they can call me sir from now on, just to get another one, while
Stratho salutes me with a limp wrist for his.

After orders, there's not a huge amount of difference between
a sergeant and a private in the field; it's all the same rubbish. If I
thought it appropriate I could shovel slightly less shit, but the
main part of the job is giving orders as passed down the line from
the brass. And, of course, to keep on with Dunc's favourite: how
are we all today, and pull out anyone who's sick or tired or not
bearing up, or all three; and I can do that now without even

asking for his opinion, just as I can read a map that's no doubt going to be fucking wrong anyway and tell others where to go. Up until a few days ago I was fairly impressed at the difference between the AIF and the BEF that means our lower-order officers are more often than not drawn from the rank and file on the basis of merit, rather than where they went to school or how long they've been around, but the fact of it for me now is not exactly comfortable. The brass is the brass and I don't want to have anything to do with them. I don't want to take responsibility for their actions. It's too hard to take responsibility for my own: I can feel France whacking me, but with the plain knowledge now that I could not have made a worse mistake, and that it's far too late for that sort of clarity.

A very big shell explodes a mile or so ahead up the road, beyond Albert, or what's left of the town. I feel the shudder under my feet. I look up at the ruined cathedral we're passing and there's a statue of the Madonna and Child on top of it hanging right over the street, tipping just below horizontal. She's had enough, obviously. She's holding her baby down to us as if to say: *Please, take him away from here.* She's famous, on both sides: whoever knocks her down will win the war. How sad is that? Others say the opposite; that's even sadder. There are craters everywhere, in the road, across the town, beyond the town and all the way to where we're going. Closer in, well within shelling range and under the buzz of dozens of aeroplanes, the bodies start; those that will stay here because there are too many to retrieve; everyone's a little busy with other things right now. I wish I had a camera so that these men could be seen by everyone everywhere: to stop this. I would want it to be in colour, though, so that you can see their bones against their pink-grey flesh, the colours of their dead eyes that stare every which way. See the trenches, collapsed, sinking back into the earth, taking these men with them. The shapes of the men, some just asleep, some stunned, some still in the moment of screaming. Some don't look like men at all; only charred shapes. And just as many horses; stinking meat everywhere, as far as you can see. I don't think my photograph would make it into the papers somehow. And even if it did, I'm not sure it would make a difference. How could anyone make sense of it? I'm looking right at it and I can't.

I think about fucking off AWL, but that's not likely to make a difference either. Except to make me a proper coward. Welcome to Pozieres, then. A proper Australian assault.

Approximately 0300 hours, well back, in some officer's empty bunker, resting for a tick. I'm in charge of three blokes I've pulled out: two of mine, a corp and a sap, who I've decided will not be making another run of ammunition tonight, and an infantry private who I don't know: he can't speak to tell me anything, and I can't prise his fingers from around his tags. I can appreciate that. He looks about sixteen. Shoved him in here a minute ago after I saw him wandering along the top between the trenches like he'd lost his last sixpence for the train home to Woop Woop. I'm still catching my breath. My blokes are all right, sort of, or will be after a break, though I think the sap is deaf: I practically had to shove him in here, because he either couldn't understand me or wanted an argument. Can't move them out yet, because the end of the world is going on above us and dead and wounded are jammed along the trench outside the entrance now. We'll stay put till … till we don't, and I can palm them off onto someone else and get along to what I should be doing now, which is further back still, with Stratho and Foley, repairing the ammunition supply lines, and hoping I get cholera while I'm at it.

Now a Tommy major sticks his head into the bunker, right in my face, and says, or yells because he has to: 'Who are you and what are you doing in here?' Like he's caught us having a sly smoko in his office.

'Ackerman, Sergeant.' It's official now, as official as my lack of a salute, or anything resembling an identifiable uniform at the minute. 'Engineers. With bewildered. Sir.' If it's any of your business.

Makes no sense to him what an Engineers NCO is doing in here with these head cases, but little of sense is going on. The Australian infantry is advancing, and is getting slaughtered. Advance? Jesus. But we must have pissed off Fritz because the retaliation is screaming: *We're going to bury every last one of you fuckers. Today.*

'Get them out of here,' says Tommy major.

'That's the idea. Sir.' And who the fuck are you when you're at home?

I realise I've seen him before, a week or so ago, overseeing the tying up of one of his corporals, to a pole behind the lines, to leave him there overnight. Very medieval. Don't know what the corporal had done, probably drunkenness, or maybe he didn't want to push on and had made his opinion clear. It's an unwritten rule in the AIF that we of the lower orders have permission to pervert the course of British justice whenever we see it, so Stratho and I waited till the major and his copper had gone then untied the bloke. Stratho stopped to have a smoke with him, and when he caught up with me later he said the corporal had decided to stay put anyway, untied, sitting by the pole. Can't credit it, can you.

Maybe this major is aware of our attempt at bad influence, because he's eyeballing me. Unbelievable, given the circumstances, but that's what he's doing. I give him some back: go on, have a go for nothing, you little shit. He goes to piss off, but then steps back and yells at me: 'You lot really are animals.'

That was a bit unnecessary, I think, but I find out why later back in camp.

Half-a-dozen of our blokes herded their twenty or so German prisoners into a deep shell hole during the night and threw Mills bombs in at them; they'd tied them to each other first, so they couldn't run. Mixed responses among us, but I'm revising the issue of my nationality again. Still, I'm not in the infantry.

Dunc is disgusted. 'That is revenge. That is the ugly Australian. The big man with a small mind. The big country with a two-inch cock.'

He's cleaning his toenails again as he says it, and clipping them, like it was nothing less than expected.

I say: 'We don't really know what it's like, though. To go over all the time, and to …'

He looks across at me like I've got two heads. 'I don't know what your politics are, Ackerman, but I can take an easy stab at them, and I'm not averse to breaking rules myself, no stranger to the frustration of wanting to make them too, but self-control should be a given, in every situation for every man beyond the very, very frontline. They had time to think before they acted, and didn't.'

Fair enough.

He adds: 'You might be interested to know that the instigator was not one of *yours*, but a filthy rich, British-educated grazier's son from Victoria. And he will not be punished. The incident won't be recorded. It didn't happen. Put that in your class-confusion notebook and remember it. The best and the most decent here are *your* lot, those with nothing but everything to prove about themselves. They are the ones the Germans are really afraid of. Because they go hard, they go together and they make a proper job of the bloody impossible. Just don't stop till they're called off. And they do not pretend that this is not barbaric enough.'

He's gone back to his toenails and there's a small splash on his knee. He meant that. Not sure what I think about that.

I want to ask him again why he's here, but it's just not the right time.

Very, very last act of stupidity performed at war. Stratho's been hit in the arse, as he deserves, and he can't move, this side of no man's land, not too far, but Foley couldn't get him back. It's not funny. Apart from the obvious logistical problem of dragging Stratho back to our line in the middle of the end of the world, Foley's got a hole in his shoulder the size of a fist. I tell him to get on and get seen to and I'll get Strath. Somehow.

In the time it's taken for Foley to get back and stumble into me, Stratho has probably bled to death already or too close to bother by the sounds of it: half his backside is missing in action. But I have to. Even if he is dead, I just don't want him to be there. I want him to be taken away so he gets buried somewhere, properly. This is why you should not have mates. I've done fairly well on that score, but Stratho is a special case. Duncan would probably disagree, but he's not here. He's snug in with the brass getting his orders. Good for him. I've just come back from camp, I'm in full uniform, and squeaky clean, hair clipped so close I'll frighten the lice; I should be on my way to the brig's digs to see what can be done to strengthen the roof, to stop it falling in on him every second night; he can wait.

It's quiet now, relatively, the sun is just about setting on this fine, early August evening, and it will be in Fritz's eyes, so there's no time like the present to make a leap over the top, belt up to the wire and find him. I do. He's dead. His mouth is slack like he's fallen asleep pissed. I sit down next to him and watch the sky change from grey to purple as the sun sets behind us. This land between us and them shows no sign of the village that once was:

it's the shadow shapes of dead men and wire and machine-gun metal sailing through the air above a kind of desert of dirt full of cracks and holes. It sits on a ridge that they reckon is just about to belong to the Australian infantry. What a victory that'll be. It's hard not to stay here and just look at it. Like I'm not really here. *You big girlie cunt.*

But not for long.

Sundown is Fritz fireworks like they are going out of fashion; bang on time. He doesn't like the dark here; flares are up before the sky is barely black. I can't leave Stratho here. So I pick him up. He's not that big, when you're not thinking, and we're off, as a shell lands a polite distance to the left and front of me. Stratho takes the brunt. Good on him. And we're flung back, into a hole. On reflex I put my arm out, like a complete idiot, and feel a sharp twist, snap and crunch as we hit the bottom, a few yards down. It's all going on. Mad. I'll just lie here for a while in the bottom of this hole, with Strath on top of me, and pretend that I didn't just do that.

But not for long.

Fritz is sitting in this hole with me. He looks like that bloke I grabbed the other night. About sixteen, maybe less. He looks like I should look: scared shitless, spragging in the dark. Except I'm a bit elsewhere at the minute. Like when you fall off your bike and clock yourself and you think, how did that happen? Before the fact registers.

I can't stop looking at him, as he's looking at me, and I'm a bit hysterical now. There's a break in the shelling as I wear myself out and fear and pain hit me.

He edges closer and says: '*Du bist 'n Australier.*'

Picked me in one. Don't need German for that, but it's amazing how quick memory can work in an emergency, or in a place so far from understanding you'll grab at anything. I say: '*Und du bist 'n* Fritz.*'

248

He says, quite seriously: '*Nein. Ich bin Johan. Johan Schultz.*'

I laugh for five minutes, I swear, despite myself. And he just keeps staring, can't blame him, and he's armed all right. Everything I can see plus more no doubt. My rifle is pinned under my back, between my back and my arm. Which is wrong in every way. Pig's fucking arse. I say, for what it's worth: 'Can you help me? *Gefallen tun …? Hilfe?*' pointing with my left hand at Stratho.

'*Ja.*' He gets up and rolls Stratho off me. Unbelievable, *danke*. He says: '*Sprechen sie Deutsch?*'

'No, just a bit,' I say and I let him know about the rest as I sit up.

He says: '*Arm gebrochen. Schlimm, ja? Das muss weh tun.*'

Hurts? *Ja.* Very *ja.* To buggery. Oh boyo, don't look at it.

Then he starts saying something else to me, but I can't understand him, apart from *heute, sterben* and *Australier:* today die Australian; which would be alarming if there was any threat in it. He's not threatening; he sounds like he's praying as he says it again; he's shaking, beyond terrified. Can't hear him above the gunning now anyway and I yell at him to write it down; at least I'll have a souvenir of this moment if I ever get out of here. He takes out a little pocket book and pencil, scribbles it down, tears off the page, then leans over and shines his torch on it for me. I read it, but I'm not sure I've got it right. I stick the paper in my top pocket, in with Francine and my compass. He says it a few more times, louder, above the artillery, to the artillery.

'Shush,' I tell him: 'Shut up. *Schnautze!*' He'll draw attention to us, and I'm happy here with my mates Stratho and Johan, thank you. He gets the point, and now I think I've worked out what he was saying: *Heute muss ich sterben und ich will von einem Australier umgebracht werden.* He thinks he's going to die today, and he wants to be killed by an Australian. Well, it won't be me who kills him, and not just because I couldn't hold a rifle let alone pull a trigger at the minute even if you asked me nicely.

So we just sit here for ten million years, hour after hour, as the shelling goes on and on and on. Oh Jesus. Jesus. I'm waiting for one to hit us, listening to the whistling as they come close, trying to guess where the next one will land and when this hole will swallow us. And I think I might be praying too. They reckon your life's supposed to flash before your eyes at times like these, but apart from apologising endlessly to Francine, which I've been doing for the last three weeks anyway, all I see in my mind is Pete, my big brother, saying: 'Don't sook now, save it for Mum — do a good job and you might get the day off school tomorrow.' I was about ten, and I'd scraped half the skin off the palm of my hand, falling back into a dry creek bed, when he saw me, on his way home from work. I think that sort of memory is called wishful thinking. Did my best: but no chance Mum was going to let me off school: '*Glückskind — nichts gebrochen.*' Well, Mum, the arm's fairly well *gebrochen* now.

Eventually, we're not dead and the rampage above us settles right down, exhausted, and I say to Johan: 'You want to come with me? *Kommst mit mir …?*' May as well make a run for it now.

'*Ja.*' He gets up. I think he knows what I'm asking him: does he want to stay here and be killed by an Australian or get packed off to prison camp? I hope that doesn't mean the same thing; maybe he doesn't care.

'Give me — *geben* …' Can't think of the word for rifle, never came up in conversation with Mum, so I point.

'*Ah — Waffen,*' he says and he hands over the lot, even his frigging knife.

There's hardly anything of him he's so skinny, but he throws Stratho over his shoulder and takes him with us. I'm crawling up the slope of the hole and he says, like the kid he is: '*Das muss dir echt weh tun. Echt schlimm, ja?'* and reaches back to pull me to the top. I want to cry; I am hurting. Seriously, for the whole bloody lot. He can't be more than fifteen.

When we hop down into the trench, who should be there but Tommy Major Nobody. Good: let the Brits have Fritz Johan; they won't kill him — they might even give him a cup of tea if he calls them sir. I see clearly now that Tommy major's younger than me too; looks as though he's only just started shaving, but then a lot of Brits look like that, don't they. I say, dumping the weaponry at his feet: 'Fritz is yours, but you can give James Strathlyn to the Ambulance.' And you'd better fucking organise it, you safe-and-sound fucking major fucking major piece of shit, or I'm going to come back and kill you myself. With something blunt in my left hand. Not sure if I actually said that last bit or not.

Tommy wants to ask me questions; I definitely tell him to fuck right off, tell him to speak to Duncan if he has a problem with anything. Johan's dropped to his knees now, with relief, I think, and I say; '*Auf Wiedersehen.*' I've had enough of this, I realise, finally. It's all over for me. I'm taking my dishonourable discharge and going home, when they let me out of prison. They won't shoot me for refusal; no one in the AIF has been shot for being a goose or a coward; in fact, never heard of anyone having been shot by AIF court martial ever. They'll just lock me up with all the others that are having problems with their behaviour. I've heard there are quite a few; more Australians than any other type of ally in military prison: we do everything in a big way.

It's just after 0300 hours, my favourite time of day, and I haven't done anything I was supposed to be doing tonight, so I start wandering off through the trenches back to the road, back to the camp. I'm so out of my mind that I don't think to hand myself in to the Ambulance and get my arm seen to, have a nice rest in dock for a few weeks or several, care of my own stupidity.

It looks like it's been put on backwards, but there's no blood, not a scratch on me, and it's not hurting any more, so I don't care. Duncan was right: I don't panic for anything on the job, don't miss a fucking duckboard, I know so clearly where I'm going, but I am definitely insane. *Saublöd*. It's not shellshock; I'm not shaking, not now; it's just me. Broken in half, mission complete. I couldn't hold one full thought in my head right now if my life depended on it. It occurs to me that my life probably does depend on it, and I have a laugh at myself as I hit the road.

It's just on dawn when Duncan catches up to me, as I'm nearing Albert. I can hear him yelling, 'Ackerman! Ackerman!' as in stop this minute you idiot, fifty or sixty yards behind me. But he can talk to me when I sit down again, when I get to the huts in camp. Got to get my kit, my letters from France are in there, and I'm cold, I need her jumper, so I'm ready for when they take me to the lockup. I'm not stopping here. Besides, you never know who's lurking around Albert; it's not a good place to stop. So I'm not stopping. Not for anything.

But I am apparently.

I can hear it coming under the buzz of the aeroplanes. The whistle sails through the air. I stop, but I am that confused I don't take cover. I just stand there as it hits the ground in front of me. Not exactly, but near enough is good enough to do the job.

FOUR

AUGUST 1916–DECEMBER 1917

DANIEL

'Just keep quiet and be still, will you,' Duncan is saying. He's pulled me into the ditch and is trying to stop the bleeding with the towel from his pack. I'm not mad any more but I'm not cooperating either. I can hear France screaming inside my head, like she did that night her father died, and I am matching her for breath and volume. I started up as soon as I saw the size of the hole in me and kept going as Duncan started pulling out the khaki and pouring iodine in it, pushing the inside of me back down. Even though we've all seen something like this before, it's a bit different when you're looking at your own; there are some things about the way you're made that you really don't want to know. I wish I didn't know, too, that a hole like this means you bleed to death fairly quickly or die of shock before anyone can do anything for you. I'm not keen on either of these, but I shut up now; try to: Dunc looks like he knows what he's doing, and he's just doing it anyway.

He's already sent off for me to be collected, and now he's shoving a piece of wood between my legs, looks like a bit of window frame, and he's tying them together with a length of rope. Always hated carrying rope in my pack: it's heavy and never long enough to be useful for anything. Dunc's found a use for it, though: an extremely painful one. Then he picks up my arm, says 'For God's sake, Ackerman,' strapping it to my side with my belt and I don't know what pain is any more. It's a whole new world in itself. Special one, just for me.

Dunc says, 'I'll speak to you later,' and the last thing I see as I'm carried off is Madonna and her baby, still hanging on over the road. I want to know if I have a son or a daughter. I'm not going to die. Not like this. France is just blinking at me now, and I'd very much like to pass out.

The last thing I hear is Dunc yelling out: 'Stop.' A motor turning over. An argument. And I'm on the back of a lorry. An empty ammo truck, I think. At the first jolt I would start screaming again if I could understand anything.

FRANCINE

Postman comes. My old friend Mr Symes delivers it personally. At first I think they've made a mistake because it says *Sgt D Ackerman*. Sgt is a sergeant. They've got the wrong man. But they don't, I know. And even though I know, it still takes a small eternity to believe it.

It says *gravely injured*. What does that mean? What does *shrapnel wounds right leg/hip, fractures femur & pelvis* mean? *Dear Madam*: it's a warning. But I'm oddly thrilled. He's alive. Because this is not a pink death telegram delivered via parish priest; this is a white letter, a slow white letter from Victoria Barracks. Which might mean he's toughed out *gravely* for weeks already. No pink telegram to tell me otherwise. Gravity rushes through me with every breath, but I can't help trembling with relief. Little Daniel smiles in his basket as I peer in at him: 'Dad's all right.' Of course he is.

Louise is in town shopping and Sarah is at her house now; I'll keep this to myself till I know for sure.

Lots of apples still left to bag and with every one I take out of the tubs in the shed I make a wish. Pretend that my thoughts can reach him, have reached him, will make him well. Not too well, though. I want him to come home. Unfit for service. Now. Grave battle wounds mean amputations, though, don't they? I'm not silly, and I haven't failed to notice the increase in advertisements for prosthetic limbs over the past year. I don't want them to have cut his leg off, but if they have, they have, and it means he can come home. How do you amputate a hip, though? Oh God. I wonder how many women are praying that their husbands and sons are merely crippled today — not too badly, but just enough. Thousands probably. This war is warping the fabric of everything.

The letter also said in handwritten scribble beneath typed warning that he'd been recommended for some award, for doing something or other with a gun *under bombardment*. I don't doubt Daniel's bravery, but that doesn't sound right: he was supposed to be digging holes, and he has an aversion to firearms. But what would I know? Then again, maybe they say things in these slow white letters and pink telegrams to make you think your dearest was a hero, to soften the blow. Maybe more so now than ever: I think the whole country is in shock at the numbers lost in France, but Billy Hughes is going to hold a referendum on conscription, to change the constitution to force All Our Boys to serve overseas. After all, at the bottom of the letter, in big bold type are the words: *IT BEING CLEARLY UNDERSTOOD THAT IF NO FURTHER ADVICE IS FORWARDED THIS DEPARTMENT HAS NO MORE INFORMATION TO SUPPLY*. Perhaps that can be interpreted as: DON'T DARE ATTEMPT TO SEEK THE TRUTH. Maybe no one's getting pink telegrams now, maybe Daniel's not even … Maybe, Francy, this war is warping your brain. Billy Hughes might be the prime minister, and he might look like a troll and act like a troll, but he couldn't make the army lie, could he. And half the Labor Party is against him and conscription. Bishop Mannix has promised thunderbolts if the referendum goes ahead.

Daniel also has *fractures right arm*, and the address given for the hospital in France was quite plain. Get back to counting apple wishes against miserable facts.

Please God, if you let Daniel survive, I will eat dirt for the rest of my life. I will sell my half of the Wattle smack on the third of May next year, my birthday, and I will give the money to the miners, pay off our greedy capitalist debts in capfuls of cash. My Daniels can live on apples and potatoes and my love. Please. But why would God listen to me and my impossible promises? I haven't kept my last one: Little Daniel will not be raised a Catholic: Big Daniel will have been through enough without coming home to discover his son is a Certified Mick.

No. Sensible, higher thought: if he survives, I know I'm not going to get the very same Daniel back, but the wish I make the most is that there is just enough. That'll do. That's reality. But as much as I can, I'll try to keep that to myself too: keep believing that my wishes make a difference.

DANIEL

'Watch him for melancholy,' the doctor says to the nurse as he walks off, as if I'm not here. As if I'm about to be anywhere near melancholy. I'd be dancing, running around punching the air, if I could. He's just told me that he's not going to cut my leg off. I have a *promising* leg, and it's staying with me. Not quite out of the woods till the wounds heal, but it's enough to make me feel like the luckiest bloke not exactly having his best day, but a bloody good one. Even if this is a new and improved experience in being arsebound. Can't get off the fucking bed bound. Can't fucking move actually. Well, that's not exactly true: I can move my left foot a bit, which doesn't mean a lot in this position, and I could move most of the top half of me if the attempt didn't mean agony, which leaves only my left arm free, to do bugger all. Fuck that, I'm here. Yes I am. And I really have to stop swearing so much. I'm going to go home, eventually. The doctor said it's very unlikely that there won't be some permanent damage. Is that so? Good-o. Stupidity has taken me a very, very long way round the block, but I've got there.

Everyone here in this ward has got there in one way or another, and I can tell you that the atmosphere is very bright today. Best get-together going on in France, even if you are minus an arm or a leg or an eye or half your guts. And we're all Australian — since they have to pen the animals separately, apparently. I've got to write to France, my France, to tell her all about it. Got to find someone to write for me first.

Foley walks in — he won't do. He's slinged up and won't be writing anything for a while either. He spots me, not difficult, and comes over. First thing he says is: 'Sorry, mate. Sir.'

I say: 'Don't be. I didn't have to go, did I. Glad I did.'

'Does that hurt?' he asks, looking at the rigging that's got my legs strung up by metal rods and rings and lines with little sandbag weights over bars above and over the far end of the bed.

'Not much.' Not at the moment. Not if I don't move. A few days ago, when I came to properly after the second operation, was another story: more than a little bit blindingly crook; some padre rubbing my forehead and holding my face in his cold hands and talking mumbo-jumbo like Dracula *en français*, shocking me back into the land of living excruciation; best forgotten. And don't ask about the arm: there's a razor at work in there on my elbow right now. But whatever you do, don't look under that dressing round my thigh: very frightening.

'How long will you stay like that?'

'Don't know, don't care.'

Then he says, shaking his head, and laughing as much as Foley ever does: 'Heard about your prisoner too and what you said to that Tommy major.'

That stops me. I don't want to think about that. About being mad, about Fritz Johan, anything to do with the front at all. I want to just forget it. He sees, and drops it.

He says: 'So I take it you're tagged for going home.'

'Yep. And you?'

'Not unless I get the plague in here. Just a surface wound.'

That stops us both.

He says: 'You're a lucky bloke then, aren't you.'

I am. Can't hide the smile.

'Well, just wanted to say g'day,' he says. 'I'll see you later.' And he's off, not happy about the prospect of being sent back to hell.

Poor Foley, Clem Foley; he's got something in his eyes that looks like permanent damage too. Hope not. I could have been a bit more diplomatic, couldn't I.

But Dunc's here now. The fun never stops. And I'm going to have to talk about it now because that's why he's here. To ask me what the fuck I was doing.

He's holding a letter, though. I already know who it's from; I can see her handwriting on the front. He says: 'Thought you might like this sooner rather than later.' He's grabbed it for me from camp, God love him. He opens it for me and hands it over, steps away while I read it; he's not just here to give me this.

It's not a letter that I read, though; it's a card that she's painted with her watercolours: Josie's, our house, on the front and, inside, apples fat on their branches, around a photo of the funniest-looking little baby you've ever seen. She's written: *It's a boy! He is you all over, don't you think? He is Daniel. Just Daniel. Whatever you're doing, well done, darlingest. That's everything you need to know. Magic flies around the world to you in relentless salvos. Your France.*

I lose it in front of him, completely, no problem at all, but I'm laughing too. He's got a look saying: *Well?*

'Boy,' is all I get out.

He looks at his watch, then he asks what he came to ask, while I'm good and raw: 'So, now you can tell me the unofficial version of events.'

'What's the official one first?' I'm not that raw.

'That in the attempt to rescue Strathlyn, who later died, you caught Fritz, disarmed him and handed him over to Tommy.'

I can only say: 'I knew Stratho was probably dead, so I shouldn't have been there in the first place, and Fritz handed himself in, and I handed my mind in after that.' He doesn't need the details. 'What did that Major do afterwards?' Am I in the shit? Do I care? Not really.

'He came after me, carried on about you threatening him. I refrained from asking him if he didn't have more important things to do and instead asked whether or not you'd given any indication as to where you were off to. He said he thought you'd probably have got yourself to the casualty station, since he'd noticed your arm. Startling: both the arm and the fact that he still found you a threat. I was on my way back out anyway, so I went looking for you there; no sign, so I pushed on. And then there you were, wandering along the road like you were out for a ramble. Is there anything else you want to say about it?'

'No. Except thanks. Not for the official bullshit.' I know why he's done that, if only for morale, for the others. 'But for whatever you did when, you know, while I was carrying on. You knew what you were doing, didn't you.'

'I'm your CO, I know everything. Including the fact that without this rather more sophisticated splint you're in now, you might not even be here. Now that's a piece of engineering.'

'Certainly is.' And I'm very, very grateful. Not just for the splint, if that's what you call this thing that's got me half drawn and quartered, but for the fact that I'm fairly certain I wouldn't be around if Dunc hadn't shoved me on the back of that motor-lorry and demanded I be dropped off here, where there's a proper bone doctor. Not too many get that service; if it had happened at the front, then I'd probably have died before I left the butchers at the clearing station.

'So, you're going home,' he says. 'Lucky chap. I shall miss you.'

That gets me. I'll miss him too. It occurs to me I might never see him again, so while we're being chatty I have to ask: 'Tell me why you're here — and don't say the same reason as me. I'm here because I am an idiot. What's your story?'

He stands there looking at me for a second and then says: 'I had a friend, a doctor, who signed up the first week, killed in

Turkey not long after I first met you. So it is the same reason, really.'

No it's not, I can hear that loud enough: he's cut, very. So I have to ask him: 'Are you queer?'

He rolls his tongue around inside his cheek and shakes his head: 'You really are special. But yes, you could say that. Does it make a difference?'

'No. I just had to know, so I don't wonder.'

'Fair enough,' he says. And he's about to leave when I ask him: 'You haven't got time to write a letter for me, have you? It won't be a long one.'

'All right,' he says, scrounges paper, and pulls up a chair.

I say: 'My France. Received your alarming news and photo of the kid. He's odd-looking enough, so he must be mine, but I hope he's not too much like me. Received all your salvos too by the looks of it. Trust you've received pleasant notice from AIF about the state of me by now. If not, I'm a bit bunged up, successfully enough to be sent home. Well done me. Don't expect dancing, but otherwise intact so far and however it goes I'll compensate by giving full effort to the things I do best, for you. Double. Please don't worry, it's just a few broken bones really. No idea when I'll be home, but look out. In the meantime stop blinking, will you. I can't stand it any more. You're champion. See you when I'm looking at you. Both of you. Slightly less stupid and very well behaved, no choice, Daniel. PS: My handwriting hasn't got neater, Captain Duncan is scribe. Seems I owe your father and his connections a fair bit.'

'That's it?' Duncan is bemused. 'What a sweetheart you are.'

'You'd be surprised,' I say.

'No, I wouldn't,' he says, and after he takes the address, he farewells: 'Well, good luck then. Might see you at home, et cetera.' And he's off. Back to the front. On those little feet.

And I am a bit melancholy now.

★

Bit more than that after a month of this. Very ugly Australian, very surly arse, very sore arse. If one more bloke calls me lucky I'll … not do anything, because I can't. And I'm screaming all over my skin to get out of here. You get too good a view of the war from this place: this isn't a proper hospital, it's a field hospital set up in a big old mansion, one step up from a clearing station really: fix them up and shift them off back to the front or to some other more pleasant place to convalesce, without the sounds of aeroplane engines and occasional distant shelling to cheer you up, and some poor bastard yelling somewhere, sometimes right next to me. I'm stuck here: Not To Be Moved. Unless for X-rays and manipulation, and I'm not allowed to be awake for the excitement of that: just the extra kick of pain when I come to again. Doctor's Pet, I am: he's very pleased with himself. Despite the cramps that sometimes make me want to cut my leg off, cut both of them off I'm that sick of looking at them, bone and muscle are floating around at his command when he blows in and blows out again with doctor mates to demonstrate his miracle *double abduction* splint that's apparently successfully stopped a piece of my hip from floating away altogether. His name is Lieutenant Lovejoy, of all things, he's a very English gentleman, and he says to me today, like he's talking about the mail: 'It won't be long now, we'll get you down and in a full cast and you'll be more comfortable.' Can't wait for that. My arm has been in a full cast all this time too, and the razor's still at work on my elbow in there. But you don't make complaints: you're too grateful that you're alive and being looked after. You grin and bear it, or just bear it. Try to.

Through the daily routine, most of which I am exempt from, except for being washed at four am, temperature taken at five, breakfast at nine and then dressing. I find this fascinating. There's hardly any of me that can be dressed, but come eleven am, nurse is there to get a blue hospital shirt on me. Why? Well, in case the King walks in unannounced. As likely as me escaping. Never mind that it's completely unnecessary, it bloody well hurts. Then, after dressing, it's lunch at one, and absolutely fucking nothing until five, when nurse comes and takes my shirt off. Jesus. I try not to be rude to the nurses, they're only doing what they're told and trying to get everything done, but sometimes I can't help it. Some blokes don't even bother trying: come lights on at four they tell them to bugger off: that's why they pen the animals separately.

Today, I can't help it. I look at her walking towards me; tiny little thing, she is, and I say: 'No. I don't want a shirt.'

She says: 'Please don't argue, sir.' Firm with her sharp Scots accent, but I think she'd rather move on to the next pain in the arse.

I say: 'You're not putting it on me.'

'Yes, I am. Or would you rather Matron sort you out?'

'Can't you just leave it today?'

'No. It's only a shirt. What on earth is the problem?'

I tell her, finally: 'It hurts.'

'What do you mean it hurts?'

'It hurts my arm, when you lift it. All the time.'

Horrified: 'Why haven't you said anything before today?'

Good question; maybe I don't know what pain is worth mentioning. 'I don't know, but I'm saying it now.'

'Right.' And she leaves me be, thank you.

But no thank you when Lovejoy returns and shears the cast off to have a look: I just about hit the roof with it.

'This is no good,' he says.

Is that right? You could have done me a favour and knocked me out for this one.

'It'll have to be redone.'

Meaning?

'It's not setting correctly. Needs surgery. But not here.'

Why not? He doesn't say. Says something under his breath instead about some 'damn fool', knocks me out for another X-ray and puts another cast on it. 'This should be more comfortable,' he says when I come to. And it is; he's changed the angle of my elbow from ninety degrees to a hundred and twenty and it's amazing what a difference those thirty degrees make. Even better, he says to my nurse: 'You're not to dress Sergeant Ackerman unless he specifically asks you to.'

'Yes, Doctor,' she says, but you should see the look she shoots him behind his back as she walks away: she hates his guts. Who'd be a nurse? None of this is her fault.

He's about to walk away too, but he stops and says to me: 'How you bearing up, generally?'

How do you reckon? Happy as Larry. 'All right, I suppose.'

He says again: 'Won't be long now, we'll get you down from the traction. You'll feel better with your legs on the bed.'

No I won't. I'm not going to feel better until I leave here. This afternoon I watch a very unlucky bloke dying of septicaemia across the other side of the room. All doctors too busy with a full load of new casualties, too many holes to patch and amputations to do today; and nothing you can do for blood poisoning anyway, apart from a shot of too much morphia, which is in short supply at the moment and can't be wasted on him. Please, someone shoot him. But nurses don't carry guns; there's probably a very good reason for that.

I go for days at a time without really speaking now. I am lucky, I am lucky, I am lucky. Doesn't help.

Bloke in the bed next to mine, congratulating himself at only losing three fingers on his trigger hand, says to me today: 'What's the thing you want the most right now, ay?' Leery, cheery, sliding his eyes over the backside of my main nurse. Her name's Sister Taylor, or Pam to me, and she's got enough to put up with herself.

I say to him: 'To piss standing up, without her assistance.' Fuck off.

And the rest. I want to go home, to be with France, to see my child. I want to stop having the dreams every night, and sometimes any time while I'm just staring at the ceiling, not looking at my stupid legs, up through the bars of my own very special little cage, or out the window over the other side of the room, and I only glance at that to see that it's still daylight, because every time I do I think I can see the flash of mortar fire under the rain clouds. Lovejoy wants me to have some brew or other to help me sleep, while I'm still waiting to be *got down*, but I'm not having it. Dad would agree: you have to work these things out yourself. You can't fight fear with anything except yourself. It's just fear and horror and not understanding why I am so bloody lucky that is giving me the joes. I'm smart enough to know that. It's only come on because I'm not in so much pain any more, and I don't have anything better to do. It'll pass.

Someone else starts nattering on about Our Little Aussie Digger, Billy Hughes, and how he saw him when he passed through the front, on prime-ministerial tour, saying the whole country was behind us, more Aussie troops on the way. I'm not impressed; but I'd like to have a word with Hughes right now and let him know all about the big parade in here. I remember reading something ages ago, before I left home, about his objections to Australia sending troops to that Boer War, once upon a time, when he was a New South Wales Solidarity Labor Party MP and president of the Waterside Workers' Union, before he was anywhere near the top job; doesn't have any objection now, does he. Little Brit Shit when it suits. Have to try to keep that opinion to myself around here, though: everyone thinks he's marvellous, putting Australia on the map, like it wasn't a whole fucking continent before he lobbed in it.

Mouth firmly shut, all I can do is read, which is something that I've not been known to do at great length. I now have far too good an understanding of the hundred per cent arsewipe that entertains people: fantasies of triumph and tragedy and love and chums forever, and sometimes just plain boring words strung along for no clear purpose. There's a boom in that industry in London, because they just keep coming. Stuff to get people to sleep by nine pm; doesn't work here. I can get stuck on a word like 'cupboard', like I've got chats come in my ear to get at my brain, and it'll keep me awake for hours wishing I couldn't read at all; wishing I could do a fucking tapestry cushion cover like the bloke on the other side of me; no I don't. Pam gets hold of copies of the magazines the Tommies are printing at the front — there's a few laughs in there; seems the officers of the BEF do a good line in sick humour on Shit River's Fluent Effluence and Serious Pointlessness when they are not being arseholes, better than *Aussie*'s We're A Lot of Larrikins Aren't We anyway, but that's only five minutes' worth and for obvious reasons there isn't a constant boom in that magazine industry. I want to draw. I know that I could get the pictures out of my nightmares and away into the light if I could draw. Or carve. Which only makes me think of Fucked Elbow, and the fact that I still can't move the fingers on my right hand very much: possible spanner in my plans for permanent good behaviour and doing what I should be doing, whenever I get out of here.

Which won't be soon. Full cast finally arrives for my lower half, and it is more comfortable too, sort of. It's an indescribable relief at first to not feel the stretch, like I just don't exist from the middle of my chest down. I'm floating in cotton wool for a day, on the biggest and best bed in the ward, before I can't believe I'm going to spend weeks like this. Six of them, at least. Not tied to the bed now, but cemented to it, with a pole holding my ankles a good two feet apart, and another holding my knees bent, reminding me not to get any ideas about going anywhere. Not in any pain at all, but already insane. I can hear Stratho laughing: *Got you good and plastered now.* Fuck off. How can it take that long? Lovejoy says, checking my toes: 'It can take as long as six months for a pelvic fracture such as yours to heal.' *What?* But I don't need telling again: smash up your hip and the top end of your leg by means of flying metal and things'll be grim, won't they. By all counts I should really be dead. 'But you're doing well, and your leg is in far better shape than expected. Count yourself lucky. I do think you should consider taking the sedative, though.'

No. It'll only be opium and brandy and I'm not spending weeks swallowing some rubbish dope old women have to take for their nerves. Pam has a go: 'There's no harm in trying it, is there?' But I'm not talking today.

She says: 'Well, let's get the covers up over you then.'

'No. Leave it.'

'It's chilly this morning.'

'Not inside this thing it's not.'

'Right.' She pulls the sheet up between my legs, to make me decent where I need to be, and says as she folds the blanket away: 'You know, you're a much more pleasant lad when you're not talking.'

She doesn't mean that, though; she's a good sort. She does whatever I ask her to do, but not on account of Lovejoy. A few weeks ago when the ward was cleared for cleaning, she tried to get me chatting, picked up my photos of Francine and said she looked far too sensible to belong to me, and I dropped my bundle right on her. I even told her how scared I was about what would happen if I couldn't walk. She told me not to be silly: Lieutenant Joyful might be an arrogant piece of work but he doesn't give false hope — wouldn't bother with me if I wasn't worth bothering; wouldn't have kept me here. I knew that, but still, he's also been careful not to say I will be able to walk, and after so long tied to the bed with your legs wasting away, you wonder. Wonder about an awful lot. She also said France was a lucky girl; don't know about that. *Glücklich, glücklich, glücklich.* Fuck that word.

She leaves me to my maggoty self now; I'm not the only prick she has to look after.

I get back to my letter from France. It arrived yesterday, and it's enormous. Thirty-seven pages filled with every detail of her and Little Danny: that she's sure he smiles when she says Daddy, that she's sure his eyes are going to be green, that he kicks and punches like he was born to it, that already he's nearly too big for his basket and all the clothes she made him; what Mum said about him, what Mim said when she came to visit, what the kids said, what Evan said. She describes the rolls of fat on him for half a page. On and on, and I could read it forever, except that she tells me she does this transport thing for injured veterans with her friend Louise, which sounds like it might come in handy for me if hopes are false and permanent damage is badly permanent, and that she thinks Mum has forgiven me for leaving now I'm safely out of action. Yep, hilarious. Almost as hilarious as the thought of Francine driving a motor car: she must be joking. She can't see two feet in front of her. She says nothing matters more than that I be well, and that not too well doesn't matter. She doesn't mention how she's really got on while I've been buggerising around for nothing and getting crippled. It's all cheery, cheery, cheery, and somehow not all of her. I want her to call me an arse, I want her to punch me in the chest and then kiss me. I want to touch her. I want her here. No I don't; I don't want her to see me like this. Instead, I've read her letter fifty-eight times since lunch yesterday, rationing myself.

Now this young woman appears over the top of the twenty-second page. I've been ignoring her the whole time she's been in here; she's not a nurse, lucky her, she's an odd little thing, a Red Cross volunteer, who's come in to help write letters for the incapable or the illiterate, cut hair, have a chat. She's a widow, I've overheard that. And she's here in the middle of nowhere not too far from the front lines in France, doing her bit for a spell. She's not frightened of diggers she's said; her husband was the hardest case; she got a round of laughs at that. She's upper crust, and there's a spill of Irish in her voice, *good heavens, absolutely*, laughing, laughing. It's too much.

She says to me: 'Oh dear, aren't you in a bother.'

Fuck off. At least she looks nothing like France: France is all slim, smooth lines and perfect red and white and blue, while this woman is blonde and plump, soft colours fading into each other, but she really is sweet. She has grey eyes, smiling at me.

I say: 'Hmn.'

She says: 'D'you want anything? Haircut, letter, bag of oranges for the show?'

I really do want to smile back but my face doesn't work.

'There's a band coming this afternoon, tea on the lawn et cetera. D'you want to see if we can get you outside?'

'No.' I nearly laugh. Do I really look fit for travel? More to the point, do I really look as if I'd like to be lifted onto a spine-bed and wheeled outside to listen to some shithouse military band that I'll be able to survive perfectly well from here? It's humiliating enough to have to have two strong orderlies lift me while the nurses change my bedding, and turn me over for a bit every other day.

'You could do with a haircut,' she says.

'No.' I can't help the Fuck Off in that. It's the last thing I want; I've just grown it back. My only achievement since I've been here. I'll get it trimmed another time, thank you.

She shrugs and floats away.

But she must have been a spy sent to inform a higher authority. Duncan's back the next day during a short leave, which for Australians means hanging about a very, very, very long way from home, playing endless games of two-up, drinking, praying, hunting down a chaplain of any denomination, or trying to talk to French girls, well not in Dunc's case, but all of them just waiting to go back to hell. He's not hanging about, though. He's come all the way here, as my CO, since I'm still in the army, to have a word with me.

Which is, first off, taking in the sight: 'God, you poor bastard. Won't bother asking.' Then he tells me he's mates with some mate of Lovejoy's and they've been chatting. He's also my mate and he needs to tell me: 'I'm sure you have your reasons, incomprehensible as they may be, but it's disturbing for others. Just take the sedative, to go to sleep at the appropriate time and not wake others up while you're at it.'

Apparently I am now at my most vocal when I am asleep. He adds: 'And your mutterings in German might be particularly upsetting for some. Note the sensitivity shown to you on this.'

Jesus; I had no idea and no one's said anything about it. All right.

'If you don't take it voluntarily, you'll get it in a needle.'

'All right.'

He looks at me like he'd rather be cleaning his toenails. 'I'm sorry.'

'What for?'

'Recruiting you, everything since.'

'I would have done it anyway.'

'Yes, you did do it anyway.' I can hear what It he's referring to, but we won't talk about that part of my behaviour; I don't ever want to remember some of my acts of stupidity, and there were quite a few of them. So he only says: 'You couldn't help yourself. In that regard, I'm glad you're hobbled now.'

'I'm glad you're glad.' Fuck off.

He laughs. 'Is there anything I can try to scrounge for you? Anything you're interested in that'll take your mind off it?'

No. But I say, half to get the reaction I'm after: 'I want something better to read, something highbrow to help the sedative along — politics, art, whatever. You know what I'm like.'

There it is: he rolls his eyes and gives me that chuckle. 'I'll see what I can do.'

Doesn't get around to it, though. Two weeks later I'm told he's dead. Shell right on target this time for Captain Richard Gregor Duncan. You really don't want to know what I'm like after that. Stratho's favourite term and I don't care who hears it.

Lots of sedative required. But not enough opium in it to cover the very serious pointlessness. Of the animals winning a piece of cracked dirt that used to be someone's home, of Fritz trying to take it back again now and flooding this place with Canadians. Of me, of hoping, anything. The world is still ending. The world needs a quick, clean bullet in the head and so do I. Hooroo.

FRANCINE

'Heard any more from him?' Evan asks me, but he's looking at Danny, leaning over his basket on the sofa in the parlour, tickling his toes.

'No,' I say and try for chipper, although I feel quite ill. 'I'm sure he's still getting through my last letter.' Which was about sixty pages or so, full of more inane twittering than the one before that, and I only posted it the day before yesterday.

It's mid-November, and I should have heard something more by now, from him, or of him. No pink telegram, no FURTHER ADVICE; nothing but a *bit bunged up, don't expect dancing, however it goes I'll compensate* and *look out*. The only thing I can work out for myself in that is the dancing bit: we've never been dancing so I wouldn't know if he could or not, but he's heavy-footed and slightly bow-legged so I don't imagine he'd have been much chop anyway. I've asked Doctor Nichols about bunged up and he suggested that the inventory of injuries was indeed fairly well bunged and that I was quite right to prepare for some sort of worst, but that Daniel's resilience should not be underestimated. As an illustration, he told me that when Daniel was seventeen he walked all the way from the Wattle, across town and up to the hospital with a huge deep burn to the inside of his leg that would have had most bellowing for mercy, and said to Mrs Moran: 'We've run out of iodine at the mine. Can I get some on this?' Mrs Moran said: 'Danny, what were you thinking walking such a distance with this?' And he replied: 'It hurt too much to ride my bike.' She took him straight to Doctor Nichols to have it properly cleaned and dressed, then he went back to work the next day, and it didn't even scar him. This was meant to help me rally? He's a tough one is our Daniel. But, so Sarah said, not as tough as his father. One thing I worked out quickly: we're not going to run out of iodine at the Wattle again.

Evan looks up at me now and says: 'He'll be all right, love. Too much to hurry home for.'

'Yes,' I say but it's a wispy weak sound that comes out of me. Doctor Nichols is the only one I've told about bunged up. I haven't had the heart to tell anyone else, especially not Sarah. I've only parroted the line: 'He says not to worry, just a few broken bones.' The look of utter relief on Sarah's face was enough to warn me off saying another thing, apart from: 'He sounds in very good spirits.'

'What is it, love? You don't look well,' says Evan. 'I can come back another time.'

'No,' I say. 'I'm fine, thank you. Just a little tired.' And tired is true: I'm trying to wean my little Danny some because he's wanting to be fed too much. Sarah said, from experience, that I'd better start putting him off sooner rather than later, unless I want to disappear; but it's hard to resist him, he's so lovely. I can lose hours and hours feeding him every day, imagining I'm sending off magic as I do. That's not why I feel so ill, though.

'Well, you could put down that tea tray, might help.' Evan's crinkled face smiles at me. He looks the toughest of the tough, till he smiles like that. And that only makes me feel worse. I haven't seen Daniel's smile for so long and now it even seems to have disappeared from my imagination. I've always been able to conjure it, even if only to give myself a fit, but now I can't find it except in his photograph. But I suppose that would be a feature of being heartsick, worried and preparing for the worst, wouldn't it. So put down the tray, Francy, before Evan thinks you really are ill.

And get your mind out of your own small world for five minutes to think of others. I'm not the only serviceman's wife left wondering, and, more immediately, there are coalminer's wives out there at the moment in a spot of bother.

I say, because Evan's not just come here to tickle Little Danny's toes: 'How much do you think would tide most over? Give me a total and I'll draw it out of the bank tomorrow.' We're in the midst of a coal strike, two weeks into it, and it's not looking like stopping soon. The dispute is over hours, over the owners wanting to increase shift times to increase their profits; thinly disguised avarice in the name of the war effort, if you ask me. There's no problem with hours at the Wattle, of course, but the men have to strike for solidarity, and every miner in New South Wales, Queensland and Victoria is on strike. Drummond is scarce with me, has been since I sent him packing over a year ago, but I've heard he's in Sydney right now lending his support to the capitalist cause: to force a relaxation of the regulations through parliament.

Evan says, aghast: 'Not taking your money, lass.'

'Why on earth not?' I can't take it out of the company account without Drummond's approval, and I doubt very much he's going to return from Sydney a converted philanthropist.

'That's Danny's money too,' Evan says, 'and you don't know if you might need it one day.'

Whack: if Daniel can't work when he comes home is what he means. Evan Lewis is not silly: he's a miner, he can guess at bunged up without my saying it; he's seen the fear of it written all over my face this afternoon anyway. And his consideration and love for his Danny makes me thankful I am sitting down now. But he is also not entirely aware of just how much money Daniel and I have: buckets and buckets, thousands of them. As I'm thinking how I might tactfully put that to him, he adds: 'You can't support more than a hundred and their families without asking him; I won't allow you to do that.'

Whack, whack: without my husband's approval. I want a fair bit more than my husband's approval. I want him to walk in here right now, call me dippy, and tell me what's what. Tell me he's all right.

I say: 'Well, what can I do then?' Hold a cake stall outside the trades hall? Bang some pots on the balcony of the Cosmopolitan Hotel?

'All I would like you to do is to see if you can't draw money from that compensation fund. Our money. But not for now, mind, just to see if it's possible, in case the strike goes on too long. We have our own funds for shortfalls, for those who need it, but inflation being as it is, I'm concerned we'll break the bank within the month.'

Inflation, yes, madness. Everyone everywhere is earning boom wages, but the cost of living is outrunning any gain. The price of coal could quadruple tomorrow and it'll only make me, and Daniel, richer: if the price of flour went up ten-fold it would make little difference to me, who's feeding two young women, me and Louise, and a baby, who's not up to bread yet; a fair few of the miners have six or more mouths to feed. As for *our money*, well, what's the difference? It all comes out of my share of the profits. I want to argue with Evan, but I say: 'All right.' I won't bother Messrs Stanley and Bragg with a request to find a loophole, though: if need be I'll just lie when I write to them and tell them someone else has died at the mine. I've done that four times now, for war widows; I'm sure my legal angels will think something is amiss, so many deaths and no official enquiries as to what might be killing the miners of Wattle Dell Colliery, but they haven't queried me. I'll make up a miner, kill him off, and ask for five hundred quid from the fund, then top up the kitty with my own money. Dippy.

Everything is. Whole country's gone mad and Billy the Troll PM is the maddest hatter at the party. He's got a new party, called the National Labor Party, after wrecking the old one over the conscription referendum, which failed, apparently because of our lack of patriotism. He's got a new best friend too, that *liberal, Free Trader, capitalist arse* Joe Cook, whom he's appointed Minister for the Navy. He's also got a War Precautions Act and he's not shy about using it: Billy and Joe have got government-contracted labour inside our coal mine right now, taking what coal is necessary for The National Interest, and the miners will bash up any *scab* they catch in town. Meanwhile, Billy is determined that we give more than our all for Blighty, who is still failing to free us from the evil scourge of Fritz, but has managed to this last Easter murder several Irish rebels in Dublin for wanting freedom for themselves. Really, is there a shred of sense in any of this? Coalminers are going for broke to protect what they should have by rights anyway; the Wobblies are resorting to random acts of arson and inciting riots against the imperialists; and 'socialism' is just about the most treasonous word around, not including 'trade union', 'Catholic' and the very worst: 'pacifist'.

And My Boy has sacrificed God only knows what for this madhouse?

I'm going to start hyperventilating now.

'Are you sure you're all right, love?'

No. A terrible, deep stab of dread drives into that soft centre of me. My heart is banging, belting in my chest and the room is spinning. But it passes just as quickly and I say: 'Yes, I'm all right.'

Evan says: 'No, I don't think you are. But you'll not do anyone any good if you let the worry make you sick.'

'How can I stop worrying?'

'Tell yourself that it'll be all right. You'll be all right and so will he. No point thinking otherwise.'

There's a circle, but it's true: keep believing that my wishes make a difference. A difference against this feeling that feels like knowledge that something is very, very wrong.

Evan winks: 'Prayers don't go astray either. Danny'll never know what chats we've been having with The Boss on his behalf.'

And that gets a feeble laugh from me: I'm sure Evan's entreaties to Our Lord have been a little less fanciful than mine.

Two more weeks sees the strike end. Miners win, for the preservation of their eight-hour shifts. Which I've since learned Billy the Troll, as a state parliamentarian, was instrumental in achieving in the first place. And I haven't had to lie and fiddle about with the accounts to take money from the company compensation fund, which no other mines have; I'm sure every other hole in the ground across the eastern states has worn down their own mutual funds to nothing too. Raise the fist. What a victory for the workers of Australia.

And I couldn't care less.

I've just received another slow white letter from Victoria Barracks, this one informing me that the award of Sgt D Ackerman's Distinguished Conduct Medal appears in the *London Gazette* at such and such a date.

I am livid.

I don't read the citation; can't. What I would like to know, all I would like to know, is very simple: how is my Sgt's health?

I leave Danny with Louise and let my fury take me all the way to the post office, not gathering any sense of obedience to AIF *IT BEING UNDERSTOOD*s along the way. Mr Symes is startled by my air of urgency but most helpful in putting me through. The line is very clear and the cretin on the other end tells me in the most officious tone: 'You must understand, Madam, that if no further report has been received, then it must be assumed your husband's progress is satisfactory. Please do not call again.' There's a click, then nothing.

I keep hold of my angry, preparing-for-the-worst tears long enough to pay for the call, and get out to the car. *Satisfactory?* What does that mean? Satisfactorily grave? Satisfactorily bunged up? Satisfactorily gazetted but otherwise vanished?

Not even in the front door and I unravel completely at Louise, and the only thing that stops my incoherent tirade is Danny's tears. Oh, this won't do, Francy. Won't do at all. Keep yourself in check, girl. If no further report is received you must assume that you're to keep wishing and not upset your child while you're at it.

Louise says, so simply: 'It's not a sin to be angry, Francine. It's probably a good thing to let it go once in a while.'

'You never do,' I tell her, and she's got more reason for anger than I do.

'Maybe I'm just more quiet about it,' she says, then smiles with the gentlest tisky glint: 'Maybe I won't be quiet about it if I miss my train.'

Oh good heavens! She's got to be on the afternoon train to be in Sydney first thing tomorrow for an interview: she's determined to become a nurse and has applied for a training position. Then shame stings: Louise has every reason to rage at the world, but instead she's decided to rejoin it, alone. About time for me to do that too, or I will make myself sick.

First opportunity comes a few days later driving out to Bathurst with a Mr and Mrs Henderson and they are just the motor start

I need, and also provide, according to my sage mother-in-law, the perfect excuse to spend a day away from Danny so I stop indulging his appetite at the expense of my own flesh, which really is diminishing alarmingly.

The Hendersons are cards, chipper to the enth, and have me in stitches from the first, despite myself. Stan Henderson is twenty-five, wickedly handsome as they come; he's lost a leg and the hearing in one ear and when he has a bit of difficulty negotiating his way around the car door he says: 'Don't worry about me, love, never had a great sense of balance to begin with.' His wife Lilly says: 'Don't listen to him — the only great thing he's ever had in his life is me, and I'm the fool who married him — and that was *after* he came home.'

We're just jaunting, going to the Big Shops so that Lilly can look at the wider selection of dress fabrics, wants to make herself a new skirt for Christmas, and we'll have lunch in a teashop while Stan meets up with some cobbers at the pub to do some further work on his balance. I've met them not through Father Hurley this time, but through the district's veterans' league, which exists now that enough of Those Who Help Themselves have returned to help each other in lieu of what they're owed: help, housing, jobs.

But betrayal is the furthest thing from their minds and mine, and Lilly is giggling away at something Stan has just said about the cows by the roadside as we near Bathurst, when all of a sudden I'm washed over by dread again. Head spinning, heart pounding, I have to pull the car up. In my mind I can see Little Danny in his basket at Sarah's and I have to get home to be with him. I'm utterly terrified, but have no reason to be. I wasn't even thinking of Daniel, for once, but something is wronger than wrong with him, with me.

Lilly says: 'What's up, love, are you all right?'

It passes. Of course I am all right.

No I'm not. I put my head on the steering wheel and lose it spectacularly. Breast milk pours out into the padding of my corset — *Deo gratia* for new and improved feminine undergarments for nursing mothers. I can't stop it all pouring out of everywhere.

Lilly gets out of the car and comes round to the side of me. 'Shhhh. It's all right.'

No it's not. Nothing's ever going to be right again. Can't tell Lilly that — doubt she'd believe me anyway. I force a laugh out and tell her: 'I'm just missing my husband. Just jealous listening to you two talk.'

'Ohhh,' she says, tears quick and real for me.

Stan reaches over and pats me on the back. 'Let's just go home, love — we'll go another day.'

'Not on your life,' I turn around and tell him. 'I should not be left unsupervised today.' I can't let these people down because of my overactive imagination.

Stan says: 'Fair enough.' But best of all he laughs right at me for the fool I am.

Then I ask him, I suppose just to know some small thing against everything I can't know: 'What's a Distinguished Conduct Medal?'

'Ah-ha. Your lad got one?'

'Apparently. What does it mean?'

'Who knows, but I can tell you this: you get a Military Medal for not losing your lunch, but you get a DCM for asking what's for dinner.'

'Oh Stanley!' says Lilly. 'What a horrible thing to say.'

But he ignores her. 'Means your lad's got a screw loose or two, and you probably should be proud of him.'

'Have you got one?' I ask him. 'I mean a medal, not a screw loose.'

'No. You get nothing at all for being shot before breakfast, but I've probably got more than two loose screws.'

'You should get a very big medal just for making me laugh,' I say.

But Stan just wants a very big beer instead, and I'll need a ladies room shortly to deal with the sticky mess under my blouse.

A few hours later it's time to head back, Lilly's chastising Stan outside the pub for becoming so pie-eyed in so short a time, and my breasts have calcified to rock, they're so full. I'll leave Lilly to wrestle her Stan into the car, while I stop in on Miriam, who only lives around the corner. I was looking forward to that when we set out this morning, but now I don't want to hear: 'Heard any more from that hopeless little brother of mine?' First thing she says as she opens the door of her big terrace house.

'No.' Immediately aching, leaking heart and breasts.

She waves away my angst in her effusive, jovial way, then says, archly: 'I'll bet money that he's only feeling sorry for himself, Francine. He's a big sook, really. You'll see.'

'How's Roy?' I ask her, automatically, because I'm lost again in wondering what awful thing Daniel must be feeling sorry about, what awful dinner he must have eaten to get that medal.

'No idea,' says Mim as a shrieky squabble erupts from the children inside. 'Wherever he is, it's probably quieter than here. Last letter, he was fixing the boilers at some hospital in Belgium — what an adventure! Chippy goes abroad to learn how to tinker.'

She's so buoyant, vivacious, nothing like her big tough sook little brother; and now she's pulling a face at me and waving at her chest.

I look down at my own: soaked right through. She hurls me a cardigan to cover it up. 'You'd better make tracks for home, before you explode.'

★

January. I haven't exploded or disappeared and Little Danny loves his mashed potatoes, what a surprise. And I haven't had a thump-spin morbid moment for a few weeks. Still haven't heard from Daniel either. But I'm doing a good line in acceptance: whatever's happened to him, it's too awful for words. It's even crossed my mind that perhaps he doesn't want to come home. That happens sometimes, doesn't it? Possibilities endless. I'll leave it one more week before writing to the Red Cross; add my little plea to the thousands of others: *To whom it may concern, I wish to make an enquiry as to my husband's state of gravity …*

I must concentrate on what I am doing, though: almost removed my thumb with the paring knife just now. I'm making a special dinner for Louise: a farewell one. She won her training position, and she's going off on her adventure tomorrow.

She's in her room now, packing. And I am not going to blubber at the wrench that's coming. It's something to celebrate for her, and celebrate I will. Celebrate her courage and her plain ambition: she wants to be a *headcase* nurse eventually, psychiatry I think it's called; she'll probably know more about all that than the doctors. Her Paul might have been ignored, but I have a good suspicion that she won't allow herself to be.

Knock on the front door: signal for Francy to drop whatever she's doing and race up the hall hoping it's mail.

And it is mail, except Mr Symes is holding it; Odysseus's prow powering across the valley behind him. I'm about to have a morbid moment, thinking he's brought a special salvo from the AIF. But Mr Symes is smiling. Never seen that before. He says: 'I recognised the scrawl — must be from your fella. Hope it's good news. Leave you to it, then.'

Breathe: 'Thank you.'

I look at it for a moment. It's Daniel's scrawly hand on the front, very scrawly. Very deep breath. Open it.

It says, in writing that's mostly barely legible, even for him:

My France

Sorry I haven't written, but I've not been very good company for a spell, and not a lot I wanted to share with you or anyone I might have got to write for me. Thanks for all your letters, stopped me going all the way round the bend. You should be proud to know that I'm famous over here for having spent almost as much time in bed being a pain than in active service. Well deserved too. Lately I've been busy learning what legs are for, slow going, but I'm getting there. I'm in London now, can't wait to see the place where the big decisions are made when I'm allowed out to practise walking around it. My arm is no good, though, managed to do a very good job of wrecking my elbow. Explains worse writing than usual. There's a quack here who is going to have a look at the damage, but it's a doubtful cause. You might get a bill from him if he has a go. Can say that I'll be on one of the next ships home. You'll get word from AIF, I suppose. But please don't bother coming to Sydney, you probably won't want to anyway. I want to make my own way home and see you there, nowhere else, not ever again. Just you and the kid. Mum and everyone else can wait in line till I find a way to forgive myself. I'm so sorry, France. I love you more than ever, but I don't know that there's too much to love about me.

x Daniel

Oh dear. I know this voice, as well as if I can hear it. Tight-jawed, morose, fierce.

First rush of thought: I won't take this nonsense from you. *Not ever again.* There was I worried I wouldn't recognise you. Ha! And you've got two legs, which you walk on.

Second rush: scream with joy.

Louise runs into the hall. 'What?'

Wave letter.

'Oh! How is he then?'

'Sounds terrible! Two legs, no good elbow. Wonderful!'

Third rush: oh dear God, maybe he's on his way home right now. I've had no *word* from the AIF, so telephone call needs to be made, and I'll camp in the post office armed with Sgt's name, rank and serial number and one serious demand, and I'll keep calling till they tell me which ship he's on. As if I wouldn't.

In any event, he's not going to get away with his lone-dog act this time.

DANIEL

If I thought Egyptians were small and scrappy that's only because I'd never been to London. Anyone who says Australia is the arse end of the world hasn't been to London either. I know I'm still *melancholy*, very, but this is the saddest place I've seen. Full of people pretending to cope, cracking hardy hard as, with a smile, a wave, a joke, got a smoke, but please, Fritz, don't bomb the Palladium or we'll be really unhappy. The French just shrug and look tired of it all as they starve and watch whole chunks of their country being razed; I could understand them better, without a word of the language, except for Frogs' reluctance for shaving and preference for long hair — why would you do that to yourself deliberately when you're living in a trench? It's an eye-opener being here, though, in this Old Dart, this great imperial capital. Does something to confuse my anger to see it: seems Blighty's own are copping it worse than anyone else, and I'm not sure how much that's got to do with the war. Even if things are bad at home, at least you've got the sun, and colour, to remind you that you are actually alive. Here, it's all little grey shapes in the fog, all of them looking like they need a good long feed. Something must happen when they come and live in Australia that suddenly makes them grow; I know they've got food shortages here, but I don't think you can shrink the overall height of a population by that much in a couple of years, even after culling all the tall ones. I know they've got goods shortages here too, but it took half of yesterday to find someone who could sell me a toothbrush: I don't think Londoners believe in that sort of thing; might make their cheery smiles more convincing if they did. And I love the cold, I really do. I love the sleet and the snow and the wind that comes up through the gully at home, but here, although it's colder by far, it's more than cold: it's dismal and filthy, miles and miles of dismal filth around a stinking wide grey river. Not pleasant for creaky bones either, the damp sinks right into you. They should put opium in the drinking water. Maybe they do.

Us animals are certainly popular here, though, at least among young females. We're the only ones with money, with our six bob a day rattling in our pockets, and a bit extra these days in my case. If another girl looks at me with half-starved eyes, I'm just going to give her the bloody money. My hand's always in my pocket anyway, since that's about the position my arm seems to prefer, even when I take off the brace I have to wear on it so it doesn't get any further beyond repair. I can hear Stratho laughing when the skirts look at me — it's not funny. I've got to go and see this other quack tomorrow, but today, to torture myself, since that's what I am best at at the minute, I'm going to pay a visit to the National Gallery in Trafalgar Square. I've never stepped inside an art gallery, and I suppose it's time to see what I should see. I still don't know anything about anything; didn't get around to further reading, since I fell down that hole full of sedative. When I first caught sight of my legs again I didn't think I'd ever be able to do without it; they were just bones, so stripped of flesh that I could feel the lump of bone under the scar where my right leg had healed. Pam told me before she said farewell: 'You might not think you'll be getting up on them, but stranger things have happened.' She was right: five minutes in the convalescent hospital here in London and they strapped me into calipers; best way to convince a bloke: no chance I was going home wearing that lot. They still feel strange, though, different, like they're not quite my legs. They do the job as well as anyone's now, and I don't even limp, not really; there's just half an inch of extra leather on the sole of my right boot to even me up a bit, and I don't know why it doesn't feel right, this *ambulation*. They do the job, they do the job, they're doing it right now, and here's Lord Nelson, pigeons shitting on him through the fog.

Grand façade across the way, flash foyer inside, halls decked with paintings and paintings and paintings and some more paintings; must be in the right place. They're mostly portraits of this noble personage or that, or some bloody religious scene, or a classical one which I reckon they must have gone for as an excuse to paint people in the altogether. Couldn't care less about how old some of them are. None of it says anything to me. Maybe it's not for me anyway. Don't know what I'm going to do when I get home. Read? Something left-handed? I've tried to draw, but it's no good. Whatever's gone on inside my elbow makes my hand shake when I hold a pencil, makes writing an athletic event: I have to take off the brace and sit on the floor to do it, foot holding the paper, while my left hand holds my right wrist to keep it steady, and I've got to put my shoulder into it to keep the whole scrawny, scrammy, crooked thing in motion. I'm not really stewing about it, or trying hard not to; it's a case of not missing what you never really had, I suppose. Still, I more than hope it's fixable. Either way, I'm sure I'll get what I deserve: seem to have all round so far.

'Magnificent, isn't it,' says this bloke standing next to me.

I look at him: he's balding, overfed and puffed-out middle class. Then I look at what he's looking at, what I've been standing in front of for who knows how long without seeing it. Don't know who the artist is, why would I, but it's a massive painting of a battle scene, gilt-framed, with far too little shit and mutilation in it. I look at the plaque that tells me this is *The Battle of Hanau*, 1813, painted in 1824 by Horace Vernet. French and Germans at each other near Frankfurt during Napoleon's shot at imperial idiocy.

I look back at the bloke and say: 'No. That's rubbish.'

A huge laugh tears out of him and echoes. Then he says, very seriously: 'You fellows are doing a marvellous job.' He means Australians; he can see what I am by my brand-new uniform, and the rest.

He goes to shake my hand, but changes his mind when he sees the brace; he says: 'Oh, I am sorry, dear boy.'

I say: 'I'm not.'

And I'm not. The good oil's finally dropped a load on me. Just like that. I know now what I want to do, and I'll teach myself to do it left-handed if I have to. I am alive. I couldn't count my blessings if I tried. Wish I hadn't written that dismal letter to France, though. I want to see her as soon as I step off the ship. Too late now. Too bad.

I tell him: 'I'm going home soon.'

He says: 'Well, good luck to you.'

I salute him with my left hand as I leave: I don't need any more luck. Had buckets of it already. I really am an arse. And cheers to that too. I've done my *penance* and she will have me *pure*. This time. Just don't fucking sink my ship, Fritz. *Bitte.*

Doctor Myer is about a hundred and two and talks like he's got to get it all said before his final moment. So far he's told me that he's really a Mr, rather than a Dr, because that's what you call them from the Royal College, but I can call him doctor because he grants it's easier, should all be called Dr, save confusion; and he's told me that his son's a surgeon too, and is working in France, knows the chap who did that *splendid* job on my leg and hip, which I know, because it was a letter from Lovejoy that got me in to see this bloke here at his private surgery, inside this old stone building that stinks of Lysol and centuries of rats' piss. Advantage of being Doctor Joyful's melancholy miracle pet with own funds at home: he visited me when he came back to London on leave to check on his *splendid job*, and when he found out that the surgeon who came to see me at the convalescent hospital had said my arm was a no-goer, he sorted this appointment out for me with Mister Doctor Myer, who's still rabbiting on now.

'… I've always said that such splinting is a life-preserver, invented by a Welshman, you know, half a century ago, and it's taken two years to get it to the battlefield. Shame. Shame there's so often so little time for more than mere preservation, especially in the orthopaedic field, lots of messy work going on there, and too much sepsis to contend with, but can't be helped …' All I want to know is if he can help me, but he's saying: 'It's been very interesting for me, however, looking at the mess brought back. There'll be leaps and bounds come out of this when it's all over.' He has a chuckle at his funny. Good for him. He finally sees I'm a bit beyond it and says: 'Yes, well, let's have a look then.'

Under the X-ray in the room next to his office. 'Hmmm.'

Prodding, twisting. 'Hmmm.'

Well?

'Hmmm.'

Well?

'Hmmm.'

What?

'Yes, well, there are two problems here. Very unfortunate for you, very interesting for me. Not surprised there's been a baulk at the challenge.' And he's off after a rabbit again, telling me about the four different places that broke and how; but he pulls himself up: 'In ordinary English I'd have to reset all three bones in your arm to attempt to restore any reasonable function to your elbow;

or in other words, your elbow is simply not in the right place. But to do that all at once would be impossible, even for me. The wonder is that it ever healed at all without surgical intervention. What I suggest is that for the moment we look only at the second problem, which is how this affects the function of your hand. This is the worst of it for you, yes?'

'Yes.' Bloody oath.

'Well then, let's see if I can't do something about that, restore some movement, improve your grip. No promises. But I can't make it much worse, hmmm?'

Hmn. Just bloody do it. 'When can you do it? I've got to leave in a few weeks.'

'Leave? Oh no.'

Oh no? Just bloody do it. I'm already on a ship and I have to leave. I have to get home. Please. 'Please.' I've never begged in my life before, except with France, but there you have it.

'Hmmm,' he says. 'Do you have a doctor at home?'

'Yes.' Quack Nichols.

'Is he attached to a hospital?'

'Yes, Lithgow.' Backyard job. Well, no that's not true, but I'm fairly properly certain that he won't know how to fix me up this time. This Myer bloke obviously does this day in day out, probably for the last hundred years. He has to do it for me. I tell him: 'His name's Doctor Nichols, he's fixed bones before, and mine.' Still begging.

'Hmmm, never heard of him,' says Myer. I'm sure you wouldn't have, I'm thinking; glad you haven't since I now recall he started his professional life as a vet.

And another: 'Hmmm.' And then: 'I'll have to give him instructions … the exercises you'll have to do later on … it's a rigmarole.' I'm a spanner in the works again. Please. And then he adds: 'It's important that I know how things go, you see, and that they go well. It's not just about your poor old elbow, it's about elbows in general. *Everyone*'s elbow.'

Fair enough. And I can't say how glad I am he cares so much about the subject. He's going to do it. Thank you. I tell him: 'I'll do anything you tell me to do.'

He squints and smiles, funny little old man, and says: 'Yes, you will, won't you.' He looks at his watch. 'Well, come on then.' Gets up off his chair.

'Now?'

'Why not? I've not got to be away today till four, plenty of time. You don't have anything better to do, do you?'

'No.' But don't you have other things to do? Apparently not. I follow him out of his room and down the hall.

He says as he's walking: 'We do it now, with any luck we'll have you out of the traction before you board your ship.'

Traction, on my arm. Good-o. Why not try all means of torture while I'm here? Rather not have the experience at sea.

I have to ask him: 'Shouldn't I let someone know where I am first?' I've been known to go AWL from convalescence a fair bit lately, but this is extreme.

'Nurse'll sort all that out later,' he says, as if nurse sorts out everything, and she probably does.

'Well, here we are,' he says, tapping the operating table. 'Get your kit off and hop up. I'll get my mallet and chisel.'

This is too strange; I don't know if he's joking. 'You are going to knock me out first, aren't you?'

He's looking at two heads, horrified. 'Of course. Don't know how it's done in the antipodes, but I'd have thought you'd have noticed we're civilised here.'

Yep. And I'm not sure if he knows that I was joking either.

He leaves to get whoever and whatever he needs, and I cross all the fingers I can. But I'm already thankful. I can hear Francine saying, *I've formed an unfortunate attachment*, and as the chloroform hits me the last thing I know is that I'm probably going to wake up with one.

Halfway home across the Indian Ocean and I haven't chucked once. Funny that. And it's not rowdy this time, in this floating infirmary. It's full of uncertain blokes, full of wondering. Who will be there, what will I find, what will I do, what have I done to myself; not that you hear it outright. I reckon it'd be fair to say that some are more scared going this way, especially those that have been mutilated, or stuck inside some other place in their heads, and I wonder who'd be more scared: those who've got a wife to face, or those who haven't got a hope of getting one now. It's just too sad, some of it, so sad you have to separate yourself from it. And you don't need to be told twice to steer clear of the big cage on C-deck where the proper nuts are fenced off from the rest of us. Keep your distance from pity, anger and shame, or take your sedative.

None for me thanks, I'll keep practising separation: my greatest skill to date. I'm aloof; here's cheers for the loofs. Practise being pleasant and civilised too. If I practise hard enough I might come out of this thing less of an idiot than I went in. You could put that on a recruitment poster: *IDIOTS! Let the AIF fix you up!* Quacks could bottle it: *WAR! Recommended for idiots. Contains fear, horror, pain, humiliation. Try it — you'll never look back.*

Be good if there was a cure against looking back. At least I'm a lot less gut-knotted, if nothing else, and the only bottle I want is the one that'll convince me to take a punt on myself. How hard can that be? I have a wife who loves me, and I love her; I have a kid I'm busting to see; I have money and a home, the best home in the best part of the best country in the world; I still don't know if I have a hand that works under the lump of cement that I'm told contains more than just the tops of my fingers, but even if it doesn't work I have no excuses. I've been entertaining myself with my attempts to draw a straight line left-handed: the results suggest that I've damaged my brain, but it's improving daily, sort of. And the only ache I have right now is that I didn't have enough of a brain to try to slip someone something to send France a telegram to tell her I want her there at the Quay: those two weeks in London with my arm tied to a five-pound weight have to be recorded as possibly the most blinding of the lot. Thank you, Doctor Myer. Thanks for the attempt anyway. Then it was straight to Southampton: who says women can't drive? The girl behind the wheel of that ambulance was either determined she get her load there on time or that she have us all killed, God bless her.

I don't know what France is going to see when she looks at me, and I separate myself from that thought; all I want to see is her. But if she could see me now, she'd see a bloke sitting outside on the top deck of a hospital ship getting sunburned again as we pass through the equator, and he's shoving a towel in his armpit to try to stop the sweat running down inside the cast. I'm sure I smell like a fish: very dead one. If she could read my mind, she'd see that I'm trying very hard not to think about torpedoes, and concentrating on trying not to look bored with the conversation going on around me.

I'm loafing about with three other sergeants and an infantry corp, all of us in various states of ticket-home disability. The sergeants are talking about who and what they saw in England and where they're from, their connections to Blighty, like a rope between home and the world and every stupid thing they've had to do to get back home. The corp is quiet; he's also been recommended for a Victoria Cross, which suggests he's been particularly, extremely stupid on the job. He's particularly fucked up too: he'll never make a move from the waist down again, that wheelchair's his to keep. And I wish I could job the next bloke I hear congratulating him on the recommendation. What poor form is that? As if it could ever compensate. Maybe that's the saddest streak through all this: permanent rank and honours. There's some poor blokes on this ship that actually call me sir — really, no guns blazing. That's not class confusion, Dunc: that's too bloody stupid for words. The AIF has ruined them for life. No, Blighty has: leave home with a healthy disrespect for authority; come home buried under the weight of it, lost in the fantasy of it. And these sergeants here, nattering on, talk like they *are* Brits. In my angrier moments, if I'd have said anything about it at all it would have been something like: 'Why don't you do me a favour and shut up.' But, practising being pleasant and civilised as I am, I choose instead to take the towel out of my armpit and fold it over the other way.

As I'm doing this, one of them says to me: 'So where're you from, Ackerman?'

'Lithgow,' I tell him. 'But I'm German really.' The goose in me just can't help himself at the minute. I've been wanting to say that to someone for months.

Silence. But the corp laughs.

I say to the sergeant: 'Fair dinkum. I'm a Hun. Not a drop of Brit in me.'

I mean it. More silence, except for the corp, who's still laughing. Sergeant says: 'Well, why'd you join up with the AIF then?' And I can see he's only confused; he doesn't hate Fritz any more, not with any conviction; we've all been round the block, heard the stories of good old Aussie lads finding a sudden ability to speak perfect Deutsch when confronted with the enemy; seen it all in our own special ways.

I say: 'Tell me and we'll both know.'

Laughs all round; good. But I do know the reason now. While it's true that I didn't want to sit on my arse at home and leave it all up to others, I also had something to prove, and it's proved: I'm Australian and I don't owe anyone anything any more. So there you go, Mum. Not a British subject any more, either; not where it counts. And there you go, Dad. Somehow I can hear even Robby giving me a slow round of applause from oblivion.

A little while later the sergeants have buggered off and it's just me and the corp. His name's Al Cash and he's got a suntan like an Abo. I say to him, and I am just taking the piss out of it: 'So now you going to tell me you've got a touch of the tar?'

He laughs; what I was after. 'No. I'm an Abdul.'

What? 'You're a Turk?'

'No. My name's Abdul. Abdul Kashir. My Dad's a Gippo from Toowoomba by way of Cairo, though my mum's Aussie.'

'Well, at least you're an ally,' I say; but there goes the VC probably, though I'm sure he'd rather have calipers instead.

He says: 'No ally. Just Abdul, mate.'

I'll pay that.

Sydney, for all the jabbering, really is something to see coming in. The heads of the harbour look like arms, wanting to hold you, draw you in, and the light here is like nothing else on earth I've seen. The difference between green and blue is so sharp and so soft at the same time, it's my whole mind. I can't believe I'm here. I know she won't be here, but I'm looking around for France in the crowd on the quay, trying to catch sight of her hair. Can't see her; doesn't matter. I'll catch the first train home and be there soon enough. Give me a few hours to find my legs again anyway. And I need to: I'm that relieved as my feet hit the dock, I'm almost crying.

I'm among the last of the walk-offs, and the place is jammed with wandering, and with a few reunions, most happy, some … I can hear tears, walk through them, I can't look at anyone. Can't look anywhere: there's that many Union Jacks flapping about you'd think we'd just arrived in England. No brass band today, though. I've got to get away from here, catch the tram to the station.

'Oi,' says some uniform at me. 'Cars to the hospital, this way.'

I shake my head at him, I'm not docking in with this lot, not even for five minutes; and he nods, smiles. 'Don't leave it too long or the Jacks'll come looking for you.'

The military police? What for? I hand him my pay book and my papers that say I am officially a cripple. 'You've got my address. Do me a favour, sort it out, will you?' The AIF can dock my pay for AWL till they work out I've discharged myself.

'All right, sir,' he says after another quick glance at my rank; but he's seen something else maybe: 'You do have somewhere in particular to go?'

'Yep. Thanks.'

I go and wait at the stop behind the quay, and I can't look at anything there either. In front of me, pinned to a telegraph pole, is a poster that says: *Will you fight now or wait for THIS?* showing a picture of Fritz, his helmeted grey men, invading the city, bayoneting women and kids. As if. I'm sure Fritz'd be hard pressed to take New Guinea back right now, and he's not shown an inclination for it either. On the next pole along is another poster, from Billy Hughes's New Beaut National Labor Party saying: *WIN THE WAR!* As if Australia can punch so far above its weight; but it does anyway; read the small print and wonder if it's a Fluent Effluence leg-pull: *Our soldiers have done great things. They have carved for Australia a niche in the Temple of the Immortals. Do your part in this greatest war of all time!* I decide to face the wall behind me, then see an even better one, an old paper poster, glued to the boards: a picture of a hooded woman stabbing an Anzac in the back, with a banner underneath saying: *The crime of those who vote NO!* To conscription, presumably. Evil nay-saying women. I remember telling France before I left that something had to give, and it has: reality, totally. Welcome home.

Suppose I'll have to practise diplomatic insubordination now, won't I, Dunc. Too many hearts hanging on Blighty's line, or being told to.

One heart's hanging particularly hard: there's a bloke not ten yards away, khaki melting against the wall so that I didn't see him straight off; he's holding a little sign that says, *Spare a bob for a blind Anzac down on his luck.* The A on the shoulder of his sleeve shows he was at Gallipoli. Not a lot of jabbering going on around him today. I put five shillings in his hand, 'Mate,' all I can get to at the minute without giving him my change for the tram, and I go back to waiting. I'd further expand my understanding of disgusting, but it's a bit too much to take in.

It's a real February stinker, and I'm melting too. I put my kit down and frig around trying to shake my tunic off, when I hear: 'You need a hand, cobber?'

I already know who it is before I turn around and see her. Just can't tell you.

FRANCINE

After I've let him go enough to draw breath, he says: 'Jesus, France, what have you done to your hair?' His hand searching for it, pushing my hat away.

'Don't you like it? It'll be the height of fashion one day.'

Kiss him again and he's laughing against my cheek: the first time I've heard it in an eon, feeling it.

'Hello,' he says.

'Hello.'

Every nerve in me is singing; I have to touch him and touch him, my hands around his too-thin face, on the tips of my toes, my face against his face. Some old Dame Wowser passes us and mutters: 'Disgraceful.' Pity to think she's referring to us, not the poor fellow against the wall. As I was walking, no, fairly running along the back of the quay, thinking I was too late, having miscalculated how long it would take to drive to Sydney and how quickly they'd all disembark — eleven am sharp I was told yesterday, and I know I got here at five past — I finally found the sense to ask the nearest policeman who said he thought they might have already left for the repatriation hospital in Randwick, which sent me into a sprint. Then a dead stop, when I saw him. Saw him approach Private Down on His Luck: I watched him for a moment as he went back to waiting. I had to take a moment to gather myself, get my bottle up. I'm determined not to be hysterical, but I am; it's coursing through me like electricity.

Tram comes and goes and I still haven't let him go. I have to keep touching him till I calm down. I do, a little. I can look into his eyes now without feeling I'm going to fall over. I can look at him properly and believe it.

He looks terrible. But he's so happy; nothing tight-jawed about him at all.

He shrugs his tunic off his shoulder as he says: 'Where's the kid?'

'At home waiting in line with your mum,' I tell him, looking at his poor cast-bound arm: good God, what are you doing at the tram stop on your own? Being Daniel. Who's helping you? Me: take his tunic, Francy.

He laughs again as I do. 'Sorry about that note. Good to see you didn't pay it too much attention.'

'Not taking any of that rubbish,' I say, but I would have. He looks a lot more than terrible: ten years older; I don't just look like a five-year-old now, I feel like one. 'Come on then, take you for a drive in my flash Cadillac.'

I lug his bag up off the ground. 'What have you got in here?' It's so heavy: what on earth were you thinking making your way home alone? Bet you'd have walked the five or so miles from Lithgow Station too, wouldn't you.

'Nothing I need any more,' he says. 'Just souvenirs.'

We start walking up Alfred Street to the corner of Pitt where I've left the car. He walks slowly, and I can see that his gait has changed somehow. I'm not going to cry, not today. I say: 'I've packed food for the trip home — didn't think you'd want to hang about here.' I also packed four tin cans of petrol and a carryall stuffed with a week's worth of essentials, just in case — I was a wreck heading out just before dawn this morning, as if I were making an expedition to Antarctica.

He just smiles at me. That smile, there it is. Don't cry.

'So how's no-good elbow?' I ask, not sure if I should but it's hanging there between us as we walk, all twenty-five pounds telegraphed remittance to extortionate London surgeon's worth of it.

'Don't know,' he says, as if I've just asked him the time of day. 'Find out in a couple of weeks.' He tells me about ancient Doctor Myer's brutal assault and that his own and Doctor Nichols's part in the war effort is now reduced to elbow's gift to medical science. Then he says: 'Whatever it is, it's all right, France.'

Something's shifted, and whatever it is, I believe him: it is all right.

Don't bloody cry.

'Very flash,' he says folding himself into the car, watching me watching him as I start the motor. 'Whoever made you did a proper job, didn't they.'

Can't respond. Crying now.

He says: 'Stop that. You won't be able to see the road at all.'

'Ha! That's what you think,' I tell him, getting out my specs and popping them on my nose.

He really, really belts out a laugh now; says: 'You look like a bloody bookkeeper.'

He's sprawled on the sofa, dozing, Little Danny asleep on his bare chest, small against his father, though he's eight months old and getting so hefty I'll be glad when he starts walking. All clean, all right. So all right I'm floating somewhere near the ceiling. All souvenirs are shoved in the back of the wardrobe, above the drawer that contains all other things we don't need to find unless we're looking. He's wearing his old trousers again; I told him they'd been very good company while he was away. Lunatic look: he loved that thought. As if he really has only been out for a very long jaunt. I'm happy to imagine that's the case for as long as he wants it that way.

I'm suddenly very tired, from concentrating on the road for the eleven-hour round trip no doubt; the mist at Blackheath and Mount Victoria was a challenge on the way back, and I hate that sweepy end of Bell's Line into Lithgow. He loved it; loved the whole trip home, looking about, taking everything in. Home. Home. Home. And look at my dippy France driving a motor car; every ten minutes he'd turn to me and laugh some more. It only hits me now what a ridiculously long and bumpy drive that was; had to be done, though: I wasn't going to share him with train passengers.

Sarah left a while ago, just before sunset, not long after we got in. The first thing she said to him when she let him go was: 'You smell like an old fish.' He does too. But then she held him by the face and said: 'It's finished now, isn't it.' Not a question. He said: 'Yep. I suppose so.' I don't know what she meant, and I'm not likely to ask at the moment, if ever; whatever, it's finished. As Sarah left, she said to me at the door: 'Now you can get on with your true life.' Then she held my face and kissed me before turning away and walking home alone through the gully. I think I can guess what she's doing now.

After that, Daniel played with The Kid, peek-a-boo, and let me count your toes, your belly button, and your four and a bit perfect tiny teeth, touch you. Matching pairs of eyes, matching marvel. Matching need for a good wash. Shock at hideous scar on his thigh dealt with here in our kitchen. It's an angry jag-edged backward S, that runs from just above his knee almost to his groin, and the muscle on the inside of his leg pulls slightly towards it; there's another small white dent of a scar above it, near his hip. 'Very attractive, isn't it,' he said, as if he should apologise for it. I told him, 'It looks an awful lot like a very fine leg to me,' and I put my hand on it as he was sitting there in the tub. But as I scrubbed his back I had to swallow the weep; not for the scars, but for the glaring pain they shout, and a sharp flare of desire in me to murder whoever caused it, followed by a wash of gratitude for whoever brought him back to me, so deep I will be saying automatic Hail Marys in my sleep tonight for them, decades and decades of them. For all of them: whoever patched you up, cared for you, nursed you, all those months, the cobbler who put the extra leather on the sole of your boot, and whoever tied your laces this morning on the ship.

And I don't need to be told he's still not too well. He's so very thin, and he's eaten so little today. Less than The Kid just now, and I'm impatient to make him well, for him to bulk up, as if that'll mean he's truly, truly back. But he just wanted to lie down with The Kid, who was getting mewly, who then collapsed in a little sprawly heap against his father's heartbeat, his father's voice saying, 'Settle down, you,' wedging his arm at the back of the sofa to keep it out of the way. And there they are. Partners in crime: unashamed bandits.

Daniel, half-open eyes, says: 'This is the second best day of my life.'

'What was the first?'

'Day I married you.'

Whack. Feet back on the floorboards. It almost hurts to hear that, does hurt, even though I know he loves me; I can feel it humming around the room. I walk over and prise Little Danny off him. Large hand tugs at my skirt: 'I meant what I said about behaving myself. I won't upset you again. Not like this anyway. Don't think your father would let me get away with it a second time.'

Suppression of urge to say: too damn right, darlingest. You arse. As all those months of wondering shiver through me.

I take Danny, sleeping, floppy, pouting angel, into my room, our room, and put him in his cot. Keeping an eye on gentleness.

On the completeness of our union. It's all right, all right. And Daniel is behind me, in the darkness, his hand at my waist.

I close my eyes and see the valley as we came in earlier today; not our valley, but Lithgow, black and seared around the edges, the sleeping women breathing in the poison, and I imagine the valley folding over the ugliness. Not by God's hand; something greater than that.

He whispers: 'I'm quite a bit more than sorry.'

I can feel it burning through his hand, through my skirt and into the skin at my hip. I believe him.

'I want to build a room off the back verandah,' he says, and that's what he's going to do. Doctor Nichols has removed smelly Thing and elbow is not exactly tiptop but Daniel is. His whole arm looks frail as glass; he can't straighten it right out, or bring it right in, but he can hold a pencil and roll his wrist. He's thrilled to bits. He says to me, fairly beaming: 'Don't worry, France; it might look a horror at the minute, but it'll get more meat on it with exercise.'

And now here he is, a month later, exercising on the roof of his creation, bolting on the tin. Resist the urge to say: 'For pity's sake, get down.' Because this is essential to good behaviour: Daniel's going to teach himself to paint in there.

A solo exercise, unlike the room, which saw Evan and at least half-a-dozen come round to help build it on Sundays. All 'G'day Danny' as if he'd never been away, except for Evan who, when he came round the morning after Daniel's return, said, right in front of me: 'You do anything like that again, boyo, and I will belt you.' Daniel said to him: 'I would have done it regardless.' Evan replied: 'I realise that. It was your sneaking off that cut me.' And for a blink Daniel looked about twelve, and belted. But now the room is finished, it's the only fragile thing about, with all its windows, flanking three sides to catch the north sun. One mustn't refer to it as a *studio*, however, because that might suggest *artistic endeavour*. Oh dear no: Daniel's going to *paint*. I don't know what the distinction is, but he's ordered in a truckload of supplies, so let's leave him to it.

It occurs to me that my darlingest is a very odd man, and possibly the most wonderful man that ever lived. Of course he is: he was hand-picked by the Leprechaun. And there's only one thing I want right now, apart from him to get down off the roof: I want to make love to him. He won't sleep in our bed, though; hasn't done since that first night home, and then he only kissed me before succumbing very thoroughly to unconsciousness. He sleeps in the spare room instead, says he has trouble sleeping and: 'I have to get some things out of my system first.' No trouble whatsoever kissing me whenever he gets the urge, and no idea of how terrible that makes the craving in me, but I'm not going to pry or push or resist a single kiss. I don't need to be told he's still not too well, regardless that he's bulked up quite a bit. Maybe he has a problem with all that; Dr Nichols did mumble something about *all manner of difficulties* associated with *pelvic trauma*, and if this is one, then that's all right; he can tell me when he's ready, or he can have me when he's ready: he can do whatever he damn well likes.

Evan says to me now: 'You won't get him down from there by looking at him, love. Why don't you make us a cup of tea?'

At the same moment Little Danny tries to launch himself off the edge of the verandah. I catch him up just in time and I laugh. My whole life is very odd. It's beautiful, just as it is. The world is dying, but you wouldn't know it here in this paradise.

'So I said to him, as everyone's heading up: *Why shouldn't you pay, maximum, for your loyal support of the war and the fact that we're making a fortune from it? I'm paying it too.'* Daniel's talking about today's confrontation with our business partner. Darlingest has taken to making random raids on the Wattle, having appointed himself Chief Spanner in the Works. The confrontation is over Daniel's suggestion that the men be paid for the time it takes to cavil out each quarter, a day's pay, four times a year, and Drummond has argued that the company can't afford it, not now that Billy the Troll has imposed a Commonwealth business tax to raise war revenue. Which, of course, is utter rot: the tax is negligible, and so's four days' pay.

'What did he say to that?' I ask him.

'Not a word, just walked away, drove off. He'll pay up.'

'How're you going to make him?'

'By embarrassment. He can't bring himself to say an outright no to me as it is; I'll wear him down.'

Daniel means by bullying, and he's enjoying it. He has a string of *suggestions* that he's going to work his way through methodically: he wants shot provided, he wants an on-site blacksmith and full pay for Christmas and Easter. As leverage he has the war veterans' card, Drummond's past taunts and an ability to appear dangerous despite no-good elbow. Evan's said that Robbenham, the manager, only gets called quickly in-pit for one reason: the sudden arrival of 'Our Danny' in the office, looking at the books, saying: 'Awch, manager's salary's a bit sharp, given these tough times, ay?' Our Danny who also only need look sideways to have the men down tools, but he wants to avoid them losing any pay over his game. They at least are finding his efforts entertaining, Evan most of all.

Whatever happened to him *over there* must have given him this confidence in his own authority, but so has the way he's been treated by his old union, I think: he wanted his membership reinstated, to give him some sort of official menace to flaunt at our partner and simply because he earned it and wanted it back, but they refused. Due to his conflict of interest as an employer, citing some objection from the eastern states federation. How truly gaga is that? He says they can go to blazes; he's only interested in the Wattle anyway and he'll take his own industrial action as it suits him.

My twenty-first birthday has come and gone, and I didn't bother asking Daniel if he wanted to sell our share to resolve his conflict of interest. He carved me a tiny jarrah key, so polished it looks like carnelian agate, and he said to me: 'Congratulations, France, you've earned your freedom; but unfortunately you still have to live with me. Forever.' Trillion times forever.

He's having too much of a lark. Mostly. We share a good laugh when the Troll declares the Wobblies illegal, *about bloody time, and as if that'll shut them up*, but it's not amusing a few weeks later when the state government tries its hand at tyranny. The railways commissioner tries to impose timecards on workers, which seems such a silly quibble, but virtually the whole of New South Wales goes out on strike in response: the whole state shuts down: hardly any food in the shops and we do live on a lot of potatoes and apples. It's not about timecards, though, it's about relentless inflation and pressure from bosses to work longer for less, for the war effort of course. Trade unionists are called the enemies of Britain and her Allies, and the outcry against these *revolutionaries* makes me think that unions are a breath away from being outlawed too. No talk of the facts: that people have simply had enough. Not a difficult two-and-two by any understanding. But this time the workers don't win; miners might be able to support each other through strikes, at the Wattle especially, after Daniel's fat cheque for mutual protection, and in Lithgow with the co-op store and Bracey's emporium doing everything to get what they can and give it cheaply, but most workers can't prepare at all:

they're starved and cowed within a month. It's not so much the scabs under police guard in our mine that upset Daniel, or that a few hundred miners in the Illawarra will not get their jobs back, it's that some poor fellow, a striker, in Sydney was shot dead by a 'volunteer' truck driver during a riot. He said, more to himself than me: 'Only been through a couple of big strikes, and no one died. The one my first year in, it was better than school holidays. Me and Jimmy … we had a good time,' and he stopped there, then he barely spoke, about anything, for two days.

It's things like this that tell me he's still not too well. And the fact he rides his bike or walks wherever he goes, avoiding the car and its tendency to backfire at the bottom of a hill. No prizes for guessing why, no need to pry. Just as I didn't when we had to miss our vote in the general election in May: Daniel just didn't happen to want to go into town that day: 'No point.' Hughes decreed that German Australians could not vote: they are behind union unrest and they are all spies, regardless of place of birth or citizenship, vague as that notion is. Held my tongue from quipping that it's bluster over nothing — after all, our most treacherous Hun *enemy disloyalist* Mr Edmund Resch, the infamous brewer of *Sydney's best*, is still safely interned at Liverpool 'concentration' camp, *concentrating* no doubt on the reinvigoration of Tooth & Co's KB lager as the state's ale of choice. Sarah defied the decree and voted *per worthless usual*, no one in town was going to stop her, but the Nationals were always going to win against the old Labor anyway. So said the papers. And thus it came to pass. And thus it all hurts My Boy and makes him silent sometimes.

It's times like these that make me want to tell him with my body that I love him, that nothing else matters but us and our paradise. It's mid-September now and he's been home nearly six months, and still he hasn't come to bed, and hasn't mentioned it at all. Sometimes he sleeps in the spare room, but more often he sleeps out in the *room* off the verandah. I can hear him rattling around out there at all hours, the light from the kerosene lamps reaching up the hall; I'm sure sometimes he doesn't sleep at all. I'm fairly bursting to know what he's up to, but he's told me, firmly, that he'll show me when he's finished. When I walk past, out to the orchard, I can see paper roll pinned up against the windowless wall and pencilled shapes strewn across it. Can't tell what it is. I can see some canvas on the floor, looks like he's been experimenting with colours; oils. I don't know what's making my skin ache more: waiting for him to come to bed, or waiting to see what this will be.

DANIEL

I worked out quickly that bullshit is the new religion of Australia, the fastest growing national movement, everywhere, and maybe strongest with those who should know better, do know better: answer the call, get yourself ruined, come home, to nothing, but still you're all for King and Country. Hand on your heart for the fallen in God's great war against evil. Evil what? Evil capitalism? Evil imperialism? Evil fucking flying metal? No: evil bloody Fritz. Who the fuck is Fritz when he's at home? No one knows, and no one gives a rat's. Neither do I, really, but Jesus. I understand it's important for these blokes to believe that they're suffering for something reasonable, but the truth would get them what they need quicker. And I can't criticise: I've got my own difficulties with the truth.

Which is why I've only been to one servicemen's get-together, for the medically unfit. Thought I'd see if I could help, even though I didn't want to go. I got a good earful about how marvellous my missus is, but that was followed by an hour or so of rubbish about the lack of heart in new recruits. While I was away, there was some mutiny by troops in Sydney over training hours or something, which got so out of hand that coppers had to bring in a few hundred returned men to help hose them down. Apparently they all walked off the job, rushed on the pubs and got very, very pissed; thousands of them: wrecked half the city, looting grog shops and even pulled apart Sydney Station.

One recruit killed, six wounded. The blokes who were telling me this were all pissed, probably have been fairly solidly since they returned. Then they said what a good thing this new six o'clock closing of the pubs is, put a brake on bad behaviour, as they sank back several more ales before the bar shut. Then they said that conscription would sort out the chokers: make them all go. I had to pull back very hard from saying: 'What? So if they make it home alive they can come here and sit on their arses needing to get as pissed as you?' Then they were so pissed they started talking about it: the things that happened that'll make them want to be pissed for life. Publican took pity and kept the bar open illegally. And I couldn't get away from them fast enough. Told them if they know anyone needing a job to come see me, if they remember tomorrow. I'm not going back for seconds. And no one's shown up at the Wattle asking for work so far, which is unsurprising in a way. I've realised one truth, as if I didn't know it: coalmining's not exactly at the top of most people's list of desired occupations, unless you're stupid, desperate, or born into it. You also need to be fit.

Just as well France is so marvellous, with her *jaunting* and helping them write letters lobbying the government. Lobbying Hughes, the soldiers' best mate, so long as you're not asking for anything. Without people like her that bother, these blokes would be completely buggered. She actually asked my permission to keep going with it; that winded me. After all the grief I've caused her, she doesn't want to do anything to upset me. She couldn't if she tried, and I'm a living miracle of bullshit in myself as I keep it all away from her. The truth is, I'm struggling with it, just about all the time. *How hard can it be?* I asked myself coming home. More than a bit hard. I have everything, plus too much I can't say, and can't do.

Despite my many conflicts of interest, back in April I did want to go to the Anzac service at the town hall, for my pretend birthday, and because I thought it might do me some good, to let a bit of it go, where it's expected. But I spent the night before doing nothing but remembering, so that by the time dawn came around I was too much of a headcase to go anywhere: spent the day in the cage. I couldn't have put that uniform back on anyway, and I couldn't have gone without it on either, not without being disrespectful. I can't even look in the bloody wardrobe at my kit. I've thought about burning the lot of it, but I can't do that either, because that would be the final act of bullshit: it didn't happen. Same reason I could never get rid of that ridiculous DCM: as much as I don't want to see it, and don't want to think about the reason for it, it was Dunc's last little word in my ear, received well after he choofed off for good. A gem of a piece of bullshit, if ever there was one. Still hobbled, couldn't have stood up without the calipers if you paid me, and I think it was the first time I'd laughed in a hundred million years, maybe since he brought me France's apple card with Danny's picture in it. Thanks, Dunc. For everything, and for allowing me to be one of possibly a very, very few to crack silly during a medal ceremony; I'm sure it was put down to my sedative consumption, but that wouldn't be the whole story, would it. Of course not. And how could I ever burn Fritz-Johan's little note? *I'm going to die today, and I want to be killed by an Australian.* That's a piece of national history, and it might well be the last written record of that kid's. And how could I ever burn my photos of France, and all her letters, and the jumper she made me that I never wore because I didn't want to get it dirty? I'd rather set fire to myself. But how could I ever say any of this, without lighting a fuse and blowing it all open?

That's exactly what I am trying to do out here in my cage off the verandah, though. Sorting out how to show what I can't say. I've never had a tooth pulled, but I think I can see where the term *like drawing teeth* comes from. Can't stop it, can't help myself. The further I go, the more I've got to drag out. Had thought at first I might just have a quiet go at this for a while and maybe try to convince myself to make an application to the Sydney Art School, I know France'd be thrilled if I did something like that, but things aren't working out that way. Of course not. And I'm not talking to anyone about any of the dippy rubbish going on in here. It's not the painting that's difficult; that comes so naturally it'd make you wonder what took me so long to catch on: it's … just get on with it.

Get on with it, and get back to what I should be doing. Being a proper husband to Francine, and a proper father to my son. Can't do that till I get rid of this: plain violent undiplomatic insubordination. Then I can leave it there and paint Francine for the rest of my life. Maybe one day even get a whole night's sleep. It's not just that I can't sleep, sometimes I don't want to, because I'm sure I'll carry on while I'm at it. It's better to pass out from the lack of it: then I don't dream. And I'm too buggered to go round to the Wattle, which is a good thing: the state I'm in at the minute I might have to be a very good boss and show Drummond what a prick I can be, rather than bother with breaking him down by slow degrees. It's probably a good thing Mum's out of town at the moment too: one less face asking me the question: *What* are *you doing, Daniel?* Mum's off in Bathurst, with Mim, who's having a fit because Roy's been injured. Not badly by the sounds of it, he's written to her, but my sister, as much as I love her, is hysterical, always, in a hundred different ways. When she came round straight after I got home, she said, 'Well, you look like you've been in the wars, don't you,' then she fussed all over me, 'hopeless little brother', telling the kids to shoo all day as if they might have broken my other arm from twenty yards if they weren't careful; I can see her fussing round her house now in a silly panic before there's a need to have one.

315

Francine doesn't fuss and she doesn't ask. She's peaceful and steady and she does bloody well everything, while I'm out here buggerising around. She's a legend, deserving recommendation. All women should get a prize for the amount of bullshit they're putting up with. Except for those like that Nellie Melba, blowing in to sing us all an *international* aria about how frightfully shoddy Australian women are for not making their men to go — I'd like to tar and feather her as Queen of the League of Bullshit. But I'm too busy, aren't I. Very busy trying to get the purple I'm after.

Knock on the door of my cage. 'Daniel?' I just about jump out of my skin. I'd very much like to stop doing that one day, since I know it's Francine. I look out the window and there she is, but with Nichols in tow.

I come outside, wondering what he wants on a Wednesday.

'How's the elbow then, Danny?' he says; wish he'd stop calling me that. Only Evan calls me Danny now; I don't mind feeling like a kid with him. But Nichols is very chuffed with himself these days, having taken instructions from eminent *orthopaedic* surgeon in London. God bless him.

'Good,' I tell him. And it is; I'm not about to throw a football or a grenade with any accuracy, or start hewing again, but it's a marvel of medical science as far as I'm concerned. It does the job.

He says, looking especially pleased: 'I've had a letter from Mr Myer in London.' He says the *Mr* and the *London* as if it's a scandal. 'He was very pleased with the way things went and my report on your progress.' Nichols took to exercising my hand with even more enthusiasm than I did, and made enough notes to write a book on The Elbow, even bought a brand-new X-ray machine to celebrate. And I couldn't be more grateful; grateful too that he sorted out my formal discharge from the army, after confirming with them that I am both physically disabled and neurasthenic, which means officially out of my mind, so they

316

wouldn't come looking; they didn't, just sent the paperwork, and a classical piece of arsewipe called Certificate of Service, thank you very much *CANCELLED* Sergeant D Ackerman, DCM. So my favourite quack's just come round to skite about my progress; that's all right, can't blame him.

No he hasn't. 'Mr Myer has suggested a surgeon in Sydney to do the further correction. And I've arranged it for you, for next month on the —'

'No,' I tell him. France shoots me a look to say I've just been *exceptionally* rude. I say: 'Thanks, but not now.'

He actually looks hurt as well as stunned. I add: 'Maybe later.'

'Later? You don't say *later* to a specialist surgeon in Sydney who's agreed to look at you. In the middle of a war, when he's got plenty of other things to do.'

'Sorry, but I am saying no.' I can't tell him why. Sorry, but I want to paint my nightmares and that might take a while; and sorry, but to be very truthful, I just don't want to have the mallet and chisel again. Not when there won't be a written guarantee that it won't turn out worse than it is now; and not since I've found out that chloroform and ether can kill you — I've heard X-rays can kill you too. Teeth pulling aside, I've come to appreciate the fact of my life and the function of my hand very much. I do owe the medical profession buckets, but no, someone else can play specimen for *everyone's elbow*. Besides, it's nearly summer, and I'm not going to spend a day of it wearing cement. Not wearing cement ever again.

France steps in with her better manners. 'Doctor Nichols, you've been so very kind, but I think we need to give it some consideration. Daniel will let you know soon.'

That the answer is no: not later, not maybe, but no.

He sighs: 'Well, you might have missed the boat by then, I'm afraid, Danny. The longer you leave it …'

So what.

He's off, shaking his head bemused. Too bad.

France says: 'Don't do anything you don't want to do.'

Don't worry, I won't. Not going to let you down now, France.

Second of November. Roy's dead. Mum's sent us a telegram from Bathurst. He'd said to Mim that it was just a nick to the back of his wrist. But it was obviously one nasty enough to go septic and kill him, slowly. He was somewhere in Zonnebeke and took the bullet sometime in early September. Just one of thousands on the Flanders Line doing a marvellous job of getting killed right now. I made the mistake of opening a paper last week: they reckon it's another Somme, already a quarter of a million Tommies gone; and it sounds like the AIF is having another Pozieres at some place called Passchendaele. Except, according to the report, it's really pissing down like there's no tomorrow. Anzacs expected to enjoy the challenge even more.

France is crying, holding the telegram, just quietly. She's crying because it's Mim's Roy, even though she'd only met him the once. She's crying because it's all too much, and it keeps going on and on. She's also crying because she had no choice but to come out and tell me this, even though I haven't been past the kitchen or spoken to her beyond the necessaries for the last five days. I've been busy being angry. I haven't been outright angry for a very long time, but I am very angry now. She's been giving me a wide berth and keeping Danny away from me, keeping anyone and everyone away. I wish I could tell her that this is the very last time I will ever be angry, that's a promise, that I'm just doing a very proper job of it.

I should go and see Mim, but I can't, not in this state. I doubt she'd recognise me anyway: I haven't slept and I haven't shaved or had a decent wash for the last five days either.

There's someone banging at the front door; France is wiping away her tears before she goes to answer it. Doesn't get a chance, though.

And into all this, right now, lobs Drummond. Here, in my backyard. He's obviously furious about something, and I just look at him as he says: 'This has gone beyond a joke, Ackerman.'

Couldn't agree more, but I've got no idea what he's talking about.

'You can't pretend you don't know anything about this.'

Why don't you tell me?

'Lewis has downed tools for your cavil-out pay for September, as if I need to tell you that.'

Has he? Good for Evan. I laugh at Drummond, not nicely. Evan wants the pay, of course, but I've an idea that he also wants me down at the Wattle, to resolve the issue and to get me out of myself. This is what's called poor timing. Or maybe perfect timing.

Drummond looks me up and down now. I know I'm covered in paint of every colour, and he can wonder if I'm barking. I hope he thinks I am. I hope he's wondering what I'm going to do. I certainly don't feel much like a pacifist right now and that's what's called irony, isn't it. And I'm an expert at irony today. I should belt him just for speaking to me like this in front of my wife; I should belt him for speaking like this in front of my wife who is very clearly upset, who is still holding a telegram from my mother that tells us my brother-in-law is dead. I won't test my left on him, though. I'm just sane enough to be mindful of the conflicts of interest here.

Instead I say: 'Well. Why don't you fuck off and pay them, you mean cunt.'

The horror on his face is only matched by the flame on France's. Drummond's horrified not at the sentiment but at my language. I crack it at this point. It's all right to murder millions and make money out of it, but we don't say fuck off cunt, do we. We're civilised here. Not me.

I say: 'Are you deaf?'

He's just standing there; France says to him, with her perfect manners: 'I think you had better go, Mr Drummond.'

He does, and he stalks off round the side of the house, but he'll do as he's told on this: no choice. Danny's wandered out to the verandah, and he starts to cry. His father is not a very pleasant chap. I can't look at him, not now, and I turn to go back inside my cage.

France says at my back: 'It's all right.' And she means it. And I know exactly how she means it. She's saying: get on with it, get rid of it. Luck takes on a new meaning for me. I'll go back inside and finish this mess, and I'll do it for her. Just her.

After all that, it's only three pictures: my Holy Trinity. One big one, of the Albert-Bapaume Road heading towards Pozieres, and two smaller ones: there's Madonna hanging over the road, and there's Fritz-Johan bringing Strath out of the hole as he turns to look back at me: *Das muss dir echt weh tun. Echt schlimm, ja?* Not any more. Not now. I know that I'm finished because I've just woken up from ten hours' straight sleep, and though I'm aching everywhere, I'm looking at the big one, which hurt the most, and I see: it's only a picture. There it is. Permanently there, and no more or less than all of the other pictures in my mind: sea, pyramids, Dunc cleaning his toes, corkscrews, my stupid legs. Don't have to get them out unless I particularly want to look at them. Won't get a ticket to any art school for them either, and I don't give a shit. I'm in control of myself, the whole machine, for the first time since … for the first time ever probably.

When I go back inside the house I wander around for a bit, looking at the things we have, so much rubbish; they're all just pictures too. I catch sight of myself in the mirror above the sideboard. Beard does not suit me; I look like a crook Frog. France is round at Mum's debriefing and sorting out how they're going to sell the house and Roy's business and move Mim and the kids back to Lithgow. She'll be a while yet, so I'll spend the rest of the day making myself respectable.

I don't want to draw or paint or carve another thing for ten years. I will, I know, but I've got other matters to attend to for a good long while. Wife, son, mother, sister, nieces and nephews, and even a brother somewhere — forgotten I had one of them. Life. The thought of touching Francine now, right now … like you wouldn't believe. Look out.

After I've shaved it all off and cut my hair a bit, I have another good look at myself. I look like me again. I look twenty-three. No wonder Dunc thought me special.

It's finished. Please.

FRANCINE

I stop when I hear it, as Danny and I are walking home through the gully. It's hot, and I'm tired and sad, scoured out, but Danny's not — to think I so desperately wanted him to walk once. Novelty's worn off, for me at least. Now that's all he wants to do; no: run. I am gripping him by the wrist to stop him from falling down the steep bank just before I can see the house. I can't take him out in the Cadillac any more: he won't sit still, wants to jump out of it, while it's moving. And he's worse in the trap; wants to ride Hayseed. He's been naughty all afternoon: I'm sure children pick up everything that we don't want them to understand and express their opinions in stubbornness, wriggling and the word 'no'. I'd smack him if he weren't so lovely otherwise. Or maybe it's simply because he's an Ackerman. They are all wicked. And adorable: even when they are called McKinnons, and especially when they are small and sane and live inside a house and don't look like a bushranger. My tether is stretched just a little too tight, and now, finally, it snaps.

Even Danny stops, looks up at me.

I say: 'That's Daddy. Playing the piano. Race you home.'

Didn't know if he could still play it. Must be able to, obviously. Does everything else with that arm that looks like it needs a good squirt of oil. I've still got hold of Danny, and his feet are fairly off the ground as I drag him along; but he doesn't mind. He's giggling at me as a tune I've not heard before floats across the valley.

322

Daniel's singing, in the fashion he does, when we clatter inside:

If you were the only girl in the world
And I were the only boy
Nothing else would matter in the world today
We could go on loving in the same old way
A garden of Eden just made for two
With nothing to mar our joy
I'd say such wonderful things to you
There'd be such wonderful things to do
If you were the only girl in the world
And I were the only boy …

'What's *that* song?' I ask him when he's finished. 'It's too sweet.'

He doesn't turn around; he's looking at the keys. 'Something I picked up in London.' He's laughing inside his voice. 'Could have been worse.'

There's no sheet music on the stand, must have memorised it; I say: 'Play something else.'

But he plays '*Funkel, funkel kleiner Stern*', double time, full chords, turns around and looks at me. Small smile. Good God.

He says: 'Did you sort things out for Mim?'

'Think so. And when Mim's ready to move, the boys will come and stay with us, and all the girls at your mum's.' Harry and Charlie are in the middle of the mix: nine and nearly seven. They need a man, and a firm hand, and I had thought they might bring Daniel out of himself a bit, or they'd be too terrified by him to misbehave. Seems there's no need to worry on that score now: he's back in the nick of time.

'Good,' he says, and the glint makes it plain that they will now all misbehave. I could not be more pleased or relieved. Timing is appalling for us as ever as we move Danny's cot into the spare room. I'm pulsing all over already and he hasn't even kissed me yet. Oh my goodness.

Speechless. Knew I would be, but if I imagined anything at all, it wasn't this. They are grotesque and sinister and transfixing, on the floor, where he painted them. Eviscerating might describe the large canvas, if I were searching for a euphemism for four square feet of … bodies and pieces of bodies of men and horses, mangled and torn and charred, coming into and out of grey mud, disaster stretching out forever under a red-purple sky. The perspective is shaped as though looking through a magnifying glass, the horizon rounded, distorting slightly at the edges. It's the world, somehow rolling forward. I've never seen anything like it, and I've never seen a painting like it, on the floor or otherwise. The colours are electrically vivid and the sphere of destruction deceptive: more explicit and intricate the closer I look down into it, a fingernail leaching its pink with lost life, a cracked hoof, more explicit than language, than reality maybe. Expression loud and clear. *He's very clever with it.* I know I'm biased, but … That book I read a lifetime ago, about those *Continental Expressionists*, those squabbling French and German pretenders, rings a faint bell somewhere. *Art or Arrogance?* Something about the invalidity of the emotional view, obfuscating truth. I don't know what this is that Daniel's done, other than intensely disturbing: *painting.* And he must have had to somehow stand right over it to reach the middle, since his arm doesn't stretch out as it should. I'd say that's doing things the hard way, if I were looking for a euphemism for the completeness of my incredulity.

The other two smaller paintings are not as immediately confronting, but maybe more so for what they seem to say. Our Lady leans over a broken road from a ruined cathedral, holding Baby Jesus down towards what looks like a fissure, but is in fact an open wound, revealing the shattering of bone. I'd like to think that's just my Catholic-afflicted imagination; know it's not. Neither is the intent in the other one: a smooth-faced, fair-haired, frightened boy, inside a grey Hun tunic, red piping like a vein down his charcoal trouser leg, a body hung over his shoulder, khaki clad and rent open from rib to thigh. The boy is looking out, directly, through the night, as he clutches the enemy's legs to his chest, pleading for something impossible; a National propaganda poster gone very awry.

What can I say? Have to say something; but avoid the unspeakable, and tears stoppered with awe ... I look up at him, standing beside me, and blurt: 'You could get locked up for this.' A joke, but a weak one, considering the War Precautions Act has now allowed for censorship of anything remotely resembling war protest. For images that should be sent straight to Melbourne marked *Urgent: Commonwealth Parliament House*, and hung above their heads.

He laughs, softly. 'Yep. So that's the end of it. I'll stick them under the house and we can forget about them.'

'No you will not,' I say, and wince: bite my tongue; I've no business telling him what to do.

But he says: 'All right.' Picks them up one by one and stacks them against the windowless wall, so that now all that can be seen is the precision with which he's pulled and fixed canvas over wooden frames. 'I'll leave them here then. But you don't have to look at anything like this again, and neither do I.'

And I think I'm more stunned by the apology in his voice than anything else.

★

We're sitting out on the front steps, in the shade of the house, looking over the valley; Danny's having an afternoon nap for once. It's the middle of December and it's so scorching you feel you can't take a full breath; cicadas deafening, flies appalling. I'm only wearing a shift, no undergarments: we can see and hear anyone who comes around the corner in enough time for me to run in and get decent, not that we're expecting anyone. Daniel's not wearing a shirt, just those old trousers, and he doesn't run anywhere for anyone; not because he can't, he just doesn't. He's not quite the same Achilles that I first saw, but he'll do, very well. It's hard not to feel that very sharp bolt of gratitude every time I see the scars: the backward S, the silvery dent; the neat slash along the underside of his forearm, the slight wasting of the muscles above knobbly hinge. Things could have been very different. For all my prayers and promises, I don't know if I would have coped, and I'm not sure that he would have either. He's quite vain, in a way, and I don't think he could have stood needing help all the time. We would not have been a Stan and Lilly duet; perhaps more Louise and Paul. Thank God, the stars, the angels, the saints and whoever else had a hand in making sure we'd never find out; thank the moon if it was you. He's not contemplating anything as pedestrian as that at the moment: he's looking at my breasts through the almost sheer fabric of my shift.

'No,' I tell him. 'It's too hot.' That's all we've done for the best part of the last month: no exaggeration and twice already this morning, the second time he sat me on the sideboard, as he often likes to, while Danny was corralled in the spare room. I love that; I am in a constant swoon for him, but it really is too hot right now. Haven't fired the stove for the last few days for fear that the house, or the entire valley, will combust; fires in the mountains have even brought somnolent koalas down here, swinging from branches to get the air going.

'This is not hot,' he says. 'Egypt got *hot*.'

I'm surprised he's said that; he's not really mentioned much about it yet. But I say, having a bet each way: 'I've never been to Egypt.'

'You were there, though. Every stinking day. You didn't mind torturing me then either.'

'Ha. I think you'll find that worked both ways, and I didn't start it.'

'Yes, you did. Minute you stepped into town. Don't know how I'll ever forgive you, Francine Connolly. The things you've put me through.'

Sublime. But I'm not relenting. 'Apart from vaporising me *later*, when it's cooler, what are you going to do with yourself …?' Daring the question, because he hasn't been out to his *room*, or off the bounds of our property for the last month either; when he's not having me, he's playing with Danny in the orchard, or playing the piano, or teaching Danny to bash it, or picking grubs off the tomatoes and green beans I planted in spring. Once upon a time I might have thought nothing unreasonable in perpetual leisure, and Evan's said to me that Daniel's the happiest he's ever seen him, and he is happy, and Doctor Nichols has said to me that *rest is best*, and he is resting, but still …

'Knock some sense into Charlie and Harry when they get here,' he says. Sarah's in Bathurst right now, and will bundle them all onto a train tomorrow; but he hasn't answered my question. 'I'm going to have a go at being a gentleman who is good to his wife and family,' he adds, and that's not an answer either.

'While I keep drudging?' I play along with a dig.

'I'll never be that much of a gentleman, dear. You can suit yourself.'

Love is not the word, nowhere near close. I'll drudge till the end of a trillion times forever on principle, but I say: 'There is only one thing I'd like, to make my life complete, and that is an indoor bathroom.' True, especially today: I want to sit in a cold bath. Arms and legs hanging over tin tub in the kitchen is not quite on the money.

'Done,' he says, wink and a nod: 'So long as you're paying. I know too much about the importance of good plumbing these days, so I'll do it myself. Special scheme, special price, just for you.'

'What do you know about plumbing?' I laugh, without thinking; I haven't pried into the knot of what's passed, and I realise too late that that's what I've just done.

But it seems that's exactly what I should have done at this precise moment in time, since a good deal comes tumbling out now. Right here, hip to hip, on the front steps of our house.

It's not funny, it's so very, *very* not funny, but he has me laughing as he tells me about all these men together in this Great Act of Stupidity. Trying to avoid flooding dugouts with sewage, the contentedness of rats and lice, first blooded by a fellow called Foley who accidentally hit him with a roll of barbed wire, moonlight jaunting with a drunk called Stratho, Captain Duncan and his little words and little feet always popping up and promoting him and nearly having him killed playing rugby against the BEF. But it's the unofficial version of what he calls his Most Distinguished Conduct that pinches off my laughter: he tells me how he tried to retrieve Stratho's body and ended up falling down a hole and that's how he broke his arm; spent his final big night of the Pozieres offensive in that hole with a dead man and a German boy who wanted to give himself up. Stifle the shudder and try to smile: because, somehow, Daniel thinks it is funny. I suspected the AIF were stretching the truth about the valorous act *under bombardment* business; I also suspect that Daniel's spinning a yarn. Longest tale he's ever told. A special version for me, for today. Compensation for the paintings perhaps. Naive as I am of matters military, I am fairly certain that you don't get a medal for falling in a hole; don't think that's what Stan Henderson meant about loose screws and asking what's for dinner.

Even more certain now: he's talking about wandering up the road towards Madonna, he's so mad that when he hears the shell whistling towards him he thinks he's slept in because it's already dawn. He says: 'But Duncan ...' and then he stops. He puts his head on his knees.

Little Danny has woken up; he's talking to himself, singing, 'Bah, bah, bah, bah, bah, bah, bah, baaaaaaah!' and rattling the side of his cot, which he is far too big for now. He can climb up and over, and he'll appear any moment now to see his father crying. He can hear him anyway. There it is. It's the worst sound. I put my hand on the middle of Daniel's back, it's such a big back and such a small hand, and he collapses against me as Danny toddles out. Danny pats Daddy on the shoulder; Daddy's very sad. I'm very fierce.

More so now. Charlie, who doesn't really know what's happened to his own dad, and didn't really know him, is missing his mum on the first night at our house. He's wet the bed, and he's so terribly ashamed, and I'm doing everything I can not to cry too, and not to punch a hole in the wall in fury at the idea that a seven-year-old should be so painfully ashamed, of any such thing. But I have my resource of good hopeful truths. I say: 'Your uncle Daniel is so happy that you're here; he couldn't wait for you to come. He has some excellent scars, too. I bet they're better than yours.' Did I really just say that? Uncle Daniel is mercifully asleep, or rather, more likely deeply unconscious with emotional exhaustion, in our bed and none the wiser. He's been jovial uncle, and good brother and good son; he held his sister for most of the afternoon, no need for other language; I don't know how he got through today at all, after wringing himself out into silence yesterday, after everything. Miriam is mute, trembling desolation; I've seen that before, of course, but somehow in Miriam it is the enth of tragedy. I can't imagine what the children have seen and understood over the past weeks since Roy's death.

Charlie pushes down the blanket and shows a scabby knee. 'Better than this?'

'You bet.'

We blink at each other in the moonlight.

'So you'd better move out, soldier. This bed needs fatiguing.'

Harry pretends to blink blearily beside his little brother, protecting him from his shame too. How much do these boys need to be hurt? My Boy and these small ones.

I think I am a bit of an atheist this minute, too: Merry Christmas everybody.

And for the first time in a long time I am making a radical decision. Everyone's asleep, or pretending to be. I write Daniel a note. I go to the linen cupboard for more sheets, then out to the *room*. I bind up each of the paintings and squeeze them into the car, wedging them behind the front seat with cushions from the parlour. And I'm gone just on dawn.

DANIEL

She's back after a few hours; she's obviously turned around at some point and come home again. I'm standing out the front with the kids, we've been kicking a football around all morning: they've never done it before, cricket's their game, but they are naturals with the pigskin, of course. I've been practising not thinking too much about my inability to pass the ball to the right, or to bowl overarm. Reminding myself that I'm too wrecked for rugby and I never liked cricket anyway, and I still have all my teeth. When in doubt, look at Danny still running around in circles near the house; I really should have done myself a favour and paid the kid more attention throughout this year: he's beyond hilarious, beyond beautiful. And he's still going as France pulls the car up inside the stable next to Hayseed; as Charlie and Harry and I stop and watch her.

She glances at me, flame face, says; 'Lost my bottle,' and storms off down the side of the house. Then we hear some thumping, she's hitting the weatherboards with her fists by the sounds of it, and then I think she's kicked the tub off the back verandah.

Charlie says: 'What's Aunty France doing?'

Hmn. I say: 'She's a bit cranky, I think.' Can't help smiling, though: she's back, properly in herself, despite all attempts to break her spirit. This is the girl I married. Nothing peaceful and steady about her now.

'What's she cranky about?' says Harry.

'The war.' No bullshit about that at least. 'But I reckon she'll be all right in a tick.'

She is. She comes back round the corner and says: 'Sorry about that. Not out of my system. But I have to plan it better next time. Got to Mount Vic and realised I don't know anyone in Sydney any more, apart from the lawyers, and even if I did they wouldn't understand your … monsters. And I don't want to be locked up for a lunatic. I'd rather be locked up for more newsworthy sedition.'

She might too. She is a lunatic but she's got more bottle than I have.

She says: 'Help me put them back in their box, will you? I'm about to fall over.'

We do, and I don't mention anything to the kids about it — bit too odd, this one.

Charlie asks about it later anyway: 'What was that thing you put in that room? What's in that room anyway?' Which has a lock on it now.

I tell him: 'They're paintings. Ugly ones. And I don't want you to see them.'

'Did you paint them?'

'Yes.'

'What are they of?' Don't you just love kids. I've decided that they should be able to ask anything, even if I can't answer it, and Charlie is taking full advantage. Good on him.

'The war,' I tell him. 'But they don't tell the full story. Just some ugly parts. They'll frighten you, so I don't want you to look at them.' I don't want to look at them either.

He has a think about that and then says: 'So are you going to paint the rest of the story?'

'Maybe,' I tell him. 'But I'd rather paint pictures of Aunty France.'

'Why would you want to do that?'

'Because I love her, and she's not very ugly.'

He screws up his face, no idea. He's priceless. He changes the subject: 'Aunty France says you've got some really good scars.'

Good on you, Aunty France. No time like the present, may as well have a wash now anyway. 'Yep. Want to see them?'

'Yep.'

I've stripped off and he's looking at the big one on my leg. 'Wowee, how'd you get that?'

'Being an idiot, not doing what I was supposed to be doing, being in the wrong place at the wrong time when a shell exploded. Spent nearly four months in bed for it. Not nice.'

'Four months!' Charlie says. 'That's horrible.' Too true. He shakes his head. 'When I got a fever once Mum tried to make me stay in bed all week, and that was horrible. I snuck off. Did you?'

'I certainly wanted to,' I tell him, then I notice Harry's snuck off somewhere; he's not interested in this sort of talk just yet, if he'll ever be. He's a bit too quiet; reminds me of someone I know.

Charlie's saying: 'What's a shell?'

'It's like a bomb that gets fired out of a gun, like a cannon, or dropped from an aeroplane. Smashes things up.'

'What's it like getting shot at?'

'Very horrible, frightening.'

'Lots of soldiers have died, haven't they?'

'Yes. Millions.'

'You didn't, though. You came back.'

'I was very, very lucky.'

'Did you shoot anyone?'

Good question; unanswerable. 'I didn't want to.'

He frowns at that, as in: where's the logic there? Spot on, but it's a bit hard to explain that one to a seven-year-old, let alone myself. He says, looking at the other obvious scar: 'Did you get shot in the arm too? Like my dad did?'

'No. Not like your dad, Charlie; and he got very sick from it. I never got sick, and I managed to wreck my arm all by myself, falling over. And it doesn't work properly now.' I show him.

'You did that just falling over?'

'Yep, into a big hole. Again, being where I shouldn't have been.' I'll spare him the details. 'Whenever you fall over, Charlie, roll with it, don't put your arm out, no matter how much you'll want to.'

He nods, like he reckons that sounds like good advice; and it is. 'Are you a hero?'

Crack it: 'No.'

He says, frowning again: 'I reckon you must be.'

As much as his poor little head has been filled with rubbish — inescapable, he'll have been getting the hero jabber at school all year, and it's all over the papers, everywhere — he's not talking about the war. I think he's telling me he's happy he's here, and not with his poor mum and million sisters at Grandma's. I think this must be the first proper conversation he's had with an adult. Even when Mim's at her best, there are too many kids to yell above; she forgets their names half the time.

I tell him: 'I'm really, really not any sort of hero, but I'm happy you think so. I reckon you're a pretty good bloke too.' That's very easy to say to him, because this is the easiest conversation I've had since I came back. I'm having a chat with someone I love, who I haven't upset. Best medicine: should be bottled.

And it gives me the shove I need to tell France a bit more of what she needs to know. I tell her outside, on the front step again, in the dark, because that talk will never go on inside the house. And I have to tell her, so she doesn't wonder, so she knows something of why I carried on like that the last time we were here. That it wasn't just what I'd put in the paintings; it was that sometimes I thought I'd be better off dead, was dead; sometimes

334

all day, day after day, and the sedative couldn't take that away. I don't tell her, though, that without the sedative the grind of it got a bit worse than that before it got better and I thought about buying a pistol in London — easier to get hold of than a toothbrush — that stupid, and I don't know the answer to that one: why you'd want to top yourself right when the fact of being alive had started to sink in, when I'd just had my first walkabout on my own without any assistance, been told by the physical therapist that was the fastest trip to ambulation he'd ever seen. Instead I tell her the answers that make sense: that it cut one time too many that Dunc bailed me out, then copped it himself; that I never thought I'd ever get home, and the want of it, the want of her, was only matched by how ashamed I was of what I'd done to myself, inside and out, in the name of nothing. All true enough. And I'm still ashamed.

She looks at me, thoughtful, calm, when I've finished battering her with it all, says: 'I knew something was wrong. I mean something like that: wronger than wrong.'

'What do you mean? Everything was wrong.'

She tells me about her morbid moments, saying it felt like I was disappearing, 'Like something being shaken and torn from my soul.'

I'm wondering if neurasthenia might be contagious, or maybe there's a special form of it called AIF Wife. 'That's a bit hocus pocus, isn't it, France? I'm not surprised you had a few panics — gave you a few decent reasons.'

'Yes you did.' She kisses me, and then there's the sweetest smile under her eyes that say: *You arse.* 'But you've got to admit my salvos worked against it.'

'They did.' I'll believe in that magic. 'I'm still getting hit.'

Everything I want to say to her about it has been said now. We're pure again. Please.

Now we're free to concentrate on how France is going to get herself locked up for sedition.

But not until I've sorted Harry out. It's Sunday, the boys have been here only four days, and he's wandered off, been gone since some time this morning. He's not at Mum's; careful to avoid mentioning his disappearance to sister and mother; just popped in to say a quick hello; no thanks, won't stop for a cup of tea. I stalk back home; France is getting frantic and so am I, quietly. Don't know where to begin looking for him and there's a lot of places to look. He doesn't know Lithgow. Glad it's summer and not winter, because the sun is going down and he'd freeze to death if he slept out in the valley. He's nine, he's smart, he'll be around somewhere, hopefully not lost, not bitten by a brown snake or fallen off a ridge, and when I grab him I will be trying very hard not to hurt him.

Tea's on the table, and I'm not very hungry. He is, though: he's just walked back in.

I say: 'Get out the back and wait there for me.'

He does as he's told and I start eating. France shoots me a disapproving look.

I tell her: 'Better he waits there for a while, than me belting him right now.'

Horrified look. I'm sure she's never been belted in her life; she's got no idea on this score.

When I've finished eating, not that I wanted it, I go out onto the verandah and Harry stands there looking at me with a challenge. Yep. Looks very much like someone I know.

I say: 'Don't ever do that again. You leave this house, you tell someone where you're going and how long you're going to be. Do you understand?'

He says: 'I don't have to do anything you tell me.'

What? Not even I would have pushed a challenge that far at that age. Not at any age with my father. But I'm not Harry's father, am I.

I say, trying to rein it in: 'Yes you do, while you live in this house.'

'I don't want to live in this house.'

'Why not? You were happy enough to be here a couple of days ago.'

No answer.

'Do you want to go back to your mum, to Grandma's?'

'No,' he says. 'They don't go to church either.'

That stops me, hadn't even crossed my mind. It's Sunday. Roy was a churchgoer, not particularly religious, but went to please his mother, though she lives out in Dubbo. Can't even remember which mob. Presbyterian? Mim had always played along, but stopped taking the kids when all this happened.

But it gets worse. Harry says: 'And you're all German.'

'Don't be ridiculous,' I say before I can stop my idiot mouth. Try again: 'I'm sorry about church, mate, but we don't go. You can if you want to; we'll sort something out.' Evan can take him to the Methodists — it's all the same thing. 'As for being German, well, a lot of people are, including part of you. But we're Australian here.'

I think I've put the pieces together: not only is it Sunday, but he can't understand why his dad's not here and I am; he wants something to blame, and he'll have a go at the lot, no matter how stupid. France and I were talking about the papers being full of hatred yesterday too; he'd have heard us: German town names changing in Adelaide, Lutheran schools being closed down, Fritz fever in the Sydney editorials and letters. Even the local rags are full of it: look out for nonexistent spies. The fear's important to keeping the machine going, because everyone's losing heart again at the losses in Flanders, twice Pozieres, and Hughes is having another referendum on conscription next week, but it's all a special poison for this kid here. Mim would make a joke of it, calling herself Fritz, but she was never serious. Harry knows that, I'm sure, but he heard me slinging off yesterday too, didn't he: at King George changing his name from Saxe-Coburg-Gotha to Windsor; I'd said to France it'd be an easier signature on all those death warrants, just to turn my own anger around. I don't know how to turn Harry around right now, though: he's still giving me the challenge. He's got a nerve, that's for sure. He's so charged, he looks like he really is going to have a go.

I say: 'You settle down. Right now.'

No. He's not going to do that. He is going to have a go. He's nine years old. I'm six and a half feet tall. He doesn't care. He's laying into me like you wouldn't believe. I don't know what to do for a second, before I grab him, trying not to hurt him. That's why he's let fly, I realise, suddenly: because he knows I'm not going to hurt him. He's bloody strong, though; and he's kicking me now I've got hold of him. 'Settle down!' He's still going, and then he pushes it too far, really too far, dropping down as he tries to get out of my grip, yanking my favourite arm with a good deal of force to where it does not like going: straight. I yell and mean it, 'Jesus fucking Christ,' not at him, but at that particular sensation, as I let go.

He stops, just stares. Wish I'd blasphemed a little earlier.

France is out here now. 'What have you done to him?' She's asking me, not the kid. I can't speak yet.

Harry's burst now, in angry tears; I could join him soon.

Penny drops for France when she sees I'm having difficulty: 'Oh dear.' Then: 'Serves you right for being brutal.'

'He went for me.' I sound like I'm nine too.

She's got her arm around Harry; he's worked himself right up now, not angry, just awful grief. I say: 'Harry, I wasn't swearing at you.' He can't hear me; he's inconsolable. Swig of opium-laced brandy and off to bed for him.

Francine takes care of him, and Danny and Charlie too, while I stay out on the verandah trying not to be angry. It's a big effort. Harry will be all right, eventually, we'll see to that however we can. But how many kids are going through this rubbish? Tonight. Never mind yesterday and tomorrow. All over the world. Sliced up by grief and propaganda. Finding it a bit hard to float away from this one.

'Are you all right?' France comes back out.

No. 'Yes.' Dull throb now, very pleasant.

She stands beside me. 'Apologies for jumping to conclusions earlier, I …'

'I wasn't ever going to belt him,' I tell her. Don't think I could ever belt a kid, any kid.

'Good,' she says, and she sounds so sad with it; I can't look at her.

But I ask: 'Are you all right?'

'Yes,' she gives me a soft little laugh. 'In spite of a few good *beltings*.'

That makes me look at her. 'What do you mean?'

'Our Lady of the Leather Strap, at school. Hideous.' She winks: 'And I never did a thing to deserve it of course.'

Gut knots again at that thought; what sort of a grub would you have to be to hit Francine?

She adds: 'You don't have to work too hard at being intimidating, Daniel, and he's only a little boy.'

'I know.' And I do, very much, so I tell her: 'Losing Harry after four days didn't do much for my temperament, did it. I've lost less to just about do my head in, and not even mates, France. I didn't have mates over there, only a few, and you can work out why, but Harry is a fair bit more than a mate, and if I was a bit rough on him when he came in, then too bad. He won't leave this house again without telling anyone where he's going, will he. He's not going to push it that far a second time to find out.' I am barking.

'No.' She puts her hand on my hip and says: 'But if he does, he knows how to disable you now.' Very funny, France, but she cracks me anyway. Then she says: 'If you're not going to paint or do anything else in particular, then maybe you should see about getting that elbow fixed, if it can be.'

No, for all the same reasons. 'Missed that boat, I'd say.'

'Daniel,' she's talking to a moron, 'a Sydney surgeon, a Sydney anyone will do anything for money, especially now. Don't think you've got a problem with cobbling together funds and just asking for it to be done; you can relax your frugality for a minute and splash out on yourself.'

It's not my frugality that needs relaxing. 'You want an indoor bathroom,' I say. 'Maybe after that.'

She laughs, loud: 'Capable as you are at everything under the sun, darlingest, I doubt you'll be able to put in an indoor bathroom on your own. Not as a community undertaking either: you are *not* getting Evan and friends to do it for their Danny for the love of it. That's immoral.'

'That's not immoral — that's the way we are.' Though she has a point. I could ask Evan to get me the moon and he would, and he'd never take anything for it. We are all idiots. Complain about the unfair distribution of wealth and then knock back a bit of equaliser. For a mate. Jesus. 'All right, I'll pay for help then.'

'This is a stupid conversation,' she says. 'I can wait for a silly bathroom. But you didn't look too well just now. I didn't realise it gave you any trouble at all.'

'It doesn't.' It does though; I've done that to myself a fair few times to know about it; done it in bed, that's why I like to put her up on the sideboard whenever I can. 'It'll be all right in the morning.'

Everything always is, isn't it.

No it's not, and it's not just the fact that grinding throb kept me awake half the night. It's more that I feel like something filthy at the bottom of a trench. It's come back and hit me like a cave-in and I don't want to get out of bed. Rats have stopped to watch and listen. I can hear France outside the bedroom door, talking to Charlie, who wants to kick the ball around if I'm not going to work, and asking why I don't go to work. She's saying: 'Oh, we sometimes sleep in on Mondays, any old days, when it's required. We do things a bit differently round here whenever we can.'

I could smile at the whole truth of that, but my face won't work. I didn't even hear the whistle this morning, and I hear it every morning, bar Sundays, even when I was going mad out the back. I should get up and talk to Harry, let him know everything is all right, or will be. But I can't picture myself actually speaking, saying something useful to him yet, apart from, maybe: thanks a lot, you little shit. The fact that I know what this is this time doesn't help. The very last time this happened was that day in London, when I went to the gallery to drag myself away from it. That worked. Didn't it. I have to do something like that now. Paint my France; dull angry throb; won't be today. Can't make a fist, let alone hold a pencil. Nothing for me at the Wattle either, apart from resuming hostilities with Drummond, and I couldn't be further from arsed. What does he do all day? Read the papers, talk to a few people, look at the books, look important, get together with other important people at this place and that and talk about how important they are and how wonderful the war is. I don't know where I fit in. And I don't particularly want to fit in. Anywhere.

I'm just thinking about how quick chloroform would kill you without you knowing about it, when France shoves open the door, closes it and whispers: 'Whatever it is that's going on in here, just stop it.'

That's enough to frighten anyone out of it. I lie there and look at her like she's a witch. Maybe she is.

She says: 'There's a boy wandering out in the orchard on his own who needs a word with you.'

Yes. Yes. Yes. Rattled out of it now.

She says: 'What's wrong?'

I say, getting up; awch fuck: 'Just sorry for myself.'

'There's no room for that here any more. If you've got a problem, for heaven's sake will you speak to me?'

'Won't happen again,' I tell her. And it won't, not while the witch is anywhere near me. Just as well she loves me. 'But I'm fairly certain Harry's broken my arm.'

FRANCINE

Oh dear indeed. He doesn't have a choice now; he'll have to see Doctor Nichols at least, since no-good elbow is defunct and he is in a good deal of pain over it, pretending he's not. Harry is silently mortified even after Daniel said to him: 'Mate, you've got no idea how much this is my fault. You didn't mean it, and I know why you let fly. So you can put it right behind you. I, on the other hand, have to do what I should have done weeks ago. The only lesson here is not to put things off. If you've got something on your mind, discuss it, don't bottle it. Always leads to trouble.'

Bravo, Daniel. If only … but let's not dwell there. Nor I in the churnings that kept me awake all night feeling your hurt, watching you pretend to be asleep, then asking you if you want breakfast in bed and getting an indecipherable grunt in reply. Nothing hocus pocus about that. It's knowledge all right: knowledge that I can look past your anger, your foul mouth, and your surly face, I can even cope with the occasional beard if you ever do that again, but I won't abide this worst of yours: this feeling of … *absence*. Perhaps a hole filled by grief and shame. And perhaps I have a will to match it, if the look on your face when I did speak my mind was anything to judge by. Is this the worst of you? Regardless, I shall exploit my power over it ruthlessly from here on. So, there you go, Father. Maybe there you go, Sarah, too.

And now here we all go, piling into the car. I ask Harry to hold onto squirming Danny, to give the lad something to take his mind off our predicament, give him an awful lot to do on the short trip to the hospital. He needs this responsibility, not being carted off to Grandma's feeling glummer than glum. Then I ask him to look after his brother and Danny while Big Danny gets Achilles' Elbow fixed up. Well, at least a more comfortably incapacitated fracture, waiting for word from this fellow in Sydney to see if and when the structural problem that caused it might be corrected. Doctor Nichols manages not to rub it in. This has to be the last time, please, for the Curse of the Thing. But not for something else; something I've been longing for.

I say to Daniel on the way home: 'Do you know what this situation is missing?'

'What.' Trying not to be cranky for Harry's sake; not quite succeeding.

'A further complication.'

'Hmn.'

'You don't sound like you want one, Daniel. What's wrong with you?'

He looks at me that way I love. 'What now.'

'I think we're going to have another baby.' So pronounced Mrs Moran while Daniel was receiving application of *cement*.

Cracked him. Beautiful.

FIVE
JANUARY–NOVEMBER 1918

FRANCINE

Darlingest Little Danny will not accompany us to Sydney. No chance but Buckley's there. He can stay with Grandma. But we will take Charlie and Harry as well as Miriam's eldest, Kathryn, who's almost twelve, since an extended tour of Babel is a good reason to delay the trauma of starting at a new school, and the children will provide good distraction for me from the purpose of our trip: The Operation. It's a glorious big blue sky morning as we tootle around to Grandma's, and I don't want to leave the valley, except that, apart from getting Achilles's Elbow brutalised by some man we've never met, I also have an act of sedition planned for the sojourn. Not completely gaga this time, given the change in our circumstances, and greater degree of rationality obtained after thought; it will be a small but significant act. I probably won't succeed, but I'd kick myself forever if I didn't have a go. Daniel wishes he could be a fly on the ceiling for my attempt; but I'm glad he won't be: better that he takes my failure lying down and medicated. I'll take it like a girl. Besides, I don't really want him to see me make a fool of myself: he can hear all about it in amusing anecdote afterwards.

Plenty of inspiration for foolishness and sedition of all kinds today, I think, but not very many avenues left for the expression of such. Billy the Troll still reigns over us, despite the failure of his last conscription referendum, and his promised resignation: he's been recalled by the Governor-General, Sir Someone or Other, because no one else was available to fill the vacancy. Not a soul in the entire parliament? If you believe that, you can believe there's a man in the moon. Suspicious by nature, as I am, I do, however, think it would be fair to say that there's rather a lot going on down the dark rat tunnels of power that we don't know about. The Troll was asking our permission to send seven thousand conscripts per month: *per month?* At that rate he'd have no one to rule over in quick time; he'd have to start sending women and children. Our population is about four million, and he's determined it be decimated: ten per cent unaccounted for. He's already unaccounted for three hundred thousand odd, so he's getting there. He is clearly deluded, but the only man capable of running the country? Very concerted efforts being taken to ensure our ignorance remains intact, too. No photographs, no words, no speeches allowed against the war effort, the government or Britannia. No complaints, no strikes, no fainting in the street allowed against poverty and exploitation. Stick your hand up and you'll get it bashed down by a pack of returned men, who are allowed to do as they please to dissenters: anyone who's served in the AIF could probably murder a trade unionist, a Catholic or even a pacifist over a penny and claim defence of the national interest. Well, maybe that's an exaggeration, but you can at the very least now be arrested by the Troll's new Commonwealth Police Force, established in response to some wicked Queenslander who hurled a couple of terrifying eggs at our PM last month; apparently the local constabulary were too busy laughing to come to his aid, so the Troll has declared the entire state of Queensland a viperous nest of sympathy for the Hun, and the other worst one, Sinn Fein; and the entire country in need of supervision against any impulse more radical than breathing.

Obscuring the real news: that the veterans still haven't been delivered their promise of land grants, housing, jobs or meaningful compensation. If you lose both legs then you get four pounds a week, good job, but if you only lose one you get one pound eight and six. The average working-man's wage is something like three pounds seven, now that inflation has pushed it to the dizzy heights. Do the equation for the fellow who didn't stand close enough to the shell to get both blown off. Do that equation for Stan Henderson, who still can't get a job to make up the shortfall, whose Lilly now works the dawn shift in the arms factory cleaning the machines. She laughs at the irony, good for her, but I think that's what you call straightforward evil; and will be more so when their baby arrives sometime in April. I'm waiting for the Troll to proclaim that compensation has been found to be entirely unnecessary, since he's made it to the top of the tree in spite of being stunted, ugly, obnoxious, demented and, apparently, deaf as a post.

The veterans' leagues hail him, though — they're the Returned Sailors' and Soldiers' Imperial League of Australia now, and express their cooperative frustrations with hatred of everything that's not British. Part of the reason I've quietly retired my association there: too tricky to sympathise with that conflict of interest, and in any case, Those Who Help Themselves are coming back in droves now to look after each other so us women are not really needed any more for much beyond cake-baking. The other part is my own sense of conflict: in deciding of late to refrain from tongue-holding where an issue burns, I don't want it to lash at anyone who really doesn't need my opinion adding insult to their injury. Enough of a small but significant victory to have got Daniel out the door to add his 'No' vote to the referendum; he said, 'I can't write,' and I said, 'You only have to tick a box.' I could feel the hurt burning all the way into town, but he did it, and afterwards when an old wag idling about under the awning of the Cosmopolitan said, 'Oi, young fella, I'd say your motor was a beauty if I hadn't caught sight of your driver,' he laughed all the way back home.

And now we're going all the way back to the Big Smoke, and he's been laughing at me all morning: 'Everything's all right, and no I don't think I'll need a jumper, Francine, not even just in case.' And now Danny's dispatched and Kathryn ensconced; Mim tells hopeless little brother to 'break a leg or let Harry have a try' — she's bouncing back — and Sarah chides for bad taste but she's smiling as she waves with the four little girls and one little boy running round the bottom of her skirt out on the street. Wish I had a camera. Push all other thoughts aside. I'm overwhelmed with a wash of joy; throat closing over for every life that's not like ours. Leprechaun pokes me in the ribs and says: Laugh! I do. And we hit the road, driver delightedly maternally deranged.

Motor backfires as we turn up off Dell, kids squeal, and Daniel doesn't even flinch; instead he turns around to them and says: 'Settle down, you lot.' Then: 'Keep your eyes on the road, Francine.'

DANIEL

Unexpected benefit of this Great War and my stupid part in it: France makes love to me, for the first time. I've always made love to her, always made it when and how. But now, in this room with no sideboard, it's her, here on this massive mahogany bed, in the Metropole, this flash squatters' palace bang in the middle of the city, making love to me. Who is this woman? With our life somewhere there inside her. I can't tell you. I can't describe her; I have to paint her. Please.

I don't know what goes on in other people's private lives; don't care; but I don't know that too many blokes get this. I think you'd hear about it. Or maybe not.

I actually tear up as I'm …

The luckiest bloke in this world, our world. Best wife. Best life.

Which will hopefully continue well beyond today. I am, if that's possible, more rattled than I have ever been. No, I'm petrified. Last time, with Doctor Myer, I was still in enough of a fog that I wasn't really thinking beyond what I wanted. But now, as we head out to Waverley, I'm a bit too clear about what I have, and a bit too aware that in too short a while I will receive a huge serve of pain, if I wake up. I tell France to drop me outside, partly because any minute I'm going to chuck, and partly because I'm thinking of pissing off. Stratho's big girlie favourite that I am.

But I've forgotten she's a witch; she says: 'Daniel, I'm not going to put you out on the footpath and drive off.' And she leaves the kids in the car and sees me right up to the front door. It's just a big weatherboard, just a nice house, a bit like home, I tell myself, except for the brass plaque saying *St Christopher's Private Hospital*, and I'm thinking I hope he doesn't hold my lack of religion against me. And then she makes sure Doctor Adinov finds me for this eight o'clock appointment before she hands me over and shoots through with a quick kiss, whispering: 'It'll be all right, darlingest.' Wish she sounded a bit more certain.

This Adinov sounds Russian, definitely when he says, 'So, how do you do, Mr Ackerman,' and I can only nod and probably guess who he's barracking for in the revolution: doesn't look too proletarian to me, with his fat gold ring and silvery silk tie, and I hope he doesn't hold my Bolshevik sympathies against me. We're not likely to have that conversation, I suppose.

We don't. It's all very straightforward according to this straightforward bloke, who's got a face set so hard from concentrating it looks painful. Good. But I'm not listening to his talk about what he's going to do to me; I'm busy thinking about septicaemia and amputation and having had probably way too much luck. And I'm thinking, mostly, what if you wreck my hand? I would like to leave, now. Leave it the way it is; it's not that bad. That's a joke: he shears the cement off and the whole thing looks on the brink of death already, after only four weeks. It's nothing in his hands, which seem like they're hardly touching me as he lifts it and turns it this way and that.

Adinov can see me wandering off as he starts talking about the range of movement, the fortunate condition of some tendon or other. 'Don't worry, Mr Ackerman, I've had too much experience. Russian surgeons are the best because we all have too much experience. Lots of war for practice, and icy streets for lots of broken bones.' He's not joking. I'd like to ask him about it, and how he ended up here, how it is he knows Myer, but now's not the time for a settling chat. He's a very busy man. Wants to hack through the end of my *humerus*, then make it happy with some *external transfixion*, and he's going to. And I'll be paying him a small fortune for the privilege.

France is fairly dancing round the tub and I flick her with the flannel, just to get the bell sound. There it is. Opium is fantastic when you're not having nightmares, or maybe it's just a better class of brew here. What is this stuff? I can understand how you could get addicted to it, how anyone could. I can look at the *external transfixion* and say that's a new shade of wrong, every time I open my eyes and look right. Fuck. But at the same time, I can say that's what an arm looks like, my one, and despite logic, not that logic is the greatest strength in me at the minute, I can say that's as it should be. The Russian was here a few moments ago and he smiled like he knows what I mean, well I think he did; it's a bit hard to tell on that face; he looks like a middleweight boxer … with girl's hands. I can still hear him saying, 'Yes, that's the heroin', and I'm thinking: where is she? And France is back again now, except I think she's actually here this time, since she's fully clothed. She rushes into view, I can smell her; she says: 'Hello darlingest not supposed to be here been very seditious see you tomorrow.' Kiss on my forehead. And she's gone again. Don't go. I want a proper kiss. Doesn't matter. Pass out again. For me and my doll. *Great big beautiful doll. Let me put my arms about you, I could never live without you …*

FRANCINE

I hadn't intended to do this today. Got plenty of time: Doctor
Nichols said we could be here for weeks. I was only going to
loiter about with the children, give myself some time to imagine
my assault upon the curator before executing it. Rehearse my
lines some more. Plan was I'd do a good show of desperate war
wife with talented, valorous, headcase husband who's on the
verge of losing arm altogether. So these paintings would be rather
rare then, and they might be. Don't think about that. I was going
to appeal to the curator's sense of cultural interest, present them
as a gift, something to keep in the vault, as curiosities: after all, do
you know he's really just a miner? Lithgow coal. Left school at
fourteen for pit. Spontaneous genius forged on the fields of
France. Of course they wouldn't be hung: apart from War
Precautions, one only needs a glance through the Art Gallery of
New South Wales to know why: where would you put the
obscenities amongst the gentle impressionism, the pastoral
landscapes and stately portraits and emphasis on British best
bland? Even Streeton's *Fire's On!* manages to make the act of
blasting through the face of a sandstone wall an idyllic,
transcendent image, wild blue sky and shimmery, languorous
gums overriding the fact: tunnel at Lapstone needed for faster
train over the mountains. I never thought about it at school, of
course — Sister Margaret, who instructed us in The Creative
Arts, was as inspiring as a metronome — but I can see it so much

more clearly now without even looking at it: a false impression: Streeton's painting is as tall as a man, but the men in the picture and their labour appear incidental shapes against the grandeur of rock and bush. Why did he call it *Fire's On!* I wonder; should have called it *More Rock And Bush: Since You Like It So Much.* Wonder what sort of war pictures he'd make *en plein air.* Pleasant ones, I suppose. So, my small act of sedition is to try to find a place for Daniel's unpleasant monsters, a place to lie with their own truth, beneath the acceptable lies: like unexploded bombs perhaps. But knowing I'll be laughed away, shown the door. Silly woman. Silly or not: you get nothing if you don't ask your silly questions.

And here I am with Kathryn, Harry and Charlie, mounting the sandstone steps of the gallery, about to give them a taste of our culture on their first full day in the Big Smoke. I can feel their boredom already, when we pass two well-preened Dame Wowsers on the way into the vestibule; one's saying to the other: 'And can you believe there's a race meeting at Randwick today? Don't they know it's banned?' I dawdle to hear the reply: 'It's not banned, dear. Only frowned upon. But it should be banned — and they should all be sent to France. But they're all Irish: what can you do?'

Hmn. Fine example of the calibre of woman who voted yes to the conscription referendums, if they voted: perhaps they're against female suffrage too. But I'm not going to bother thinking about that: I'm having a flash of inspiration as I take the children into the first hall. They are not all lazy bog Irish no-hopers at the races, are they? And some of them are my father's old associates. I know the name of at least one who might be there right now too: Captain Duncan's father. He'll be a Mr Duncan, won't he. And he'll be a gentleman.

I'm standing in front of Longstaff's portrait of Henry Lawson and I swear the old soak winks at me: Go on, Francine, the snakes at the track won't kill you. But Mr Lawson, I have no idea what I'm doing, I tell him. He replies: *Who ever does?* He's got a good point there. No courage, no reward. Oh Leprechaun, what are you laughing at?

I say to the children: 'This was a very silly idea. Too dull by half here. Let's go to the racecourse instead.'

My heart is thumping not with morbidity but with the fear of doing something I don't know Daniel would approve of: because Captain Duncan is someone sacred to him. This is a man's world, though, and I will have a better stab at succeeding if I have a man's support, a man's introduction to someone who can introduce me to someone who must know someone who can assist me with a proper introduction to the curator. Just now I was preparing to embarrass myself in front of a complete stranger; why do that when I could do it in front of a man who already knows my name? And what if he's not there? Not interested? It won't matter; just give me more time to get my bottle up.

'You're in charge, Harry,' I tell him, handing over some money for a treat from the shop across the road, as well as the law to be upheld: 'Don't stray too far from the car. I won't be long, I just have to deliver a message.'

The three of them look at me with complete bewilderment; can't blame them, can't explain either. They are not having a very interesting day so far, but I'll make up for that later. I can't take them with me; I have no idea what will happen when I step up to that entrance gate, and, besides, I realised on the way here that Daniel, as such a confirmed abstainer of vices, would most definitely disapprove of me taking the children to the races. Poor Kathryn looks especially flummoxed; she used to be a little chatterbox; not any more: she's taken her father's death very hard, and she's also very fond of her Uncle Daniel, who was so beside himself this morning he didn't even manage a 'see you later'. I'm supposed to be distracting her from her worries with the wonders of Sydney, or at least the summer circus at Coogee, not my own erratic behaviour. I'll pay her particular attention when I've finished making a fool of myself, or at worst prodding a terrible wound in a man I don't know.

There's the members' gate: seen it hundreds of times before from the road, never been inside it. There's a man there: just walk right up to him and ask him to find out if, among the throng inside, there's a Mr Duncan, a gentleman, old acquaintance of the late Frank Connolly in attendance and, if so, could he give him this message, please. The man on the gate looks like a wiry grey rat. He's looking at me now, a question on his face already. 'Can I help you, miss?' He's got one of those nasal voices, so twangy and high I'm sure that's exactly how a rat would sound if it could speak.

My request bumbles out of me, my little note trembling in my hand, and I wait to be told there are a thousand Duncans here. This is the most preposterous thing you've ever done, Francy. Congratulations.

But Ratty says: '*The* Mr Duncan? Sure he's here. Been here all day. Saw him come in. I'll give him your note, miss. You don't want to come in yourself?'

I shake my head. Ratty scuttles off, my two bob for the favour jangling in his pocket. I've gone far enough as it is; possibly too far. Close enough to the heart of Babel right here, where I'm sure I can hear the punters being skinned beneath the hubbub beyond. Anyway, if this *The* Mr Duncan is not interested, or has never heard of me, he will not come out to meet Mrs Francine Ackerman nee Connolly, daughter of Frank. I'll give him twenty minutes, no, fifteen, and then I'll take the children for a drive along the beach roads, so they can pick which one we'll go to tomorrow.

He's here in less than five. He is enormous; pinstripe swallow tail, stiff collar, massive shirt front a wall that fills the space in front of me as I turn to the sound of my name, look up from under the brim of my hat. And I can't speak: I simply lose it on the spot: cap blown off a bottle of Brainless Girl Schweppes fizzy. For everything. For the awful presumption I am making, for every stinging nerve. Because I suddenly miss my father so sharply I can't breathe, and because, to be plain with myself, I've been a flea in a jar of absolute fret since I left Daniel at St Christopher's Never Heard Of It Before with cold-eyed Foreigner for Ortho-Whatsit molestation.

But this Mr Duncan is so kind. He says, 'Oh, my dear, dear girl,' with a soft, disappearing burr and guides me to a bench nearby, sits down with me and waits while I compose myself; try to, quickly.

Force out: 'Please excuse me.'

'No need,' he says: 'But you can tell me what's the matter.'

Couldn't possibly, but must ascertain: 'You do know who I am?' Other than strange and overwrought.

'Of course.' He smiles as I look up. 'And I was very sorry to hear of your father's passing, sorry when he vanished from Sydney, to be more precise. So please, tell me what I can do for you.'

Face-slapping embarrassment will not let me tell him any such thing; searching for return condolences, I blather instead: 'My husband knew your son …' Can't get further.

'I know,' he says.

Stare: *You know that?*

'Richard mentioned him rather a lot in his letters to me. How is he?'

How is he? The intimacy of the question, mentions in letters throws me, then jolts me back to my senses. 'Not the best today,' I tell him. 'He's having an operation on a bad elbow. But other than that he's … well … mostly. He grieved terribly for your son, and he still does, I think. I'm so sorry for your loss, Mr Duncan.'

He smiles again, but with the wound. 'Thank you, Mrs Ackerman. So am I. Richard was my only child, a very loved one. But I must say that he was most relieved when your husband was sent out of it. Your chap gave him all sorts of trouble, and as many reasons for admiration.'

Dare: 'What do you mean by that?'

Mr Duncan chuckles gently at my ignorance. 'He hasn't told you about it at all?'

'No.' Not much.

'No, don't suppose he would have. It's hard for one to know what to say, to anyone, these days, isn't it?' And I'm sure he's drifting three sheets to the wind, just as Father no doubt would be if he were here.

'Yes.' Indeed it is, but can you please be sober enough, or perhaps soused enough to tell me something more of what Daniel hasn't, or can't?

He considers me and his words for a moment, before divulging: 'Well, I think I can say that your chap appears to have made a hard habit of following his own orders when things got rough. And whatever the record says is not entirely accurate: less to do with holding his post than with abandoning it. Took some dreadful risks on account of the safety of others; so many, Richard thought he must be bulletproof.'

I have no idea of Daniel's *record*, beyond the cryptic, gazetted citation, which sits folded up under my old missal in the back of the wardrobe drawer with the *Dear Madam, Sgt gravely injured* letter, and pronounces his *conspicuous gallantry and devotion to duty on all occasions … blah, blah, blah, in particular something to do with a machine gun one day in July, blah, blah, blah*; and the present illumination suggests that it's probably a good thing I don't know more: not sure whether I'm monumentally impressed or somehow furious at multiple *dreadful risks on account of the safety of others.* He was supposed to be lamenting his *stupid decision* while getting on with it, and ensuring he came home in one piece. Seems Most Distinguished Conduct involves deliberate actions contrary to that; several loose screws and a predilection for dinner, perhaps. I say against the clattering reel: 'Well, he wasn't shell-proof. Did you know that your son saved his life?'

'No.' Almost a laugh, fond and bruised. 'Only told me about the mess he was in.'

So, while we're swapping clandestine unmentionables, I tell him what I know: that his Richard gathered the mess of my Daniel and waved down a motor-lorry to take him direct to the nearest hospital that wouldn't decide he was already dead or legless before looking. I don't tell him that my Daniel remembers his Dunc as saying to the driver: 'Take him or I'll rip your empty English head off your shoulders and post it to your mother.' Nothing unseemly as that.

Mr Duncan says: 'There needs to be a new term invented to define how it is that we should be sitting here talking like this, that this is the way things are.' Indeed again. He adds: 'Though presumably this is not the reason you've sought me out.'

Time for confession to intimate stranger. 'No. I …' still can't say.

'Please,' he says. 'I don't mean to be impolite, but I haven't put a bet on for the three o'clock yet …'

He breaks through my hesitance and makes me giggle: it's only half past eleven now. 'All right, then. I want to know if you have any connections in the … art world … perhaps the Gallery of New South Wales?'

Thick greying eyebrows jump; then: 'I have connections everywhere,' he says, roguish. 'But as for paint slappers and ink scratchers, you could say I'm rather well connected there.'

Stare: *you're not serious.*

Now he does laugh. 'I'm a principal contributor to the gallery.'

Gasp: 'You're an artist too?'

Guffaw: 'No, my dear girl: I throw money at the place, along with the odd item of interest. Why do you ask? Are you an artist?'

Only if you'd like to purchase my last watercolour of a wombat, which isn't too bad, but you'd hardly call it art. I tell him: 'No, but Daniel, my husband is, I think.'

'You think?'

'He is. But his paintings are … not the usual fare.'

'Good. I want to see this unusual fare.' He does, too.

No baulking now, Francy: 'Anytime that's convenient for you, over the next few weeks or so. I have them at the hotel, the Metropole. There's just three of them.' Sent along by exorbitant express freight mail, crated up and marked all over *FRAGILE*, day before yesterday in my fit of super-optimistic maternal derangement; they're sitting in the guests' storeroom now.

He says: 'Well, shall we go?'

'What about your three o'clock, Mr Duncan?'

'What about it? I don't really need to lose another ton on the dog meat — already spilled four this morning. I'll call for my car.'

Car: children: abandoned by roadside. 'If you don't mind, I think we'd better take mine.' Good heavens. And did he mean that he'd lost four hundred *pounds* this morning? Good heavens again.

★

'My word, I see what you mean,' he says; they are lined up against a clutter of trunks and parcels in this narrow room that barely fits us as well; Mr Duncan is leaning so as not to keep bumping the 'Forgotten Coats' rack behind him and his feet crunch on the bumpy sea of brown packing paper all over the floor. He turns to me, blank-faced, and his first adjective is: 'Repulsive.'

I gape, knees about to give way: how dare you.

But he nods into my stunned glare, turns back to the paintings, and adds: 'Adamant about it, isn't he, but the subtleties … Extraordinarily confident, in every way. And the boy is … well, simply exquisite.' He edges closer to young Fritz who's asking his eternal impossible, then turns back to me again, eyes alive again, glittering. 'You say he's never painted *anything* before?'

Knees about to give way with stunned relief now; recover yourself, Francy: 'Not that I'm aware of, apart from the weatherboards of our house.'

Then he clears his throat, returns his attention to the paintings and says: 'Name your price.'

Pinch me or excuse me? I wouldn't have the faintest notion of price. 'There isn't one,' I blurt: 'He doesn't want to sell them, just to get rid of them. But I want them somewhere where they'll stay, perhaps mean something one day …' A couple of fat tears blob down my face, along my neck, into my blouse, but that's all right; it's as it should be, because I'm not gaga, and my bias is good: Daniel's paintings are important, and not only for what they express: he is clever. 'I want them at the gallery, archived or whatever they do with items of interest.'

'Where at best they'll only collect dust? They'd be better off staying here as lost property. I know of a collector, however, a European chap, who would be most interested, most interested indeed. At the very least he'd want to meet your chap; I'd be more than pleased to arrange that.'

'No. Thank you.' Too fast, too far from the plan and my grasp of what's happening here. A collector? 'I'd have to ask him first. I mean, you know, well, it'll be a while before he's up and about.' And at a guess I'm afraid he'll deliver an outright no: as far as Daniel's concerned, this is my mischief, and he's not a proper artist; which is the crux of my caper for him. He is not going to want to meet a *European chap* for a chat about it.

'Of course. Until then, may I look after them for you? They can't stay here.' Mr Duncan smiles, one that deepens as he explains: 'No more than I would have them at the gallery. I could walk them into the dusty depths for you myself, but I'm loath to do that: it's not unheard of for items lacking sufficient *appeal* to be misplaced these days, if you understand?'

Oh. 'I understand.' The depth of my naivety, at the very least, and from Mr Duncan's tone I think I'm being told that I would not only have been laughed away by the curator, but reported to the Commonwealth Police on my way out: it didn't occur to me that censorship could reach that far. Quick prayer of thanks to Mr Lawson and the Leprechaun for timely encouragement; but to this *The* Mr Duncan, champion of monsters: 'I'm much more than grateful for the advice and the offer, so yes, please, I'd very much like you to look after them.'

'Good. I'll arrange for their collection.' He looks at his fob. 'But now, if you don't mind, could you get me back to the track? I need a drink and a flutter after viewing this lot.'

'Of course.' I could probably do with a drink too; don't need a flutter though, feel like I've just won four hundred pounds worth of something right, whatever it is. So instead I indulge in a natural impulse: stand on the tips of my toes and kiss him on the cheek, saying above the scrunch of paper: 'But there's a proper thankyou first, and a request that you have a malt and a bet for my father.'

'No need to request, Mrs Ackerman.' Chuckling away his surprise, at both the kiss and his collision with coat rack: 'I'll have one of each for you as well, and another for your chap's elbow, eh?'

I am so, so teeth-gnashingly sorry, children: abandoned at the hotel now, in their room next to mine, for around about two hours, and they must be starving for lunch. But I must make one last detour: Daniel.

'Just one minute, please,' I beg Matron, who is Mrs Moran to the power of ten. 'I only want to see him.'

'Not on your life, Mrs Ackerman,' she says. 'Not today. Doctor would not approve.'

I say: 'Yes, on my life. One minute, that's all.' Woeful beseech.

St Christopher intercedes and she relents: 'One minute.'

And there he is. Oh —

Propped up on pillows, unconscious, fortunately, so he can't see me gag at the first sight. There's a sort of scaffold on his upper arm, attached to two pairs of bolts that appear to be driven into his flesh either side of a stitched-up wound, and he's encased in plaster from shoulder to waist, and from elbow to wrist, with more scaffold from elbow and wrist to waist holding his arm out at an angle in front of him. There's also a thick dressing around elbow and I can see blood seeping up to the surface of it.

Lunch very doubtful for me now; perhaps Matron had a point. No; had to see him, and it's not going to be any less what it is tomorrow.

He opens his eyes and smiles, mumbles something, then closes his eyes again. Compulsion to wash his face, but Matron ahems and my minute is up. Kiss him and see you tomorrow; don't think he even knew I was there anyway. Leave with a heart full of tight screws and loose miracles.

Must be a miracle that drives me back to the hotel, I'm so distracted. Charlie bounces about in front of me: 'Can we see Uncle Daniel yet?'

'Not yet, kiddo.' Certainly not while Uncle looks like he's being attacked by a Thing that's grown fangs. 'What about fish and chips at Bondi Beach instead?'

Famished children rip open newspapered treat and while they lick greasy, salty fingers and the seagulls screech and swoop about us, I take my first long, steady breaths of the day. Thank all my angels. *Ave* anyone who's watching. Send some rapid-fire salvos for quick healing up the steep hill behind us for St Christopher to catch, and imagine that this shorter distance means they'll be even more powerful this time around.

Kathryn comes and sits next to me while her brothers build a sandcastle. 'He is going to be all right, isn't he?'

Her huge brown worried eyes swallow me up, and I cuddle her, half to hide the weep: 'Course he is.'

Motor start of love and anger: how dare this world have made her so afraid.

DANIEL

First thing I ask the Russian when I come to properly is: 'How long will I have to stay in bed?'

But he says with that face I'm still not sure is a smile: 'No need to stay in bed, better to be as mobile as possible, though you will not be travelling far for a while. I'll be back later to show you how to get up without falling over, yes?'

Yes. Good. No stay in bed, very little pain, and no traction: apart from the inconvenience, very impressed. But I haven't got a clue how I'm even going to sit up with this lot.

He says: 'The wounds look very good, and as soon as there is sufficient correction and union of the bone here in the shaft, I can take away all this metal. The pin at the base of your elbow, however, is permanent, so you must tell me if there is any pain there at all, beyond what you have now, of course.'

'There's a what in my elbow?' Serves me right for not listening in the first place; or maybe it's better I wasn't.

'A small pin,' he says patiently, 'the most important piece of metal here. You see, the interior prominence at the end of the humerus, otherwise known as your funny bone, was fractured completely, and malunion occurred, which means, for you, when it healed it had moved out of position. I have moved it back again, and it is, if you like, *nailed* there with this pin. As a result of that and the alignment of the shaft above, you will have an elbow that works. Better than ever, yes?'

Will I? This bloke's got some serious tickets on himself but I'm more than happy to believe him. Might take some time to believe there's a permanent piece of metal in there, though. What if I rust? Don't ask.

Can't now anyway: he's off, busy man, and I'm alone again. Completely. Except for a tall potted plant by the window, some sort of palm. Can't even hear anyone about, it's that quiet. Of course I have to have a go at getting up straightaway. Can't. Stratho has a good long laugh. Go back to staring out the window at the sea beyond Bondi and the sky that's so clear it looks flat enough to walk on, and I'm feeling envy for the plant that's swaying a bit in the breeze: got more freedom of movement than me. Have another go. Nearly roll off the bed. Just leave it. Wait.

Wait for France; she's come in twice a day for the last few days but I've either been asleep or in the land of Best Brew Ever. Wonder what the time is now; wouldn't know, beyond morning. I've had my breakfast, been shaved, and Nurse even asked me if I wanted to clean my teeth. Yes please, and the service here is amazing, thank you. So it should be for the cost. I should track down Sister Pam Taylor one day and tell her about this for a laugh. I even got a copy of the *Herald* with the slice of lemon for my cup of tea with breakie. Haven't read it, though: apart from news from the Western Front, front page is news of a cyclone wrecking several towns on the Queensland coast. I haven't had a nightmare or a daymare for more than two months and I'm not going to give myself one by reading the details.

Got to do something, though. Probably only been ten minutes and I'm bored already. There is something wrong with me in that respect, I'm sure of it. A bloke should be able to be still, and not fidget. But I am so bored I'm scrunching the end of the sheet in my toes and my left hand is twisting the end of the cord in my pyjama duds. I do these things without thinking: I can stop doing them, but as soon as I don't think about it, I'll start doing them again. What else is there to do? Resist the temptation to touch the *external transfixion*; just because it's right there and I can't work out how it is it doesn't hurt. My elbow does, a bit, but not the fat pins going through my skin and into my bone. How can that be? Doesn't matter: all the fingers on my hand work, that's all that matters. Make a fist to prove it, sort of. Awch: that does hurt.

But now here's footsteps, at bloody last, save me from disappearing up my own arse.

It's France. 'Hello,' she says. 'You're with us,' and she's glowing, little bit sunburned, brought the sun in her hair; her eyes are so blue against the sky behind her and blinking: no cranky nonsense, Daniel. I'm not about to give her any, unless she doesn't hurry up and kiss me. Reliable as ever, there she is. She tastes of peppermint and Francine taste. 'Poor darlingest,' she says. 'Is it too awful?'

Wonder what she's referring to for a second; laugh: 'No.'

'Sure,' she says, and there's a trace of my mother in that *sure*. She thinks I'm having her on.

I say: 'Really, it looks a lot worse than it feels.'

She's not convinced; can't blame her: it does look revolting. 'Well, that's almost as credible as my mischief-making,' she says.

Here we go, this'll be entertaining. 'You've done it, then, have you?' Not that Francine can't do anything she puts her mind to, but I didn't think she'd have a hope of getting in the door of any gallery with my rubbish, let alone the state one. Still don't expect she has. I'm waiting to hear all about the *debacle*, and she says: 'Not exactly …' But then looks a bit guilty about it.

'What happened?'

'I ran into a certain Mr Duncan, father of your Dunc …'

'Ran into him?'

'Not exactly ...' And she tells me all about it. Then: 'I hope you're not cross.'

'Cross?' Jesus, I'm still taking in the tale, but I'm thrilled she's off-loaded them; wouldn't care if she exchanged them for a chook under the counter at a pub. If Dunc's father wants the mad, ugly things, he can have them.

Then she says, 'Um ...' and she never says *um*. 'He was quite impressed, you know, quite very impressed actually. He mentioned a collector he knows, whom he thinks would be even more impressed, suggested this fellow would be keen to meet you.'

Keen to meet me? What for? A laugh? 'I'm sure he was just being polite, France,' I tell her.

'No. I don't think so,' she says, staring at me. Blink, blink. Waiting.

'Well, I do think so.' Think about it: if this Mr Duncan is really interested himself, then it's probably only because he's lost his son and I knew him; and if France believes it's anything more than that, it's only because she wants to believe it, or maybe needs to; and Mr Duncan would have seen that plain in her big blue eyes, as anyone would, so he'd have said something extra nice to her about them: *I know a fellow who knows a fellow, et cetera and if you ever mention it again, I can say oh what a shame, he's just left town.*

Now she looks cross. 'Mr Duncan knows what he's talking about. He wanted to *buy* them, first thing: *name your price*, he said. I told him they weren't for sale, but neglected to add that the *artist* is averse to anything which might suggest he is of value. I don't know why I bothered with the *caper*.'

I do: because you love me. But I don't say that; can't anyway, she's not finished.

'Anyone would think you were afraid of praise, though Mr Duncan also knows very well that you're not a coward. And so do I. He knows all about your *record*. Record of *abandoning*.'

Whoa. 'What would you know about it? What did he tell you?' And I am a bit more than cross now myself: whoever he is, he's got no business having an opinion of me, let alone having chats about it with my wife.

She grabs my hand. 'He didn't tell me anything, I promise. Just that his son told him about you. Please, can you pretend I didn't say any of that. I don't know what I'm talking about and I don't want to know.'

No, you don't, and I'm never going to tell you; very good thing you can't read my mind right now. I tell her: 'But you know enough to work out why *I'm* not interested in the Holy Fucking Monsters, don't you.'

'Yes.'

'Shouldn't you be off somewhere with the kids now?'

'Yes.'

And I've made her cry. She leaves me like I've kicked her.

And I'll spend the rest of the day thinking about how I'm going to apologise for that.

FRANCINE

Bravo, Francy. You *fucking* cretin. That was not a ruthless act of devotion; it was … schedule ten minutes for immersion in boiling oil for that misguided salvo, then arrange to have tongue cut out. But in the meantime, stick a smile on your face: 'All right kiddos, let's head for Taronga Park Zoo. Who's up for an elephant ride?'

Kathryn asks: 'Is Uncle Daniel feeling better?'

'Oh yes, much better,' I tell her. Nothing like a visit from his dutiful wife to make him feel just grand. 'He could do with a present, though. How about you help me choose something for him later on?' See if you can help me get that half right.

DANIEL

Longest hours ever: me, the pot plant, lunch at one and then slow destruction of the cord in my pyjamas; feels like days before she's back. And when she comes in she says straight off: 'I'm not going to say sorry, Daniel, because I don't expect forgiveness for that depth of error.'

I tell her: 'It's not you that needs forgiveness, France.' Can't get past that for a second; tell her what she wants to hear and what's true: 'You can tell Dunc's father that I would like him to have the paintings and he can do whatever he wants with them, so long as I don't have to talk about it, to anyone. All right?'

She nods.

Then just to make it clear: 'And soon as I can, I'll paint something else: you. You can lock me in my room if I misbehave.'

And when she smiles, I feel twice as ashamed of myself for having shouted at her, sworn at her. She kisses it away, and her tear hits my cheek, slides into the pillow with mine and my promise to myself never to do that to her again, for any reason.

'Well,' she says, sitting down on the edge of the bed, and there's a breath of wicked in that *well*: 'It remains that blokes should beware of wives bearing gifts. Got you this.'

She pulls a small, battered, leather-bound book from her bag and hands it to me. It's a copy of, of all things, *The Manifesto of the Communist Party*, by Karl Marx and Freidrich Engels.

I just look at her; she blinks, as if to say: don't you like it? And she's having more than a bit of fun with me.

I say: 'I'm sure the Russian'll be pleased to see me with this.' Whenever he turns up again to show me how to get out of bed.

There's the bell, and she lets me in on the lark: 'Look at the inscription.'

Flip open the cover with my thumb; it reads, in writing that's bad enough to be mine: *Mr Hughes, Is Australia a model of bloodless political Evolution? Only History will tell.* A signature scribble, then: *Lenin, 1913.*

'Where did you get this?' And I'm still reading over it, as if it's double-dutch.

She says: 'On the two for a penny secondhand shelf at a thrift shop round the corner at the Junction, just now. Only went in there to buy some puzzlers for the children. How's that for a puzzler. And incendiary. Fancy Mr Hughes is our little Troll? I'm rather tinny for it at the moment, aren't I?'

'You're not wrong there.' Though I reckon she's whipped it out of her magic hat. 'But Hughes is common as muck; have to be a goose to turf something like this, though.' Real or otherwise. I know that Comrade Lenin gave his two bobs' on this place, and I know it was in 1913 because I'd just turned nineteen; I remember thinking who the fuck is he, and what's a Bolshevik; it was something in some rag quoting him, saying Australian socialism was a bourgeois European fantasy, that our parliament was full of workers' reps that could shut down the Cook government but that had the hands of the plutocracy so firmly up their arses communism couldn't happen here. I remember being shitted-off at this Russian nobody calling Australia a young British *colony* that didn't have any socialists worth anything in it. Fair call, as it turns out. And Hughes would have been one of them at the time: not likely to have sent off abroad for Lenin's autograph; and even if he did, he wouldn't leave it lying around in a personal copy of the Manifesto: more likely to have burned it since Russia's signed a truce with Germany and left Britannia in the lurch for its Workers' Revolution. But then again, he did once run a Socialist League bookshop in Balmain or something, didn't he? Maybe he was an under-the-counter communist-autograph collector in his spare time. Who knows. Maybe it's someone's idea of a joke. Pretty funny one as it turns out. Or pretty sad.

She raises her eyebrow, giggles at me. 'Yes, common as muck. Have to be a goose to sell Mr Lenin's signature for half a penny. What's the world coming to? Anyway, knowing how much you love to read, darlingest, thought you'd appreciate such a slim volume.' And it is tiny; seems too slim to be anything much at all. Then she adds: 'I've had a quick look and I can recommend chapter three for hypnotic bombast if you're having any trouble sleeping.'

'Thanks, dear.' Who is this woman?

'Try to do my best for you,' she says, reaching in her bag again and handing me a parcel. 'But this is your proper present. Kathryn chose it.'

I look at the knot in the string round the wrapping and hand it back. 'You could do me a favour.'

'Oh?' she says; then: 'Oh, of course.' Dippiest girl in the world, my girl.

'Your niece knows something about gentle treachery,' she says, picking it undone. 'For adored ascetic uncle it must be luxurious, currently extremely expensive, and outrageously delicious.'

It's chocolate. What else do you have with your communism? 'Tell her I love it: just what I wanted.'

She says: 'I should do that now, get back to the kiddos and stop bothering you.' Don't stop; but then she kisses me again, properly, and I think it wouldn't be a bad idea if she left immediately.

'Is there anything you need for the morning?'

Get my head out of right now for long enough to manage: 'You could run a new cord through for my pyjamas.'

She looks at the damage. 'How'd that happen?'

'I don't know.'

But she smiles like she's made a fairly good guess.

Dinner and half the box of chocolates later, sun's going down, no sign of anyone coming to turn on a light for me, so I skip to the end of the Manifesto, like it'll have a wind-up; but it does: *Let the ruling classes tremble at a Communistic revolution. The proletarians have nothing to lose but their chains. They have a world to win. WORKING MEN OF ALL COUNTRIES, UNITE!*

And then do what? For this country's proletariat the answer might be: bog into the good stuff left behind by the ruling classes, then complain about headache and indigestion for a while before whingeing come Saturday: *Where's the fucking boss pissed off to, I want me fucking pay*. Not really, but there'd need to be a few changes to the Manifesto for Australia: with confiscation of all property of all emigrants and rebels, there'd be very few left with anything, and with an equitable distribution of the population throughout the country, we'd all be starved for each other's company; hand's up for not living in the desert too. And I have a more fundamental question for the Communist Party of the World: in your *forcible overthrow*, unless you execute all the mean arsewipes, across all classes, then where's your advantage? There's always going to be thickheads, across all classes, that have no idea, and I should know; so how do you educate, protect and make equal that which can never be the equal of an arsewipe intent on taking his own advantage? Manifesto of Ackerman: the world is divided into two main groups: a large group called Idiots, and a small one called Selfish Bastards. The Selfish Bastard, like most parasites, can only be exterminated by means of something which will probably take half your skin off while you're at it. This is why I am not a philosopher, or a politician. I am, regardless, a member of the ruling class, however uncomfortable that fact still is. I'm not trembling, though, except maybe from too much chocolate, which I would have shared if there was anyone about.

Footsteps: please, whoever you are, come and have a hazelnut thingo before I make myself sick.

'Apologies for the delay, Mr Ackerman.'

Of course it's the Russian; it would be, wouldn't it, while I'm holding The Red Rag. He's come to get me up and about, no doubt, and I forgot to ask the nurse to change my pyjamas so they don't fall down when Frankenstein's monster stands; embarrassing enough to have to ring a little brass bell to ask her for anything. Strange day, very: why not end it with an extra dose of embarrassment.

I say: 'Don't worry about it.'

'I was not worried,' spade face smiles; it is a smile: 'But I do enjoy Australian idiom.'

Idiom? Close enough to idiot for me. He's rigging up a length of rope, over the bar above the bed, for his monkey right now.

But goose says: 'You've had a busy day then?' Couldn't Nurse have done the job? Jesus: he could've just given the rope to me and I could've thrown it over, worked it out for myself, maybe.

'Yes,' he says, as in aren't I generally very bloody busy. 'I treat public patients at Sydney Hospital when necessary and this afternoon I was necessary, and busy.'

'Why's that?' Half for want of chat, half for wonder.

'Little boy fell off the roof of his house, two storeys. Did a good job on himself, as you might say.'

Awch. 'Is he all right?'

'He will be.' He snorts and shakes his head. 'But I thought we might have to admit his mother: distressed for her child and terrified she could not afford a bill.'

Out before I've thought it: 'Well, I could pay for it.'

He laughs. 'You already have. I bill you as much as I can get away with so that she does not have to pay, for me at least.'

Fair enough.

Then he says: 'What are you reading?'

'Just a bit of rubbish,' I tell him, and shove it in the drawer of the bedside table. Expand my manifesto to include a third, probably even smaller group called The Decent. 'You want a chocolate?'

'No, thank you. But I'm sure you would like to be out of bed.'

'Not till I've changed my pyjamas.'

He looks concerned. 'What's wrong with your pyjamas?'

Could've said that a bit more clearly, couldn't I. 'I've wrecked the cord.'

Spade face nods like he's sure I must have had a very dull one; but I haven't, not by any stretch. And not now I've got a *specialist* surgeon changing my duds.

'So,' he says when I'm ready, 'pull yourself upright, swing your legs over the side of the bed and stand up, slowly.'

Is that right? Have to say: 'I hope you didn't make a special trip back here for this.' Then I nearly keel over against him.

'Yes,' he says, righting me; and I'm sure he's come for the entertainment. 'Now sit back down and then do it again.'

I do: 'Well, there you go, thanks.'

'Good,' he says. 'But bear in mind, Mr Ackerman, that I charge double for further repairs.'

He's got a laugh out of me. I suppose I could end the day by falling over and causing myself another injury, Doctor Adinov, but that's one event I think I might try very hard to avoid.

★

'So what is it you do, Mr Ackerman?' Adinov asks me the next
morning, and he's holding a little spanner as he's looking at my
external transfixion. And yes, he's going to use it on me. I'm
getting ready to bite down the scream, and the only thing
stopping me from closing my eyes is disbelief. But when he gives
a short turn to the nut that holds the two bars at the tops of the
pins, it doesn't feel like anything, except what it looks like. I can't
make head or tail of that.

I say: 'What?'

He says: 'I asked, what is it you do, for a living.'

I'm a professional orthopaedic experiment, I'm thinking, but
I say: 'Not a lot at the minute.' Or nothing, to be honest. Ask him:
'What did you do just then?'

'Moved the edges of the bone by the smallest fraction, to
straighten the shaft; I'll do this every other day for a few weeks
until it is correctly positioned.'

He's put his spanner down and now he's dabbing wet cotton
wool around the bottom of the pins.

'What's that you're putting on it?' I sound like Charlie.

'Boiled, salted water. Revolutionary antiseptic, this one. And
you are free now for another day of not a lot.'

And off he goes to amaze someone else.

Off I go on my first slow trip out to the balcony, wishing I
had my boots on so I wouldn't lean that extra half inch to the
right. There's a couple of other blokes out here, or young
gentlemen I should say: silk dressing gowns and slippers, one's
smoking a pipe and the other's wearing a couldn't-miss-it-at-
midnight dark pink cravat, or should I say *cerise*. I can't be missed
either: they've seen me, in my best Francine-made-to-measure
pyjama duds and nothing else but my cement and metal.

'Hullo. Here, that's impressive,' says Cerise.

Pipe waves.

I could probably do with some more practice at being civilised and polite; at least try not to be so quick to judge others. See how we go: smile: 'G'day.'

When I've lowered myself into a chair, chat in Universal Bloke follows: comparison of ailments. I win: not hard. Cerise has twisted a knee coming off a horse in a game of polo. *Polo?* And Pipe's knocked a couple of ribs coming a cropper while *motoring*. I'd like to ask them what they are doing hanging about in a hospital, even if this particular one appears to double as a gents' holiday resort, but think better of it: they're doing their duty for Adinov's public service, possibly while avoiding military service.

Pipe says to me: 'So, you must have a tale to tell about this arm of yours?'

No: 'It's a very long one.'

'We've got all day,' Cerise chuckles.

Fuck off: 'I buggered it at Pozieres for the AIF.' Stratho's rolling around pissing himself at that.

Conversation stopper: they don't want to know now. But they are patriots nonetheless.

Cerise says: 'Only one thing the damned war's good for — Blighty's still pushing up the price of our wheat and wool. I'd put some money in the golden fleece if you haven't already.'

Thanks for the advice, and the note I've just added to my manifesto: Cerise is the Idiot that is produced when Selfish Bastards breed.

'So, what is it you do with yourself when you're not being tortured?' Pipe asks me; it's clearly the question of the day.

'Fuck all,' I say, and they think that's hilarious.

'Here's to fuck all,' says Cerise, chuckle, chuckle, chuckle.

Pipe says: 'What's your business then?'

'Coal,' I say. That's what it is, and a big fat penny's suddenly spinning on the floor between my feet. I can hear it but I can't see it. Fact: Francine and I own half a coal mine. I can hear Evan saying: *if you were any slower on this, I'd say you were backward.* Francine and I have to buy out Drummond, and then … not sure. It'll come. And I won't be looking to Messrs Marx and Engels for advice on how to overthrow myself. I might not be much chop as a bourgeois Kraut intellectual, but neither of them ever hewed coal, did they. Neither has Lenin, or Hughes for that matter. They can all go to buggery, along with the miners' federation. I'm going to do something very radical: talk to my wife, when we get home, after I've had more of a think about it.

'You'd be doing well then,' says Pipe.

'I suppose so.' But I really don't know what's in the capital kitty. Francine looks after our accounts.

'Oh, there you are.' And here she is now, my saviour, in a thousand different ways: 'Should you be out of bed?'

Yes, but: 'Not for long. Better get back in it.'

Cerise and Pipe are looking at me for an introduction. I say: 'My wife.'

France gives me that look: *exceptionally rude, Daniel.*

I give her one back: *So what.* But I have a simple engineering problem as regards escape: I'm stuck in this bloody chair, trapped by curved, sloping armrests that were not made with me in mind: I'll topple it as soon as I push up. 'You could do me a favour.'

'Yes?' she says.

I say, quietly: 'Just stand there and don't move, will you.'

I put my hand on her shoulder and haul. I'm up and she cracks a beauty of a smile. 'Well, this is dancing, isn't it.'

And it is.

★

'I was somewhat distracted this morning. So, it's fortunate I did such a *good job* on it, hmm?' Adinov says when I come to, and this, I think, is Russian humour, which I might appreciate another day. He's just told me I'll be like this till the tenth of April, that's fifty-three days away, no metal, except for my permanent, most important, funny-bone pin, but no moving shoulder either: cement stays, it's fixed my hand on my heart, or near enough; here's cheers for remembrance, King George. And it must be a hundred and five degrees in the shade and a hundred and four and a half here indoors. Bastard. I am seriously *impatient, seriously* beyond this. You'd think I'd have learned something about compliance, acceptance of time as my bones know it. No. Think about the other poor blokes worse off? No. At least it means I can leave prison, though: France can take me home tomorrow: lucky, lucky, lucky girl.

But now spade face says: 'Fortunate it survived the whole journey, I thought, when I realised who you are.'

'Who am I?' Apart from not keen for a game of Guess Who.

'The artist responsible for three paintings I saw yesterday evening.'

Good thing I'm horizontal and weighted down. Thought I might have been beyond surprise. 'Am I.'

'Yes. Don't worry about it: Edward Duncan has only shown them to me. No one else. Your wife made it very clear to him that you do not want to acknowledge them, and I can see why. But you should know that if you don't continue with it I would want to amputate my *good job* for the waste of it.'

'And who are you?' I'm somewhere between not here at all and knocked for six.

'Someone who perhaps understands something about waste, loss.'

Go on.

He sits on the bed as if he owns it and I'm sure he does. 'Well, if losing my country can be considered a loss. I left St Petersburg, or Petrograd, or whatever you want to call it, almost two years ago, after taking my leave of the carcasses on the Eastern Front. Easy for me to do, but lacking in foresight. I no longer have a home there, it is now the possession of the state. Whatever the state of Russia is now. It has been expropriated from me, I was fortunate to get most of my money out in time. I do not care that peasants have probably brought their pigs to winter inside my home — I wish them every happiness together — but I do care that inside my home, on the ceiling of the main bedroom, is a fresco painted by my grandfather for my grandmother. It is not masterly, a brilliant mess of angels and doves and too many flowers, but it is a priceless expression, and my inheritance, or was. You understand?'

'Yes.' That I must be due another riddle, but I can see Dad's kitchen cupboards, and the bedhead he carved for Mum and I think I know what he means. At least I know that I would be ropeable if it was *expropriated* from her.

He goes on: 'As irreplaceable as any treasure — my collection of artworks, from all over Europe, all those years picking up this and that. It's all gone. It would be interesting to know what the Soviet has made of them. My taste runs a little to the *innovative*, shall we say. Taste in art as well as transfixion apparatus — not always appreciated by those who know so much better. Like your work, yes? Unlike any other work I've seen here.'

Work? Jesus. And, slow off the mark as I am, I realise this must be that collector France mentioned; it wasn't bullshit, even if that's the main word going through my mind at the minute. Stumble into it: 'They're just pictures, flukes. I'm not really ...' Anything, and I'll never do anything like that again, be that mad again; I don't ever want to be.

'Flukes?' he says. 'They appear deliberate to me. Your opinion is not at issue, just as my opinion of what you do with your arm is not. I can only tell you what I think, and hope that you take my advice. I am aware that you do not wish to discuss it, so that, shall we say, is that, Mr Ackerman.'

Is it? Doubt it; at the very least: 'Can you not call me Mr Ackerman?'

'What would you prefer?' he laughs, having a go like he was born here.

'Daniel'll do.'

'All right, Daniel. And I'll let you call me Anton in exchange for another of your *flukes*. You've got fifty-three days to think about it.'

'Fair enough.' I'll think about it, once I've come round to believing it. But for now I have to ask, mostly just to check we have actually had this chat: 'What made you set up business out here?'

He says, standing up and glancing out the window at three hundred different shades of green and blue: 'If you had the choice between London and Sydney for your exile, where would you go?'

No contest, even if I am melting inside my cement straightjacket. He doesn't wait for an answer; gone off to be amazing and decent to someone else, and on a Sunday. I'm not supposed to get up today: bugger that. I'll spend some time frigging around to see what I can and can't do in this thing while I wait for France; practise not being a pain in the arse. Even if she is late, or maybe already come and gone, probably taking a ferry ride or swimming with the kids or what have you. Even when it takes me ten years to get my trousers on, or mostly, apart from the bottom two fly buttons, five seconds to work out the rest is fairly much impossible and I'm going to be a pain in the arse anyway. So practise being a *pleasant* pain in the arse, Daniel. Poor France. Must be well past midday now, and a hundred and ten degrees: where is she?

FRANCINE

I most definitely had not intended for this to happen today. Two harbingers of immense debacle should have told me to be suspicious of my promise to the children that our final day in Babel would be the best: beginning with an excursion to the Domain to hear the nuts in the park on a sunny Sunday morn. And here I am, in Phillip Street Police Station, contemplating all that brought us here.

First ill omen occurred after an innocent decision to tootle round to Rose Bay first, to have a look at the old house where I grew up. I wouldn't have thought to go there at all, except that Kathryn asked me at breakfast where I used to live. We pulled up outside the gigantic monument to excess, all sprawling sandstone down the incline towards the sea, box hedge and banks of agapanthus and clivia still framing frangipanis in full heady bloom out the front, and I was just thinking how odd it was that I could no longer see myself in this place, and yet it seemed I could still hear Father thumping away on the piano, being gorgeously vulgar, as if he were there inside, when Harry said behind me: 'You left this for Uncle Daniel?'

Too incredulous, and too curtly said for my liking, young man, especially since you haven't once shown an interest in Uncle this entire holiday. I think I know why this is: because he still feels responsible, and because he's probably not looking forward to seeing Uncle tomorrow, Uncle who will need some looking after for a while yet. If we're released by the metropolitan constabulary so that we can see Uncle, let alone look after him.

Anyway, I was going to try to explain to Harry that it wasn't so simple as me leaving a house for a man when Kathryn said: 'Why wouldn't Aunty France have done that?'

And I was going to try to explain that Aunty France was actually once a stuck-up little so-and-so who thought Uncle Daniel too far beneath her for acknowledgement as fellow human, when Harry muttered under his breath: 'Bet they're not even properly married.'

Oh? Never had a desire to scold a child as I did at that moment: despite the fact that he's only about three inches shorter than me, and towers over his elder sister, he's too young and too fuddled to know anything about it, but if we'd been anywhere near a washing facility I'd have rammed a cake of soap into his mouth. Just as well we were standing on the footpath in a genteel neighbourhood. Very short walk to Our Lady, though, and I almost, *almost* thought to drag him over there for a quick cheerio: hello, it's me, Francine, come to have the devil frightened from this child by Sister Simon-Peter. Couldn't do that to an enemy; besides, they'd all have been at Mass. So instead, I steadied myself and said: 'Perhaps we should go to church this morning, *Catholic* church, where your uncle and I were *properly* married.' You sour little Presbo.

And I was only going to try to give him a sense of the ludicrous with a stop-off tour of the Gothic catastrophe that is St Mary's Cathedral, just across the road from the Domain. But we got a bit more than I'd bargained for.

Second ill omen. Pre-Mass parade: clutches of women gossiping around the forecourt, their men looking over their shoulders for their bookmakers, wanting tips before the performance, when I took the children up the steps, their wide eyes all fixed skyward at the edifice. Then it happened. Galloping horses. A cry of: 'Filthy Micks!' And a small plague of eggs. One of which hit the masonry at the side of the entrance, splattering back a good deal of its contents across my face, but mostly in my ear. Where are the Commonwealth Police when you need them, hmn?

Don't know if it was my discombobulation or inherent lack of reverence, but I stepped straight through the vestibule and lunged at the font with my handkerchief. Dipped it in archbishop-blessed water and scrubbed at the sticky muck. Just egg. As if I thought it might have been something worse. And then I was a horror-struck Mick for a second, awaiting thunderbolt for my gross sacrilege. But none came. Course not: it was saving itself for later. I said to Harry, not hiding my contempt: 'Well, there's religion for you. Now would you like ice cream and ginger beer?' Meaning at the Domain.

He said, nine-year-old boy but standing *at me* like a man, in the middle of the aisle: 'Do you even believe in God?'

Dear God, does Uncle Daniel have to sort you and your rude little mouth out. Catch that thought: your rudeness is quite possibly — what's that new science of inheritance called? *Genetics*.

I said, dabbing yolk from the brim of my hat: 'No. Not really. Not this sort of thing at least.'

'Why?' Truly asking and needing to know.

My attempt: 'Because I doubt that even God would approve. Perhaps it would be more *responsible* for us all to fear the power of us, without the convolution of the hand of God.' Ten points for clarity under duress, Francy; a hundred points for prophecy as it turns out.

'What's convolution?' said Charlie.

Second attempt for seven-year-old: 'Making things seem more complicated than they are, so that it's harder to work out what's true and what's not, for yourself.' If only you knew the half of it, kids.

Harry said, unrelenting: 'How do you know what's true and what's not without God?'

And Kathryn replied, her small voice clarion bright in the massive vault: 'That's what your conscience is for.' Indeed. Touche. Not quite twelve-year-old who's had her world turned upside down and yet she knows what's what. But then she whispered, or rather hissed, loudly: '*Heinrich.*'

Oh dear. Low blow, Kathryn. Harry's christened Henry Hubert McKinnon, after his grandfathers and in that order because, as Miriam has said, you wouldn't call a child Hubert for any reason. No: neither is he Heinrich. But his sister's swipe shut him up, and I could have cuddled him, except for the threat of violence in his glower at her.

We'd got through just over three weeks together without so much as a hint of squabble, and I wasn't about to allow one to break out now as an encore prelude to the Mass, so I marched them up to Mary, lit a candle and told the three of them to kneel and pray to her for peace. And they did, before I whipped them out the side door and onto the street to save them from the main show.

But Our Lady is overburdened presently, isn't she. Or she has a sharp sense of the comedic, reserved especially for Presbo kiddos and lapsed Micks.

No sooner had our truce been ratified with sweet treats in the park than it was Aunty France's turn to lose her head when we ambled through the throng. Perhaps it was the rising mercury; perhaps it was the residue of egg in my ear; perhaps it was a surge of maternal derangement, and I am straining against the seams of my skirt already, as the heartstrings are straining after these weeks without my rascally Danny; perhaps it was even a bit of disappointment at the absence of a more entertaining soapboxer in this our last bastion of free speech; but undoubtedly it was the attendant conscriptionist that provoked it.

'It is a duty,' I heard him say with quivering ardour, 'as a child to its mother, that we serve her, as she has nourished us. A man who would not fight for his mother's honour against the Hun is not only a coward, but should be deemed, by all morality, a felon, and by God damned to hell.'

Or perhaps it was the devil that made me shout into his dramatic pause: 'And what does all morality call a mother who murders and maims her own children? Is there a place in hell for her?'

Wave of 'Oooohaaa' swelled from sweltering crowd: might as well have burned the Union Jack. And self-induced flabbergast might have put an end to my outburst had the speaker not replied: 'Where is your husband cowering, woman, while his countrymen suffer his spineless betrayal?'

I know where the expression 'to see red' comes from now: too much blood too fast in the brain. I sort of had a vague notion that his question was rhetorical, and even that the crowd was enjoying this preacher for his inadvertent parody of himself, but I could not prevent my action. Could not find words with which to vent the whorl of outrage, or the dignity to walk away. Instead I hurled my peppermint ice cream at him. And it didn't miss. His face.

'Top shot!' Cheer erupted. As did demand from speaker: 'Police! Police!'

A man said from behind me: 'Don't worry, love.' And I didn't have the wit to worry as a wall of men surrounded us. The children all looking up at me: *what?* Charlie tugging at my hand: 'Aunty France?'

But Mr Parody's outrage was more than a match for mine; pushing through the throng: 'That's her! She's a troublemaker. I've seen her before.'

One word found: 'Liar!'

Man behind, quietly: 'Shush, love.' Then he said to approaching policeman: 'The lady didn't do anything, officer. It was someone further back.'

Parody, still wiping at milky goo: 'I saw her with my own eyes.'

Policeman, to me: 'Did you throw the ice cream, madam?'

Still can't believe the fact of it, or that ability to fib deserted me precisely then: 'Yes.'

Policeman, to Parody, wearily: 'Are you injured, sir?'

'My word, I am. I want her arrested for assault upon me.'

Policeman: 'Wouldn't an apology from the lady be more appropriate?'

Parody and Me in chorus: 'No!'

I said: 'I'm not apologising to him. So arrest me.' Really should have had tongue removed.

Policeman: ''Pologies, madam, but it seems I'll have to. At least sort this out at the station.'

And so here we are, the children and I, not in a cell, but in an airless oven of a room, waiting for me to be sorted out. Chewing over my words that *I'd rather be locked up for more newsworthy sedition*. Parody maintaining that I am not only his assailant but that he's certain I'm a member of the Socialist Party.

Policeman, very weary now at playing go-between: 'I'm not aware that being a member of the Socialist Party is a crime yet, madam, but he claims that you've a habit of taking part in subversive activities. Any truth to this?'

'No, and I'm not a member of any party.' Merely victim of Mad Hatter's one.

'Didn't imagine so. But he still wants to press the charge of assault, and he's within his rights to do that, pointless as it would be. I have suggested an alternative: that a fine be paid by you for disturbance of the peace, to settle the matter today, and he's considering it. Have you got a fiver on you?'

Five pounds! Rattle through purse. 'No. Two pounds, three shillings. My money's at the hotel, Metropole.'

'You're not from Sydney?'

'No.' Not any more, cobber. 'Lithgow.'

'Husband about?'

'No. Yes, I mean, he's at St Christopher's, hospital, Waverley.' And by now no doubt woken up with fresh cement and wondering where I am.

'That's no good. Not well, eh?'

'Not not well, exactly …' I give him a brief version of the tale of no-good elbow acquired *over there*. 'That's mostly why I took objection, and, well, you know …' Incendiary ice cream; cringe.

'He's a returned man, then. Right.' Policeman scratches his head, says: 'Excuse me for a moment, madam.'

Within a moment, returned policeman: 'He's decided against any charge.'

'Oh?'

'Yes,' and weary smile: 'I've told him to mind his words or you'll have my permission to throw a brick at him.'

I can hear Father hooting.

'Well, kiddos,' I say on the way out, 'can't complain of nonevent, can you?'

Charlie says: 'Let's go back and see if you can get him with a brick.'

Bless that boy: I laugh so hard I do burst a bit of a seam. 'The policeman didn't mean that, he was just being funny.'

'Aw,' says Charlie.

Harry rolls his eyes. 'Goose.'

Kathryn says: 'We should probably hurry now, shouldn't we?'

Yes, we should.

★

Bless my darlingest most of all: there he is, sitting on the bed trying to get a sock on his left foot, making very hard work of it.

I say: 'I'll do all that.' Didn't realise he'd be quite so helpless.

Neither did he: he looks up; miserable: 'Suppose you'll have to. Where've you been?'

'Oh, out and about,' I say.

'And what does that mean?' Got a bit of a smile.

'Means good deal of morning spent in police station, avoiding arrest.'

'Is that right? What'd they nab you for?'

'Assault.'

'Good-o. Do I want to know?'

'Depends on whether you think you've got the stomach to hear about what I can do with an ice cream when riled.'

'Just try to shock me, France.'

Do my best, but he's still miserable. 'What you getting up to this afternoon, then?'

'Just the beach, I think. We've had enough excitement.'

Doubly miserable: 'Have a swim for me, won't you. But can you help me get back into my pyjamas before you go?'

Forlorn to break your heart. Maybe he's still drowsy from the ether this morning, or some sedative; he'll be better tomorrow.

Sort of. Monday morning, and I've almost got him ready, buttoning his shirt, thinking, fortunate you prefer a generous cut across the shoulders or we'd never get this round you, when I remember.

'Your shirts. I haven't picked them up.' From the tailor on George Street in town; Father's old tailor, who does a proper job, though I don't think he does too many collarless jobs sans matching collar these days. That's what Daniel wears, however, plain white cotton and no collar, like a protest against fashion, any fashion, and gentleman tailor far too professional to question this lady's order of four of them in finest fabric. Lady too sensible to mention cost to gentleman, too; instead, I told Daniel that this lot would last for centuries. And they will.

He says now: 'I'd rather go straight home.'

'I know.' He'd rather hibernate and wake up without Uncomfortable Heavy Thing. 'But what's five minutes in a five-hour trip?'

'Five more minutes,' he says, terse.

This'll be a fun trip, won't it. Would you like me to put you on the fast train? Don't say anything, Francy: just pack his bag and get going.

I'm hunting for Almighty Toothbrush when Doctor Adinov puts his head around the door. 'Fifty-two days to think about it now, Daniel.'

Daniel? They're chummy?

Daniel says: 'Yep.'

Doctor waves goodbye: 'Safe journey.'

Daniel: 'Yep.'

Doctor bows slightly to me: 'Mrs Ackerman,' and he's gone.

'What was that about fifty-two days?' I ask Daniel.

Grunt: 'Tell you later.'

Right: 'Are you going to be this cranky the whole time?'

'No. Sorry. I'm just …' then he smiles. 'Cranky.'

Rub it in: 'Well, just remember, darlingest, cranky kids get castor oil for supper.'

And he's still chuckling at that as we hit the sunshine outside. Kids waiting in the car not chuckling, though.

Charlie, aghast: 'Oh, Uncle Daniel, where's your arm gone?'

Kathryn, blanched: 'Charles Robin, you shush.'

Daniel says: 'Don't worry, I've still got it. Somewhere under this.' And knocks on his shoulder.

Harry's looking away, pretending he's not here, but he's so pink-cheeked that when he glances at Daniel lowering himself into the front seat, he looks as if he'll burst.

Kathryn doesn't appear much further off bursting either. She looks positively slapped. But for a different reason, I've suddenly seen. She's not a kiddo any more, and profound concern for uncle is perhaps not only another burden of the war and the awfulness it's brought her: she *adores* adores him. Can't blame her there. Goodness me, I'm a breath off slapped too, just looking at her. Stop that: concoct diversion immediately.

I say: 'Daniel. It's just occurred to me that we haven't got a present for your mother or Miriam.'

He looks at me: *so what?*

Persist: 'Since we have to stop in town on the way, Kathryn and I can pop into David Jones, get some little somethings.'

He says: 'I think we've spent enough money lately, Francine.'

'We won't spend much.' As if we can't afford it.

Frown: 'What am I supposed to do while you're at it? Sit in the car and fry?'

Masterstroke: 'You can sit under a tree in Hyde Park, with the boys. They'll look after you. We won't be long: straight in and out.'

'Do I have a choice?'

'No.' But if I look at the pout a second longer, I'll have to be very unmindful of the children and lean hard on the pedal for home to put you straight to bed.

DANIEL

Charlie's still rabbiting on about Aunty France's top shot yesterday. 'You should have seen her,' he's saying, but over the last half-hour he's already given a blow-by-blow account detailed enough that I may as well have been there. 'Never seen a lady shout out like that, or a girl; never seen anyone do anything like that. And the man was so rotten — he called Aunty France a troublemaker and brought the police. Just for a bit of ice cream. If it was me I wouldn't have wasted my ice cream. But she stood up to him …' Here we go again.

And Harry's wandering off along the path towards the street, not because he's had an earful, I don't think. He is as impressed by France as anyone is, if you're looking.

'Oi, come back here,' I tell him. He doubles back. I tell Charlie to pipe down and go chase the pigeons away from the bubbler for a while. Then I sit there, looking at Harry as he scrapes the side of his boot against the gravelly dirt of the path, determined not to look up. If he could give me a wider berth he'd be in Queensland. I say: 'Stop doing that, you'll wreck the leather.' He stops. Still staring at the dirt. Try again: dredge up a memory of not talking to Dad for weeks after breaking a window and getting belted for saying it was an accident. It was an accident, but as far as Dad was concerned carelessness at sling-shooting magpies off the roof did not make an accident: an accident is what happens when you have no control over events. He had a point, but this

394

little Harry has no idea of the difference: that he didn't have control, and that that's more than forgivable, considering.

'Sit down,' I say, and can just reach to pull him by the shirt sleeve onto the bench beside me; he doesn't resist. My hand on his shoulder, I can feel the too-big bones under his skin; he's all bones and little else; little boy growing very fast. 'You can't keep this up forever, mate. Believe me.'

He says: 'I won't. Keep it up, I mean.' Looking at his knees.

He used to be the first kid to take a running jump at me; fling himself at me to get thrown higher. I touch the back of his head to feel my own paintbrush hair, and he curls against me. To clock his forehead right on the edge of the cast.

'Awch,' he says, rubbing his head. Looks up at me. And he doesn't fail me now: he starts laughing like it's going out of fashion.

Charlie wheels back and says: 'What's so funny?'

'You, you goose,' Harry says.

Champion. Both of them.

Charlie says, patting around my chest to find my arm: 'Geewhizz. Wowee. So are you going to get a good scar out of this too?'

I tell him: 'Best one yet: looks like I've been bitten by a giant snake.'

'Really? When can I see it? Bet it's not as good as the one on your leg. Never seen a scar as good as that one …'

Here we go again. And he might as well keep going: no sign of France and Kathryn. They've obviously been detained by David Jones, and I'm not sure that France is pleading for quick release.

FRANCINE

As if the deferential doorman, the swish hydraulic lift, the plush velveteen chairs and long marble-topped tables weren't enough of a giggle, in which we indulge at first with our eyes and then quite openly, the camisoles we're shown are too exquisite. I want her to have all of them. It's funny to think I used to take all this for granted; stranger still to realise I haven't missed it. Funniest of all is that although these days I might know more about motor mechanics than my husband does, there's enough Rose Bay left in this little engine for me to be as swept up as the young lady beside me on the velveteen.

Kathryn says, scandalised murmur: 'I can't choose.'

Neither can I. There's a ban on luxury goods now, but not, apparently, when it comes to feminine undergarments. Let's be scientific and mindful of the fact that although we've left Uncle Daniel in the shade, it's already a very warm day out there. Kathryn, with her thick dark hair and fire-brown eyes like Sarah's, is not suited to absolute plains, but fairly plain it has to be at nearly twelve. 'This one,' I say: it's broderie, with a slim ribbon at the waist and a tiny beige butterfly beneath the centre of the subtle V neckline. Perfect, in prettiness and purpose: to acknowledge her growing up. She thinks so too, and now it's her pleasure to choose something for her mum and grandma. Mim needs new gloves and her daughter picks a palest blue-grey pair with a single pearl shell button at the wrist. Grandma doesn't need anything, never does, so she gets something completely frivolous: three of the most divine lace handkerchiefs known to woman, which she'll put in a drawer and never use, but love anyway.

Done. Remind the saleslady we're in a hurry, so please package up at speed. Bolt off back to ground floor for scribbling journal I've decided is another essential for young lady. There really is only one choice there: it's bound in mauve kidskin impressed with a border of daisy chain. 'You have to have that one,' I say to her. 'That is a journal for some very high thoughts, hm?'

She says, in her soft clear voice: 'My thoughts are plainer than that.'

I say: 'Even better. Celebrate the contradiction. Done?'

She giggles; loveliest sound. 'Done.'

'Anything else? Let's give ourselves two more minutes' shopping frenzy.'

'There is something else I'd like.'

'Excellent. What?'

'A haircut like yours.'

Good God. Not on your life. I say: 'I doubt your mother would approve of that.'

'I know,' she says, and I see she's having a laugh, with me. She adds: 'But I will, when I'm older, have a haircut just like yours. I think it looks elegant, and different.'

Throat closes over. You couldn't buy that, could you? 'Yes, I'm sure you will. Meantime, how cross do you think your uncle is by now?'

'Fairly cross,' she nods.

'Let's get cracking, shall we?'

Bolt through payments and packaging and back out onto the footpath. Fly into and out of tailor's, then dodge through the traffic along Market Street back up to the park.

But Daniel's not cross at all; asks when he sees us: 'Released without charge or out on bail?' Smiling as he heaves himself up; sun in his eyes, makes me want to fall into them. And Harry's smiling too: well done, Uncle.

'Charged,' I say, 'but released on grounds of good character.'

'Judge must have been drunk. That looks like a lot of charge, France.' Raising an eyebrow at the packages as we all head for the car.

Kathryn's blushing now. For heaven's sake. I say: 'Anyone would think you were mean, Mr Frugal.'

Pout: 'I'm not mean. We just probably shouldn't be spending so much.' And he's serious.

'Why?'

'Tell you later,' he says.

And that's two *tell you laters* I have now to keep my imagination busy on the long drive home. Fifty-two days to think about it, shouldn't be spending money, and chummy with Russian surgeon. No, completely baffled.

DANIEL

'Shush.' France is shoving me awake. 'Snoring.'

I know, I know. And I know how very, very irritating it is to sleep next to a snorer. Only six days left of this, for me and poor France. Doesn't matter what I do, I usually end up snoring; you're just not meant to sleep on your back holding a slab of cement. And lately when I wake up like this or she wakes me up I remember Anderson, Keith Anderson, and know that his wife and sons would give anything to hear him snoring. Float away from it; it was an accident, not even Fritz intended it, but I still don't know if I believe it was an accident or my fault.

Force myself to think of other things, what I do know, what I can control. What I want to do. I start ticking off the plans we've made for the Wattle and balancing them against the fact that however you look at it underground mining is probably second only to warfare in filth and risk. No revolution or truce will change that. Accident waiting to happen. The Wattle's had three in the last twelve months, requiring a doctor, none too serious: that's pretty good. But that's lucky. Somewhere along the line something out of control will happen again. It's a matter of being properly prepared, for it and against it, and of me going back to work to take responsibility for it, whether we can buy out Drummond or not.

France groans now: 'Go back to sleep.' She reckons she can hear the wheels turning.

But I can't go back to sleep, I'll only start snoring again. So I just lie here and look at her instead in the dark. That's not hard; I can do that for very long stretches. She's four or five months pregnant now and it's showing all over her. There's no way I can describe what I feel about that. When she gets dressed in the morning and I see her body, rounder and smoother and softer everywhere, it's not an image I'm looking at, it's the whole incomprehensible privilege of seeing her. How do you paint that? Worth every second of this spell of uselessness to be able to wonder about it, watch her every day, except that I'd prefer to be of more use to her. She's half asleep half the time, and not just because I keep waking her up; she's heavier and looks further along than she's supposed to, apparently. Mrs Moran said straight off that France's going to have twins this time, and Nichols agreed, reckons he definitely heard two little heartbeats in there, and he told me our timing is good this time, since I'll be back on board when she should be taking it easy. And he said I should insist she does, because it's important she doesn't do anything that might make the babies come too early. That thought sets the wheels turning in me again. Twins. Jesus.

And I've woken her up properly now.

There's the whistle; dawn soon anyway.

'Uxorious,' she says, *exasperated* kitten, snuggling against my left shoulder and I would very much like to rip my other arm free so I can hold her properly. In six days' time I will. A spell of gentle exercise before I start doing everything for her.

She's taken to calling me Uxorious I, Cranky King of Uxor and Benevolent Dictator of Wattle Dell. She's the best lark, dreamy half-asleep lark. I had no idea what uxorious meant when she first said it a few weeks ago. It means foolish wife-lover, from the Latin *uxor* for wife. That's me, except I don't feel like any kind of fool for it. She said it's the ugliest word for the most precious thing, and I said no, you can't beat *frau* for that.

Danny wakes up in the next room: 'Mummm, Mummmaa.' He'll come tearing in in a tick.

France yawns as she sits up, snorting a laugh through it. How could you not be uxorious?

FRANCINE

What have you done for Lent this year, Francine? Well, God, as you're probably aware, my husband and I have been writing The Proposal, or rather I've written it. Even if he could write, or muster a basic grasp of formal grammar, no one should be made to decipher Daniel's scribble. Proposal is the reason why we're being careful with money, and, should Proposal be successful, we might have to be careful for many years to come. So, in a roundabout way, I've come half good with one of my fanciful promises, *Deum Patrem omnipotentem*: we're not going to sell our share and give the money to the miners, we're going to try to buy the whole company and sell back shares to them. Turn the Wattle into a kind of workers' collective run on socialist principles, in a capitalist economy, at the end of the world. You've got to chortle at the ambitiousness, but after these weeks of nutting it out together, it appears that it is actually possible.

So long as we can find a temporary replacement partner who is willing to have a go at some experimental philanthropy, since no bank would be able to give us what we need. According to my legal angels, any respectable banker would run a mile as soon as we presented the plan: for small loans for the miners, guaranteed by Daniel and I and our lion's share; and interest low enough that we can cover it ourselves, while the miners pay their bits of principal in instalments. Without that, it won't work: it's not feasible for us to buy it outright, at a price Drummond won't be able to refuse, and Daniel doesn't want anyone to have to put their savings into it, or anyone who doesn't have savings to miss out.

'That's revolutionary,' I said to him when he first told me about the idea; and he said: 'No. It's anti-revolutionary. Commonsense, really.' Uncommonsense, *really.* I asked him if he'd discussed it with Doctor Adinov, and he looked at me askance. 'No. Why would I do that? He's a surgeon.' And so I asked: 'Well, what was the *fifty-two days to think about it* about, then?' He said: 'Oh that. He saw the paintings, at Dunc's father's; he's that collector — how's that, ay. Wants me to paint something for him.' *Oh really?* Still attempting to digest this confounding explanation; they say Sydney is a small world, but *really?* And I was simultaneously appalled that Mr Duncan had allowed that to happen, and intrigued, most of all by Daniel's nonchalance. I asked: 'Well, are you going to?' And he said: 'I don't know. Maybe. Probably.' Don't you just want to smack it out of him sometimes, Lord?

And don't you sometimes simply delight in him? If you exist, treat yourself and look at him now, sitting at the kitchen table, being *useful*: he's got Danny wedged between himself and the edge of the table and he's shovelling porridge into him, while I make second course of breakfast for him and the boys. At the same time, he's talking about the need to insure the company and the workers against stoppages and price fluctuations without going broke. He could have been the author of *Bituminous Coal*, except for the interjections: to Danny: 'Don't wriggle'; to Charlie: 'Show us your teeth — have you cleaned them even once this week?'; to Harry, with glint: 'Do that lace up. Or you'll trip and break something.' Then finally: 'Go on, get off then, you'll be late for school. See if you can't come home with more sense.' It's nearly five miles from here to school, and he makes

Harry and Charlie walk, *does them good,* and they pick up their sisters on the way.

Boys gone, I'm washing up, and Daniel's said something about wages and dargs. I'm nodding off on my feet again. What's a darg? Oh yes, quota. Quota? I'm finding it harder and harder to concentrate with every day. Not that he's boring; well, to be truthful, it is fairly dull stuff, but it's dull stuff I should be abreast of if we're going to go into this business on our own. And he's got to talk about it, whether Proposal succeeds or not, to be certain he knows exactly what he's doing; what *we're* doing, Francy. Most words he's ever uttered and they're all about coal, coal, coal. Coal? A giggle escapes. He'd get more sense in return if he went through this with Evan, but he doesn't want to go to him until we've dotted every i and crossed every t. Tea. That's what I need, another cup of tea.

He says: 'France, why don't you go and have a lie-down.'

I look at him. Senses smack me. I look at Danny, who's heading straight for the stove; estimate that it takes his father a good two seconds to get up from his seat. And I shake my head.

'Tuesday,' I tell him, 'as soon as we get to the hotel.'

In Sydney, where Doctor Adinov will give Achilles his right arm back on Wednesday, and where Mr Edward Duncan will be approached with Proposal on Thursday. He's the only unconscionably wealthy person we know, or at least I know, a little, who might at least have a look at it, or might know someone who'd be interested in helping us; also according to angels Stanley and Bragg he's the fifth richest Sydney landholder on the roll, not including dubious activities in gaming and 'entertainment', and I personally think he owes Daniel some kind of a favour for underhanded art show. Not that he knows yet that this is the purpose behind our visit: I've told him we'd like to pop in for morning tea on our way through, and he sent back a note: *That will be lovely.* God, if you do exist, you'll make Mr Duncan say yes to experimental philanthropy, you'll make elbow a perfect hinge when it's got its meat back, and you'll make Daniel paint something for Doctor Adinov that'll prove his talent to both of them, to Daniel most of all. There's a dare for you. But if you can stop the war this afternoon, I might be impressed. And if Daniel doesn't snore tonight, I'll go to Mass on Sunday.

Careful what you dare, facetiously or otherwise. No snoring. Instead Daniel wakes me up with mumbles, then yells out something in German with '*Achtung! Achtung!*', then: 'Don't shoot. For Christ's sake. I've got you, I've got you. Just shut up.'

He grabs at the bottom sheet and wakes up with a shudder that shakes the bed; looks across at me through the dark and says: 'What?' And he sounds frightened; I've never heard that in him before.

I say, calm as I can muster: 'It's all right. You were dreaming.'

'Did I say anything?'

'No. Just mumbles.' He's so desperate for me not to know, I want to say, *Tell me and I'll make it go away*

But then he says: 'I'm sorry.'

You're sorry? 'Don't be.'

Last time I ever have words with God, facetiously or otherwise.

DANIEL

Jumpy kids get hot milk before bed, and at least I can fix that for myself. Seems to do the job; I haven't had another bad dream. Very jumpy this morning, though, and it's no dream: France trips up the step getting on the train and I nearly follow her, trying to catch her. I'd rather she wasn't coming with me, but someone's got to *look after me*, and she's not going to get any rest at home without me anyway, since even with Mum's help Danny wouldn't leave her alone. Besides, the proposal we've put together is just as much hers as mine, every question she's asked making my answers clearer, and if I ever thought I was quick with figures, France can calculate interest in her head, then chew the end of her pencil for a bit and tell me what tonnage and what price we'll need to keep up to pay for it. I want her to hand it over to Dunc's father with me. Or to be more honest, I wouldn't do it without her: I don't want to meet this bloke on my own. Jesus, we must be a sight as we stumble into the carriage. The guard brings our bag on for us and makes sure we're safely seated, and I can tell you if I had a knife I'd cut my way out of this bloody straightjacket right here. That'll be Adinov's privilege, though, tomorrow at ten o'clock; don't be late.

France says to me now: 'Stop scowling — you're getting a big wrinkle right between your eyebrows.'

She's hilarious, looking at me as if this wrinkle is a serious concern. Does the trick; I've stopped *scowling*, and she says: 'That's better. Look like that and you'll frighten the other passengers.'

So I look out the window as the train starts heading up, steadying myself; my heart's still pounding from seeing her trip. Then it pounds some more with the thought of freedom tomorrow; try not to get too excited about that. But I fail: I am excited. After calculating that my arm has been in some arrangement of cement for nine out of the last eighteen months and that I've spent nearly a year out of the last nearly four years in some state of useless, I am fairly desperate never to be useless again. But what if ... don't think about it.

Not going to think about Mr Edward Duncan, either, till we're there in front of him; that'll only lead to more scowling. Not going to think about what it'll mean if he says yes to the proposal. What it'll mean if Evan baulks. And there is a chance he might: it's one thing to fist-thump about the issues, and another when you're going to be asked to put your money where your mouth is. Money you don't really have. Even if France and I are the ones taking the main risk; even if the miners' outlay will be offset by their profit share over the three years, maximum, it'll take them to own their stakes. Even if it means that company profit can start being spent on the things we really need and that they'll have a say in what those things will be. It's still a matter of asking over a hundred workers to put their trust in two people who don't exactly have a reputation in business. Even if the charter of checks and balances France has drawn up is as long as the Constitution. I won't blame them if they choose known security over promising unknown, or if they say piss off how far on yourself are you asking us for money. But I realise it will cut if they don't go for it. Don't get that far ahead of yourself. Don't think about Drummond saying no to our offer either: he couldn't possibly say no. If everyone else says yes and he says no, I will have to have him killed. Not really, but I don't think I've ever put so much plain hard thought into anything and come up with what looks like the right conclusion from every angle.

France tugs at my sleeve. 'Daniel, what's that terrible racket?'

'I don't know.' But she's having a go. 'You tell me.'

'Them wheels turning,' she pokes me in the hip. 'Stop it.'

'Can't.'

'Can — look at the scenery.'

A million gum trees. Fascinating. I'd rather look at her, but looking at her and her too-big-with-twins belly only gets me wound up again.

What else is there to think about? Painting: there's five minutes' worth. I know what I want to paint as soon as I can: her. Don't think about painting for Adinov; that's part of what that dream was about, I'm sure. *Nicht Schießen*: don't shoot; don't want to go there again. Maybe I'll give him a picture of Francine, as a nod at the loss of his grandfather's ceiling. I think he'll be expecting something more than that. Don't think I can give it to him, but something in me wants to, or feels obliged to.

Look at the scenery: more gum trees. And we're only at Mount Vic.

Have a chat, play a game; I say: 'France, I spy. Something beginning with G.'

No answer: she's kipping again. Holding my arm, head against my shoulder: she's the sweetest thing ever made. Not at her most entertaining at the minute, though.

Think about how entertaining she is when she's awake, telling me yesterday that Billy the Troll's off to London again and she's thinking of sending a telegram to the war conference suggesting that the last wool clip Blighty bought from us be used for shell casings: *soft, durable and reusable, and, being Australian, Fritz'll quake at the mere thought of them, force him into a truce.* It's the pinch of spite behind her funnies that makes me laugh — she hates

Hughes more than I do. To me, now, he's just the official Two-Inch Cock; but to her, if he stepped onto this train today, I think she'd wake up quickly and throw more than an ice cream at him. She has a point, though: the world must be going broke. I can see those cheery starving Londoners, and that was more than a year ago. Can't be so cheery now. The French must've disappeared altogether. But if you believe Hughes you'd think the AIF was about to win the war single-handedly, if only we'd let him send more idiots. He sings God Save the King and Advance Australia Fair out of either side of his mouth drinking a glass of water. That's politics, isn't it. Doesn't bear thinking about at all.

Look across the carriage instead: bloke with his head in a newspaper; front page saying *ABOUT TIME*, referring to America, lending their Associated Power to the war against evil these days. Not news, just more Aussie is Best propaganda, and old news. Doubtful America will ever live down coming to the picnic so late. Not here anyway, where the idea of an independent country is foreign. America: the big choker, the big DT, with a pacifist for a president. And Russia — Jesus — they will definitely never live down abandoning the Eastern Front, much less going Red. Shame on the lot of them. Or shame on us? Does anyone really give a shit? Probably not. Not here, where France would say: *How much thinking could you realistically expect from a nation whose best-selling book of the year is a ditty about a loveable larrikin and his bonzer tart Doreen?* Look out the window again at the million gum trees. Too much sunshine for thinking, maybe. Spend more time in argument over whether there should be six or eight balls an over in cricket: I'm with Blighty's rules there: six is definitely enough. No argument at all on the blinding fact that the reason for the whole disaster is so that Blighty can stay top capitalist monster. And maybe he will, with a million or so fit, un-starved American idiots helping. Bully for him. But it's never going to end, is it. Not really.

Well, that's lifted my mood. Good job, Daniel. Very frightening. Just as well France kips on all the way to Sydney so she can't see my wrinkle.

Very big lift, very good job at around half-past ten the next day. My arm looks in urgent need of a good feed, but it goes all the way straight, and I can nearly touch my shoulder with my fingers, with help for the moment. Adinov looks pleased with himself. Let him; he's a genius. Even Stratho's impressed.

Adinov actually says: 'I told you so.'

Yep.

I'm still looking at the skinny thing on the table, and I get that feeling like it's not mine, same as I still get sometimes about my legs when I'm walking. He's bandaging round the length of it, slinging it up. 'It stays bound and supported for a fortnight. You are not to lift any heavy weights for at least six months. And you'll do the exercises every day, yes?'

Just try to stop me.

Then he says: 'I'll be visiting Bathurst in June. I'll inspect my painting on my way through then, yes?'

Yep. 'I suppose so.' And I think I might even have an idea now for what I'll paint for him.

Then, saying farewell, he grabs my face and kisses me on both cheeks. Very European. I know he likes me, but I think he likes my arm more. Surgeons are strange people, God bless them, and Adinov is probably at the top of the scale there.

I float, practically, with the weight gone. I can breathe without knowing I'm doing it. I can give France a cuddle — here she is, waiting — and touch her belly with both hands and not care who's looking.

We catch the tram back to the hotel and France has a lie-down. She's tired again. She's asleep in five minutes; still got her

410

shoes on. I take her shoes off and lie down with her, but I don't sleep. I'm holding her: my most precious thing.

I'm remembering the night Dunc threatened to shoot me. He didn't of course, wouldn't have. But he decked me. Just about separated my jaw from my face. He might have been queer but there was nothing girlie in that connection. We'd just started opening up some shallow sap tunnels ahead of the advance, at night, so Fritz couldn't see what we were up to. Sure. It was quiet for a moment, and I could hear a bloke yelling out; no, just yelling. Disadvantage of being tall, apart from having to duck so much so as not to get my head blown off, is that I only had to look up and I could see him, sitting there, about fifty yards away. Orders were not to help the wounded across no-man's-land at that time. I couldn't keep to that, even though Dunc would have had every military right to shoot me for it. I'd just shovelled through one corpse too many; you could hear metal scrape bone. You don't get used to that. Seeing a man about to make himself another corpse made me plain insubordinate. Dunc grabbed me by the leg, 'Keep going and I will shoot you,' and I kicked him away as I went up: 'Fuck off.' I wasn't a complete idiot about it: I crawled the whole way; grabbed the bloke, got him down, got him to shut up; got him to crawl the whole way back, with half his foot shot off. Didn't take that long, considering.

Dunc waited till dawn, when we'd finished and were heading back. He dismissed everyone at the second trench line, except me: 'Ackerman. You stay where you are.' He waited some more, looking at me, beyond anger. I was looking back at him, beyond everything. Then he grabbed me, both hands nearly ripping my collar off. He said: 'You will not do that again.' I was still jumpy enough that I couldn't hear who was talking to me, and I pushed him off. Too quick for me to see it coming, he laid me flat out then, and said: 'I mean it.' And he walked off. I was still picking myself up off the ground when Stratho came back to stickybeak; laughing his head off.

That's what I'm remembering as we get off the tram at Edgecliff. The things I'll never tell France about. No one. Even I can't believe I did that. And that was only the first time I went AWL for a tick, in my own special way. Dunc would bail me up after that, but he never hit me again; didn't bother. Instead, he'd fiddle a few facts to give reasonable explanation for why I so often wasn't where I was supposed to have been: covering my arse and, apparently, trying to promote me away from myself. He didn't succeed in getting me packed off for officer training school, doubt he ever would have, but he got me decorated, Christ knows how. The citation there is true, sort of: I did lie down behind a Lewis gun for a spell as Fritz was pounding the advance of reinforcements behind me. What's not noted is that I didn't fire a round, couldn't possibly have, not least of all because I failed at the Just In Case study of practically every piece of machinery more complicated than a rifle, and Fritz must have taken pity on me for that because he didn't take a single shot at me either. What's not noted is the reason I was there at all: I was the last to clear out of the sap, or supposed to have, and I heard the gunner up top get hit; went back to have a look and he was very *kaput*, no sign of his second either, just the pile of magazines next to him. He asked me to write a letter for his mother, and we got a few lines in before he couldn't speak. So I lay there with him while he died; then I just lay there with my finger round the trigger, looking at Fritz, thinking about giving it a burl and waiting for the bullet that didn't come, till a bloke wormed up behind me and said: 'You can piss off now, mate.' Why did Dunc see that I got a bells and whistles souvenir for that one? I don't know. Maybe it was love after all, but more probably it was because you don't get a medal for not firing at the enemy or for being inclined to duck off from the job, and the *perversity* of my *conspicuous gallantry and devotion to duty* amused him. His parting sentiments certainly amused me, exactly when I thought I'd lost my sense of humour forever.

Why did I do any of it? As Frank Connolly said: *does strange things to people.* But don't think I wasn't sticking with rule number one: I was that scared the whole time that I couldn't sleep, even on the few days' break Dunc made me take in the middle of it. I had to pass out from lack of sleep, and I did not need coffee to look lively again five minutes later. I just couldn't help it, and I know now that's the main reason I wanted to get locked up. That was the only way I wasn't going to do it again. I know I'm not alone in my behaviour, but it's not the sort of thing you natter about, is it, because you can't explain it. Maybe I thought I was buying my own life by it, thieving the only thing I could; or maybe that's just the way the anger came out in me in that circumstance, caught between two hatreds: them and us. Either way, any way, I don't understand it, and France shouldn't ever have to try to. What would I say to her? For three long and very eventful weeks in hell I did my best to make myself a target? It's better forgotten, and for the most part I can manage that. The only reason I'm thinking about it now is obvious: Dunc would write whole novels home to his father, and, take a wild stab, he'd have included one or two details about me.

Strange, isn't it, that I'm nervy about it, as if Dunc's father might belt me for being an idiot today. He can only say no to us; and if he does, well, he does. And he'll be polite about it, since he thinks I'm impressive already. Sure. He's got my monsters in his house, and I'm expecting to see them. Waiting for one of them to hit me on the head. I can't believe I'm doing this. When France suggested it, it seemed perfectly logical, to just walk in and ask the question, nothing to lose but Drummond, and a whole coal mine to win, but now …

'You all right?' says France; she can feel everything she doesn't know in me anyway. Very good thing she's here, and wide awake; she can be impressive for the pair of us.

No, not all right. 'Yep.'

You should see this house. Jesus. It's not a house, it's a suburb.

So's Mr Edward Duncan when he comes down the hall after we're shown in. He's as tall as Dunc but broader, thicker, everywhere; he might be sixty-odd but you wouldn't want to try to put your shoulder into him. France looks like a pretend human between us as she makes the introductions. He's so pleased to see us, 'Mr and Mrs Ackerman,' I'm frustrated that I can't shake his hand. He slaps me on the shoulder in lieu of it, making me glad I'm not slight either; he'd knock a small man through the wall.

He takes us into this sitting room that's indescribable. You don't want to sit on the furniture and the carpet on the boards is so thick that you're not sure if you're actually walking or hovering above it. I'd be a bit revolted if I could comprehend it properly, comprehend that this bloke lives in this huge place alone too, but at the same time I'm thinking it'd be a novelty living in a house where you'd never ever clock the top of your head on a door frame. Not a monster in sight; but there's a big portrait of a young Dunc, wearing a kilt, above the mantelpiece: he's saying to me: *After everything, you're not seriously going to lose your nerve now, are you, Ackerman?*

His father's saying: 'Sit down, sit down. Now what'll you drink?'

'I'd like a cup of tea, please,' says France.

'And you, Mr Ackerman?'

'I'll have a glass of water, thanks. And call me Daniel. Please.'

'Not a Scotch?'

'No thanks.'

'Don't be shy.'

For Christ's sake, what is it with some people? It's only eleven o'clock in the morning. I say: 'I don't drink.'

'What, not a drop?'

'No. Thanks.'

'Oh. Well. Good for you.'

France is looking out the window trying not to laugh, so she can keep the small talk going, about the *gorgeous* garden out the front.

Tea, cake and shocking water arrive in seconds and he says: 'So, I'm sure you didn't stop in just to see old me and my fuchsia hedge. What can I do for you?'

No flies on Mr Duncan.

France looks at me: *Go on, then.*

All right; I tell him: 'Francine and I need to borrow some money.'

And if France could kick me in the shins she would: I was supposed to mention the idea first.

But Mr Duncan says, 'How much?' as if I'm going to ask him for train fare.

I say: 'Fifteen thousand pounds at four per cent interest fixed over three years.'

He doesn't blink. 'What for?'

So I tell him all about it, and once I get started, the words just come. It's different when you know what you're on about, isn't it.

France interrupts: 'It's all set out in our proposal, Mr Duncan,' handing over the fat envelope, blink, blink, blink. Maybe I was banging on a bit too long.

Mr Duncan puts it on the table beside him and smiles at us both. 'Thank you. My solicitor can read that, and draft up terms.'

You're saying yes? Just like that? Fuck. You really do have a spare fifteen thousand pounds? I know you're filthy rich, but thought you might have to at least think about it.

'But there'll be a personal condition as well,' he adds, to me.

Anything.

'I want a painting, when you're up to it, of Richard. Or something of Richard.'

Too easy. No thought involved from me either. 'Sure. I can do that.' Already: Dunc, out the back of the huts in camp, cleaning his toenails, with the tear splash on his knee. His father is a very large man, and I'll give him the best of the truth I can offer.

He says to France: 'Must beg your pardon, my dear, as regards my sneaky divulgence to our European collector; couldn't resist. But I swear I had no idea he was our elbow doctor too — that's what you call providence, is it not?' But he's not asking for any sort of pardon; clearly someone who decides his own providence. And to me: 'Trust no harm done, eh. Trust you gave the pair of us more of a startle than we did you. He's always at me to let him have one of them in particular, you know: the Virgin in Albert. He was here last night, looking at her again. Funny chap, good man, avid about his interests to a fault. You still want me to hang onto them?'

'Unless you feel inclined to burn them.' Out before I could shove my fist in my idiot mouth. For whatever reason, I think they mean more to him than me; maybe something of Richard. How else would he know it's a picture of Albert? Shit.

Yes: he's appalled: 'Why would I do that?'

I'm that embarrassed I can't say anything.

But then he adds: 'After I've gone to the trouble and expense of having them framed, my boy?'

And he leaves it there, Francine's bells doing the rest. But I'm caught in a thought that sounds like someone else's: I'd never imagined them framed; hope he's not bunged them in anything fancy; hope it's plain, timber. Don't ask: I don't really want to know. Do I? No.

I look at Francine, chatting away; but I'm not listening, just thinking: if I get any luckier I'm going to have to start paying an extra tax somewhere.

FRANCINE

Desperate to kiss him, I mean properly, indecently. Can't wait till we get home: that's hours and hours away. So I pull him into a lane that runs between two not-quite-finished apartment buildings on New South Head Road.

He pulls away, glinting badly. 'Stop it, France, you'll make me dangerous.'

I know. Doctor Nichols's orders: nothing that will make the babies come too early. But I'm craving him so terribly. He rubs my tummy through my clothes and that only makes it worse. I've recanted a little from my atheism again and decided that there is a God or god: that one who put Daniel on this earth to torture me, mercilessly.

I say: 'That went well, didn't it.' Ackerman business instinct: whack it down and say there you go, then bludgeon benefactor with ten minutes' solid facts and figures, then insult his generosity and sensitivity. If coal's an industry for the uncompromising, then perhaps the King of Uxor won't have trouble with future negotiations at the top end.

'Mmn,' he says; and he's the cat that ate the cream, seventeen rats, five rabbits and a side of beef.

To celebrate we eat, of course. At least he does; I can't eat too much in one go, already. Unbelievable: what am I going to be like when the babies do come? I'm enormous already. Mrs Moran said second babies are always bigger; but these babies are … don't think about it. Watch their father attacking his plate. Elbow on the table, no problem: emancipated hand wielding knife by Ackerman's strongest instinct against weakness: food. I love watching him eat: it really is heroic. I ask him how his flash-Metropole capitalism feels now and he says: 'The crackling is especially tasty today.'

Heading for home on the three o'clock train and I'm dozing pleasantly. I really will lie in in the morning, for a little while. Daniel can manage breakfast: gentle exercise can begin with stirring porridge, cracking eggs, flipping bacon and buttering bread.

He says to me now as I wake at the approach to Parramatta Station: 'No more drudging for you, my *frau*.'

'If you insist.'

'I do. Mum'll help, and maybe Kathryn'd like to come round after school sometimes. I'll get that bathroom put in, too.'

'We can't really afford that now.'

'Last splash, ay? Can't have you bathing in the kitchen in this condition. You'll frighten the children soon.'

The babies seem to shift around in laughter with me, and again when he adds: 'And I suppose you should teach me how to drive that car, while you can still fit behind the wheel.'

I'd punch him on the shoulder for that if I wasn't sitting on the wrong side of him because there were no left-side seats free when we got on and he wouldn't have me sit on the aisle, ever. Instead I screw my nose up at him and find I want to kiss him indecently again. Fan face in the stream of afternoon sunlight.

Then I have the oddest moment of maternal derangement yet. We're still stopped at the station and I glance out the window at the town. Well, it's not really a town now, but more the outer bounds of sprawling Sydney. I can see a kookaburra sitting on the top of a telegraph pole next to the stationmaster's house; it's in profile, looking towards the countryside beyond. When I look down again, there's a woman right at the window, staring back at me. She's stout and plain and reminds me a little of Polly, the housekeeper Father and I had when we arrived in Lithgow, but even though I haven't seen Polly for years, I know this woman isn't her. This woman is much older, white hair, but a plump healthy face. She smiles broadly at me, grey eyes, a missing eyetooth, and says: 'Goodbye. Don't come back.' Muffled but clear through the glass. The train pulls out and she waves.

I say to Daniel: 'That was odd.'

He says: 'What was?'

'That woman. Look.'

'What woman?'

Of course he can't see her now we've chugged away; I can't see her any more either past the clouds of steamy smoke.

I say: 'She said goodbye, to me.'

He looks at me: lunatic.

I say: 'She did, and she waved. She said don't come back.'

Lunatic, in need of a good lie-down. Indeed. Except I am quite sure that did just happen. Don't come back. Hmn. Not likely to return to Babel unless we really have to. I decide that this is my imagination merely confirming what I know is true: goodbye Sydney. For good. I snooze some more, then wake at Penrith and see the mountains. The wave of forest rising from the plain, the wide Nepean River purpling in the almost dusk. The babies swim around again, and I feel a deep surge of excitement as the train pulls upwards after Emu. Then I close my eyes and see the men shovelling and shovelling and shovelling our coal into the fire that drives our engine. Too exhausting.

I wake in the night as we head down into Lithgow, the furnaces of the ironworks glowing to light our way. Sarah is there waiting for us at the station, lamps on the trap; Hayseed snorting mist. Dear Hayseed, lugging us all the way home in the dark.

★

'But Aunty France never puts that much butter on.' That was Charlie, in the kitchen.

Daniel says: 'Aunty France isn't making your crib, is she. And if you wake her up with your whingeing, you'll go to school without.'

Don't worry, Charlie, I've been awake for ages: babies woke with the whistle and have been trying to have a game of tip inside me ever since. I've been lying here, gestating, relishing this sensation, wanting them to keep at it until Daniel comes in, so he can feel them too. It's June now; three months tops before we see them.

Daniel won't come in for a while yet, though, not till he's completed his routine. Every morning, he gets up, washes, shaves, gets all fed, watered, dressed, combed and toothbrushed, sends Harry and Charlie off to school or to do some job or other, then he ties Danny by a rope at the waist to one of the back verandah poles while he exercises, no, *exercises*: like penance for the worst sins.

Babies have given up their play and I haul my great self out to the verandah to see Achilles at it. He's already done the sit-ups, and has moved on to pressing himself up against the boards. He enjoys this; wouldn't stop for a fire. No oil needed in that corrected hinge, just horseradish and eucalyptus liniment he rubs into it every night and the whole house smells of it. It's positively freezing, there's still a sheen of ice on the boards near the house, but his hair is wet with sweat. And nearly-two-year-old is trying to mimic him; not quite succeeding: slapping his palms on the boards and rocking back and forth on his little fat knees. Good morning.

First time I saw Daniel do this, must be nearly a month ago, I queried the wisdom of punishing elbow so soon; he said that it

421

wouldn't do it if it couldn't and he wants to be fit again; he does another round before bed, says that it wears him out so he sleeps better. Hmn. However, I have to admit that, shirtless, the benefit is already obvious and more than a bit pleasing to behold. And somehow he looks even larger for it. Or perhaps men just take longer to grow than women; I wonder if he's stopped growing: he's not twenty-four yet. Maybe his new shirts won't last for centuries.

When he's finished he wipes his face on an old towel, kneeling, sees me at the doorway. 'It's too cold, France. Get back inside.'

I laugh at him, breathy because these babies don't think a full breath is a necessity. But then he stands up and all of a sudden I'm weepy. I see those boys, so long ago it seems, in Hyde Park and on the train: how many of them have not become men; how many of them can't stand up? The jumble of scars on My Boy's arm are pink from the exertion; I see his right boot needs resoling again, as it wears down so quickly on the outside, and he is perfect, magnificent as the first time I gasped at the sight of him.

He says: 'What's wrong?'

I want to tell him, but it's too vast an emotion; I can't articulate more than: 'I'm so happy you're here.' That says it all anyway. His arms around me say it twice.

Doctor Adinov has a face that's so flat it only has one outstanding expression: inscrutable. But at this moment he's making up for that with a look of very easily discernible delight; a look that's at odds with what he's looking at. And I'm looking at him, so as to avoid looking at what he's looking at: the painting.

It's macabre. Worse than The Holy Monsters, for repellent, overwhelming. It's the first time I've seen it too, close up, since *room* is invitation only: not that Daniel says so, I just know so. I feel disloyal, avoiding it now, but it's stomach-turning, and there's not much room inside me for that. Force myself: try to see the gore as masterful for its … goriness. A cruel lesson in anatomy. Look at the light instead: it's coming from somewhere outside the picture, illuminating the blackness of the tunnel floor, the curve and roughness of the wall behind, the smooth edges of the skip tracks and what looks like a dusting of yellow wattle pollen collected in the cracks of the sleepers. Be astounded: how does one teach *oneself* to do that? It doesn't seem possible; but perhaps that's only because I could never do it if I studied for a thousand years. And I haven't seen the things that Daniel has, to be able to imagine, no, photograph in my mind a scene like this.

Look at the boy: gangly, coal-scuffed arms and legs, squiggle of a bootlace undone, face turned towards me not in pain but in the disbelief of having been hit. And he has been: almost ripped in half. Like the German boy, he is beautiful, and asking something unanswerable. The only clue to what's done this to him is the rusty iron wheel his other boot is resting on: a skip wheel, without its skip.

'Does this fluke have a name?' the doctor asks.

Daniel says: 'It's Jimmy. Boy I started work with, killed our first year in.'

'It is a tribute, to a friend.' The doctor's eyes are filled; so are mine: is this the Jimmy he had a good time with during the big strike, *better than school holidays*?

'Yep. Suppose it is.'

Dear Lord, what have You done for Lent this year? What do You do to Your lambs?

'And you would give this to me?'

'Yep. If you want it.'

The doctor shakes his head, wipes his eyes with his silk handkerchief. Looks around the room. There's the fastidious

organisation of tubes and jars and tools, even folds the rag he
wipes turpsy brushes on, on the bench he made, and there's a riot
of paint all over the floor, from the monsters, still showing their
square outlines, though Daniel's graduated to using easels now. I
watched him make the first one, and asked him why he didn't use
easels before, and he said: 'I don't know, too barking to think of
it, I suppose.' There you go. And there's the portrait of Captain
Duncan that's not quite finished, over the other side of the room:
he's bent over his extraordinarily little feet, as if he's about to roll
into a ball, with sadness, some secret sadness, and the only thing
stopping his momentum is his toenail scraper, like the flourish of
a joke against it; there's a smudgy scrape at his right knee, which
Daniel evidently wants to have another go at. And then behind
his Dunc is paper roll pinned against the windowless wall full of
drawings, mostly of my great self, mostly nude.

Daniel says, wry: 'So can I call you Anton now?'

'You can call me whatever you choose. But I'll let you call me
Sweet Fanny Adams if you'll come to Europe with me one day.'

'No chance,' says Daniel, deadpan. 'But I think I'll call you
Fanny anyway.'

Doctor Adinov's laughter is a rich warm sound; funny old
world: first friend I've seen Daniel with who isn't a miner is a
bourgeois to the tiny diamond in his tiepin Russian surgeon,
who says now: 'When the war is ever finished, Fanny wants to
return *over there*, particularly to Berlin, if he can, and might like
to take some of your work with him, yes? Some more flukes?'

'I don't know about that,' Daniel frowns, back stiffened. 'I've
got proper work to get on with soon; don't think I'll be doing
any of this sort of thing for a long while. You going to go back
to Europe for good?'

'No. Too partial to sunshine and Bondi Beach now. I'll only
go to indulge myself in the essentials unavailable here. To visit

some old colleagues and to enjoy what some artists might call their *proper* work.'

Doctor Adinov stares at him, waiting. So do I: is Doctor Adinov suggesting he wants to take flukes on a tour to Berlin? What for? Oh. Goodness me.

Daniel shrugs. Doctor Adinov shrugs back and shakes his head again, but mystified. I can sympathise, with them both. Doctor Adinov is looking at a work of art, but Daniel is looking at a painting, which took him a month to do, and it can't have been easy, technically or emotionally; not that he's likely to admit to either.

He says to me, my Uxorious, avoiding further chat: 'You look a bit tired, France. Come on.' I am too; always.

And back inside we go; I waddle, fall into the sofa in the parlour, Danny released from corral and now trying to find purchase on the mountain I have become. While Daniel makes tea, Doctor Adinov says to me: 'You should try to change his mind about *work*.'

Ha! If I do have magical powers, I doubt they extend that far. He laughs at my expression, full throated.

When Daniel joins us we talk about the Wattle and what on earth lawyers do that can make a straightforward transaction take so long. I'm sure Mr Duncan's lawyers have requested the last amendment to the loan document just to squeeze another bill from their bottomless pit of revenue: it's taken them two weeks to discover that my middle name was missing from the front page, and that *thereby*, the entire thing has had to go back and forth again for *Veronica*. Messrs Stanley and Bragg have done their bit so promptly, even sending a young associate all the way out here, twice, but then, they're angels, aren't they. Daniel's impatient to get it all over with and to get back to *work*. He won't go to the mine or talk to Evan about it until he's got the offer in his hand;

then he'll approach the miners, then he'll approach Drummond. And, fingers crossed, we'll then be swimming in debt. We will be anyway: if the miners reject the idea, we're going ahead with the offer to Drummond, and if he refuses, Daniel will bully him until he capitulates into giving us the entire debt, up to our ears; and with our own savings at virtually nil, the slightest downturn in the price of coal could then send us all to the poorhouse, and generous as Mr Edward Duncan is, I'm not sure how pleased he'll be if we are bankrupt.

Doctor Adinov does not appear overly interested; he seems to be more interested in Daniel's forearm, exposed by neatly rolled sleeve and at present engaged in raising teacup. He says: 'You look fit enough to tear this Drummond's head off. Do you mind if I have a look at that arm?'

'What for?' Daniel is the rudest man that ever lived.

'Because I gave it to you,' says the doctor; and he's rude too: 'Take your shirt off.'

Daniel does as he's told; Doctor Adinov says, before he's risen from his seat: 'You did not get that biceps lifting a brush, did you.'

'No.' Twelve-year-old caught pinching a biscuit before dinner.

'This is a foolish risk.' Doctor is examining hinge; very scrutable disappointment. 'I said at least six months.'

'I haven't wrecked it.' You'd better not have, darlingest.

'No, you haven't.' But Doctor Adinov gives him a hard stare before adding: 'Although any reasonable person would think that was your intention.' Then he laughs: 'But you're not reasonable, are you. Daniel.'

'Suppose not. Fanny.'

And it's time for Doctor Adinov to go now, to catch the train through to Bathurst, to visit the hospital there.

'Don't get up, Mrs Ackerman,' he says and kisses my hand.

Don't worry, I can't.

Daniel drives him to the station; he'll pack up Jimmy and send him on to the doctor's home tomorrow. I'll wait here and play clap hands with Danny till Daddy comes home and can use unreasonable biceps to pull me up off the sofa.

I really can't get any bigger, can I? I'm in the bath, in our luxurious new indoor bathroom, off the kitchen; it's a massive, deep cast-iron bath, but it barely accommodates me. Daniel is rubbing my back with a flannel, trying to ease the pain with the hot water; not labour pain, just pain pain, like one of the babies is pinching the base of my spine. It's around midnight or so; it's the sixteenth of August and I just want them to come. It'll be safe now, and Sarah will be coming to stay with us from tomorrow; she'll sleep on the sofa, no argument she said, ready to help when they do come. But I want them to come now; I even try to push a bit, pointlessly, since neither one has moved down yet. Daniel is kissing my shoulder, and the late-night stubble on his jaw is as soothing to my skin as anything could be; at least I can't see his face. he looks more scared than I am. And I am very scared now.

DANIEL

There's not just a little bit of snow out there, the usual dusting that disappears with the sun: it's a good foot deep. It's been snowing on and off for three days. At the end of August. Why now? Just to be sure I won't miss how much I'm panicking. I can't get the fucking car to start. Fucking useless fucking pile of American shit. In lieu of being able to ask France to get the thing going, I've kicked a dent in the side of it. So much for teaching me to drive, when I don't know how it bloody works; should take the trap, but it'll take too long to get Hayseed fitted up now. One last go before I take the bike instead: start, you bastard. It does. Grab the kids, who've been watching my performance, frozen on the front steps, even Danny, and not just because it's fucking freezing; still in their pyjamas, shit, chuck them round with Mim.

France woke up just before the whistle, with the proper pains. I wanted to get Nichols straightaway but Mum's been holding off. For what? Till the pains get worse. Where's the logic in that? She even told me to leave the bedroom, said I was upsetting France. Jesus. I've already decided she's not ever going to have another baby: this is horrible.

It's three o'clock now, in the afternoon; I'm on the front steps watching the snow melting. Of course. One baby's out. A boy. Of course. Mrs Moran brought him out to show me, but I'm a bit

428

distracted at the moment. The other one is stuck. France is screaming; she's been at it all day. No one's telling me anything.

She screams again; it's not like any sound I've ever heard. That's it. I have to go in there.

Mum stops me in the hall; says: 'No.'

'Yes.'

'No.'

And everything's gone quiet now.

He is the saddest little thing; a proper heartbreaker. He's perfect in every way, except that he's dead. Mum shows him to me before she wraps him up again. Puts him in the other basket in the sitting room. France doesn't know; she's still out to it. And she's not too well. She's lost a fair bit of blood and, though she's stopped bleeding so much now, Nichols is giving me a warning: she'll have to go to the hospital if she doesn't rouse out of the ether soon; he's concerned she might be having a bad reaction to it, and that she needs blood. I can't really hear him. I can hear the other baby crying, though. Can't look at him.

They let me in now. Can't tell you.

Just us, and that little oil lamp of hers. The room smells of blood, though I can't see any.

'Wake up, France.' Begging. Much more than that.

I kiss her face and squeeze her hand, but she just goes on sleeping.

'Please, France.'

A thousand years.

Behind me, Nichols: 'We'd better take her, now. Her breathing is too shallow.'

No. No bloody way.

FRANCINE

My plump little hand is enclosed by Mama's; we're going to David Jones, and she'll buy me a chocolate there. My favourite one, with a caramel centre. She bends down to me outside the doors and wipes some spot or other from my cheek with her handkerchief. I can smell hyacinths, her hyacinths. She's saying to me: 'Francy, you must not come to Sydney again.'

I say: 'I don't want to, Mama.'

She says: 'Good. You've always been a good girl. The bestest. I trust you not to come back. All right?'

'All right.'

'Now, when you get home, you must look after Danny.'

'Daddy?'

'No, Danny.'

'You don't know my Danny,' I say to her.

'Course I do. Big fellow with the green eyes.'

'Oh, Daniel?'

'Yes. Him.'

'He doesn't need looking after any more,' I say.

'Course he does,' she says, and stands up again.

We go through the doors; I can see the doorman's shiny black shoes, and his hat all the way up there on his head. But there's nothing in here. It's all black beyond the doors.

Mama's still holding my hand.

I'm crying. I'm so frightened.
And now she's gone.
I don't know where to go.
And it hurts. Everywhere.

DANIEL

Just as well, or I might have followed her. She's moaning awake and I couldn't be more relieved at the sound of that. I really don't believe in any of that Irish Catholic rubbish, or spirits or whatever, but I do believe I would not be here without her. And if she's not here, I'm not here. How could I be alive without her?

Nichols wants her to go to the hospital anyway. He's not confident.

No bloody way.

She's not going. Not to the local. Could be anyone there, with who knows what sickness; and I'm not letting her out of my sight. Mum can help me look after her, or I'll pay someone.

He says: 'Danny, be reasonable.'

I say: 'I am. Couldn't be more reasonable.' Considering. 'Treat her here.'

Mrs Moran says: 'All right, Danny, I'll stay tonight. But just tonight, and in the morning we'll see.'

Good. And you can stop calling me Danny.

FRANCINE

Danny. There he is. Frowning, fierce Danny. It's dark but I can see him clearly, his profile. And it's his big rough hand around mine, not Mama's. Mama? Josie? Can't catch the dream back to hear it again; can only hear whimpering, mine.

He's looking at me now, pushing the hair back from my face. The pain is going to shake me apart any moment. Tearing me up from the centre, but it's everywhere; burning. I am inside it. Fire trapped in glass.

He looks away and says to someone else: 'Give her something for it.'

Yes please.

He's still there. I can feel his hand around mine before I open my eyes. Bit more properly awake now; not shaking any more. Just hurts, there, lots. I can hear a baby mewling. Mine. How long have I been asleep? I have to feed them.

He says: 'Hello.'

'Hello.' Ow, sore throat. 'I want the babies.'

He strokes my face with the back of his hand and says: 'There's only one, one baby, France.'

One …

One baby … what does that mean?

It's still dark but I can see the tears in the lamplight, running down his face. It was so perfect last time; not easy, but perfect, and

Daniel wasn't here. But this time it's … the devastation on his face. That's all I can see. I did everything I was told to do. I don't understand. I couldn't push any more. *One baby?* That means one baby is … is not. Not here. I know, but I don't understand. It didn't matter what I did, the baby just wouldn't come. 'I'm sorry.'

'Sorry?' he says. 'Jesus, France. You couldn't have done anything more; he was the wrong way round. Nichols couldn't get him out. He had to cut you a bit and pull him out backwards. But his brother is fine, beautiful.'

He. Brother. Two boys. My baby is still crying; I have to feed him. The one I have. I want him now. 'Can I have my baby then please? Now.'

DANIEL

She's barely conscious, and she takes him and feeds him. That's more than a little humbling to watch.

Mum says I should give her some privacy for a bit. No, I'm not leaving her. I'm not leaving this house until I know she's safe. Not leaving this room unless I have to.

In the morning Mrs Moran says France'll be all right, so long as she doesn't get an infection. Mum's given a list of instructions, and the lecture, as if I'm not here. Excuse me, women, but I think I can manage this myself. No one is going to help France wash or dress today but me.

Her poor body is so sore, as if it wouldn't be. Doesn't matter how gentle I am taking her nightdress off; and she's embarrassed when I first see her and the little bit of blood that keeps coming. I tell her I've seen a lot worse and looked a lot worse, and remind her that the second time we ever met I chucked up all over her floor, and I sound like an idiot and it doesn't matter. I keep talking into her stare, I tell her all the ways she's looked after me, I tell her it's stopped snowing, I tell her I'll have to get some paint to fix where I kicked the car, I tell her I love her, I tell her nothing matters more to me than that she is well. She looks so sore at that, she says: 'But I am well. I'm all right, darling.' No she's not. I'd like to tell her how sorry, how cut open and gutted I am that she feels the need to say that, but I don't think that would be helpful right now. She doesn't want to cry and I'm not going to make her.

Instead I leave the room to scrub out the bathroom and the toilet with bleach, so that later, when she needs to use them, they'll be cleaner than clean. She can't sit up yet, and she's not walking anywhere in this state today, so I'll carry her there. I'll change the sheets and her nightdress every day and boil and bleach them too. And I'll scrub my hands every time I leave the bedroom, before I come back in. I'd scrub my soul if had one. I know that I'm still very much beside myself, but that's all right, in the circumstances. Mum doesn't argue; she can help me or keep out of my way.

France wants me to bring the other baby in to her now so she can dress him and say goodbye. She tells me what to get from the drawers and as I watch her put the tiny clothes on him, I think this is what's called grace. She asks me if it's all right that she calls him Joseph Francis, after her parents, and I can only nod. Then she kisses him. She doesn't carry on about it when she gives him back to me, but I might in a second.

Evan comes round and he and Mum take our little Joe out to the ridge beneath the paddock. That's where France wants him buried; no priest, no funeral, no cemetery, just looking into the valley that runs into ours. When she says she wants him to keep my father company down there, I have to leave the room for a tick again; need to get her something to eat anyway. But I go out into the orchard first and bawl for a good little while.

She's not hungry, but she's got to eat something, so she forces it down.

Baby cries and I lift him over to her so she can feed him again. She says: 'What shall we call him?'

'You choose.'

'What about David?'

'That's very Taff, very Lithgow.' She can call him whatever she likes, and that'll do: 'Dave.'

She's very pale and weak, even her eyes are so pale they are barely blue, but she manages a sharp little go at me: 'You don't call a baby Dave. He's Davie.'

'Davie, then. What made you think of that name?'

'Close to Daniel. He looks just like Danny did, just like you, just like …'

And now it's too much. He looks just like his twin did too. She cries now, not loud, just forever.

I stay where I am, I hold her hand, till she's asleep again, and while she sleeps, I watch her.

She wakes up a fair bit in the night from the cramping, low in her belly, makes her catch her breath; Mum says it's nothing to worry about, often happens with second babies; means she's healing inside. Mrs Moran and Nichols agree. But I remember cramps I'd very much like to forget, when I couldn't move to flex them out, and I want her to stop hurting. She hasn't cried again, but I know it's more than the cramps that are hurting her. For want of saying something more useful, I tell her maybe she'll heal quicker if she tries to move around a bit, just gently; she does, a bit more every day, and the pain gets less every night.

After seven days she's declared out of danger, but Nichols orders bed rest for at least another two weeks. France winks at me when he turns his back: *see, I'm all right*.

When everyone leaves us alone, she comes out onto the back verandah with me. The sun's streaming over the hill behind the orchard and it's warm here, golden. Her hair has grown to her shoulders now and it's flaming in the light; she's got her yellow-striped dressing-gown wrapped round her: she is the sun.

She says: 'I think you can stop sleeping on the floor now.'

Hmn. Don't feel I should ever be in her bed again. But she has a point: I can't do that forever.

She adds: 'And you can stop bleaching the life out of everything, too. For someone who can't abide unnecessaries, you can do a decent job of being excessive.'

That's true. I say: 'But you wouldn't have me any other way.'

'No. Couldn't, could I?' And she's a bit sharp with that.

'No.' Poor girl; my girl.

Her hand on my shoulder: 'Mim must be run ragged with all the boys over at your mother's.'

'You're not well enough for that,' I say. And she's not: Nichols hasn't even taken the stitches out yet.

'Daniel,' she says, talking to her favourite moron. 'I miss them being here. And shouldn't you go back to work?'

Work. She means the Wattle. Since the sale went through a month ago. Everything we wanted to happen has happened. Evan gave himself a moment for shock before saying, 'As if not,' and calling a meeting on the spot; three quarters of the miners have taken up shares; those that didn't are those that don't trust the boss because You Don't Trust The Boss, and I can't say I cared about them: more interested in getting back home to France that day, to tell her everything was good; still don't care about them, mostly the sort who can only ever look at me like I'm about to threaten their grog money. Jesus, who'd be an alcoholic coalminer; it's hard enough work without a headache. But it takes all sorts, doesn't it. And Drummond proves you can't ever be too certain of what a man will do: he rolled practically before I'd opened my mouth. I didn't consider how happy he'd be to get rid of it, me, us; I think he was relieved, but he shook my hand, even wished me luck, all's water under the bridge with the cheque in your hand, and now he's gone, off to make a bigger profit elsewhere, with partners that won't demand such horrors as cavil-out pay. Needless to say, I didn't have to ask Robbenham to resign; quickest he's ever moved. So now I need to run the company. Sign for licences to keep printing more money. Not been very interested in any of it lately, strangely enough. But France is right. Danny and Charlie and Harry can come back tomorrow, and I'll go back to the Wattle. Mum'll look after France.

I'll go back to … responsibility; first collective decision: blasting at the bottom of three. It'll stop production there for a while, but it should have been done a long time ago, to bring down all of what wants to come down. That pinch, where Dad and the others were killed, is still there, though it's unworkable now; men walk through it every day, or duck. Beyond it the seam has opened up, as if Drummond didn't know that five years ago when he had the leaseholding extended to include it; but it's haul by hand up to the pinch, too tight for ponies, up to the roof that still bumps like there's dancing upstairs. So, get rid of the pinch altogether, stabilise the roof, increase production: blast a proper hole through two hundred yards and follow what appears to be an easy, ten-foot thick run for who knows how long. But I've put it off, till after France, well, till now. Because I want to see to it myself; get the slow job done quickly but properly, carefully. Haven't mentioned it to her, though; not a conversation we need to have, and certainly not now.

But France is still a witch; she says: 'Penny for your thoughts.'

Not for a million pounds. 'I just don't want to leave you.'

'Don't be silly.'

No. I'll try not to be.

FRANCINE

'It'll be just as it was, Francine,' Doctor Nichols says, taking out the stitches, only three of them: urgh. 'But no, er, *relations* for another month. Still a possibility of infection, inside. There, all done. Good girl.'

Good girl. Do I get a pat on the head or a lolly? Certainly won't be having *relations*. I get a kiss on the forehead from my husband in the mornings and if he touches me at all it's as if I'm made of china; barely spoken to me beyond the children, food and the weather all week. A campaign to keep France safe from anything and everything that might distract her from … I know he's trying to do all the right things, but when he ironed the boys' school shirts last night, he looked so slapped when I asked him not to any more, I could have slapped him. I don't have anything else to do. And I don't know what I want him to do. But I know how I feel: like I'm not a woman any more. And resentful, and twisted up … Oh, stop it, Francine, it's only been a fortnight since … Sarah said I should try to give myself something she could never give much to her own self: time, to let my thoughts return to normal. I don't want time; I don't want normal thoughts; I want my Baby Joe to be alive. That's not going to happen, is it, and babies die every day, fact of life, you're not the only one, so pull up your drawers and try to be sensible, at least.

But Doctor Nichols now sits beside me on the edge of the

bed, not-to-worry tone replaced by grave and kind: 'I should say, though, that it's unlikely you'll be able to have another child.'

Oh.

He talks about the *trauma* to my *uterus*, the inevitable scarring in there, says it's best not to have expectations. I want to shout: do you have a crystal ball, then, to go with your medical degree? How can you say that to me? Because you're a doctor, my doctor, and you're trying to be kind and fair. I want to cry, I want to wail and wail and wail, but the sadness has lodged itself direct in my womb. No more babies? I am not a woman any more and I have no expectations.

I am not sensible. Can't even remember letting Doctor Nichols out the door.

I am rubbed out. By my lack of attrition? I can hear myself snort. That's what they call this war now: a War of Attrition. Not much fearing of God's Wrath going on there, I don't think: merely a phenomenal excess of death. A rolling abomination of infinite abnormalities. But oddly, I can feel God weeping into my soul, somewhere past emotion. No, the universe is weeping. It weeps as it tilts and tilts, throwing out stars like tears. *Über aller Welt.*

Who am I to mourn my small bundle against this vastness? No one. Davie's bleating for a feed: get on with it.

Sensible now, sort of: kiss on my forehead and Daniel's come home with that smell on him, that smell he had when we were first married. It's not coal; more acrid than that. He's bending over the stove, sampling dinner, and I ask him: 'What is that smell on you?'

'What smell?'

'That sharp, dusty smell.'

Sarah says behind me: 'Shot powder.'

'Shot powder? Why do you smell of shot powder?'

He says, 'I don't know,' around another mouthful.

Sarah has an idea: she's just made a sound that's half a laugh, half a sigh of scorn, and now she's left the kitchen.

I say: 'How can you not know why you'd smell of shot powder?' Since it's a volatile substance with a very specific purpose ... *Oh.* I realise before he replies. He's not just running the Wattle, is he: he's working *in* it. That's why he looks so tired, too; and bleary-eyed, from the dust. And he's hiding the fact, must be washing before he comes home, he must even take a change of clothes: because he's done this before, hasn't he, smelled like this lots before, when he was managing the mine. Sniff, sniff: smell from the blasting sticks in his hair. Oh. Oh. Oh. This was not part of our proposal.

He says, reaching for a glass, not looking at me: 'I hang about a mine. Why are you bothered about it?'

Because ...

There's no completeness to our union.

I say: 'I'm not bothered.' I have no expectations and no valid opinion; even if I could speak. Everything I've ever done for you is negated now in this deceit, and I don't care if it's well-intentioned: you are a moron.

'Good,' he says, then kisses me on the forehead again.

So much for promises, so much for locking you in your room if you misbehave, so much for true love. Kookaburra cackling sunset somewhere in the orchard: thanks for the note of ridicule.

Bit more than sensible now; it's been ten weeks and I am declaring myself well. I'm fit, physically, and inspired by my own epiphany in the bath this morning: while my body has resolved itself to be what it will be henceforth, bit bunged up but in good working order, so has my mind: I have decided that there is no

442

such thing as a normal thought, not for me, when I doubt very much that there was ever much that was normal in me to begin with. Promise to myself then: proceed henceforth as I wish to continue. And I wish to do so as intrepidly as I can. The AIF have broken through Fritz at the Hindenburg line, and even the Troll has demanded they now be pulled out of the cauldron for a spell. I have my own line that needs to be broken through, my own demands as regards enough being enough, and it's going to happen today.

'I want to go to the paddock to visit Joe,' I tell him.

He looks up at me from the little truck he's carving for Danny: sad lone dog. Not at all surprising: I've barely spoken to him since The First Night Of Shot Powder, as if I thought I might play him at his own game; make *him* talk to *me*. As if the words 'yep', 'no', 'don't know' and 'nothing' could be used against the expert. I can't bear this any more. Bleary and weird with my own grieving as I have been, I can't blame him any more either. And I have sunk that low, if only to myself: it's all your fault. If I hadn't accumulated so much worry and so many tears on your account, then I wouldn't have lost my baby. I wouldn't feel as if I've been dragging myself through the gelatinous soup of my own guilt for weeks on end. Sinking low enough within it that when I discovered through Sarah via Evan that he's been carving a big tunnel underground, appointed himself Chief Navvy, I even thought: I hope you do blow yourself up, since that seems to be a particular ambition of yours. Watching him picking at the savage blister on his thumb and thinking, I hope that hurts. Watching him sleep so deep he doesn't stir a muscle even when Davie squawks out in the night, and thinking: you exhaust yourself deliberately because I am repulsive to you now. Juddering glimpses of throwing myself under a train, not to follow Joe, nothing as romantically daft as that; no, just murderous. And worse: imagined throwing Charlie under the next Mail instead just because he'd dragged me out to see the blue tongue he'd found under the verandah and wouldn't stop his jolly burbling about it when I wanted to be stringing beans. Very ugly load of abnormalities. I want to cancel it all out; I want peace.

'I want to go now. Today. With you.' Because I have been avoiding this: the final proof that Joe is truly not here. I've told myself I don't visit graves: not Father's, in the Mick section of the cemetery which is always kept spick and span by donation to the tiny colony of mute nuns in town; and not my mother's, not ever, because Father couldn't bear it. I've told myself I don't need to visit Joe's because I see him every day, in David. But that's only another reason why I do have to go, isn't it. And I can't do this alone, not only because it's not my grief alone, but because I'm frightened.

'All right,' he nods, and the fear becomes a clenching round the swallowed cataclysm in my belly, but I will do this. He says, 'Good,' and I know I can do this, because I can hear that he is coming with me.

It's Sunday. We leave the boys with Sarah and Mim and drive round to the Wattle, past the office, the sheds, the toot, the black holes in the hill, and pull up on the flat, still mowed short like a rugby field by the pit ponies. A monument to Nothing's Really Changed.

We walk across it to the edge of the ridge and Daniel helps me down the rocky slope to the small flat at the bottom; he hasn't said a word, and neither have I. Can't; just need to keep hold of his hand. Whisper to myself: this is where our son is buried, this is real. And yet it's not at all; fear falls away from me like the bark peeling from the trees. This place is too beautiful for fear, and somehow the thought that our little boy keeps Daniel's father company here comes immediately to me, as a gentle fantasy, one I can keep. About two who live in this place, looking directly into the bronze-green skirt of the escarpment on the other side of the valley, who live beneath the gums that rustle above us, red-tipped with new growth, who live among the golden banksias and bright pink orchids that range up behind us. I can hear my whimpering, feel my knees buckle, feel Daniel's arm catch me round the waist, feel the warm solidity of the rock he sets me down upon, hear myself ask: 'Where is he?'

'That little peppermint,' he says, raspy and soft and warmer and more solid than the rock. 'See, near that scribbly? That's Dad.'

I say, 'Peppermint,' as I see it. About three feet tall, with three very sturdy sprays of bright young leaf. *Eucalyptus piperita*, Sydney Peppermint Gum, and it's very happy here. Thirteen to the dozen, but for the sprinkling of tiny, tiny daisies beneath it, so tiny … don't know what they are. Except … too lovely.

He says: 'I thought you'd like it. You know, peppermint.'

Like it? That I now know he's chosen this tree for Joe, for me, that he's nurtured it, that he's been waiting, all these weeks, waiting for me … I don't know anything. Except the pain washing and tumbling through me, waves and waves of it, overtaking me, and Daniel keeping hold of me and saying nothing because there is nothing to say. I am inconsolable, I will always be inconsolable for Joe, and that's all there is to it; and that's all right. My pain is soaring and circling out into the trees with my breath, my existence, the particles of my loss permanent in the atmosphere, permanent as this valley, and I want it to be. I howl for this injustice. I howl into the earth at my feet, between me and my child. I howl until I don't, until I feel his arms around me tight with his acceptance, gossamer and firm, until I am quiet and I feel his breath through the back of my hair, until we are sitting, hip to hip, just here.

And into this stillness I find I can say something I have to say, simply, with no tangles: 'I don't want you to work inside the mine any more.'

I can feel his jolt at my voice, at my knowing that; but he only says: 'It's nearly finished, and I won't after that.'

Whatever that means, at least I've said it; and something else: 'I don't want you to come to bed and just sleep any more, either.'

Silence. But I have to know this, now, today.

'Daniel?'

Into the earth: 'I didn't imagine that you'd ever want me again.'

'I do.' *Please.* Please don't let this have wrecked us there.

He looks at me and smiles, just, that heart-sore barely-there smile, and he stands up. 'We should probably get back.'

No. Yes: I need to feed David, probably a few hours ago. But … I take his hand and follow him up to the top of the ridge with my impatience stinging: this is hardly the time to have raised the subject. I have desecrated everything, us, everything, and somewhere across the paddock I blather: 'I'm just awful, I'm twisted up and awful.'

He stops and stares at me, and I don't know anything and I don't know him, and I want him to let go of my hand. I want him to stop looking at me, but I can't stop looking at him. Heavy storm clouds are arcing above the valley, behind his face, and the low sun at my back strikes the gum leaves blood red, the peeling branches luminous white. A black cockatoo is screeching cold derision; a wallaby thuds away somewhere into the scrub and I'd like to follow it. I wriggle my hand away.

He catches up my wrist and says: 'No, France. Never.'

Words are less than useless for what happens after that, except that I can say nothing is as it was, and I know now that's all right too. It is fierce and it is infinitely gentle. *Gloria.*

DANIEL

'You won't be making a habit of this,' Evan says, following me in.

'A habit of what?' I'm still thinking about Francine yesterday, two miles backwards and about twenty yards up; I'm still watching her eat breakfast and hearing her saying: 'That was a very good egg.' She ate the whole thing, and two pieces of toast, for the first time since —

'Labouring here,' he says: *yur*.

'No,' I tell him. I'm that full of aches I'm never going anywhere near a shovel again after this, and for the last few weeks it's felt like someone's been drilling into my hip while I wasn't looking: doesn't matter how strong I've made myself, it's the turning that does me in; I've got calluses inside and out. 'But what's your issue with me now?'

Evan's still the real boss here, and he's the manager, unofficially, so that he can stay union; I'm just the majority shareholder and signature provider. He says: 'It's neither appropriate nor entertaining any more that you do. Puts some off.'

'Puts some off? Who?'

'Me, for one.'

'Why?' I don't need a ticket or a union card to break rocks in my own company if I want to. How's one free scab upsetting you, when I'm not taking anyone's coal? Jesus, how dippy does that sound?

Very: Evan says: 'Because I don't want you to, and that's all I have to say about it.'

And off he goes, to labour, whether I want him to or not: he's put himself on down the bottom stalls in section two with one of the younger blokes whose dad's not well.

And off I go: idiot. But I can't drop it now. Here's my mess, lads: you clean it up, since I've got a bit tired of it, you finish the blasting, since my wife doesn't approve, just about the first thing she said on rediscovering her power of speech. Only a few days to go and it is finished. Thank Christ.

By the end of the day I don't know what's got me worse: Francine, Evan or the limitations of my hopeless body. I'm that keen to be off and home and in the bath, I've come out into the light too quickly. Wish I'd brought the car today, I don't feel much like a bike ride. I'm still squinting when I hear: 'Danny!'

Stops me dead: my father's voice. And there he is. It *is* Dad. Marvellous: now I'm hallucinating.

Squint some more.

No, it's not Dad.

Flaming hell.

It's my brother. Peter. Must be. I haven't seen him since I was fifteen, but it's him all right. Couldn't be anyone else who looks like that: fair hair, like Dad's; only other one in the whole family. And who walks like that, straight at me, slamming the ground with his feet.

'What do you look like?' he says, like I look stupid.

That's what you say to someone after nine years. He's smiling, but I've got an instant urge to deck him, like I'm thirteen and he's just pinched a chop off my plate. And I could too, now: I'm bigger than him. Except it's doubtful I could lift my arm that high.

Instead I say: 'Well, hello to you too.'

'Yep,' he says. 'Hello all right. Jesus, just look at you. *Just* look at you.' What am I? A frigging bunyip? Then he says: 'What are you doing back in the hole, you goose?'

What is this? Make Sure I Get The Message Day?

I say: 'Is it your business?'

'No,' he says. 'But Mum's not happy about it.'

What? again. 'Mum's got you down from Newcastle to come and tell me this?' I'm still having trouble believing my brother is here at all. I've been meaning to write to him for a year now; don't know why I haven't. Yes I do: haven't known what to say. I'm good at that.

He's not having any trouble with it. 'No,' he laughs, just like Dad. 'I only stopped in on my way back from Orange; we're moving there, next month. Mum filled me in on the latest; had to come and see for myself.'

He's still looking me over: yes, so I'm filthy. I'm looking him over: he looks very flash: nice suit, nice tie, very nice pair of boots. The docks have clearly been kind to him. What is he? Thirty-four? He looks like a bit of a sharp one, and I'm having trouble believing that too.

I say: 'Orange, ay? Gets even colder there in winter.' Next big town on from Bathurst, not too far away. Don't think you're going to make a habit of coming round here and bailing me up like this. 'What are you moving there for?'

'Setting up a here to Woop Woop transport business: trucks. Not a lot doesn't fit on the back of one. The money'll help me cope with the weather.' But then he drops the laugh. 'Mum's really had enough of you. It'd be a good idea if you stopped giving her things to worry about. I know you've had a rough ride, and maybe you think the job gives you something to control, but —'

'What would you know about it?' Stop right there: there's nothing about you that says you're one to lecture me.

'Danny, I know about it.' And he's dead serious, there's blokes all around us, heading up; Pete doesn't care: he has come here to tell me something. 'I know that at Kembla I lost my brother, our brother, and that it probably would've killed Mum if she didn't have you to keep her busy, and to try to replace him. And that even still, I went in with Dad, because Dad had to replace him too. And I know that he didn't have an option but to keep on: a nobody Kraut with strange politics and no religion and his heart ripped out six ways every day before sleeping wasn't going to get a job worth anything anywhere else. But I thought he was so staunch then, the way he handled himself, though he must have been that shredded, I thought he could walk on water if he wanted to. Then when I was seventeen we were helping cart bodies, or what was left of them, after the blow-out, which I can still hear, and feel: it cracked windows in Wollongong. I found a mate's leg; recognised his sock — his sister was shithouse at knitting.'

He stops there, rubs his hand across his mouth, looks into the drift behind me. I don't know whether I hope he's finished, or whether I want him to keep on for the next nine years. He looks at me again and he looks nothing like Dad; he's got brown eyes, like Mum's.

'And even still, it took me eight years to get out, to leave Dad. Jimmy Skelton was the decider, though: when I saw the look on your face, as you were looking at him laid out; Dad telling you to run on to his mother; you doing it, as you'd do anything he told you to. Then Dad using Jimmy to bargain with Drummond over lamps, like it would count for something against the loss. Drummond giving in only because he'd lost too much on the strike the quarter before. It made me retch.'

'What? That's what happened?' That was *no one else's business*?

'Yep. And everyone keeping shush about it, for your sake. You didn't speak for weeks after you got home from the Skeltons that day; I tried to talk to you, and Dad told me to leave you be, that you had a mind of your own; you couldn't even say goodbye to me. Don't you remember?'

'No.' I don't remember that bit. But I believe him. And I think I already know the answer to the question I have to ask: 'Why was Dad so dark at you leaving?'

'I don't know, really,' he says, 'except that I think grief does strange things. Took me a fair while to come to it, but I think Dad was off his trolley with it; couldn't see that I wasn't leaving *him,* letting *everyone* down. I don't blame him now; it's sad, is all. I'm still cut, over Kembla, and over Dad, sometimes so sharp I … How can you not? When Mum wrote and told me about the loss of your boy, to add to all you've … then told me today about you coming back in here, firing and *labouring,* in the worst hole in the place, where Dad … I thought: here we go. Tell me if I'm wrong.'

'You're not wrong,' I realise, barrel of this more than good oil smacking me in the head. 'But I'm not Dad, am I. Too much of a sook: it's the last time I'll be doing anything like this.' Then I have to laugh at the fact, at the truth of what I have done. 'I am fairly off my trolley, though.'

'Runs in the family, and you're supposed to be the smart one,' he says, smiling again, and looking very much like Dad again. 'But you're winning the sook competition: I've heard you've been *painting* — how sooky is that?'

Not very; not at all, actually: you try it. But I say: 'Not as sooky as my sorry arse: I'm that fucking sore. How'd you get here today?' Please have a trap.

He says: 'I drove. Got a little model-T Ford to go with my filthy middle-class life these days. Fell off the back of a ship.'

'Champion,' I say. 'Can I get a ride home?'

'I don't know, Danny, you'll grubby up the upholstery.'

'Do you want to come for tea?'

'Can't. Got to get back to Newcastle by the morning.'

'You can stop for a minute; you haven't met Francine yet.'

'Yes I have. Met her this morning at Mum's. Probably shocked me more than anything else, that did.'

'What did?'

'That an idiot like you caught one like her.'

Prick. Good one, though. And I feel about half a ton lighter now; lighter still when he puts his hand on my shoulder. I've got a brother, haven't I.

And I will feel even better shortly. Down to the final hours now: everyone's knocked off from day shift, but I've got half-a-dozen boys down here with me, to move the last few tons off the floor, and getting a taste of just how boring breaking and shovelling rubbish for fuck-all is: they'll never complain about shovelling shit in the stables ever again or the ragging they get from the miners if their skip tokens aren't exactly where they should be. Of course I'm going to pay them quite a little something extra for the trouble; haven't told them that yet, though. Sent one of them off to run up through the valley to tell France I'll be late: for the last time. Very late, as it turns out: whose bright idea was it to let the boys at it? Like watching paint dry, in the dark.

But it's done now: good job, lads. Leave the skips for the ponies in the morning, leave the last stretch of cementing to someone else, knowing this roof isn't going to fall down for anything. Time to knock off. Forever, for me: go home. Get clean, get into bed. Give France a kiss or several, or maybe just lie there and look at her, with that little light back on inside her, thinking about the things I know I can do to try to keep it that way.

Then the whistles blow for evacuation.

'Aw no,' says one of the boys; they all look at me.

Aw no, all right. I say: 'Don't run, don't fall behind. And stay put when we're out.'

Spend the next half-hour wondering what's happened. No one to ask down here; just us. Can't hear anything, no one calling down to us, not that that means anything necessarily. But whatever it is it's probably not big. Hopefully. Whatever it is it'll be bad enough. Can't see anything amiss along the way up the drift; not that that means anything either. But I can hear a huge racket above now, coming through the air shaft ahead: running, yelling. Jesus, it must be a fire, or gas; I'm sniffing the air thinking I can smell it, knowing, where we are, there's less than a fart between us and anything that might have happened. That's just too bloody marvellous: I missed every kind of gas on the Western Front, but I'm going to be asphyxiated or incinerated now, last day on the proper job, and I'm going to take six boys with me.

I tell them: 'Run, and hold your fucking breath while you're at it.'

I do, grabbing the slowest of them, all the while thinking that France has heard the whistles and how pleased she'll be to hear of my final achievement. Nearly as thrilled as Mum

Don't breathe till pit top.

Here we are, one two three four five six, thank fucking Christ. And I can hear Billy above the pandemonium, still with that high voice, though he must be eighteen now, yahooing. Yahooing? And then I see all the lamplights, spinning through the night. There's a couple of rifles going off; ponies raring up in fright. Mad. Billy runs up to me; he's so skinny and slight he still looks fourteen; he looks like he's about to piss himself, he's that excited. He grabs me by the arm and says: 'It's over. The war's over. Mr Drummond called, from Sydney, for you. On the telephone. He said we've won. Germany's surrendered.'

I'm that confused, and starved of air, I just look at him. Drummond? Telephone. That's right, we've got one of them now, for emergencies. And I've put Billy in the office, 'assisting the night deputy', because he's too useless for anything else, and Campbell's not my best mate for it. Where the fuck is Campbell? His nephew's in Syria, that's where he is.

Billy says: 'Didn't think you'd mind coming up in a hurry to hear that.'

No.

Didn't have to blow four whistles, though, you little shit. Don't say that, though. Can't speak. Just manage: 'Going home.' Let go of the kid first; he rubs his arm like I've nearly ripped it off on the way up.

Walk home.

Shut the lamp off; just let it be dark, and quiet. But it's not quiet: I can hear more rifles going off in town.

I get halfway home before I have to sit down. Didn't think I'd feel like this. Thought I'd be happy. I've got to have a few moments here to believe it. A week or so ago Turkey surrendered and there was talk of the end coming, a lot of talk about the Light Horse and Aussie Captain Ross Smith in his aeroplane practically pulling off the victory on their own too. Talk of ceasefires, the German navy mutinying, Austria hoisting a white flag. There's been that much bullshit flying around through this whole disaster that I didn't let myself believe it. But you don't bullshit about it ending, do you. That's either a fact or it's not. Must be true. You don't hear that many guns going off in town every night, do you. And why else would Drummond telephone, to tell me; that was good of him. More than good: above our bullshit. Maybe even an apology, of sorts.

I am happy, I tell myself, and relieved. But everything I've ever reined in now just floods out. Better to do this here, on my own.

It's too much to think about in one go. Just too much. Wear myself out till I can only see the pictures, flicking one after the other. Fair few of them.

Then I have to sit here a while longer, with the anger. It sits hard in me like it'll never shift from my gut. I'm that full of blinding hatred at the minute, for those that let this loose. So Britannia stays top monster: now we can all get some sleep. I wonder where Johan Schultz is, if he's alive, wonder what he's thinking, about going home. I wonder what it must be like to be an ordinary German today, hearing this news. Can't imagine that: I've never picked a fight and then lost. Only been decked the once, thanks Dunc, and deserved it. I wonder what people will say and think here as they wake up to the extent of it; they'll be relieved, and proud, for sure. Will they feel shame for their part in it? I doubt many will: why would you when there's so much to be relieved and proud about? Just as you don't need to be a fortune teller to see Hughes pressing the advantage now it's over: the government will ride the victory for all it's worth. That's politics.

Feel the breeze on the back of my neck and float away from it. Let it go. I do, violently. Another good reason to be alone right now: I lean forward and chuck like the earth's shifting beneath me.

And then that's enough. Long piece of string, that was, and I can see both ends now: how lucky am I? Never forget that. Ever.

Go home, Daniel, clean your teeth and appreciate every break you've been given.

I run the rest of the way home through the silver grey dark; haven't run anywhere since … since I picked up Stratho that night. And for the first time, seems like forever, they are my legs. It feels good, very good. And I decide that I'm going to run a bit every day from now on, just because I can.

FRANCINE

He clumps into the kitchen just on dawn, goes straight to the bathroom. I leap out of bed, run down the hall and then stand at the door, watch him cleaning his teeth. He reaches down to turn on the bath taps.

He's so thoroughly filthy, I say: 'You're not going to make a mess of my *indoor bathroom*, are you?'

He says: 'Just this one first and last time — special occasion.'

'Mmn.' Very special occasion. I tried to stay put when I heard the whistles, but ended up waking up Harry to fib to him that I had to go round to Grandma's with Davie, trying not to sound panicked, with a thousand different kinds of hysteria surging, main one being: *Holy Mother, he has blown himself up, and I willed it to happen, didn't I*; but then I saw the scene up Dell Street: singing, dancing, shouting; blabbered incoherently at Sarah and Mim, then came back home to wait. No morning whistle today: everyone's having the day off so they can go completely berserk when the official announcement arrives. I say: 'There's no hot water, though.' I don't light the heater round the side till four o'clock.

He says: 'Doesn't matter, I'm boiling anyway.'

He must be too: his shirt is sweat-drenched. What's he been doing out there all night? Don't ask. I watch him take it off: rush of relief and delight at the sight of that pair of shoulders, that back: it's a small country. I watch him take off the rest and hop in the water and I watch him wash. He flicks the flannel at me: gets me right across the face with the perfectly aimed spray.

He says: 'Go and tell the boys to look after the littlies for a spell. I have to take you somewhere.'

'I'm just about to make breakfast.'

'Make it later.'

'If you insist.'

'I do.'

We go round behind the shed on the far side of the orchard. The sun is just peeking into our valley and everything is flushed through soft dusty pink.

This is the way to end a war. No need for any other language. I imagine there's a fair bit of this sort of thing going on right round the world; I certainly hope so. I won't contemplate any other possibility, not now. Let's pretend that this love cancels out everything else. Highest thought ever.

SIX
JANUARY – DECEMBER 1919

DANIEL

If there is such a thing as the gods or whatever, this is what they do for a top cracking laugh.

I'm doing exactly what I should be doing, I've been so well behaved even I'm impressed. In the last few months I've been a good boss: staying out of everyone's way, doing all the boring rubbish in the office, and getting plans for a proper bathhouse organised. And I've got some fat contracts underway for electricity production to kick in next quarter, to pay for a good deal of debt and bathhouse over a couple of years; found myself negotiating with none other than Drummond at one point too: he's bought into a new mob manufacturing motor parts and bodies and approached me for supply; he thought he could get it for nothing, and I thought he'd come to love me: armed with France's bottom price, I told him to bugger off and thieve from someone else.

I've been a good *artist* too, sending off Dunc to his father, without making myself any dippier over his knee: no one but me could see the splash for what it is beyond a stain, and Mr Duncan sent me back a letter full of happy tears anyway. And I sent strange Fanny Adinov my first portrait of France — she's just got up, sitting on the edge of the bed, blinking awake for the baby — to see what he thinks of me without horror. He thinks he wants some more pretty. All right, I'll see what I can do.

I've been a good and proper husband for my France, too, in all the obvious ways, as well as suggesting that she find something better to do with her own time, eventually, if she's not going to have that big family. She's not just going to be my wife, that's certain, and she's well earned her Certificate in Housework. I would like her to give that up altogether, but when I suggested that she send the washing out, she gave me that sharp look and said: 'No, couldn't now.' So, instead, she's driving down to Sydney today to talk to her *angels* Stanley and Bragg to see how she might go about studying the law, without having to go to university — Stanley and Bragg won't live forever, it's amazing they're still alive, and France wants to be on top of that side of the business herself: contract, insurance, liability, company, industrial laws, all that palaver. Good on her. She's taking Mim and the three eldest girls, Kathryn, Roz and Bronnie, with her, so she can haul them all before the court of David Jones. She's had to take our Davie too, of course, since he has to go along with her for the food. What a legend she is as always. My only disappointment is that she's cut her hair again. Can't have everything. They'll be back sometime day after tomorrow. And I'm not even thinking about the cost of the hotel and inevitable unnecessaries, since she presented me with a *budget* for them, entitled *The Essentials of Feminine Indulgence*, including *Swishest French knickers, as of yet indeterminate value*. It's all all right. Better than all right.

I'm busy being an all right boss this morning. Seven o'clock and everyone's about to head in and I'm looking at a skip I've moved onto a flat bit of side track, out of the way. It's funny looking at something you look at all the time for the first time. Really look at it. It's a very simple animal, the skip: four iron wheels with a hardwood crate on top. I'm looking at it because I want to work out if it's possible to somehow put a brake on it, to avoid the need for spragging. Spragging is also very simple: shoving a piece of hardwood between the spokes of one of the wheels to keep the skip stationary. It's a finger-losing exercise for boys, as a few blokes here could attest, apart from being very inefficient at times, as Jimmy Skelton might say if he was here to tell you more about it. There must be a smarter way of doing it. Wouldn't have a clue how, though: I'm no engineer with this sort of thing; I don't even know how the brakes on the car work. I could build a house that wouldn't fall down for a thousand years, but anything mechanical: ask France; and I will when she's back, and she'll no doubt tell me, again, that we should look at investing in a whole box of safer mechanised cutting, loading and hauling like they have everywhere in America; and I'll tell her again that the union wouldn't have us put wheelers, let alone colliers, out of jobs; neither would I. So, now, I bend down to have a look underneath, as you do when you have no clue. And there's absolutely no explanation for what happens next.

Something makes the skip move, very sharply, like it's been kicked by a pony, very cranky one, right smack into the side of my head. That's all I know for the moment as I hit the deck.

I can see stars and hear Evan say, very slowly: 'Oh boyo. Nasty.'

FRANCINE

We pile into the car and I'm still feeling a little queasy; have been since I woke up. There's a smell of coaldust and something sweet in the air, some sort of chemical perhaps floating across from one of the fat cigars in town, and I think, yes please, let's get out of Lithgow today. I don't really have to go to Sydney; I could have simply written to my angels and asked them to send books and advice and they'd send back the entire College of Law library and pay the freight. They're an odd couple, don't know how they make money out of their practice. For all the advice they've given us, they've never sent more than the slimmest of bills, a token. I suspect, being old acquaintances of the Leprechaun, they play stocks and horses to make up the shortfall. They don't look much like gamblers, though, those sweet old men; but you can't ever tell who you're looking at, really, can you.

It's Mim we're really making this trip for; she's so excited as she climbs in next to me, holding Davie, and it's not about the DJs experience much at all. There's a few ships due in to Sydney Harbour sometime tomorrow and she wants to see them come in. She says it's because she loved going in to Wollongong and Port Kembla as a child, seeing all the steamers and the bustling round the docks. Not coal steamers coming to the Quay tomorrow, though; they're troopships, and I think I can fathom another reason why it might be important for her to see them. To see the soldiers disembarking, perhaps to make Roy's absence real and sharp and bathed in the joy of others' reunions. She is back with a vengeance: impossibly jovial. The Ackerman stern-stoic trait missed her entirely. Praise be.

She says now: 'The first thing I want to do when we get there is go to one of those fancy *continental* bakeries I've heard about. Must be the Fritz in me because I had a dream about strudel last night.'

Ackerman obsession with food didn't miss her at all; I say: 'Strudel? Haven't you had enough apples? I want something crammed with chocolate and walnuts and laced with brandied caramel.'

One young lady and two little girls behind us say: 'Oh, yes!'

'No, no, no,' Mim says, as serious as she gets. 'You can't have too many apples, Francine. Humble but perfect in every way.'

I glance at her as we turn into Main Street.

She adds: 'So long as they come with lashings of brown sugar and honey and cinnamon and buttery pastry.'

I'm still laughing as I pull up outside the grocers, to grab a bunch of bananas to tide us over till morning tea, when I hear my name: 'Mrs Ackerman.'

I turn around and see Polly, it's Polly Rogers, after all this time. 'Goodness, Polly. How are you? Please, it's Francine to you.'

'Yes,' she says frowning, her great bust on the verge of heaving up a sigh, except she's in a bother. She says: 'I think I should tell you I've just seen your husband, on my way down the hill. He didn't look very well.'

'What do you mean?'

'You should go to the hospital.' She means now.

Mim says: 'What's he done this time?'

Don't wait for the answer Polly seems too shocked to divulge. Head up the hill, here we are. Mim stays in the car with the children while I go in. Dreading.

And there he is. Big gasp.

He sees me and says: 'It looks a lot worse than it is.'

Couldn't look much worse. Looks like someone's thrown a bucket of blood over him. He's holding a towel to the side of his forehead and that's soaked through too. There's a puddle of blood on the floor.

I say: 'It looks fairly bad to me. What did you do?'

He says: 'You don't want to know.'

'Yes I do.'

'I hit my head is all. You don't have to be here. Keep on to Sydney, I just need a stitch.'

'No,' I say. 'I won't go to Sydney.'

He says: 'Don't be ridiculous. It really isn't anything.'

But it is something, with a shiver: some kind of two and two? The smell, the sweet smell ... it's here, stronger than blood or bleach. It's hyacinth, unmistakable, like a perfumed hankie under my nose; and an odd collection of memories hits me quick as a flutter of playing cards ... fresh linen, lilac glitter of amethyst, Mama dabbing a spot from my cheek ... I *did* call her Mama. Odd moment for epiphany and this one feels like a warning: not for Daniel but for me. Don't go to Sydney. Don't come back. Look after Danny.

Can't tell him that, can I, it's all a fluttery figment, so I say: 'Don't you be ridiculous.'

He belts out a big laugh then and says: 'Apparently I can't help it.'

Poor darlingest.

But a week later I'm just about prepared to accept bizarre extrapolations as clear and direct instructions. Timely ones. The soldiers returning from the Middle East have brought with them a different kind of rapid and brutal destruction: influenza.

Hundreds have dropped with it within a few days and it's well out of control in Sydney; papers say Melbourne and Brisbane too. The thought that some of those men made it through all that, only to die of the damn flu, or bring it home for the family: must be somewhere near the zenith of unfair. To make it through bullets, bombs, dysentery, cholera, pneumonia, malnutrition and who knows what else, only to … Grateful to be an atheist and not prone to thoughts of God's wrath.

I tell Daniel what I think about my 'rescue', mainly just to lighten the news.

He says, and he's still got a corker of a black eye below the bandage: 'So you think your mother pushed a skip into my head so you wouldn't go to Sydney and get the flu?'

'Yes,' I say, and I'm teasing him now, but who knows? It's as reasonable an explanation as any. Kinder than the thought that he's simply inexplicably prone to injury. Kinder than the thought that I was inexplicably destined to see him drenched like that, like a vision come back from the depths of old terrors.

He says: 'You really are barking, aren't you.'

But I can see he's considering it too. He considers it fairly seriously in the months that follow, when the flu begins visiting Lithgow, closing the schools, churches and even the pubs — even the arms factory shuts down completely with a mass outbreak. He forbids me from going beyond Sarah's, even as he tells me the only ones dying of the flu in any numbers are alcoholics and those on their way out anyway. Daniel, of course, doesn't get the flu, doesn't wear a mask in town, doesn't need to, because he's infection-proof. I have to wonder if that might not be true. Fate might have had a decent go at mangling him, but he's never had so much as a sniffle. Neither have I for that matter. But I obediently stay under house arrest at Josie's with the boys till the threat passes, not prepared to push our good fortune an inch further.

Fortune. That's a tangle, isn't it. At least I've come to recognise there are antidotes available against the worst of it, and they are really rather easy to obtain when you need them; you only need look for them: David's seven months old now and he has a little dimple in his chin when he beams, a little dimple that no one else has. I can wonder all I like if Joe would have had that dimple too, but I don't wonder too long, because I have a choice, and I do have a power. Sometimes I like to imagine that Joe made that little dimple on his brother, with his tiny, perfect pinky finger, when they were playing tip inside me; sometimes I wrap myself in the gentleness of an old man with a deep raspy voice saying to a small boy: *Look at the sun on the hills;* and I don't care if that makes me a nut. It has its own logic, one that makes sense to me.

One that means I have now taken my mother's photograph out of the bottom drawer in the wardrobe, so that she sits on the mantel in the parlour next to Father — whose photograph I had left inside a packing box with that tatty old piece of embroidery I never finished, all this time. Mama. *Good gracious, look at the girl you raised, Frank.* And imagination or not, I can hear her laughter somewhere. True enough I would have heard it once: she was married to the Leprechaun, after all.

Look at them there together, Mr and Mrs Connolly: hard not to imagine they've been in cahoots here all along. Fanciful but beautiful notions. My *Insurance,* if you like.

DANIEL

In the real world the barking is getting harsher and louder, right here in front of me. In the paddock, where we're having a collective meeting, or were until it became a brawl. Verbal at the moment. Probably a bit more than that in a minute. I should do something authoritative. Say something. But it's too stupid. I'm looking at it in *morbid* fascination.

It's started because there's been a riot in Brisbane, more than five hundred miles and a whole state away from here. Apparently a thousand or so returned men pulled apart the Russia Association building, doing a very proper job of it, because the trade unionists had marched the day before against the War Precautions Act continuing, keeping wages low, the cost of living high and mouths closed in continued censorship as well as hunger. The Queensland constabulary, who are not Hughes's best mates and who act under the only Labor state left in the country, opened fire on the Anzac rioters. No one was killed, but the police were not being careful to avoid hitting anyone with bullet, bayonet and fist. I'm split.

I can appreciate the returned men acting like animals, because that's what some of them are now, if they weren't animals before the AIF taught them how to be. They were carrying on about the unionists being in bed with the Bolsheviks and Sinn Feiners; said they were all waving the red flag. And The Red Flag, as we all know, has been banned by the Federal government. Better

469

keep my autographed copy of the Manifesto under the bed from now, if I can find it in France's *Islands of Slovenliness* as she calls her bookshelves in the sitting room. Our government has also, just a few weeks ago, finally come through with a housing plan for the veterans. Hard not to see some sort of a connection between this momentous event and the riot. France, when she mentioned it last night, is convinced they'd been encouraged to stir things up, to set an example against disloyalists — she would: she'd find a connection between the ends of a rainbow if you gave her a moment to think about it. But if this particular thing's supposed to be a Hughes show, it backfired, because the so-called enemies of the state were well behaved on their march, just saying their piece; the Anzacs' attack was actually unprovoked, so the response of the police would seem fairly appropriate. I'm inclined to shout above the brawl: 'No one died, so who fucking cares?' But clearly a lot do.

There's about thirty or so blokes in front of me who are frothing for the returned men, at the police brutality, and a few are returned men themselves. Then there's about fifty who are frothing for the unions and for Russia's right to run its own game, without Australian communists getting belted for having an opinion. But then there's every two-bobs' worth being thrown in, from the blind murder in Ireland, to Hughes deliberately inciting trouble in all unions to prevent the One Big National Union, which some poor bastards still think is a possibility. One bloke's even going off about Welsh independence. Jesus.

All of these men work at the Wattle, where, regardless of whether they have a stake in it or not, they are all on the best fucking wicket in the country probably, when it comes to coal anyway. And every single one of them is a paid-up member of the union. Thought I was an expert at irony. Not today. No class confusion, Dunc, just confusion. All I can see is about eighty different flavours of anger, banging away, letting off four years' worth of steam and more, and I'm thinking how well this sort of thing must suit the Nationalist government, state and commonwealth, and right across this wide brown land of ours. Solidarity is dead, even if it was only ever half alive. Who's going to hold a mourning service for that? No one. Mateship was born in the AIF, wasn't it: not in a mine. Eureka. True blue. Never forget.

I look at Evan next to me. He's looking off at the sky above the hill, thinking about rugby no doubt. It's a look of weary contempt. He's saying on that hard old stone face: *Let them brawl and think about it tomorrow, when they've hurt themselves for no purpose.* Ten minutes ago, before the brawl took off, I'd been talking about the bathhouse going ahead. Your fucking *heated* bathhouse, and probably the first one in the state. Thank you all very much, lads.

Punch is thrown, rowdy now. All in.

Evan says: 'Come on then, Danny, let's go and have a cup of tea.'

Yep.

And anyone who doesn't turn up tomorrow won't be paid injury time. I've half a mind to order that box of machinery and get rid of the lot of you.

Anzac Day, my pretend birthday. This time, it's fear of the national reverence that keeps me at home with my own mourning and silence. That and the service medal I received in the post last week: thanks for the reminder. Got shoved straight in the kit, still in the back of the wardrobe. I realise there's not a lot of room for those who'd rather forget. There must be thousands who don't show up to services and get-togethers, so we're invisible; won't be anything in the papers about the abstainers. I don't show up to work either: I go for a run and come home and paint instead.

France comes back from the shops in the afternoon, says it looked more like Lest We Forget The Publicans in town. That'd be right.

July is Anzac Month for me this year. I don't know why; maybe it's because drought has brought the wattle out early and my eyes are full of water as soon as they're open. Doesn't help that I don't sleep more than a couple of hours a night. No nightmares, no dreams at all, but when I wake up it takes me a moment to work out where I am. France can hear the wheels turning, but she doesn't rag me about it this time. She wraps herself around me, I think to remind me where she is; not that I need telling. She's always with me, somehow: how did an idiot like me catch one like her? Who doesn't question why I'm not going into work much at the minute, and why I can't seem to get into town at all. Just the thought of going into town makes me sweat, because I know I'll run into someone who'll make me lose it: one of the permanently damaged, and there's something like a hundred thousand of them all over the country. It sounds more than backward, but I find it very hard to accept that I was spared. That grinds into my mind more than the thought of the sixty thousand who died. I really want to believe in France's magic, I really do; I'd want to believe that her parents were *in cahoots*, that Frank said *kill him* and Josie said *no, just hurt him so he knows about it*, if it wasn't just one of France's funnies against *miserable facts*. I'd even believe Hughes's jabber about Australia's sacrifice being the largest of any of the Allies, if that would help me sleep through. But, over there, there's millions dead, and more millions damaged; and I wasn't one of them. And then there's more millions that starved to death. The hollowed-out faces of little French kids, not asking for money, just food. Starvation. That thought will never stop horrifying me; personally, I couldn't think of a worse way to go. France reckons more will have died of the Spanish flu in the past year, but it's not the same, is it: we don't make the flu.

I'm not *melancholy* exactly, not mad like before; but I am in a very strange place. I try to paint it, not even sure what I am painting. They don't look like pictures. There's one that makes me laugh, though: a headless woman in a wedding dress holding a wooden leg like a baby. I don't know why it makes me laugh; something about the way she seems to be smiling, in her hands. She's grateful to have that leg, over the moon, and I suppose she's slinging off at the disgust that made me think her into being, having a joke with herself, without me. France thinks it's the most obscene thing I've ever done. It is. I'll definitely send this one to Doctor Fanny; see what he thinks of this pretty. He's going off to Europe at the end of the year; wrote to ask if he could take the monsters along, to show some mate of his, said Mr Duncan was keen that he should; I wrote back telling him I don't care if he takes them on a tour of Mars. And I don't.

It's a letter at the end of July that shakes me out of it. It says:

> *Dear Sir, not sure what else to call you, mate,*
>   *I just wanted to let you know that I'm still alive, despite myself. I'll be passing through Lithgow on Sunday the tenth of August and would like to drop in to see you, not for the conversation, just to say g'day. Let me know at the above address if that's all right with you.*
>   *Clem Foley*

The thrill this little note gives me just about knocks me over. I'm sitting on the front steps and I see France, running around with Danny and Charlie and Harry. They're chucking slushy snow at each other. Davie's holding onto my trouser leg as he laughs at them, staggering like a drunk, wanting to run out there too.

France sees me smiling at her and chucks a handful at me. 'Good news?'

Yep.

FRANCINE

Mr Clement Foley is precisely the sort of man who makes you wonder what the AIF were thinking when they were recruiting. He's around thirty-five, with huge brown, thoughtful eyes and wispy fair hair, and so tall and reedy slim you feel you should ask him if he'd like to sit down to save him the trouble of standing. The absolute sweetest gentleman, too, polite to a fault. And he is, funnily, a bookkeeper by trade. No specs, though. Very hard to imagine him going through all that; hard to imagine him digging a hole. But it's true. And even more surprisingly, he's ridden his horse all the way from Sydney; camped out last night in the mountains.

He and Daniel are sitting on the back verandah now, and I'm finding it very difficult not to eavesdrop. I'm hovering in the kitchen, near the back door as much as possible, overfeeding the children, while I check Sunday lunch every five minutes. Stop it, Francy, or the beef'll never cook. I pick up that Clem got back in March, that *things weren't too good for a spell*, and that he's got a job and a house in Mudgee. Stab of sadness at the thought that he appears to be on his own, but maybe he wants to be, or has to be. They talk about Dunc and Stratho and some others I've never heard of, but not about each other I don't think. Daniel's not one for talking about himself much anyway.

Then Daniel clumps inside and says: 'Clem's staying for lunch. That's all right, isn't it.'

Goodness, my darlingest can raise a giggle out of me; I don't think he knows how to ask a question. He tries, I'm sure, but just about everything that issues from his mouth sounds like statement or command, just can't manage the upward inflection. You have to look at his eyes, and the position of his eyebrows to see the enquiry.

'Course it is,' I say. What difference would it make when there will be twelve Ackerman overeaters at the table already? Sarah, Miriam, Kathryn, Roslyn, Harry, Charles, Bronwyn, Jennifer, Isobella, Large Daniel, Small Daniel and David. Plus me.

Besides, ever since Daniel got his friend's note, he's slept like a bear in winter. I'll feed Clem Foley for the term of his natural life for that gift. Meantime, hope he survives the experience of Sunday lunch at our place.

He does. His large sad-sleepy eyes float around us and spark with delight at the noisy chatter of the children, twinkle at a squabble over the last of the bacony bits of the creamed spinach. He doesn't say much but he spends the afternoon smiling, and despite his rangy frame he puts away his food like it's his last meal.

Charlie, who wouldn't sit at a table for the length of lunch if you tied him down, wanders over to our visitor and asks: 'Are you really a soldier too?'

And Daniel cuts him off: 'Was. And don't be rude.'

Clem chuckles and tells Charlie: 'I wasn't much chop at it, young man.' He taps his nose. 'Don't tell anyone, though.'

What a lovely man he is. Miriam clearly thinks so too; she's barely taken her eyes off him, and has been unusually quiet today. I sniff the air for hyacinths. Say a prayer for all the lonely lovely ones. Get up with some dishes; splash some water on my face.

★

We're celebrating Daniel's birthday this Sunday, for September the twenty-fifth, and he's twenty-five. We've just given him a good teasing about the fact that, as we've recently discovered, he shares his not-pretend birthday with none other than Billy the Troll; I sent the prime minister a lump of coal through the post a few days ago to show how much we care; attached a note saying: *Don't eat it all at once. Lots of love, Lenin.* Here and now, we've just completed feeding time of industrial proportions, all seventeen of us, since Peter and Violet and their too little and too adorable to be naughty daughters Rose and Daphne are with us. It's raining buckets, and women and children have retired to the parlour, listening to Sarah play the piano, or trying to above the din of raindrops and chatter. She's playing Liszt's *Consolation,* D bloody flat, and I'm trying not to look too much at Violet, who's quite pregnant. I'm trying very, very hard not to be jealous. Failing miserably. I should be pregnant now; it's been five months since I stopped feeding Davie. I just can't accept it. I can dream my sweet fantasies of Joe; even yearning for him now, when I do, is more a tender affirmation of my acceptance of it; I usually stick my head in the linen cupboard to do it and the smell calms me. But barrenness? Resentment curls up through grief again. Just not fair. It's not that I want to make up for Joe, either; it's that I want … I don't know. I think I want ten babies against all the loss. New national pastime I can't take part in — can't go anywhere without seeing babies — everywhere. The too lovely, too pretty music is eating into my brain. I know that I'm a bit menstrually deranged today, but I'm suddenly not coping at all. I wish Father would materialise from his photograph and start playing something vulgar.

Try to let my mind drift and linger upon pleasant, funny things … Received the most beautiful letter from Louise Beckett last week. She's in Brisbane now: sub-matron in a headcase hospital; one of the doctors there keeps bothering her, and she said she might go to the pictures with him if he'd recommend her for some physical therapy course. She's got radical ideas of her own on the benefits of touch and gentle exercise aiding the mentally distant. And the poor doctor said yes, so now she has to come good and go out with him. She said that if he's not too much of a pain, then she'll look into what other courses he might like to recommend her for. She also thanked me, profusely, for our lunatics-together interlude, said she wouldn't be so at peace or anywhere near where she is today without it. Good for her. And now I'm not coping again.

Kathryn, wise and peachy little woman that she is, wafts over and snuggles against me on the sofa. That does me in. I squeeze her tight and kiss her on the head; fib to her I've a sniffle and need to find a handkerchief.

I go out to the kitchen, because it's as far away from the parlour as I can get, and look out at the apple trees, streaky in the rain, streaky like me. Should be happy about all this rain; we've had the most dreadful drought all year and the tanks were down to nearly nothing. I can hear Daniel and Peter talking on the back verandah; they usually go for a walk after lunch when Peter comes over, but it's too wet today. Their voices are so similar, I can't tell who's saying what, when one of them bellows: 'He asked you if he could *what?*'

The other one laughs: 'Write to her. Isn't that special?'

Special; that's a Danielism.

'Have you told Mim?' Peter asks him.

'No. Not going to. She'll be more hysterical if it comes as a surprise.'

What? And why haven't you shared whatever this is with me? Brothers' business evidently.

Peter says: 'He is a good bloke, this Foley character?'

Very audible gasp from shameless eavesdropper.

'The type that asks a woman's brother if he can write to her.' Daniel laughs some more.

'He does know that she's got seven kids, doesn't he?'

'Yep. Met them last month when he stopped here. All the hard work's been done for him.'

'Is he insane?'

'Yep.' I can hear Daniel slap his thigh with laughter now.

Peter says, serious: 'Don't you let her get upset.'

Silence, then: 'I won't.' Daniel switches to fierce so fast I flinch at the sink. I can appreciate his attitude, though: he adores his sister and Mim's sons have virtually become his own, so he's hardly likely to be flip about this, regardless of the joking.

Now Peter laughs: 'All right. Settle down.'

'Don't tell me to settle down,' says Daniel, but he's back to joking too.

'I'll tell you to settle down and I'll make you.'

'Go on.'

'All right.'

And I can hear chairs and feet scraping and a few thumps. The sounds of boys. Very large ones. 'You bastard.' Someone falls off the verandah. 'Watch your language.'

Clump, clump, clump, here they come. I make myself busy at the sink filling a glass with water. Slightly less glum now. Daniel gives me a sly slap on the bottom as he walks past, heading for the parlour. I stay where I am, and hear him say, 'Give it a rest, Mum,' before bashing out some ragtimey dance tune. Quite a bit less glum now. Done my dash with magic; what more could I possibly want? It's Mim's turn to have a little. Hope so.

DANIEL

Hysterical doesn't say it, not by any stretch. Mim is actually in some kind of shock when she tells me Clem Foley has written to her with *a view to forming an acquaintanceship*. I would be too, I suppose, just at the breathtaking formality and gentleness of that turn of phrase.

But that's what he's like, where women are concerned at least. If he was any *nicer* he'd make you sick. I only ever saw Clem become anything but once, and that was when we'd stopped in a little cafe–bar type place on the road south of Albert, to try to scrounge a feed with real food in it, or at least something missing woodchip bickies and tinned dog. There were a couple of blokes there more interested in the red wine when we walked in, and they were harassing the girl behind the counter. She was alone: in a room full of Australians, Kiwis and French Canadians, all of them apparently ignoring the fact that she was distressed and didn't want to serve the two idiots in front of her. She clearly didn't speak much English, and the idiots could barely speak anything approaching any language, they were that out of line. It was when one of them reached over and grabbed her by the arm that Foley went off. I took a second to watch his hand meet the back of the bloke's collar before I followed him outside but he didn't need help; and the other idiot wasn't going to take me on, especially since a couple of Maoris had started crossing the road for a gander. Clem went back inside and apologised to the girl, in French. She shrugged in reply; you have to love the French.

As for the rest of the duration, I don't know how he coped; he says he didn't, but obviously he did. Enough to get home anyway, with his quiet sense of humour and loud sense of chivalry intact.

I say to Mim: 'Well, are you going to write back?'

She says: 'You don't leave a letter like that unanswered, do you.'

No.

She turns away to take the kettle off the stove, pours the water into the pot, sits down at the table to plait Isobella's hair: last kid left at home. I've come round to Mum's with Charlie and Harry, who've just taken the rest of their million sisters off on the walk to school. I only stopped in to finally pick up those boxes of Dad's old records, to shift them to the Wattle where they belong, but I've forgotten all about that as I watch Mim, wondering what's going through her mind. She could plait hair in her sleep; she looks up at me and says: 'How's he stayed a bachelor so long?'

I say, and I think it's probably as true as anything is: 'He might have been a bit shy once. Maybe he's not so much now.'

'Well,' she says, and my sister's never been known for shy but here she is: speechless and full of amazement. Good. She deserves every breath of that. I get a glimpse of what Clem must see in her; you don't really see your sister that way until it's suddenly important: she is very beautiful. Some women would be wrecked after going through all that; she's not.

The hysteria doesn't come until November, when Clem writes to tell her he's coming up for a visit, and bringing an extra horse because he'd like to teach her to ride, *with a view to us teaching the children eventually.*

Mim and France flap about as if he's going to walk in in the next five minutes. What's she going to wear to go riding, what will they make for lunch. They both look and sound about fifteen. Mum's sitting there, arms crossed on the table, laughing at them. Better than a show in town, this is. I've never seen this kind of female carry-on before: it's fascinating.

About to leave, I finally remember the boxes and tell Mum. I follow her into her bedroom to get them. Haven't been inside this room since the day I got married and came in here to look myself over in Mum's mirror. Today, the first thing I see is Dad's comb and razor still on the dressing table, toothbrush in the cup behind. Like he's about to wake up and need them. We might be that odd mob who lives round the end of Dell, but we do a good line in devotion, all of us, in one way or another.

Mum says, bending down, pulling out one of the boxes: 'What are you going to do with them?'

'Just keep them where they should be, and keep it going, you know.' Make a note of how and why each time someone's injured, sick, sacked, retired and hopefully never killed on the job. No other mines that I know of keep official records of these things, it's always up to the union to bother, but the Wattle will.

'You're going to write up records yourself?' She looks round at me.

'Yes.' And tell me why not.

'No one will be able to read them.'

Thanks Mum. I tell her: 'Since you can read my writing, you can make a neater copy of my scribble if you like.'

'All right, I will.'

'Good.'

She laughs: at me. I love her too.

FRANCINE

Armistice Day, the eleventh of November. Daniel signs a hefty cheque for the Returned League, for the widows' fund, and will post it tomorrow. No note. Reminds me of Father, the way he'd send off yearly cheques to the Society of St Vincent de Paul, not out of penance, I don't think, but because he agreed on principle with the *good works*, if not the holy doctrine attached.

Daniel's too busy to post it this morning, or pause to observe the two minutes' silence. He's got me standing by the far windows in the room off the verandah, in the sun, trying to match the colour of my hair, says it's darkened slightly and he just can't get it right. Tells me for the umpteenth time that I am a very bad wife for cutting it. Still, every painting of me is true: short hair. Except for one: I'm eighteen, leaning around the pole of the lean-to at the back of Sarah's, with the gully behind me, a wayward strand floating over my shoulder in the breeze. I don't know what he's going to do with this ever-growing monument to his uxoriousness. He says he can't send any of these ones to Doctor Adinov, and they're too big and too me to hang in the house, so they sit stacked in this room; seventeen of them now: don't stop. Sometimes, I think this run on Francine is funny for everything it says about his indulgence, but mostly I think what a treasure it is that I can see how he sees me, how much of me he sees. I'm not particularly pretty, in a conventional sense, too many angles and freckles; but he makes me beautiful, in the shapes, the colours of me. I think he's a genius, of course: I would.

We're at it again on the last Sunday of the year, except that I'm standing here completely naked. The children are still at Sarah's; we'll pick them up later. Daniel told her: 'I want to see her skin in that light. See you round five.' You have to wonder how many sons say that to their mothers after lunch.

I want him to paint my expression of desire right now, but he's busy doing whatever it is he's doing with the white, a splotch of which is dribbling down one knee. He is a picture in himself, in his summer painting attire, which consists of an old bespattered shirt, cut-off trousers and those always everyday boots, no socks today, though. It gets very hot in this room with the afternoon sun.

Busy, busy, busy. So busy, we've been lately, that we didn't even manage to vote in the federal election two weeks ago. Hughes has been returned, of course, and there was simply no one else to vote for who could win or who wasn't clangouring for The White Australia Policy. An idea it appears the labour movement dreamed up to protect the Aussie worker from treacherously cheap Chinese *blow-ins* a generation or so ago, but which now is our new Galvanising National Fear: Fight the Yellow Peril! It would seem absurd if it hadn't been so effective at the polls. Not that the National Party needed it when they hold the trump card: the delicate economic situation requiring the steady management of the government that saw us through the war and put the country in the red by some three hundred million pounds, a figure we're to be chuffed about: a war bill greater than that of New Zealand, Canada and South Africa put together. Now, if you want to live here, you have to be prepared to work for a subsistence wage or less, so the Chinese would be mad to come here anyway, wouldn't they.

Those who do live here are fed on jingo-jangle still: chests outthrust now that we're a little empire in ourselves, having been apportioned the entire former German colony of New Guinea, as a lookout post against the Yellow Peril perhaps, and now that we're a fully paid-up-in-blood member of the soon to be inaugurated League of Nations. I can still see the Troll's words swimming before my eyes after his triumphant return from the Paris Peace Conference: *Paradise is there for those who are willing to enter in. Let us not range ourselves under the banner of intolerance. Men have gone into the pit of hell to save for us the title deeds of Australia and of liberty. Australia is free and will remain free.* Too many mines of hypocrisy in that snippet of mind-boggling cant. While his signature is on documents that say Germany should be pulverised into poverty and humiliation with reparations and embargos and occupation forever and ever amen; not a very tolerant way to treat the vanquished. Why should every German have to pay for the sins of a few? While their kaiser's skipped off to stay with friends in Holland, to recover from his embarrassment. Hear, hear to the stripping of arms, but it's only the losers who've been stripped. While winners strut: just look at Joe Cook — *Sir* Joe Cook these days, thank you very much. Not bad for a Lithgow coal worker.

Look at mine, and smile up through my centre: no slavery going on here in our paradise, is there, except for the endeavours of this little muse to please her master. I'd do anything, absolutely anything for you. Just as well it's a reciprocal arrangement. He flashes back a grin before he's busy again.

I stare out at the orchard: the apple trees are a little droopy in the heat. I imagine for a moment that they are sorrowful, gazing as they do at Odysseus's prow, sailing away from Calypso, who'll wait there forever, for all the justice that never comes. What did she want from the gods? If you can stay awake through Homer and Critical Studies to find her you'd think she was a temptress, a sorceress, a shallow device to keep the hero from his destiny; but I think she simply didn't want the father of her children to return to war and the world of men. I can understand that; I can hear her say: *Aren't I enough to stay at home for? Stay safe for?* Use all my magic to make it so; and fail. I don't have to ask why Sarah calls this place Calypso. Bereft in acquiescence but still defiant.

Daniel says: 'Stop frowning, France. Look at me just as you were before.'

Cracks me: thanks Kookaburra, thanks Leprechaun, thanks everyone.

SEVEN

AUGUST 1920

FRANCINE

There is to be a wedding. Of course. Today, in the first week of August, as if the powers that control our destiny had to complete a six year plan to the precise second, in accordance with the laws of romance.

Barely dawn, I wake, as I so often do, to the sound of grunting coming from the back verandah: darlingest at his morning ritual of self-administered physical punishment. Then footsteps down the hall, Clem's; he says to Achilles: 'You're still a maniac, I see.'

Daniel says between grunts: 'Nothing wrong with being fit.'

Clem says, in his sleepy way: 'There's fit, mate, and then there's heart failure.'

Daniel has to stop then, to laugh. 'You saying I've got a mental problem?'

'Yes, sir.'

'You might be right, Foley.'

'I am right, sir.'

'All right, I'll come quietly. Make yourself useful and put the stove on, will you. Anyone'd think you were getting married today.'

Shoop, shoop, shoop, razor on strop. Shave. Wash. Clean teeth. Clump, *clump*, clump, *clump*, shaking the floorboards with bare feet up the hall, with that lean to the right that Doctor Nichols thinks is heading towards a limp, could do with an X-ray, but which Daniel says just means his favourite quack is missing his best customer, and here he is, showing full benefits of Almighty Toothbrush.

He says to me, donning his collarless best: 'What are you looking at.' And he knows very well. No time for that, though: got to get up, get four boys washed, fed, watered, combed, toothbrushed and shirts tucked in. Very special boys, all of them.

Specialest today, though, is Clem. As we pile into the Cadillac he looks as I imagine he might have done that day he dropped the roll of wire on Daniel. Setting off for the proper job, terrified. No manufactured terror going on here today; just the most terrifying thing of all: love. Whack.

Clem is a Christmas- and Easter-only Mick, and since the law says you've got to get married somewhere, it falls to Father Hurley to do the honours. He's more than a bit special too, my old friend the priest, smiling in his weary eyes at this collection of Ackerman atheists and Lewis Methodists, I suspect because he simply loves marrying people. I think he'd marry Hindus if a pair asked him to. Dodgy Catholicism aside, this pairing-up is the highest sacrament, however it's cobbled together. I wouldn't take back a second of our marriage, not even the horrible times, and you couldn't get much more cobbled together than ours; good heavens, we married the day the world declared war on itself, and we've never celebrated an anniversary. Maybe we should from now on. There's only one prayer for today, and that's that Mim and Clem have what we have for as long as they both shall live: completeness of their union; a love that's stronger than anything else.

And here she comes. I can hear Clem breathing, or trying to, steadily, from where I'm standing. I can hear his heart beating, I'm sure. She is breathtaking. She is already crying, trying not to; so am I. With this incredible blessing.

The children do not move; not a shirt needing to be tucked or a plait minus its ribbon. They are awed as they watch their mother marry this lovely gentle man who was all alone and never will be again, who is about to take them all to live in Mudgee. He's found a bigger house, with a paddock for the horses. Mudgee's not very far away, we'll see them once a month or so, but after today Harry and Charlie won't live with us and the wrench is already terrible.

Daniel's lost in the brickwork, determined not to look at anyone; clearly he feels the same way. I try to think of something funny to stop these blasted tears. Did you know that Monash, our most celebrated general — who won the war and all that — is the son of Prussian Jews? Real name: *Monasch*. Kept that quiet, didn't they. What a difference the dropping of one little letter makes. That tickles. And did you know that Matilda's real Jolly Swagman was a German shearer called Frenchy Hoffmeister who drowned himself on Dagworth Station in far-flung North Queensland? And there I'd been thinking it was all a jingly whimsy Mr Patterson wrote for the Billy Tea Company. I'd also thought that Matilda was his sweetheart — not his *swag*. And now I've got the giggles. Badly. Stop it, Francy. Think of something sobering: that's easy. The complication I'll have to tell Daniel about, soon, mental problem or not. Maybe tonight. Can't have a wedding, or any other kind of accident without a complication, can we.

Focus on Sarah, the most serene person here; what's she thinking? I think I can guess: she'll be sad to see them all go, but glad to have her peace and quiet back. Hmn.

DANIEL

She's put the boys to bed, and now she's tucked up under a blanket on the sofa, reading about wage cases. That's what you do after a wedding, don't you, if you're Francine; book's almost as big as she is. I've just come in from a long walk, been thinking that it's a good thing Clem loves his rugby and won't let Harry and Charlie let it go; rugby *league*, though: don't tell Evan. She looks up at me with her specs on, since she needs them for reading now. We should get the electricity put on out here one day too, so she doesn't go blind squinting under the kero lights, especially since more than half of next year's contracts will go off to make the stuff.

She says: 'D'you know, if the Arbitration Court ever hears another *sufficient wage* case, I'm going to make a scandalous submission to it, on the advantage of collectivisation.'

Really. Good for you. She's got a point, though: after more than a year of failed strikes here and there and all over the place, workers are travelling backwards. The economy is nowhere near as bad as the government keeps insisting it is; we're doing well enough, we'll be free of the debt by the end of next year, unless coal goes out of fashion overnight; a few are even planning debts of their own to buy their houses off us; the profit share is keeping everyone's head well above — well, except for those who couldn't float if you paid for their swimming lessons. But everywhere else most are too hungry and too desperate to hang onto the jobs they have to argue about wages and conditions. And whoever you are, don't ask about the disgrace that is the new beaut soldiers' rural settlement plan: granting city blokes Crown Scrub beyond the back blocks of Woop Woop, where no one can hear them at all. Fair go? Or maybe equitable distribution of population? I doubt that.

Got to say that I'm far more interested at this point in time in the bit of France's breast I can see and hopeful we'll be off to bed shortly.

I say, of her inevitable submission to the court: 'You do that. Meantime, there's a local issue that needs your attendance. Very local one.'

Bell. Beautiful.

Except she's biting her lip now; she's got something else to say. She's looking at my boots like she's waiting for them to say something first.

I'm looking at the apple cores, three of them, on the little table beside the sofa: seditious thoughts have increased her appetite, as if she didn't eat enough round at Mum's today. I think I know what she's going to tell me, and though I can't say the thought fills me with a sense of calm, she treats me too carefully sometimes. I'm not that mad. Come on, out with it.

After another ten years, she says: 'Daniel.'

'Yes, France?'

'Magic's on the loose again.'

'What's it done this time?'

'Made me fruitful again,' she says and she actually blushes with her plain happiness for it. What courage is that?

It really is impossible to describe this woman in words. And now that she's told me, now that she's looking at me like this, all I can think of is that this time I'll get to paint her as she grows, with us, from the beginning.

Funkel, funkel kleiner Stern, danke, danke, danke schön. She is a star. Mine. Makes me want to get that first painting I did of her back; but Fanny's off-loaded all that *work* I let him have with his mate, or the son of his mate anyway, who happens to be a patron of this Kunstakademie over there, wrote a few weeks ago when he got back, saying that they have *a most appropriate home now*, and I'm sure he has no idea of the cracking irony in that statement. Not even sure if he knows I'm a Kraut; maybe Dunc never told his father that bit. Somehow *kunst* sounds easier to me than 'art', or maybe more appropriately harder, but the invitation from this *patron* to come over and study gives me a kick of something like panic, not helped by the advice Mr Duncan sent without me asking: that you don't turn an offer like that down, it's the most prestigious academy in Germany if not Europe, according to him. I've never heard of it, unsurprisingly, and it's a long way to go to school, isn't it. Especially given the address: Dresden, of all places in the entire bloody world. Still couldn't point to it on a map. What would I say to Mum about it? Haven't even told France yet. Haven't even seriously told myself. Fanny also sent along a cheque, as his mate insisted on *something*, and a fair bit more than Sweet Fuck All it was too: sent it straight back to Fanny for someone else's poor bones. What else could I do with it? Jesus. I want to tell France, I know she'll be hysterical for it, but not till I know what I want to do. And now she's pregnant again … that's timely, isn't it. I can put it off for a good while longer.

Look at her. She's still blushing, getting teary now. Stop looking at her, you idiot, and give her a kiss.

SIX MONTHS LATER

Dawn: Josie's

'What on earth? ... Daniel? Oh dear ... Are you all right?'

'Yep.'

'What happened?'

'I slipped.'

'Slipped?'

'Off the roof.'

'What were you doing on the roof?'

'You don't want to know.'

'Yes, I do.'

'There's a rat, in under the chimney pot. Wanted to get it out before you got up.'

'Did it bite you?'

'No. It's a dead one. Smelled it when I went to put the fire on.'

'Did you get it?'

'No. I slipped.'

'You're not all right, are you.'

'No. It's ... twisted.'

'Can you get up?'

'Just give me a minute. Don't blink at me like that. I'm already sorry.'

'It's not that, Daniel. It's ... pains have started.'

'Awch. Fuck.'

'Charming. I can drive ... Sarah! Going into town!'

★

Dusk: Lithgow Hospital

'Champion, France. He's a beauty. What are you going to call him?'

'Well, I'm not sure … But since this one looks just like you too, how about we call him Stupid Arse?'

'Very funny.'

'You are.'

'Someone's been having a lark, though.'

'What do you mean?'

'Well, if I hadn't fallen off the roof, then I'd have gone into work today, you'd have been at home with Mum, and I'd have missed this. Missed you.'

'Aw, darlingest. What's the verdict on your knee?'

'Sore. Nichols'll be laughing for the rest of his life, but I won't be going anywhere in a hurry for a few weeks.'

'Good. Lock you in your room for the duration.'

'Hmn. All right. You're the boss.'

'And don't you forget it.'

'Never again, France.'

'Hmn.'

'Francine, I …'

'Yes, Daniel?'

'There's something I should probably tell you …'

AUTHOR NOTE

Black Diamonds is fiction, a ballad of two spirits inspired by history, but not confined to it. In order to sing it freely, I invented Wattle Dell, and my omission of any reference to specific units or regiments in the AIF is deliberate. I made these decisions not only for freedom to tell the tale, but in order to avoid dishonouring the memories of those whose true stories ignited my imagination, including those of my forebears, both German and Irish.

This story is my celebration of my funny, beautiful country, with its quirks, imperfections and mistakes as I interpret them, and its deepest truth is its allegory, its love song, for my own darlingest, Andrew, the real hero of my fractured fairytale.